BEYOND THE HORIZON

THE SONS OF TEMPLAR MC #4

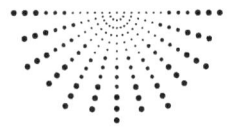

ANNE MALCOM

DEDICATION

To everyone struggling under the weight of grief, depression or anxiety. You are not alone. Light will shine through even on the darkest of your days, you'll get through this. Remember, nothing lasts forever.

CHAPTER ONE

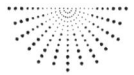

I YANKED the covers over my head the moment my alarm jolted me out of a troubled sleep.

"Ten," I whispered.

Ten seconds was all I was giving myself. All the time I was allowed to shut out the outside world.

"Nine."

I hated mornings. *Loathed them.* I wasn't someone who hopped out of bed every day with vigor. I dragged my sorry and cranky ass out, every morning.

"Eight."

For as long as I could remember, I'd never woken up without the ear-splitting ringing emitting from my phone.

"Seven."

I wasn't one of those people that got to lie in. That got lazy Sunday mornings. That got to decide not to get out of bed and spend the day binge watching their favorite television shows.

"Six."

No. I had responsibilities. People depended on me. Well, a *person* depended on me. I depended on me. Without me, we didn't eat. Without me dragging my sorry ass out of bed every damned morning, we wouldn't survive. Bills would go unpaid. Electricity would get cut off.

"Five."

But this morning was different. I wasn't dragging myself to the coffee pot then off to school, the hospital or the bar. No.

"Four."

I was going to a funeral.

"Three."

My mom's funeral.

"Two."

The person that depended on me. The person I had taken care of for the past two years. For the past sixteen years.

My person.

"One," I choked out, not letting the tears strangle me. My body already did its best to rob me of breath, I didn't need the sorrow of my soul doing it too.

I threw the covers back and stared at the ceiling for a split second, embracing the detachment, the feeling of nothingness. Numbness had spread over my body since I got the call. Since that detached, emotionless voice on the phone informed me of my mother's passing.

It had been expected, but in that vague, it'll never actually happen type way. She'd been sick. For just over three years, she'd battled cancer. I mean *battled*. Fought with every fiber of her being, not only the disease but the poison they put in her body to try and cure it. The poison that hadn't cured a thing. She had put it in her body for me, even though she didn't believe in it. She had tried every alternative medicine, every other solution until I pleaded with her to let medicine save her. I had been convinced it would. It might have given her more time, given me more time, but it had also sucked every inch of strength out of my strong mother before it let the disease win in the end.

And even though the doctors had continuously told me with

a clinical detachment that she was living on borrowed time, I never believed it. I'd held back her hair through the sickness of chemo, taught her how to tie a jaunty headscarf when her long locks fell out, changed and bathed her when needed, but I never let myself consider the real reasons for these things. Never let myself think of the evil disease that was slowly taking my mother from me.

And it did.

A demon in the night, death came and stole her away before I could even say goodbye. She died alone. Without me.

I sat up and pushed myself out of bed, my body having that tingly feeling when numbness starts to subside and pricks of pins and needles threaten to bring feeling back. That first prick of pain shocked me, it was an omen of the agony that awaited me. That I'd been running from.

I froze, standing in the middle of my bedroom. It was decorated as well as one could with little to no funds. In one corner sat a cheap wooden desk with coffee rings serving as an unintended pattern on the surface. Forgotten textbooks were crammed into a bookshelf beside it. Brochures and printouts of alternative cancer treatments littered the surface. Mismatched frames crowded the walls, pictures of Mom and me throughout the years.

I couldn't look at those.

By recognizing all that I had left of her was images in a frame, it would make it real. I wasn't ready for real. I continued my sightless gaze of my room. My old ottoman in the corner was a find at one of Mom's favorite vintage stores, the patchwork pattern almost invisible since it was buried underneath clothes. Fairy lights draped around my uncomfortable bed, in an effort to lighten up my space. An attempt to somehow trick me into thinking it was better than it was.

A huge mural took up half the wall behind my bed. A beautiful vibrant sunset, every color you could think of dancing in the rays. My mom had painted it on one of her good days. It almost looked real, like you could step through it to some magical and better world beyond. That was until you looked, with cynical eyes like mine and saw the crumbling wall beneath it. It was just paint. There was nothing beyond it.

Amongst all that, I stayed frozen, terrified that feeling would come back. That pain would blindside me. A few seconds brought back that blessed numbness that allowed my feet to shuffle into the living room.

I went to the pot, bleary vision only focusing on the one thing that made me half human, that woke me up enough to contemplate the dreary day—coffee.

"Morning, sweetie," a voice from the sofa had me jumping out of my skin.

Luckily, my unpoured coffee did not scald my arms, which I was surprised about. Fate usually loved to screw with me. Second-degree burns would be the cherry on top of my shit sundae.

"Aiden," I croaked, my voice shaking off sleep.

He straightened off the sofa and stretched, the fabric of his tee lifting with the movement. My gaze flickered over the washboard stomach for a moment before I moved to his eyes.

"You didn't have to stay," I said, pouring coffee and then retrieving another mug.

Aiden skirted around our shitty sofa and padded into our equally shitty kitchen. He took the mug I offered and lightly rested his free hand on my hip.

"Yes, I did, Lil," he murmured looking at my eyes.

"You didn't," I protested. "I'm fine, I don't want you risking your back muscles and having a horrible night's sleep for me."

The hand on my hip tightened and his attractive brows furrowed. "Your mom died, sweetie," he said softly, as if to remind me. "I care about you. Therefore, I stayed. And I'm not going anywhere. You're not alone," he told me firmly.

I looked into his clear blue eyes. We had been friends since my freshman year. A month ago it had turned into something else. In the midst of my nightmare, Aiden had somehow turned from friend to boyfriend. Not that the handful of dates and makeout sessions constituted an actual relationship, but my schedule didn't exactly give me the luxury of time for a boyfriend. I spent every moment I could with Mom, until she demanded I go out and have some fun.

As if fun was even a plausible prospect when my mom was dying in a hospital room. But I played along, let Aiden take me out, faked a smile while my insides were shredding. I'd never let anything go further, go deeper. My time and my heart were dedicated to Mom.

Until now, I guessed.

I had a huge gaping hole in my life, one I couldn't even contemplate right now. One I knew Aiden wanted to fill. One that I knew he would never fill.

"Thanks," I whispered, realizing arguing was pointless.

He was wrong, though. I was alone. Completely. My mom had been the one and only person on this earth who actually loved *me*. The me, the one that was plagued with anxiety, and felt like I had a dumbbell on my chest twenty-four hours a day. The me who barely spoke around new people, and got nervous in crowds. Everything that made me ordinary she found extraordinary, and subsequently she made me *feel* extraordinary. It was just me and her, against the world.

Now it was just me. I had friends, good ones too, ones that I loved. But nothing like what I had with Mom. Even Bex, the best of them all, would never be what my mom was to me.

He nodded and kissed me lightly on the cheek before searching my eyes. He was waiting for me to break down, I knew. For days, he and Bex had been watching me like I was an unexploded grenade, ready to go off at any moment. He seemed to be satisfied I wasn't in danger of exploding any time soon and moved to the breakfast bar, to perch on our rickety bar stalls.

I stared at him. Even after a no doubt terrible sleep on our lumpy sofa, he looked good. His sandy blond hair was mussed, but in a way that looked like he'd taken hours to do it. His face was classically handsome, and his body was lean. He looked like an all-American boy, *Abercrombie and Fitch* style. He was from a good family, was in law school and a genuinely nice guy.

Too bad he didn't make me burn.

Didn't consume my mind and soul. Like someone else had for the past three years. Someone that definitely wasn't a genuinely nice guy. Someone who would never be mine.

Asher.

Time didn't mute the memories I had of him. Of us. I indulged myself a moment of escape into that memory, one that offered a respite from the horror of the present.

THREE YEARS AGO

I liked margaritas, I decided. No, I *loved* margaritas. The handicap that stopped me from unleashing my true self seemed to fall away with the help of this magic drink. I was uninhibited by the shyness that had plagued me my whole life. The weight on my chest.

I stumbled slightly but righted myself.

I was at Gwen's, my new boss's place, dancing with people I barely knew. Beautiful women who had no qualms being themselves, and may have been slightly insane. I *so* wanted to be like them when I grew up. Well, firstly I wanted to be like my mom, with a sprinkling of these fab ladies. Mostly I wanted to be someone different than who I was. Someone better.

As I whirled to the music, my gaze landed on men rounding

the corner of the house. Hot men. I narrowed my eyes. I couldn't tear my eyes off them. I'd seen them around town and more recently at Gwen's store. I knew who they were. Heck, everyone knew who they were. They were the Sons of Templar. The motorcycle club that had unofficially owned the town since before we moved here. Some around town hated them, and everything the club stood for. Most respected them. Like Mom.

"Those boys may be a bit rough around the edges, but they've got good hearts. People like to judge based on what they think a good person should look like. Good people come in all shapes and sizes, just like bad. Don't you forget it," she'd instructed me years ago. Her eyes had been faraway, no doubt thinking of the bad man that had been wrapped up in a suit and tie. Who'd seemed like a good man, a family man, until the doors to our home had closed and the monster inside had been unveiled. So she didn't shrink away from men wearing leather. She didn't shrink away from anyone, not anymore.

I had always been fascinated with the men. The life they lived. The freedom they seemed to have. I'd longed for that kind of freedom, to be who I was, to figure out who I was. I would never have that though, not with my emotional disability chaining me to my uninteresting self. I'd admired them from afar, entertained notions of going to one of their infamous parties. Those thoughts stayed rooted in fantasy, as did any possibility of interaction with the club.

My social skills went from lacking to non-existent when faced with attractive men or intimidating people. The men in the club were the embodiment of both. Though not every single one was mouth-droppingly attractive, they all held an aura, a certain presence that seemed hypnotizing and dangerous at the same time.

That was all admired from afar. I'd never seen them up close, definitely not in social situations. But now they were here. Getting closer to my uninteresting self with every moment.

"Lily," I heard my named whispered urgently.

I reluctantly tore my gaze off the approaching men and moved it to settle on Amy, who was looking panicked sitting up awkwardly from her sun lounger. I was thankful to have a reason to escape my own head. I'd get trapped in there if I wasn't careful.

"What?" I half yelled at her. I would never have yelled, half or otherwise at anyone, had I not had tequila in my system. I would've mumbled something, gone red and most likely embarrassed myself.

Tequila equaled zero embarrassment. It ruled.

"Come here," she hissed, her eyes darting to Brock, who was chatting to Lucy, his attractive eyes kept moving in Amy's direction. She looked seriously freaked.

No wonder. I did crappy around people in general most of the time, hot guys like the ones I was presented with were in danger of turning me mute. I didn't see why Amy was so panicked, though — the chick was drop dead gorgeous. She radiated confidence and didn't have any trouble conversing with the sex god bikers. I had witnessed her exchanging witty banter with the men since I started working at her and Gwen's clothing store.

"What?" I asked when I got to her side.

Her eyes went from Brock to me one more time. They were that kind of drunken alert that I had seen on my friends. You knew you had to get your shit together, but you were also struggling to stay upright.

"I need you to go and get the booze off Brock," she ordered quickly.

My stomach dropped, the idea of approaching him, and the arguably hotter guy with him, had me wanting to break out in hives.

"I've never spoken to him—he kind of scares me. Why can't you do it?" I pleaded.

Tequila may have burned away most of my crippling shyness, but it hadn't taken away all of my self-preservation. At least not yet.

"It's a long story," she said, her eyes narrowing. "It involves a sex marathon and his stupid man bun. Will you do this for me? Please?"

She didn't wait for me to reply and gave me a gentle shove. One that wouldn't normally have moved a sober Lily, but drunk Lily went tottering off in the direction of Brock.

I was in front of him and the dark-haired man before I even knew what was going on. I blinked a couple of times to get my eyes in focus. Brock was his name. I'd seen him around before. He was big, way taller than me in my bare feet, and muscled like some kind of Navy Seal. His sandy blond hair was fastened into a bun, and tattoos covered most visible parts of his muscled body.

I quickly glanced at the Sergeant at Arms patch on his leather vest before moving my gaze elsewhere. It was the guy beside him that had me momentarily mute. His hair was dark and closely cropped to the skull on the sides, and slightly longer and mussed on top. I couldn't see any visible tattoos on him, though he had a matching vest to Brock, with a crisp white tee underneath that hugged his impressive torso.

Cut. A little voice whispered the word to me.

Cut, not vest. That's what they called it, the leather they wore with the club's patch embroidered on it.

I swallowed and moved my gaze up again. He had a strong, clean-shaven jaw and wasn't as tall as Brock, nor as muscly. That didn't mean he was short or lean. He just wasn't *Giganto.* Which was good, I wouldn't need a ladder to kiss him, just high heels.

Wait, why in the heck was I thinking about *kissing* him? You had to be able to talk to hot guys in order to kiss them.

"Hey, it's Lily right?" Brock addressed me with a smirk, though his tone was kind.

I jerked, tearing my attention away from rich chocolate eyes. Oh shit. I'd been standing in front of them, silent and staring like I should be wearing a helmet to bed or something. Mortification commenced, but luckily I had tequila on my side.

"Yeah, Lily. That's me, my name I mean. I'm not an actual Lily because that's a flower and I'm a human named after a flower," I babbled, realizing only just now the extent of my drunkenness. Or maybe my social awkwardness.

Brock grinned, the dark haired one stared at me, his eyes roving my bikini-clad body.

I ignored the feel of his eyes, the dip in my stomach at his gaze. I swallowed and focused my attention on Brock.

"Sooo, are you having a good night?" I asked, trying to remember why the heck I'd come over here. I struggled not to fidget with my hands, and my eyes darted around in search of an escape.

Brock's grin got bigger. "I wasn't, till now. Lucky you gals need your liquor, or I would've missed out on all this," he said, waving his arm around the party.

A light bulb lit atop my head. "Liquor," I exclaimed in relief. "Yes, liquor. That's why I'm here... not here in this house, but *here.*" I pointed to the ground then gestured between us. "Like here in front of you. Amy wanted me to get the booze." I pointed to her, hoping to get the attention off me and what a bumbling idiot I was.

Brock's smile dimmed slightly as he followed my eyes. He shook his head.

"I got it, darlin'. Amy shouldn't be sending you over here to do her dirty work. I'll take care of her. You have a good night now." He winked at me and then moved toward Amy, who tried to ungracefully scramble off her chair.

I wanted to watch, but my brain was looking out for me

when I realized I was standing alone with the hot biker. One that hadn't stopped staring at me throughout the entire painful exchange. I attempted to move to make my escape, before I did something that would require me to die of embarrassment tomorrow morning.

A firm grip stopped me. I jolted at his touch. Not in a "he's manhandling me" type of jolt, but a "my panties are on fire from his hand touching my arm" type of jolt.

God. I was *such* a virgin.

"Not so fast, Flower," his gravelly voice swept around me like a physical thing.

I tottered on my feet as his grip tightened and he pulled me closer to him, his eyes on mine. Up closer he was even more beautiful. His eyes were almost as dark as his hair, and his skin was tanned and flawless. I wanted to run my hands over the stubble covering his sharp jaw.

"Are you new in town too, like Gwen and Amy?" he asked, his hand now trailing down my arm softly.

I swallowed, my mind on his casual touch and my not so causal reaction. Realizing he was staring at me waiting for some sort of answer, I shook my head slowly.

He grinned, showing a row of perfect white teeth. Movie star perfect. "You care to articulate on that?" he asked, teasing.

"You have nice teeth," I blurted.

Holy shit. Did I just tell him he had *nice teeth*? No. I didn't. Tequila did. I searched the backyard for a hole to crawl into, and not leave until I was eighty.

The hand tightened again as if he was sensing I'd bolt. "Easy, Flower," he murmured, pulling me even closer. "These teeth don't bite," his eyes turned hooded, "unless you want them to."

His voice was full of such sensual promise I felt my knees shake. Like actually shake. What the heck did you say to that?

"Um," I whispered. "I think I like my skin sans bite marks, you know, for now," I added in a small voice.

For *now*? Did I just flirt?

He grinned again, but this time there was a serious heat to his eyes. "I'll hold you to that, flower."

His chocolate eyes continued to hold me hostage while his huge hand trailed up my bare skin. I shivered in desire from the casual touch. He seemed to notice my response because his eyes flared.

"So, since you're not new around here, how is it I haven't seen you before?" he continued. "And trust me, I would remember seeing you." His eyes left fire in their wake as they swept across my scantily-clad body.

I wanted to cover myself with my hands. My bikini had seemed perfectly appropriate in a party full of women. Now, I understood I was practically naked in front of this beautiful man. The power of his gaze had me feeling uncomfortable. Another part of me wanted him to look, wanted to imagine the desire in his gaze wasn't a figment of tequila muddled imagination.

"I don't um, get out much," I told him truthfully.

Understatement of the century. At high school, I wasn't exactly what you'd call popular. I never got picked on or anything, in order to get picked on, you had to get noticed. I didn't. I was forgettable and didn't stand out. There was nothing special about me. So I had a handful of friends, studied a lot, read a lot, and hung out with my mom a lot. I also had to study my ass off in order to get the grades to qualify me for a full ride at college.

My mom and I weren't exactly rolling in it. She was a free spirit, an artist. And although she was talented, she didn't make a huge amount off her art, enough to keep food on the table, only with me helping out with a part-time job at the supermarket. No way was I getting college tuition paid for. Not that I was bitter. My mom gave me a wonderful life, a beautiful life. She got us out of a nightmare to do that.

I got it, the full ride. It was at a college thirty minutes away in Tasman Springs. A lot of kids wanted to cross the country to start their foray into adulthood. Not me. I couldn't leave my mom. Couldn't stand being so far away, not when I knew neither of us would be able to afford the airfares to visit often enough. The idea of moving somewhere unfamiliar where I didn't know anyone terrified me. Plus, since I was this close I could work for Gwen on weekends. So between college, working, Mom and my newer college friends, I didn't have time for much else.

The man regarded me.

I say man.

Every other member of the opposite sex I encountered I thought of as *"boys."* The only ones I ever really encountered were ones from school, and they were mostly concerned with drinking, sports, and getting girls into bed. *Boys.* But, even though he couldn't be that much older than me, he was definitely a man.

"That's good," he muttered, stroking my arm.

"What's good?" I squeaked.

His eyes bore into mine. "That you don't get out much. If you did, I expect I'd be fighting every one of my brothers for your attention." His gaze flickered over to where Amy had stormed off, Brock following. "Well, almost all," he added, eyes back on me.

My mouth dropped open. Then I closed it, realizing how unladylike this was.

"No one would be fighting for my attention, trust me," I mumbled with certainty. The men I'd seen connected to the Sons of Templar were hot. Hot with a capital H. "Hot with a capital H" men did not bother themselves with plain, mousy college girls who were so shy they turned mute in their presence.

His brow furrowed. "Trust *me*, I'm counting my blessings

13

right now that I'm the one who laid eyes on this beautiful flower before anyone else," he promised, voice husky.

I swallowed and felt my face redden. I wasn't used to compliments, didn't know what to do with them. My mom told me I was beautiful, but she was my *mom*, and it didn't count. Moms were biologically programmed to find their offspring beautiful. Ditto with my best friend Bex, who was definitely someone boys would fight over. She was my best friend, it was part of her duties to try and inflate my non-existent ego.

"I don't know your name," I blurted.

I couldn't very well be calling him "The Panty Dropper" when I relayed this story to Bex at the dorms on Monday. I would also need it for the short novel I planned on penning in his honor.

"You definitely need to know my name, babe," he grinned.

His other hand went to my waist. I was pretty sure I stopped breathing when he pulled me even closer. Close enough I could feel the heat from his torso. For once the absence of breath felt like a pleasant thing.

"Asher," he whispered, his breath tickling my face.

I gazed up at him. "Asher," I repeated, tasting the beautifulness of it on my tongue. "Cool name," I added dreamily.

His gaze burned into mine and he regarded me intently. He then shook himself and his face relaxed slightly, there was a glint of heat in his eyes.

That moment, right then, was when I started to fall. Fall so hard that the pain of the crash to the ground still stung three years later.

CHAPTER TWO

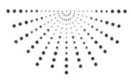

PRESENT DAY

"COFFEE," a husky voice ordered.

My cup was snatched out of my hand by a sleep-rumpled Bex, her dark black hair messed into a bird's nest. The dips of purple at the ends were uneven due to it sticking in all direction. Her mascara was smudged around her eyes, and the tee she was wearing had holes in it and barely covered her butt. Somehow, she still looked good, if a little ragged.

Aiden regarded her, his gaze blank. The two had never really gotten on. Straight-laced law student Aiden, and wild child, med student turned stripper Bex didn't exactly mesh. But they both pretended they liked each other for my sake.

After Bex had downed her (my) coffee she blinked to regard the scene with slightly more alert eyes. We both rivaled each other in the caffeine addiction department. We both got little to no sleep, and required the stuff to do things like talk and not bump into walls.

She blinked at me for a couple of moments, then her eyes watered slightly, and she embraced me.

"How you doin', kid?" she asked my hair.

I sank into her embrace. She smelled like perfume and

cigarette smoke, it was comforting. She'd called me kid since the first day we met, even though we were the same age. She'd said it was because I looked like a lost child on the first day of school. The loud and boisterous girl had taken me under her wing ever since.

"I'm okay," I told her, once I'd been released.

Both Aiden and she looked at me skeptically. One thing they could agree on at least.

I whirled around, getting myself another cup since Bex stole mine. "I'm fine okay, guys?" I told them after my mug was filled.

Again, I was met with disbelieving stares.

"We knew this was going to happen. I knew it was going to happen. I said goodbye. I was prepared," I lied, the words feeling sticky on my tongue.

Bex opened her mouth, seeing right through me.

"I need to shower and get dressed. I can't be late to the funeral," I interrupted, before she could say something that would risk that pins and needles feeling coming back.

I didn't need that. I needed to get through today. I had no choice. That was my life. I didn't have the luxury of breaking down. I had to keep going. Keep running from the Big Bad that threatened to break me down. I couldn't break down, only rich people had the luxury of indulging in breaks from reality. Normal people, people like me had to keep going, keep running, keep upright. As soon as you stopped, you fell. It was over. So I kept going.

Bex gave me a sad look then nodded. "You do you, babe," she muttered. "I'm going to go and stick my head in the refrigerator. Hopefully, that'll make it stop pounding," she added, kissing me on the cheek.

We had tied one on last night. Well, *Bex* had tied one on. I had one glass of vodka, my mind already in a perpetual state of numbness. Aiden had sipped on a beer while watching Bex down almost an entire bottle with an ill-concealed scowl. He was judging her, I wasn't. My mom was like a second mother to Bex. No, strike that, only mother.

Bex grew up in the system, her life as rough as it could get. She barely knew love, affection, or tenderness. The world had chewed her up and spit her out before she was out of diapers. Somehow, she still knew how to give love, even though she never received it. The moment she became my best friend was the moment my mom took her in as a second daughter. It hit her hard. When you'd never had anyone to count on before, then get that taken away, it seemed like all the light and sunshine in the world had been sucked away and that you were living in a night that would never end. I knew because I was living in darkness, scared I'd never feel the warmth of a new day, that the sun would never rise for me again.

So, that's why I sat with her, letting her drink herself into a stupor while we talked about inconsequential things. How shitty she got treated at the club. How I had to contact my college and get back into study before my scholarship was yanked out from under me. How our landlord wouldn't get our window fixed. Anything but the dreaded elephant in the room that had already stomped on my soul.

Aiden had carried her to bed after she passed out. I was surprised she was able to function this morning. The one time I got wasted, I felt like death warmed up. Plus, I had woken up to a hot biker who'd just taken my virginity.

Shush Lil. Mustn't think of him. Not now. Not when your fractured soul is barely hanging on. Thinking of him, of what could have been, that will tear it to shreds.

Aiden gave me a long look before he moved in front of me, putting his coffee cup down so he could frame my face with his hands. His eyes searched mine.

"You're strong because you think you have to be," he started softly. "But it's okay to let it out, be upset. I'm here for you, sweetheart."

I plastered on a fake smile. "I'm okay, really," my voice sounded weak to even my own ears, but I soldiered on, "Thanks, Aiden. You've been great. The best, I don't want you to have to drop everything in your life because of what's going on in mine."

Aiden frowned. "It's not dropping everything; this is where I want to be. With you. Supporting you. Taking care of you," he responded firmly.

"I'm here too," Bex cut in from the refrigerator. Everything was a competition for them, even who was the most supportive.

I frowned, on the inside at least. My outward smile hadn't dimmed. It was on autopilot, a separate entity from my actual emotions. I didn't need anyone to take care of me. I took care of myself. My mom took care of me in her own slightly eccentric way, and when she couldn't do that, I took care of us both. Now it was just me.

"I'll go home, shower, change," Aiden interrupted my heart-breaking thought process. His hands tightened, and he bent slightly to catch my eyes. "I'll come pick you and Becky up, take you to the cemetery, 'kay?"

I nodded, not feeling like protesting anymore.

He looked at me once more, nodded, almost to himself. He leaned in to kiss me softly on the mouth. It was nice, comforting almost. But no fire.

"You got me through this, you know that right?" he asked against my mouth.

I nodded mutely again.

His hands tightened, and he pulled back. "I'll be back just before we need to be there," he said.

"Thanks," I replied softly, meaning it. I couldn't exactly process whatever our relationship was right now, but it was nice having him here, however selfish that was.

When he shut the door, Bex made a farting noise with her

mouth sticking her head out of the refrigerator where it had been stashed.

I gave her a look.

She looked back. We had a wordless conversation about her not saying mean things about my *kind of boyfriend* who was hot, caring, nice, and completely perfect—also completely not right. I didn't add the last bit into our non-verbal conversation.

She rolled her eyes. "Whatever," she said, sticking her head back into the refrigerator.

I grinned, despite myself. It almost held a bit of true amusement, deep down. I stumbled toward the shower, coffee cup still in hand. I didn't drink, smoke, or take drugs, but coffee was my vice. Hence, me taking it to the shower. Plus, it was a requirement in my normal life when I was lucky to get five hours sleep. Ever since the news, I'd been functioning off what felt like five minutes. I regarded my reflection in the bathroom mirror setting my cup down on the cracked sink.

"You're a mess, Lily Smith," I muttered to myself.

My blonde hair was parted in the middle, and the side braid I'd put in last night was half falling apart, strands of my long hair escaping down my back. The skin on my face was sallow, almost transparent it was that pale. My blue eyes were lost in the bags and dark circles surrounding them. They were the one thing I liked about myself.

Everything else was just ordinary. My height, my weight, my face, even my freaking last name. My eyes had always been something I'd felt made me different. They were blue, ice blue, and my mom always said they changed color when I was in different moods. If that was true, then I feared they'd always be this dull and lifeless.

"You can do this," I whispered to the defeated girl in the mirror.

"You can do this, Peanut," my mom's voice whispered in my ear.

19

A single tear trickled down my cheek.

"I can do this."

WE ARRIVED EARLY. I had this thing about being early. I had to be early. If I wasn't, the ever present weight on my chest got heavier, the later it got, the heavier the pressure was. Which was funny, considering my mom was always late. No one got annoyed with her whenever she finally arrived, smiling, beautiful, and full of life. I spent most of my teenage and adult life hurrying her, dragging her along so we'd be on time. She'd always said she'd be late to her own funeral. It was some kind of sick irony or cosmic joke that she hadn't actually *"arrived"* yet, considering the hearse was running late.

"They should fire the dude," Bex declared from beside me, her dark glasses obscuring her face. "I mean, it's a pretty fucking stressful day to begin with. You've got people like ... fucking *mourning*, ready to say their last goodbyes, and it's like ... sorry peeps had to stop for a latte. Body'll be here soon," she babbled, sounding disgusted.

I failed to be offended by her demeanor. It was Bex. She didn't have a filter.

"There's no one here, Bex. We're good," I reassured her, squeezing her arm.

She pushed her glasses up, revealing her kohl-rimmed eyes, which narrowed on me.

"*You're* here, Lil. The grieving daughter. I'm giving that guy a piece of my mind when he gets his creepy ass here," she declared angrily. "Anyone driving dead bodies for a living's got a screw loose," she added, wrinkling her nose.

I smiled, something catching my eye. I held out my hand. "Look he's here, and she's here," I choked up when I realized the *"she"* I was referring to was my mother's body. It wasn't her. Her soul. That was gone, I knew. Squashed out like a burnt out candle. This was just the shell that was left.

Bex squared her shoulders, her eyes narrowing. "Right." She looked like she was going to point her combat boot in the direction of where a thin looking guy was getting out of the driver's seat. She could definitely take him. Though she may have been short and skinny, she was a fighter. She had to be, the way she'd grown up.

I reached to grasp her hand, stopping her. I was about to calm her down when Aiden, who'd been silent, cut in.

"I'll go talk to him, sort things out," he muttered. He focused on Bex. "Stay with Lily," he ordered tightly.

Bex looked like she was going to say something, then her eyes met mine and she nodded.

Aiden kissed my head, then left.

Bex and I silently watched him walk over the grass, holding hands.

"She's really gone isn't she?" I asked the air, my eyes glued to the vehicle holding the last physical remainder of the woman that raised me. Saved me. Saved us.

Bex's hand squeezed mine. "Yeah," she replied quietly.

I nodded. Yeah. She was gone. I felt the pins and needles threatening to bring back the feelings. That big sadness that lurked in the corner of my mind, like some kind of assassin, waiting for the perfect moment to strike.

"Nice place for Faith to catch her last sunset," Bex said finally.

"Yeah," I agreed, watching the sun move closer to its hiding place beyond the horizon. "She picked it," I continued.

"Of course she did." Bex smiled at the horizon.

My eyes prickled as I thought back to that day, that conversation.

. . .

21

I'D BEEN READING one of Mom's favorite books to her, she was losing the ability to grasp the edges, focus her eyes on the words. Her ability to hold a paintbrush had long gone, I think a piece of her heart went too, not that you'd ever know. Not that her cheerful smiles would betray a hint of sadness, or of defeat.

"I want to see the sunset, on my last day on earth," she said suddenly, interrupting my sentence.

I looked up from the book, failing to stop my inward flinch every time I laid eyes on my fading mother. Her hair was gone, a tie-died head scarf fastened like a turban around her bald head. Her skin was yellow, a sign of her organs shutting down. Black circles rimmed her eyes. Her cheekbones protruded, she was a bag of bones underneath the thin polyester blanket. She looked like a skeleton. Her eyes never lost their sparkle, though, or their vibrancy. The one thing cancer couldn't steal from her. It was robbing her of her life, it was yet to rob her of her soul.

"Okay, Mom," I said, choking on my words slightly. "We'll watch the sun set every night," I promised. "I'll make the nurses wheel you out," I added, knowing it would be a feat, but I'd make sure it was something I'd get done.

Mom smiled warmly, the expression the only familiar thing on the alien face apart from the eyes.

"No, Peanut. I don't want to see the sun kiss the parking lot of this place." Her eyes moved around the room. It was covered in flowers, in color, but nothing could disguise what it really was. "No, I want to be in the fresh air, with not a sterile wall in sight," she joked warmly.

I put the book down. "Okay, I'll see what I can do," I replied slowly, knowing how unlikely it would be to be able to take Mom out of the hospital. She might not even survive the short car trip. An excruciating pain stabbed through my crumpled heart at that thought.

"Peanut, I mean after I'm gone," she murmured softly, holding out her hand.

I leaned forward and grasped it gently. It was cold. I was worried if I gripped it too hard the bones would shatter.

Her eyes searched mine. "I want the day you say goodbye to me to be when you can watch the sun set, and know that I'll be going somewhere beautiful, following the rays to somewhere you can't see, but you can always feel," she said, her voice croaky.

I nodded, through the tears in my eyes, unable to speak. My throat swelled up with pain and grief.

"I want it to be on the top of that hill at that cemetery we used to go to, amongst all of those beautiful old tombstones," she continued.

We visited graveyards together. Weird, most people would say, but I'd never known different. My mom was beauty from the inside out, and she found beauty in the most unusual of places. A lot of her best works were inspired by graveyards. She was fascinated by them. I liked them because they were quiet. I could be alone with my thoughts while Mom sketched furiously on her notepad.

"I want you to wear a yellow dress," she announced, her eyes dreamy. "Rebecca too," she added with a grin. "You look so pretty in yellow, and I don't want you wearing some depressing color like black. I want yellow," she decided.

"I can do that, Mom," I said, outwardly trying to disguise my utter despair over discussing my wardrobe choices for the funeral of my mother. My best friend. My hero. My everything. "Though Bex will curse you for making her wear such a cheerful color," I added, maintaining my charade.

Mom grinned. "She'll curse me, but she'll wear biker boots and excess eyeliner and look like the beautiful girl she is," she said, her eyes warm. She squeezed my hand. "Sunset and yellow, Peanut," she repeated.

"Sunset and yellow, Mom," I promised.

So, here we were. In a cemetery, at dusk, wearing bright yellow dresses.

Mom was right, Bex wore her signature combat boots and heavy kohl eyeliner, her black hair messed in choppy layers, the dipped purple ends brushing her shoulders. She looked completely and utterly her.

Me, not so much.

I didn't even know how to be me, let alone create a look that represented who I was. My yellow dress used to be snug on me, tight at the waist and ballooning out into a fifties style skirt, kissing my knees. Now, it was loose, my long hair lay flat around my shoulders. The tan I normally had to complement it was long gone, considering I spent my days in a hospital room, and my nights in a bar. But I wore it, even though the color I identified most with was black. I got why people wore it to funerals. So their outsides matched their insides. To cloak the despair.

People had started arriving, and I had to commence my duties as the daughter, greeting old friends, acquaintances and fans of my mom's work. We didn't have family. She had a lot of friends, though. My mom was likable, a ball of light. People radiated toward her.

People that by chance did not find black appropriate for a funeral either. Most of them were hippies like Mom, so a lot of flowing skirts and bright colors decorated the graveyard. It was kind of poetic and beautiful. Well, it would have been if I hadn't been drowning under the weight of my grief.

The clearing of the priest's throat had me stop my conversation with my mom's artist friends and turn my attention to him. My gaze flickered to the coffin, one that I'd avoided looking at. Covered in flowers, letters and drawings it looked like something my mom would've loved. I wanted to feel warm about that, about the fact my mom would have loved every part of this. I couldn't. My mom would have loved this—past tense— she can't love it. Because she was dead, right in that beautifully disguised coffin. I averted my gaze, feeling the pins and needles stronger now. Bex squeezed my hand. Aiden took my other. I focused on the priest.

"Now, I understand Faith's daughter, Lily is going to say a few words," he declared, after his monolog.

Both Bex and Aiden jolted beside me, I knew they were surprised. They both knew I avoided public speaking as if my life depended on it. Knew the depths of my shyness. The crowd here must have been big, I didn't really look, but didn't need to. Like I said, my mom was loved.

"Lily babe, you don't have to do this," Bex whispered. There were streaks on her face from the tears she'd already shed. My face, I knew, was streak free. I was still numb.

I smiled woodenly. "Yeah, I do."

Aiden moved beside her. "She's right," he murmured. "This is too much."

I silenced him with a hand. "I'm doing it," I said firmly and quickly, aware of all the eyes on me, and hating it. I didn't give them any more time before moving around to stand in front of the crowd. I wasn't wrong. It was big.

"Thank you, Father," I mumbled.

He bowed his head and gave me a soft gaze filled with sympathy. I took a breath and faced the crowd. I was prepared. I could do this.

I thought I could, until my eyes caught the glimpse of chrome reflecting off the dim light. A small group of Harley's were parked in the distance. My eyes met familiar ones quickly, a rich chocolate gaze momentarily paralyzing me.

Asher.

He was here.

Along with Lucky, Amy, Brock, Cade, Gwen, and Rosie.

I sucked in a breath, aware I'd been silent. I ripped my eyes away from the man who I hadn't stopped thinking about in three years. The man who took up the fantasy world I escaped to when I couldn't stand the real one.

Don't focus on that now, I told myself. *Be strong for her, one last time.*

"My mom was the greatest person I ever met," I started, my voice clear. "She was everything I want to be, everything I could wish to be," I continued, my voice wavering. "She found beauty in every single thing that she laid her eyes on. She made every single thing she laid her hands on beautiful." I moved my eyes from the crowd, from the stare that burned into my soul to regard the horizon. To watch the sun slowly move away. "She had it till the end," I said to the horizon. "Beauty. The ugly disease failed to take that."

I took a breath as sorrow threatened to overcome me, the weight on my chest threatening to bring me to my knees.

"She wanted to see the sun set, on the day we all said goodbye to her. The sun setting does not mean it's disappeared, it just means its light's shining somewhere else, that's what she told me." I watched the sky dance with the last of the light. "That's where she is, shining her light somewhere else. Somewhere better," I finished almost choking on my last word, but able to keep my head straight, my eyes clear, so I could watch the last of the sun's aura disappear.

"Bye, Mom," I whispered to the horizon.

CHAPTER THREE

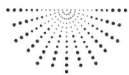

"THANK YOU FOR COMING, you didn't have to," I said to Gwen after she had finally let me out of her embrace.

The pity on her face did not fade with her narrowed brows. "Honey, of course we did. You lost your *mom*. I wanted to be here. We all did. I can't believe you didn't tell me." Her voice wasn't accusing, only sad, full of pain.

I shrugged my shoulders. "I didn't want to trouble you, you've had a lot going on," I explained.

A lot was an understatement. I may have quit working for Gwen a year ago when Mom got worse, but that didn't mean I hadn't stopped seeing them. I knew things in their lives were always intense. Kidnappings and shootings were more than intense. Which was why I never told them about Mom. They were good people. They'd take it upon themselves to help, even with all of the trouble in their life. They didn't need that. I valued their friendship, but I didn't want to be that burden to add to the drama.

Gwen frowned at me. "Trouble me? Lil, you'd never trouble me. It only troubles me having you go through this alone. Why didn't you tell us your mom was sick?"

I ignored the intensity I felt from a stare from behind Gwen, from where I know *he* stood.

I puffed hair out of my face and shrugged my shoulders, "I don't know," I said honestly.

Why hadn't I told my glamorous ex-boss and current friend that my mom had been battling cancer for the last three and a half years? Maybe because if I verbalized it to that part of my life, it'd make it real. It felt nice being able to have some sort of feeble escape whenever I met Gwen and Amy for coffee or drinks, and not be the girl with the dying mom.

Amber may have been small, but my mom operated out of the *"normal"* community and lived out of town, in a little rundown cottage by the sea. I knew her friends weren't likely to shop at Gwen's store or hang out with the Sons of Templar. So I was able to pretend when I was with them, pretend I wasn't battling every day. Pretend that hospitals, cancer treatments, and watching the strongest person I knew fade into nothing was only a distant nightmare.

Her face softened with understanding, she brushed my hair from my face. "We'll talk later. Your words were beautiful, honey," she told me softly.

I blinked away the tears that threatened with the collision of the two parts of my life. The collision that shattered any pretend world I had constructed.

"Lils, the dude with the dope dreadlocks is asking if we're heading to the farm now? I'm voting a massive yes," Bex interrupted boisterously. She gave Gwen a small smile and her eyes stuttered on what I knew were the bikers behind her. I felt her form stiffen slightly, and her eyes harden, I knew she was remembering the not so pleasant ending to my night three years ago.

"Bex, this is Gwen, Rosie, Amy, my friends from Amber. Gwen and Amy own Phoenix," I introduced quickly before she could cause a brawl. "This is Becky, my—"

"Best friend, roommate, drinking buddy, sister from another mister, and so much more," Bex interrupted on a grin.

Bex hadn't met my Amber friends, even though three years had passed since I met them, I didn't exactly hold parties for everyone in my life to mingle.

"Lilmeister has told me all about you. Your lives could totally be turned into movies," she continued with her usual lack of filter.

I cringed and my face reddened. I didn't want Gwen to think I'd been gossiping. Luckily, she laughed.

"Yeah, well only if *Rachel McAdams* plays me," she answered.

"I'd totally be down with *Amy Adams* for me," Amy piped in.

"*J-Law*," Rosie added with a wink.

Okay, so my friends from two different parts of my lives were equally crazy, and made it somehow possible to seem like we weren't standing in a cemetery after the burial of my mother.

"Lil?" Aiden's voice interrupted while Bex continued chatting to the women.

"Excuse me a sec," I said to Gwen and I failed to ignore Asher.

He was watching from further back, his eyes intent on me. He seemed like he was never going to approach, only hang back and torture me with his stare. His face turned blank and hard, at the same time I felt pressure on my waist.

Aiden turned me, both his hands resting on my hips. "You want me to give you a ride to this farm place, or do you want to go home?" he asked quietly.

The Farm was an actual farm, it was where a big group of Mom's friends lived. Words like *"commune"* were not used to describe it, though that's what outside society regularly referred to it as. It wasn't that, but it was like a second home for me. Everyone there was like my mom—free spirits, creatives, artists. People that didn't like the mainstream world. That didn't fit.

A little like the Sons I guessed, although they didn't ride Harley's and engage in questionable activities. They mostly made art and smoked pot. Mom was a free spirit, but was not as hardcore as them. Hence, me being raised in a house with just her and me, it was still our adopted family. It was also where the reception, if that's what it was called, was being held.

"Um…" I began, not knowing what I wanted.

Yes actually, I knew what I wanted. My mom not to be buried in the ground. Instead, for her to be in front of me, teasing me about the fact my "boyfriend" was from a family who didn't recycle and were —*gasp*— Republicans.

"It's been an exhausting few days for you, scratch that, three years. Your words up there were beautiful, but they'll understand if you want to go home. You need sleep," he said.

As much as I didn't like Aiden telling me what I needed, I agreed. I was tired to my bones. Though I didn't think sleep would cure much. Sleep couldn't cure an exhausted soul. It at least promised a welcome oblivion.

"Yeah, maybe I should go home," I declared finally.

Aiden nodded, his grip tightening.

I said my goodbyes to Gwen and the rest of them, eyes avoiding Asher like the plague. He didn't approach me, just stayed rooted to the spot, his eyes burning into me. I felt them on my back as I said the rest of my goodbyes, and as I walked with Aiden to his car.

The residue of his gaze, his proximity, followed me most of the way home. I welcomed the pain that came with it, since it was nowhere near close to the agony that promised to ruin me the moment I let it in.

I woke abruptly. My jerk hadn't roused Aiden, who was sleeping soundly next to me, his arm thrown lightly across my midsection. He'd fallen asleep with me, atop the covers, after lying and talking with me after we got home.

No funny business.

There was never any funny business, and he seemed content with that. It had only been a month after all, and I hadn't exactly been in the mood that month.

I knew it would come, though, and it scared me to death. I hadn't been with anyone since *him*.

Three years of pining.

I was like some sad, weak girl who held onto some desperate hope. Only that wasn't what it was. It was that I didn't want some boy to ruin that perfect memory of that night, the way Asher touched me, held me. It was the only memory I clung to after nights spent at the hospital. After having to bury my head in books on medicine after I'd watched it fail my mother. Later having to work my ass off, and keep a smile off my face even when I was dying inside. I needed it. I needed the memory of the way he made me feel.

I knew I couldn't sleep, even though Aiden's form kept me company in the small room, I felt more alone than ever.

I knew where I needed to go.

IT WAS 3:00 A.M. Who went to cemeteries at 3:00 a.m?

I didn't know. I didn't find it scary, though, the silence of the dead was comforting to me. I didn't do well in the company of the living, so I was happy with the solitude the tombstones offered.

I shivered against my jacket in the crisp air, the ground crunching beneath my feet until I stopped at a fresh grave. There was no headstone, that would come later. For now, there was only a plain white cross, with daisy chains slung around it.

"Hey, Mom," I whispered, sinking down to my knees.

31

My hand pressed into the mound of dirt. Then it came. The pins and needles finally disappeared, replaced with by the pain, the utter agony of loss. I sucked in a strangled breath, a vice tightened around my chest. Tears fell onto the dirt where my mother was buried. My sobs wracked through the silent night. I knew the pain would be bad when it got to me, when it caught up. I didn't realize it would radiate to every part of me, and that I'd drown in it.

Arms circled around me, engulfing my shaking body.

I jolted in fear, a momentary bout of terror paralyzing me until a husky voice tickled my ear.

"It's me, Flower," Asher muttered.

I sagged against him, letting him lift me to my feet and tuck me into his strong body. It didn't matter we hadn't spoken in a year, that I hadn't been pressed against his body in three. It only mattered he was here now, to catch me when I started my free fall into the pit of grief.

"I've got you," he murmured into my hair. "I've got you, babe. You can feel now, you can let it go. That mask you're wearing, you don't need it with me," he continued softly.

And with that, with his words showing he saw straight through me, I lost it. The control, the self-preservation I'd been clinging to. I clutched his cut and sobbed, letting my tears run down the soft leather. He held me tightly against his body, murmuring into my hair, kissing my head, giving me someone. Someone to hold on to. If only for a night.

He pulled me back slightly, his head nodding down so he could meet my eyes. "Ever been for a ride on a motorcycle, Flower?" he joked lightly. It was dark, but I knew there'd be a twinkle in his eye, a reference to the night we first met.

"Once," I replied quietly.

"You like it?" he asked.

"It was one of the greatest feelings in the world," I whispered back, unable to hide behind a mask of shyness like I usually did. It fell away with him. Everything did.

His body jolted. "Yeah," he said, squeezing my hips. "I can think of one thing that feels better."

Before my stomach could dip at that statement, he'd clasped my hand and directed us to the curb where his bike was parked. After he handed me a helmet, I hopped on silently, happy for the absence of words. I didn't need that. I needed to plaster myself against the one body I'd known truly and intimately, the body that made me feel safe. That made me feel whole.

The ride left my worries, my grief, all of it at the curb. The only thing that existed in that moment was my body pressed against his. I didn't know how long we rode for. Time didn't matter. It didn't exist. Only the road, the freedom it gave, existed in those moments.

We pulled up to a shoulder on the lonely highway. It seemed we were the only people left in the world, up on the slight incline, looking at the dim morning light beginning to kiss the desolate landscape.

The motor of the Harley left us bathing in the special kind of silence only offered by early hours of the morning, before the sun was even awake. We sat like that, me still pressed against him, my head lying on his shoulder, my eyes on the horizon. Without warning, he twisted, standing to lift me and sat back down so I was straddling him.

My whole body did an internal convulse at this new intimate position. His hands framed my face.

"This is why?" he asked abruptly.

I screwed my nose up in confusion. "What is why?"

His hands seemed to tighten, and the silhouette of his head turned to regard the same horizon I had been focused on. He moved to look back at me, becoming more seeable as the light began to bathe the valley.

"Your mom, she was sick. Had been for a while I'm guessing," he clarified.

A knot formed in my stomach at the mention of her. I only nodded.

"She'd been battling for three years, am I right?" he continued tightly.

I nodded again.

"So that's why," he said, his voice both hard and soft. "Why you shut down, why you didn't let me in," he surmised.

I took a deep breath. "I-I ... yes," I stuttered, unable to figure out how to explain.

I'd never felt closer to someone, even though our time together had been short, it had been magical. But with that closeness came distance. When you say goodbye to someone you'd never felt more connected to, you severed something that turned you into strangers. I felt so deeply for him I didn't know how to approach this.

"Breaks my heart, babe, you chose to follow that road," he clipped, his voice hoarse.

I was silent. What could I say?

"But I get it," he said finally. "I'm mad as fuck you thought whatever you thought to take this road alone, but I get it."

I chewed my lip, tearing my gaze away from the sunrise that was dancing beautiful colors along the barren landscape. I met chocolate eyes. Something moved behind those eyes. A flicker of understanding that could only come from someone who'd stared into the abyss of grief in which I was currently residing.

"We were together one night, how can you say things like this?" I mumbled, feeling infinitely scared at the fact that whatever it was between us hadn't dulled in three years.

His arms tightened around me and his eyes flared. "It was a fuck of a lot more than one night, Flower, you know that. Don't try and pull that shit on me. You've done it for three years, no more."

I sat up a little straighter. "What shit?" I clipped, surprised at the sharpness of my tone.

His eyes searched my face. "Whatever shit you got brewing in that beautiful head to talk yourself out of this." His hand snaked up my side, and my breath did a little hiccup.

His mouth buried itself in my neck. "I haven't tasted you in three years, Flower. I know you need time. Also, know you need it, too. Need us," he muttered, moving his head.

I sucked in a breath. I couldn't argue. Every sensible thought had left the building, and right now the only thing that could salve the burn of my heartbreak was Asher. His touch. The crazy connection we had erasing everything there was ... out there, beyond the horizon in the background.

"I'm taking that as permission, Flower," he growled.

His mouth captured mine in the next second, and I melted into his touch immediately. His arms pressed me to him, and I moaned into his mouth as the thin fabric of my leggings brushed against his hard length. I needed this, more than oxygen. More than anything at this moment. His hand went to my breast, his cool palm snaking up under my tee and tweaking my nipple.

"Fuck," he hissed, leaning back. Desire was etched into his face. "I forgot how fuckin' amazing it is," he muttered. "Tasting you, having that little body set alight for me and me only."

I looked at him through my lashes. Arousal had me feeling bold. "I haven't forgotten," I whispered. I tightened my hands around his neck and pressed my body against him. Regular Lily had disappeared. This new Lily, the one I didn't recognize, replaced her. And she was horny. "I haven't forgotten what you feel like inside me," I murmured against his neck.

His entire body tightened at my words.

"I need you to fuck me," I whispered in his ear.

Asher grasped my hair roughly, pulling my head back so he could meet my eyes.

"You can't say shit like that," he growled. "Not when I'm hanging on by a fuckin' thread, trying to be a gentleman, respectin' the fact you're grieving," he said tightly.

I watched him. "I don't need a gentleman, I need you, I need us," I whispered. "You're better, you make it better."

Asher paused for a split second, then his mouth was back on mine. This kiss wasn't like the last, it was intense, frantic, leading somewhere better. His hands were everywhere, my body responding to his touch like it was born for it. Without warning, I was lifted and set lightly on my feet.

Asher grasped my neck, his hand bit into my hip. "Sit back, baby," he ordered, his voice rough.

I did as he bid, my whole body blazing with electricity, my panties already soaking. I sat up on the bike, leaning back so he could pull down my leggings and panties. I should've felt mortified, paralyzed at the fact that I was naked and exposed on the side of the road. I felt none of that. All I felt was need. Frantic, desperate need for Asher.

His eyes devoured me, looking at me, there. He ran his hand over his mouth. "Fuck," he muttered. "So fuckin' beautiful. All I want to do is taste that sweet pussy... I'll do that, later," he decided, stepping forward and unbuttoning his jeans.

He grasped my hips and I was up again, straddling him once more, this time sans pants. There was no warning, no build up, he slammed straight into me, right to the hilt. I was ready, primed. I cried out at the magnificent feeling of him inside me. The twinge of pain I felt from his wide length stretching me was nothing next to the pleasure.

He grasped my neck roughly. "Ride me, baby," he commanded in a voice thick with desire.

So I did. With the morning rays kissing our bodies, I rode him. Rode him with abandon, this new Lily letting everything go but the two of us. Asher's eyes never left mine, and his fingers bit into my ass, one hand clutching my neck so my face brushed his. Our feverish lovemaking was made all the more intense with our gazes locked on each other, his chocolate eyes searing my soul.

"Come, baby, let go," he demanded hoarsely.

On his order, my entire body convulsed and I cried out through my release. The pleasure unleashed was like nothing I'd ever felt in three years. In my whole life. It was almost blinding. Asher's arms tightened around me as I milked the release out of him. He captured my lips as he pulsed inside me.

We sat breathing heavily, our noses touching.

"Fuck, Flower," he murmured against my mouth. "Being inside you, it's the best feeling on the planet. But you riding me on my bike"— his hands tightened and he shook his head — "launches me right into the stratosphere." He nuzzled my neck.

My heart was beating furiously and I vaguely registered his words, my heart leaping at them. At the fact he was inside me once more, his hands were on me. I didn't get much closer to any form of coherent thought. As he gently lifted me off him and set me on my feet, reality trickled back in at about the same rate as something leaked down my leg.

Hmm. Sex in the middle of nowhere without a condom, not so glamorous as you'd think, I thought with a certain degree of detachment. I was lucky I was on the pill as I realized our lack of protection.

Asher snatched what looked like a tee from one of the bags on his bike, gently cleaning me. His head moved so he could stare at me as he did so. My heart skipped a beat at the expression on his face, the tenderness of such an action. My lips stayed pursed. Nymphomaniac Lily was slowly disappearing, the regular, awkward shy and decidedly not nympho Lily was returning. Shame would be well on its way. For now, I bathed in the warm glow of the sunshine, of Asher's touch, chipping away at my ice cold grief.

I pulled on my leggings awkwardly when he handed them to

me. Once I had myself decent, Asher stepped in front of me, hands at my neck. He searched my face with worry.

"You okay, Flower?" he asked softly after a moment of silence.

That was a good question.

"Right now, in this moment, yes," I told him quietly. "On the whole ... not so much." The honest statement came out of me automatically. I couldn't hide with him. It was the first time I'd made any kind of admission I was struggling. That this was real.

He furrowed his brows. "You need to get home. To bed," he decided. "My bed," he clarified.

Bed.

Home.

"Fuck," I exclaimed loudly, remembering who I had in my bed at my home.

Asher's brow rose. "Did you just curse, Flower?" he teased.

I didn't have time to revel in how attractive his already smoking face was when amused.

"I need to go home. To my home, like now," I demanded quickly.

"Okay, we'll go there, if that's what you want," he agreed, beginning to turn us to his bike.

I clutched his hand. "Not we ... just me," I told him firmly.

He frowned slightly. "Not leavin' you, babe, not again," he declared roughly.

"Well, you're not coming into my house. I've got ... um ... company," I mumbled.

I cringed at how that sounded. It sounded like I was some kind of hussy. Red crept up my cheeks.

Asher's face turned blank. "I fuckin' know that," he ground out. "That certain visitor will be learning just how unwelcome he is when we get back."

I gaped at him. There were a multitude of things wrong with that statement.

"How do you *'fuckin' know that'*?" I used air quotes, mimicking his voice with sarcasm I didn't know I was capable of.

"I followed you home. Sat outside your place, waiting for fuckface to leave. I was dis-fucking-pleased when he didn't," he ground out.

I only stared at him. "You followed me home," I repeated quietly.

"Yep. Not surprised you didn't notice, state you were in, the fact that Abercrombie didn't is a testament to what a douche he is.".

I let out a breath. "I do not need this pissing contest right now," I snapped. "I also don't have time to educate you on the fact that sitting outside someone's house all night is firmly in *Criminal Minds* territory," I added seriously. "I need to go home, alone and sort out my head."

Asher's face softened a smidgeon. "Fuck, babe, I know that. That you need time. It doesn't mean I'm gonna like your boyfriend being the one comforting you, not me," he said fiercely.

I pointed to the bike. "Pretty sure that wasn't Aiden just then, that was you," I informed him, and myself.

Mental forehead slap.

I was a horrible person. I shelved that bit of self-loathing for later when I wasn't on the side of a road.

Asher's face turned stormy. "I'm not having this shit out here. Get on the bike, babe," he echoed my internal sentiment.

I let out a breath of relief and took the helmet he offered me.

On the ride, the usual feeling of freedom didn't sink in. Pressed into Asher's warm and hard back, I realized the magnitude of everything that had just happened. Asher and me. After three years.

It was amazing, life shattering, like no time had passed. He seemed to feel something for me. More than I'd thought. Not what I felt for him. The depth of feeling that had settled in my soul after one night wasn't something he could possibly feel. I was embarrassed I even felt it. It wasn't just that, I had tears prickling at the corners of my eyes and shame burning in my belly.

I had a boyfriend.

A boyfriend who was caring, supportive, and in my bed right now. I'd just let an ex ... whatever Asher was, have sex with me on the back of his bike in broad daylight. Or the beginning of daylight. I hadn't even let Aiden past second base. I wasn't exactly a brazen hussy, I knew that considering I'd slept with only one person, but I was a bitch. Aiden was in my bed right now. He had supported me through my nightmare, patient and caring. This and the ever present weight of grief on my chest had my cocktail of emotions turning sour in my stomach.

Getting off this bike meant going back to reality. Saying goodbye to Asher. Whatever it was between us was not something I could deal with. I could barely breathe after what had just happened. I couldn't deal with it long term. I had to think of Aiden. But in that moment, I indulged in fantasy, traveled back to the memory that would chase away the complications of the present with the beauty of the past.

CHAPTER FOUR

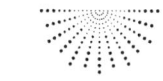

THREE YEARS AGO

NORMALLY, I wasn't one to drink into the early hours with a group of bikers and beautiful women, who seemed to radiate everything I wanted to embody.

But I did.

I may not have spoken much, but my silence didn't seem to be noticeable, nor did it distance me like it normally would. Maybe because it didn't stick out much, the scary biker Bull, beating me with his lack of words. I felt a sort of camaraderie in our mutual silence. He was battling demons of his own, much scarier than mine I knew, but it was comforting to know that being trapped in your own head wasn't something that only happened to weak college girls, big bikers could be brought mute if the demon was big enough.

To my disappointment, Asher had left midway through our conversation, one I thought had been going well.

He had frowned down at a text. His eyes moved to me and he regarded me soberly. As I was far from sober, I didn't do too well registering what lingered beyond his gaze. His hand had bitten into my hip. I sucked in a breath at the contact, never feeling attraction like I did from his simple touch.

His eyes darkened at this.

"Fuck," he muttered under his breath. "Babe, I've gotta go."

I tried to hide my disappointment, though I was afraid that alcohol might work in taking away my shyness, it also hampered me masking my emotions.

Asher grinned, he brushed a wayward strand from my face. "I'm happy that you seem to feel about the same as I do about my departure," he said quietly.

I stared at him. Couldn't stop, even if you paid me. This might be the only time a guy this hot ever paid any attention to me, looked at me like this. I was soaking up every part of this moment like a sponge. Especially his hand at my hip.

"I'll be back for you," he promised darkly, his eyes glinting with desire.

I swallowed. "What?" I squeaked in surprise.

The hand at my hip tightened. "You stay here, don't drink anymore." He frowned down at the glass in my hands. "You're cute as fuck drunk, baby, but I want you to be able to sit on the back of a bike." His eyes darkened more. "I want you to be able to remember how hard I fuck you tonight, and I want you to be able to suck my cock."

It took a full couple of seconds for his crude words to penetrate my foggy mind. They penetrated my womb the moment they left his beautiful mouth that wasn't inhibited by alcohol.

I sucked in a breath.

No one had ever talked to me like that before. I didn't think people actually talked like that. I loved it. The image of him ... *fucking* me, of me doing that to him, had my panties dampening. It was a feeling I was not used to. I knew what being turned on felt like, I wasn't a completely innocent virgin, but I didn't know what this felt like. Feeling like my whole body was on fire as a *Hot with a capital H* biker stood in front of me saying dirty things.

"Fuck," he muttered again, hand at my jaw. "See that my little flower likes the sound of that," he said, eyes on my lips.

I didn't say anything. I licked my lips, feeling them drying out.

His eyes narrowed. "I've got to leave. Like I said, I'm coming back. You're on water till then. Then you're on the back of my bike, then in my bed," he declared hotly.

I kept my silence, that all sounding good, but in a fairytale sense. I couldn't actually believe this guy was saying this stuff to me. Plain Lily Smith had a sex god telling her dirty things and promising her to take her to bed.

Did alcohol also cause hallucinations?

His thumb brushed my lip. "I'm gonna need some kind of verbal confirmation before I let you go, Flower," he instructed. "I know your body's telling me yes in a million different ways, I need your mouth to say it."

"I'm affirmative on ... all of that," I said quickly not even registering how cringe worthy my words were.

Affirmative? What was I, a commando in a bad action movie?

Asher smirked. "Good."

Then, to my utter amazement, he leaned in and pressed his lips firmly to mine in a closed mouth kiss.

I shut my eyes, trying to imprint the moment in my memory. When I opened them, he was gone.

Did that really happen?

Hours later, this was one of the reasons why I was sitting here with people who were both strangers and friends at the same time. I was clinging to the hope that conversation was not only real, but that he was coming back. Well that, and also because I was having fun.

I never had fun around big groups of people. I was too shy. They made me anxious, had me feeling sick to my stomach. This group, this motley and disgustingly attractive group, had me feeling the kind of ease that I only felt around my mom or Bex.

I glanced down at my phone that had started ringing. Speak of the Devil. I grinned as Gwen was carried into the house by Cade and stood to answer the phone.

"Hey, Mom," I greeted brightly. Although I had done as instructed and kept to water, my brain was still swimming in the depths of tequila.

"Heya, Peanut, it's after midnight. Just calling to make sure you hadn't turned into a pumpkin or anything," she greeted lightly.

There was no sternness or judgment in Mom's voice. I was almost twenty-one and a grown adult. I didn't have a curfew, I'd never had one in fact, but me staying out this late wasn't exactly normal.

"My glass slippers are still firmly on my feet," I joked. "I'm having a great time with Gwen and her friends..." I paused, chewing my lip. Asher hadn't arrived, and I felt he might never. I had to prepare my mom, though. "I ... um ... might not be coming home tonight," I said quietly, moving even further away from the remaining group. My wanderings led me to a dark corner at the side of the house.

There was a pause, then I was pretty sure the sounds of clapping were heard in the background on the other end of the phone. *Yes, clapping.*

"Are we talking a real life male-female sleepover?" she gushed as if the thought of her daughter potentially having a one-night stand pleased her.

That was my mom.

"Well, I don't know, I may still come home," I hedged, not wanting to keep my hopes up.

"Pish posh you'll be home. Whoever it is that has finally gotten my Lily to open her beautiful self to, will be unlikely to be letting her go home alone," she stated decisively. "Though, do use protection. I know you're on the pill, but that's not one hundred percent. As much as I want to be a grandma, I know you seem hell bent on that college education."

Such conversations with my mom were not unusual. She was a free spirit. Open about everything in life and all about free love.

I still felt awkward talking to her about this. Boys had never been on the scene, so we'd not had the opportunity to talk about this. Actually, we had, she'd given me multiple sex talks, but since sex was never a real possibility for me, I'd merely gotten embarrassed at her blasé attitude toward it all.

"I'll text you," I promised.

"Okay, hon. And I know it's your first time. So be sure. Be comfortable. Make sure he treats you right ... and that he takes care of you before he finishes," she added mischievously.

I rolled my eyes. "Okay, gross, Mom."

"Text me if he does turn out to be an idiot and stand my beauty up. I'll come and get you," she offered.

"Mom, it's late. I'm not doing that," I protested.

"I'm up, not likely to be going to sleep, I'm feeling inspired," she told me brightly.

This too was not unusual. My mom was an artist and came with all the idiosyncrasies of being creative. When she was inspired she was usually in a sort of trance, not eating, sleeping, or anything until she was done. This happened routinely over the course of my childhood, and when it did happen, I'd take over all of the household chores and responsibilities.

I guessed a lot of kids would resent their moms for obsessively painting for days at a time and leaving them to shop for groceries and pay power bills, but I didn't. It was part of what made my mom who she was. She accepted every part of me, even the parts I couldn't accept.

"Okay," I relented, knowing how embarrassing it would be

to get my mom to pick me up when Asher realized that he could do much better than me.

"Love you, baby," she said.

"Love you too," I whispered back.

I rang off and stared into the darkness, the sounds of laughter and music carrying slightly.

Who was I kidding?

Asher wasn't coming back.

"You're an idiot, Lily," I muttered to myself, lifting my phone to call my mom and request extraction from this situation.

"What are you doing hiding in dark corners talking to yourself, Little Flower?" Asher's voice came out of the darkness.

I jumped and let out a muffled squeal as his hands circled around me. His arms tightened on my mid-section and brought my back flush to his front.

"Not that I mind being in a dark corner with you, baby. It means I get to put my hands wherever I want without unwelcome eyes," his voice tickled my ear, and his hand ran up my side to the bottom of my breast, his other hand dancing at the top of my pants.

I sucked in a strangled breath, wanting his fingers to move, needing them to, but also vaguely aware of the people not far away. It didn't even matter to me he was a virtual stranger, and his hands were roving in a way that was decidedly familiar. It felt right. Or maybe that was my hormones talking. Or tequila. Or this was an invasion of the body snatchers type situation. Either way, I was enjoying it. And my little holiday away from the shy and anxious Lily.

He stayed like that a moment, before he spun me round, quick enough to make my head spin and his hands spanned my neck. I could make out his silhouette in the darkness, but not much more.

"But," he continued, "someone like you, is not someone to be quickly taken in a dark corner. Someone like you needs to be savored, worshiped, in the light, where I can get a full view of your magnificence."

My stomach did a little flip. I didn't even care that what he was saying was impossible. Me, magnificent? He was obviously using some line to get me into bed. He didn't need to. His words and his deep husky voice hypnotized me nonetheless.

"So, we're leaving. Are you good with that babe?"

"Um, yeah," I muttered. "Does this mean I get to ride on your bike?" I asked as he clasped my hand and yanked me out of the darkness.

He gave me a sideways grin. "Only way I ever take you anywhere is on the back of my bike," he answered firmly as we rounded the house.

It didn't even matter I was leaving without saying goodbye. I knew it was rude, but I wasn't about to ruin my chances of handing my V card to a sex god for mere pleasantries. I needed him now before he realized just how plain I was. We stopped in front of a beautiful sleek bike, illuminated softly by the street lights.

I gaped at it. "Wow. I like your bike," I declared, running my eyes over it.

I moved to an arguably better view. Asher looked at me with something like amazement. I suddenly felt self-conscious at my uncharacteristic chatter. He yanked on my hand to pull my body flush to his.

"I can't have you on it without knowing what you taste like," he muttered against my mouth.

Then he was kissing me. I mean, *kissing me.*

Not chaste like before. This was the kind of kiss I read about in romance novels. Ones people wrote sonnets or pop songs about. One I didn't even know existed. His tongue plundered my mouth, he lay me to ruin with one kiss.

I'd been kissed before.

I may have had social issues, but a couple of guys had

foraged past that to awkwardly kiss me in a way that had me uneager to repeat the experience.

This was not one of those times. I would have been quite happy to be standing there with Asher kissing me until, oh, I don't know, the end of time. When he released me, my knees were jelly and I felt like my whole body was tingling, I was pulsing in between my legs.

Asher stared at me. "Fuck. Someone like you, kisses like that? I can't wait to see how you ride my cock, Flower," he said hoarsely.

I swallowed roughly at his words.

He reached into a compartment on the bike, straightening and standing in front of me once more.

"You ever ridden before?" he asked as if he hadn't just rocked my frigging world.

I shook my head as he fastened a helmet on it. I resisted a giggle and the double meaning to my answer.

His fingers paused at the clasp. "Just lean with me, I promise you, it's the best feeling on the planet," he told me quietly.

He mounted the bike, and without any hesitation, any over-thinking that usually crippled me, I swung on behind him, pressing my body against his.

We hurtled off into the night.

He was wrong. Riding with him wasn't the best feeling on the planet. His lips on mine was the best feeling. The bike came a close second.

On the bike there was no way to talk. No need to be aware of myself the way I always was. I was free. Free from the shackles of my self-doubt, of my anxiety. There was only the road and Asher's warm body.

It was over all too soon, when we pulled up to a gate beyond which I knew lay the Sons of Templar clubhouse. Everyone in Amber knew this place. The girls I went to school with, the beautiful, popular ones, made it their mission to go to the parties they held there every Friday, though they weren't successful. The club was strict about underage girls, so they'd been snubbed — until they were eighteen anyway.

Asher nodded to someone beyond the wire fence and the gate opened to us.

Here I was, getting a glimpse into the place that had both fascinated and feared me throughout my life.

I hadn't been like those girls at school, desperate to get the notoriously attractive men in the Sons to notice them. I hadn't been intoxicated with the idea of a romance with an outlaw. Romance, in general, wasn't on my radar. In order to have a romance, you had to be able to speak to the opposite sex. I wasn't crash hot on that. I opted for steamy books instead and focusing on my studies and my future.

After Asher had pulled me off his bike, we walked to the clubhouse in silence. It was a structure separated from the garage that was also within the compound, it had a big wrap-around porch and some fire drums which had a couple of people milling around. It was mostly deserted.

As was the room we emerged into, one that looked like a huge living room, with a sofa, a big television, a bar and a pool table. My wide eyes didn't get time to inspect this, Asher's hand was tight on mine, and he all but dragged us into a hallway then into a room which ran off it. When he shut the door behind us, I barely had time to take in the small, tidy room which didn't have much other than a bed and dresser.

I was yanked around, and Asher's mouth was on mine before I realized I was alone. In a room. With a hot guy. All thoughts that could cripple me were silenced with Asher's mouth on mine. With his roving hands that ran down my body, roughly cupping my breasts.

I moaned into his mouth. No one had ever touched me, kissed me like that in my life. I pressed my body into his, mindless need dictating my emotions. Nothing else. He was treating me like a *woman*. A woman he desired. One who was beautiful. Even if this was only for a night, I'd suck out every piece of tonight I could.

His hands went to my ass, and he lifted me so my legs wrapped around his waist.

"You taste so fuckin' good, Flower," he murmured, mouth inches from mine. "Can't wait to taste that pussy," he continued, then he dropped me onto the bed.

I lay there, my mind swirling with desire at his words, at the hungry look on his face. A look that was directed at me. I stared as he quickly tossed his leather vest into the corner of the room, and my eyes widened when he yanked his gray tee over his head. Abs, like a fricking six pack assaulted my eyes.

"Dude," I whispered. "It's like you're photoshopped." I unintentionally quoted one of my favorite movies, but that was how it looked to me right now. It couldn't possibly be real. A man like *that*, wanting a girl like *me*?

A grin rippled through the hunger on his face, and he moved to lie on top of me on the bed, his bare, hard skin pressing into mine while he watched my face.

"You're full of surprises, Flower, it's hotter than anything," he murmured against my lips.

He kissed the bejesus out of me, then moved his mouth downward. He nuzzled my neck a moment then lifted his head. He regarded my button up dress for a minute, then his hands went to either side and, I kid you not, ripped it apart.

The buttons went flying everywhere.

I didn't even care about the fate of my dress, about the fact it meant I'd be stumbling out of here in only my bathing suit. Nothing mattered the moment he hissed as he exposed my breast and sucked on my nipple.

Every nerve ending in my body tingled, I rubbed my thighs together at the feeling building in between them. I'd never known his beautiful mouth would feel so good on my breasts.

I knew what orgasms were. I'd given them to myself before. I knew in this moment, whatever was coming would eclipse those pitiful excuses.

"You gonna come with just my mouth on your nipple, Flower?" Asher muttered, and cold air bit my naked breast.

I didn't have the constitution to mutter anything intelligible, only looked at him through my lashes.

"You're gonna come in my mouth," he growled.

My stomach dipped.

"You want that?" he asked his voice hoarse.

His hands trailed my stomach and I sucked in a breath as he dipped down my bare skin. I could only nod as his fingers explored the skin no man had ever touched.

"I want you to tell me what you want," he murmured, his finger making lazy circles.

"I w-want," I stuttered, and my breath came in pants as he kept making those circles.

He stopped, his eyes on mine. "You want what?"

"Don't stop," I moaned.

He grinned. "Tell me what you want. Then I'll eat you, baby, taste your honey on my tongue."

"I want that, I want your mouth," I whispered.

His entire face darkened. "Where, baby?"

His fingers began to move again, this time dancing at my entrance.

"My pussy," I whispered, just as his finger plunged into me.

His entire body froze as I cried out in pleasure, on the edge of climax.

His eyes locked on mine. His face turned blank.

"Tell me you're not a fucking virgin," he clipped, the cords in his neck tight.

I froze as I realized the look on his face. I felt my face redden. "I'm sorry, I forgot to mention," I said in a small voice.

All I wanted to do was scramble away, hide my embarrassment, and never look at another man again. But his body was on mine, holding me hostage the same way his stare was.

"How the fuck," he ground out, "does someone *forget* they're a virgin?"

I tried to move, but his free hand, the one not inside me, pressed against my chest.

"You don't need to move to answer," he stated firmly.

I stared at him, feeling my eyes prickle slightly, residual arousal from his body, his finger, making it hard to think straight.

"Well," I started, unable to tear my eyes from his, "first it was the tequila, I was kind of drunk off that. Then it was you," I whispered and his eyes flared. "I got drunk off you. Off the fact that you talked to me. You wanted me. You kissed me. All I wanted, all I want is more. You made me forget I hadn't had more before," I admitted in a small voice.

I was embarrassed. No, mortified. The sexy outlaw biker was probably disgusted at the naïve, plain virgin in his bed. One that could hardly string a cohesive sentence together. Whatever was working behind his attractive eyes right now was probably along the lines of how to get rid of me.

"I'll leave. I'm sorry," I whispered brokenly.

Asher jolted. He gently began to move the finger inside me. I sucked in a breath. His hand cradled my face and his expression gentled.

"You're not going anywhere," he growled, his finger moving slowly. "Are you sure this is what you want, Lily?" he asked seriously, his finger still moving. "To give this to *me*, someone you barely know. Are you sure this is how you want this to go?"

My eyes rolled back slightly, pleasure starting to radiate to my toes with the work of his fingers. My eyes found his. In that moment, I was lucid. "I'm sure. I want it to be you," I whispered with certainty.

We were silent for a long moment, something impossible

passing between us, something that could only be a figment of my imagination. Because the connection that I felt was not a connection you made with someone you'd just met.

Asher's eyes were glowing. "You just gave me the greatest fuckin' gift, one I don't deserve, but one I'm taking nonetheless," he murmured. "You got no idea how fuckin' hard it makes me, knowing no one else has been in here," he said, pressing into me.

I made a little sound as his finger built the fire inside me, stretching me as another one joined it.

"I might not deserve it. Might not be the best one to take this from you," he continued, kissing me softly. "I don't do gentle"— his hands, his kiss contradicted him — "but I will own you, possess every inch of you, and make sure you feel me for a week after this," he promised.

He moved down my stomach, and all of a sudden, his mouth fastened against my clit. I didn't even think, I screamed at the pleasure that came from his mouth, his fingers. It was foreign, something I'd never imagined. It felt bad, naughty. So bad it was so good.

My breath was coming in pants, and I really hoped I wouldn't have to lean over and scramble for my inhaler. That would totally kill the mood, and cement my nerd status in front of this sex god for the rest of eternity. But this was a different kind of breathless, the good kind. I didn't think a pleasure this good existed, one that made me forget to breathe—where breathing seemed unimportant.

Then it came. An explosion, an earth shattering orgasm that made me see stars, and that caused my whole body to convulse. I called out his name at the peak. Asher was gone a moment, I heard a drawer open, foil crinkle, then he was back on top of me.

His hand spanned my head, and he kissed me slowly, the

taste of me on his tongue making me twitch with arousal once more.

"I'm going to fuck you now," he told me with dark eyes.

I sucked in a breath. I wasn't nervous. I was impatient. "I want you inside me. Now," I ordered, with a brazenness I didn't know I possessed.

Asher's eyes flared. "You need to tell me, babe, if it hurts," he instructed as he positioned himself at my entrance.

I knew it would hurt. I'd read the literature, heard the horror stories. Listened to Bex recount the disaster of her first time. But the man on top of me, the post orgasm cloud I was floating on, made this prospect inconsequential. I needed to be filled with him. Needed him to claim me. I'd treasure it forever.

"Fuck me," I whispered, my arousal causing me to utter a phrase that would never have normally come from my lips.

His eyes turned hooded and then he was inside me. Not slow, not gentle, he plunged right in. To the hilt.

It hurt. Mingled with the remaining pleasure was a sharp jolt of pain. It wasn't pleasant. It hurt like a bitch if I was honest. For a split second, I was unsure if I would be able to handle the pain, if this could ever feel good. But I knew it would evolve. Be good. Be great.

His whole body was tight, his eyes on mine. "Flower, you okay?" he asked softly.

I wrapped my arms around him, clawing at his back, focusing on his eyes. "I need you to move," I ordered hoarsely. I needed him to do something, make me think about something other than the pain, help build up the pleasure I hoped was coming.

I had barely uttered the phrase when he did as I commanded, thrusting into me hard and slow. His eyes never left mine as he fucked me, my body growing accustomed to him, welcoming him.

"So fuckin' tight, baby," he ground out. "So fuckin' beautiful."

I wrapped my legs around him, needing more contact. "Faster," I ordered.

Asher immediately complied, pushing into me with an intensity that stoked a fire that burned within me.

It was coming. I knew it. Another orgasm that would shatter my world.

Asher's body knifed up slightly, so he could thrust into me even harder, my hips moved in tandem with his, meeting him for each beautiful thrust.

"Fuck, baby," he ground out through his teeth. "For a virgin, you take my cock like you were born to it." His head bent forward to capture mine.

The moment his kiss began to ravage me was the moment I exploded. It was better than with his mouth, I milked his own release, and he shuddered on top of me as I rode the last of my waves of pleasure.

We lay there, him on top of me breathing heavily.

He leaned up and kissed my nose. "You okay, Flower?" he asked softly, his eyes searching my face with worry.

I smiled dreamily at him. "Yeah. I'm okay," I whispered the biggest understatement of the year. The century.

I was sated, happy, elated, and everything in between. I had just lost my frigging virginity. To a smoking hot biker, who I never thought would even give me a second glance let alone take me to bed and look at me like I was some supermodel. Someone special.

He pulled out of me gently and cupped my jaw. "Don't move," he commanded softly.

I smiled at him again. "No chance of that, buddy. I'm delightfully content staying in this spot for oh ... the rest of time," I joked, in a manner that was so not me. But somehow was at the same time. The me of this moment at least.

He jolted slightly and his eyes sparkled while he watched me. He shook his head and turned so his back faced me.

I restrained a gasp. His back was corded and muscled, but with the rest of him it didn't surprise me. His shoulders were broad and absolutely delightful. What amazed me was the huge tattoo spanning the entirety of his back. It was similar to the patch on the back of his vest. A grim reaper, riding a bike and brandishing a sword. Underneath, The Sons of Templar MC was written in a kind of ancient script. It was amazing.

I didn't get time to run my hands along it or lick it, because after pulling on his jeans and giving me one last look over his delightful shoulder, he left the room.

I sank back on the bed, looking at the ceiling.

"Did that really happen?" I asked myself.

Before I had the chance to ponder the entirety of this night, Asher came back in. He watched me with his hazel eyes and sat close to my hips. They didn't leave me as he gently cleaned me between my legs with a warm washcloth.

I flinched slightly, more out of reflex than anything else.

Asher's frame tightened. "You in pain?" he asked.

I took stock. I felt tender, different, but the pain was a dull ache, not enough to mention. Plus, my emotional elation trumped any pain at this moment. I shook my head.

"No, I feel ... good," I said quietly.

His eyes flared, he continued, while his gaze flickered over me.

I belatedly noticed I was naked. We'd thrown the covers over the bed in our lovemaking, and I had nothing to hide my modesty. No one had even seen me like this, certainly no man. I tried to shrink away, yank the fabric to cover myself.

Asher's hand stopped me. "No, babe. You're stunning. I don't want anything obscuring the view I've got right now. Not when I wanna fuck you all over again," he hissed through his teeth.

My stomach dipped and arousal replaced embarrassment.

"That's if you can take me, if you're not in too much pain," he added, his body pressing into mine.

"I'm not," I said quickly, not wanting any excuse from stopping him.

He grinned. "Good," he muttered. "Cause I wanna show you everything."

And he did. All night he made beautiful, glorious love to me. Educating me on my body, on his body, and how they worked together.

It was the best night of my life.

CHAPTER FIVE

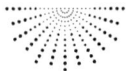

THERE WAS no sleep that night, not a wink.

We made love into the early hours, discovering each other's bodies, Asher worshipping every part of me. I gave him every part of my body in those moments. And in the moments after, the moments where dim morning light peeked through the edge of his blinds, I gave him the rest. My heart, my soul.

I talked. Talked more than I ever had to anyone. I told him about how I was studying to be a nurse, how the work kicked my ass, but I loved every second. I told him about my eccentric best friend Bex and how she was my complete opposite, and how we made total and utter sense. I talked about how close I was with my mom, and her lifestyle.

"What about your dad?" Asher asked gently when I'd finished telling him about the various marches Mom had dragged me on since I was a kid.

My body tightened at his question, and he didn't miss it. The muscled arms around me squeezed, and his hands lightly drew circles on my back, as if to give me support. As if he knew this story wasn't a happy one.

I kept my gaze down on his defined chest. "He's dead," I whispered.

Asher's hands stopped moving.

"Shit, Flower. I'm sorry," he murmured, pulling my chin up to meet his eyes.

"I'm not," I replied, surprising myself by verbalizing something I'd never told anyone.

His body jolted, and his eyes turned hard, but he waited for me to explain.

"My mom didn't always wear tie die and swear off prescription medicine," I explained quietly. "She used to be a housewife. Apron, hairstyle, court shoes, everything. She always had a free soul, but he put it in chains," I whispered, pain in my voice. "He beat her," I choked out. "My first memory is of him backhanding her for burning a pot roast. The next time he was yelling at me for leaving my toys out for him to trip on. I think he might have been going to hit me, but Mom stood in front of me, protected me. Took it for me."

I knew he was a memory, that he couldn't hurt me, but the fear that came with his memory was real. The urge to curl into myself, to be invisible, so I could hide from his wrath. I didn't know why I was telling Asher this. Why I was uncovering the darkest part of me, that hadn't seen the light in eleven years.

Maybe I did know why.

Because, as insane and completely unbelievable as it was, I loved him. Already. Something clicked the moment our bodies connected. Something more. Something indescribable. I was different. He made me different. So I wanted him to see me. All of me.

Asher's body seemed to turn to stone. I avoided his eyes, so I didn't see the fury burning in them.

"Everyone looked at us on the outside and saw the perfect family. On the inside it was a nightmare. Every day I wondered if it was the day when he wouldn't be able to stop. When I'd have to watch him kill my mom and not be strong enough to help her," I whispered.

"How old were you? When the fucker finally met the reaper?" Asher ground out, his tone blank.

My eyes flickered up to his hard jaw. "I was nine," I replied, my mind traveling back to the day when my father had a heart attack. The elation I felt when we realized he was gone. The shame I carried with me as a result of that elation.

"Fuck," he clipped. "Nine years," he said, almost to himself. "Nine years you had to live with that, and you still turned into this." His hand trailed along the side of my face, his eyes regarding me in what I could only describe as amazement.

I swallowed. "I was glad," I blurted. "Glad when he died. That my mom and I could escape. That she would be free of his chains. I'm still glad. What kind of person feels happy when their father dies?" I whispered with shame.

His fingers grasped my chin and forced me to meet his eyes. There was no disgust in his gaze. I'd been expecting to feel a new wash of shame as Asher digested my words, but nothing. The look on his face seemed like, pride. Respect.

"The most magnificent creature I've ever met, that's who," he murmured softly. "The woman who hides the ugliness of what a monster did to her under the most beautiful surface I've ever seen. That beneath that surface lies more blinding beauty, untainted by that ugliness. Strength."

A tear trickled down my cheek. Asher's hand swiped it away.

"I've never told anyone that before," I confessed.

He watched me with a gaze I couldn't decipher. "As sorry as I am that shit happened to you, Flower, I'm glad I get that. Another piece of you that's for me and me alone. I want all of you, but I'll treasure the pieces that you choose to give to me and no one else," he said, intensity drenching his beautiful words.

We stayed silent for a long time after that. It was a silence that spoke a thousand words at once. That seemed to create a connection I couldn't even understand, not at that moment. Three years later I'd still puzzle over it.

I trailed my hand across Asher's forearm. My back was pressed to his front, him holding me close to his naked body.

"Why don't you have any ink?" I asked suddenly. "Apart from on your back, the club emblem, why nothing else?"

Almost every other member of the club was covered in tattoos.

Asher's arms tightened around me. "Tattoos are for life." His breath tickled my ear. "Apart from the club, I've never loved anything that much to commit to a lifelong reminder of it on my body."

He pulled me onto my back and moved atop of me, holding his weight so his body only just skimmed mine. His eyes searched mine.

"Why? Are you disappointed I'm not covered in ink like the rest of my brothers?" His voice was teasing, but there was a hardness underneath it, almost vulnerability.

I stroked his jaw, feeling bold, like I'd been ever since we'd entered this bed. It was like my shyness melted away and I could be the me only a handful of people made me be.

"No," I said decisively. "I'm nowhere near disappointed. You're perfect," I added in a whisper.

"No such thing as perfect, Flower," he murmured back. His fingers played with my hair. "If there was, I'm so far from that end of the spectrum it's not even fuckin' funny." He looked at me. "Though, if perfect does exist, I'm looking at the embodiment of it right here."

My stomach did something weird at his words. Not weird wonderful, but weird like I ate a bad tuna sandwich.

"You don't have to lie anymore, you've already got me into bed," I said lightly, trying to hide my own vulnerability.

Asher's brows furrowed. "What the fuck are you talking about? Not one thing in this bed, not one thing between you and me is a lie. You know that shit. You also know how fuckin' beautiful you are," he clipped.

I felt my face flame. Anger coiled in my belly. "You don't have to say that, I know I'm not. I'm okay with it," I responded in a hard voice.

Asher's face turned stormy. "You know you're not what?" he asked slowly.

"Beautiful," I snapped, using my anger as a shield for my insecurities. I never snapped at anyone. It was another thing I surprised myself with.

"You're fucking kidding me, right?" he ground out.

I opened my mouth to respond that... no, I was not, in fact *"fucking kidding,"* when a pounding at the door made me jump.

"Fuck off," Asher yelled, not moving off me.

"Bro, we need you," a deep voice called through the door.

Asher's eyes stayed on me. "I'm fuckin' busy," he bellowed.

"Steg's orders," the voice yelled back.

"Fuck," Asher muttered. He looked down at me. His finger trailed my jaw. "I've gotta go, Flower, but this shit's not over," he declared, frowning.

I frowned too. Not because of the conversation, but at the prospect of him leaving. All I wanted to do was cling onto him and beg him not to leave, but a little thing called self-respect stopped me.

"You stay here," he ordered. "I'll come back, we'll finish this ridiculous conversation, and after I've told you how stunning you are, I'll show you, too." His hand trailed down to lightly dance over my breast.

I sucked in a breath and my nipple hardened in anticipation.

Asher's face turned hard. "I do not want to leave this bed, but club business..." he trailed off as if *"club business"* served as an explanation. I guessed in this world, it did. "Sleep. And I'll be back," he promised.

"Okay," I heard myself saying.

He nodded, pushing up from the bed to dress.

I watched him silently. It wasn't uncomfortable silence. Which was something different. I loved silence. My own company. Most people didn't get that, had to fill every void of noise with words, it made me anxious, the constant need to measure time with words. Not now.

He was slipping on his cut when he turned to look at me. Something worked in his eyes as his gaze ran over me. The bed depressed when he leaned in to claim my mouth. It wasn't hard to get lost in the kiss.

"Do you really have to go?" I whispered against his mouth, self-respect be damned, I didn't want him to go. Didn't want the spell to break with the harsh light of day.

He regarded me before sighing and straightening. "Yeah, babe, club shit."

I tried not to let my disappointment show.

I think I failed because his face softened. "I'll be back. Stay. Sleep. Don't fuckin' move outta my bed," he commanded hoarsely.

He waited for my nod, then left the room.

I didn't know how the heck I managed it, in an unfamiliar room, in a biker clubhouse, but I fell right to sleep.

I AWOKE TO A POUNDING HEADACHE.

I blinked at my unfamiliar surroundings in confusion before realizing where I was. What happened last night, no early this morning. What I'd told him—about me, about my life, about my father. Holy shit, it was real. The fact I was waking up in Asher's room in the Sons of Templar compound was proof enough. And the tenderness between my legs served as more evidence. The pounding headache was an unwelcome reminder.

Since I hadn't exactly slept last night, I was guessing I was experiencing a delayed hangover. They weren't fun.

Note to self—don't drink.

Though, if the tequila was the reason I was waking up here, was the reason I turned into somehow desirable to Asher, I'd put it in a sipper bottle and take it everywhere I went.

Last night was something more than just sex. Through the haze of residual drunkenness, I could still see it. I knew that girls were desperate to find a connection to their first time. Maybe that was what I was doing, desperately seeking something more than just losing my virginity to a guy I'd only just met, and letting him own every inch of my body. But that was just it. I felt owned. Possessed. In a good way. I belonged to him. Already.

I pushed up out of bed and put my palm on my forehead. "Ouch," I muttered as the motion sent sharp pain through my skull. My stomach rolled slightly.

I searched the floor for my dress.

"Great," I muttered to myself, picking up the garment that would be useless in covering my modesty thanks to its lack of buttons.

I had to admit, Asher ripping the buttons off my dress was fricking hot. It did hold a slight dilemma as to clothing choices now, though. He did say he'd be back, and the clock told me it had been three hours since he left. I was only using the facilities, so I shrugged on a tee that swamped me, covering more than the dress would have.

I reluctantly opened the door, emerging into the empty hall. My heart pounded with nerves. I was in a biker compound and felt heaviness in my chest as the reality of this settled. Now that Asher was gone, that demon that clenched its fists around my personality, muting me, returned. I didn't do well with all-girl sleepovers, feeling awkward and on the edge of a panic attack the one time I did it. How was I meant to navigate *this*?

I took a deep breath, found my strength and found the facilities without encountering anyone. With luck, everyone would either be sleeping off hangovers—like I wished I was still doing —or out on this elusive *"club business."*

My luck ran out as I almost collided with a girl as I approached Asher's door.

"Sorry," I apologized quickly, stepping back.

The woman regarded me. She had bleached blonde hair, it was haphazardly thrown into a messy ponytail. Her makeup, likely from the night before, was slightly smudged and there was a lot of it. She was wearing heels and the shortest red dress I'd ever seen. And she was looking at me like I was the dirt on her stiletto heel. The pressure on my chest intensified, and I felt panic bubbling in my stomach.

"Watch it, bitch," she sneered.

I shrank back into myself at the hostility. I wasn't prepared for it, and it hit me like a ton of bricks.

Her kohl-rimmed eyes ran over me, I knew the look. It was one a predator gave its prey, she identified that I was weaker than her, someone she could assert her dominance over. I'd had it happen to me. Not often, but a couple of times, from girls who thought I was trying to *"steal"* their boyfriends. Which was a joke really when I'd never even had a boyfriend, let alone had enough romantic skill to steal someone else's.

When they'd unleashed on me, I'd turned mute, tried to make myself small and quiet, the way I'd survived when I was escaping my father's wrath. The woman glanced at the door my eyes were darting to. I yearned for the solace that Asher's room offered, and she let out a cruel laugh.

"Asher's really scraping the bottom of the barrel," she mused. "He likes his women sexy usually, not Mormon mutes. Wouldn't be getting myself comfortable there, Jane. He's probably already abandoned you, hoping you're gone when he gets back," she hissed icily.

My face paled at her venomous words. I tried not to hyperventilate.

She raised an eyebrow. "That's what he did, isn't it? Left at the crack of dawn? Honey, take a hint. He's not into you. You should go back to the convent." She patted my arm condescendingly and smiled with venom before turning on her heel.

I quickly darted through the doorway, blinking away the tears. Though the woman had been horrible and unnecessarily bitchy, she had been right. It was as if she'd spotted every single one of my insecurities and attacked them.

I couldn't survive here.

Where I would have to live on the edge of panic every time I needed to use the facilities. I wished I wasn't like this. That anxiety didn't dictate every inch of my life, but wishing didn't get me anywhere. The certainty that I would never be able to survive this lifestyle washed over me like ice water. No matter how I felt about Asher, he'd quickly lose interest when he realized how weak I was.

I scrambled to find my things while I scrolled through my phone with blurry eyes.

"Whoever has the audacity to call me at this hour is going to have a size nine stiletto embedded in their shin bone," a cranky voice hissed into the phone.

"Bex," I whispered through my tears. "I need you to come get me."

"Where are you?" she demanded, instantly alert.

"At the Sons of Templar compound in Amber," I choked.

There was a pause. "Fuck," she finally muttered. "Do I need my Glock? I don't care if they're an outlaw motorcycle gang and all around bad ass motherfuckers, I'll pop a cap in all their tight asses if they hurt you," she said into the phone, anger saturating her tone.

"No, no one hurt me. I just need out. And clothes," I added cringing at the thought of leaving here in Asher's tee. Of being any more exposed than I already felt.

There was another pause, another curse. "Sit tight honey, I'll be there in ten."

"Okay," I whispered and rang off.

I focused on breathing, on convincing myself that the struggle to get air was mental, not physical. That the reason for it was my mind's inability to handle unexpected situations.

My weakness.

BEX WAS THERE IN TWENTY, no matter the fact, it was over half an hour to our place in Tasman Springs.

All I had wanted to do was curl up in Asher's bed, hiding from the world and that horrible woman's words until Bex came. The reason I didn't was twofold. Bex didn't know her way around the clubhouse, and I didn't want her to have to navigate it. I didn't trust her not to bring and brandish her gun, causing all sorts of drama to add to my mortification.

Plus, I couldn't curl up in Asher's bed, the bed I'd lost my virginity in. The bed my shyness fell away in, and I spoke in soft whispers to the man I'd only just met, told him more than I had anyone. I couldn't lie in the bed that I'd fallen a little bit in love with Asher in.

Or a lot in love.

So I sat with my back pressed against the door, my head on my knees, willing myself not to cry. Reminding myself that the heaviness in my chest wasn't the work of asthma, but of my mind. That my mind was responsible for me feeling like no air could make it into my lungs. I pushed off reluctantly when my phone pinged alerting Bex's arrival.

I took a deep breath.

"You can do this," I muttered to myself.

I opened the door, holding my shoes and creeping down the deserted hallway. I inwardly cringed at the fact I was doing this, the walk of shame. I didn't feel shame over what I did, moreover who I was. I wished I were someone different. Someone stronger. Someone who could have sparred right back with that woman, someone who could have let those words roll right off and slide back into bed and wait for Asher, but I wasn't. Those words pierced deep and punctured every one of my insecurities.

Though luck hadn't been with me before, it seemed to be now as I slowly walked into the wide common area of the compound. I was almost home. I could see Bex leaning against her car, pushing her sunglasses off her head and squinting into the building.

I scurried to meet her.

My scurrying was hampered by the fact I slammed right into a brick wall.

I looked up.

No, not a brick wall, just a wall of human muscle. The man in front of me, one I recognized, and even though he was the one that intimated me the least, my heart still pounded out of my chest.

I stepped back quickly, my eyes wide.

"Sorry, I didn't see you, I was just leaving," I said quickly, my eyes darting anywhere but his.

I watched him look me up and down, and then his features turned stormy. I cringed that I was the reason his carefree face was contorted in such a way.

"Lily, you came out of Asher's room," Lucky observed in a hard voice.

My already wide eyes gaped. He knew me? Of course he

knew me, he was at Gwen's last night, but I hadn't realized he'd remember me, though. But he did. And he saw me in Asher's tee, clutching my shoes and trying to gather my dignity. I inwardly cringed and felt my face flame.

I tried to step around him. "I'm sorry, I've got to go," I whispered brokenly and desperately.

His body stepped in my path.

I looked at him through my lashes, trying not to cry.

Be strong, Lily.

"Stupid fuck," he bit out, his humor still absent.

"Wha-what?" I stuttered, unsure of how to handle the anger directed at me.

His eyes softened slightly as if he realized the effect his tone was having. "Asher. He's a stupid fuck. Did he hurt you?" he clipped, looking at my state of undress in distaste.

I self-consciously tugged the tee down. I furrowed my brows. Lucky seemed to be concerned for me. His apparent concern didn't dampen the panic crawling up the edges of my throat. I'd kept it at bay, but I realized I couldn't fight it for much longer. I didn't need to lay any more parts of myself lying around this place, an anxiety attack would shatter me in this moment.

Be strong.

"Lil?" a sharp voice penetrated my confusion and caused relief to ripple through my body.

Lucky stepped aside, his head turning to where Bex stood in the doorway. Her arms were crossed and eyes narrowed on him.

Even though I guessed she'd just gotten out of bed, she looked good. Her black hair was messed in the bed head look, thanks to her choppy layers that dusted her shoulders. There was a bright blue streak along the front of her head. The color changed routinely. I guessed she was still wearing last night's eyeliner, but it still looked good. Her white ripped jeans and cropped tee showed off her body.

I watched in amazement as Lucky's eyes took her in with hunger in his gaze. Well, not amazement really, she was hot, and he was a renowned ladies' man.

She was having none of that.

She pushed off the doorway, glaring at him. Taking my hand, she gave me a worried glance before directing her anger at Lucky, stepping in front of me and right in his grill.

That girl had no fear. It would be the death of her one day.

"You keep your biker mitts off her. I don't know what you fuckers have done to her already, but if it's anything bad, I'll be coming back here with Molotov cocktails. *Capice?*" she hissed, not intimidated by his hard stare, his size, his muscles, or the general air of danger around him.

She didn't wait for his response before she dragged me out the door as gently as she could. Before we reached the gravel forecourt, she turned to me, thrusting flip flops I hadn't noticed she was holding. She took my wedges.

"Put these on, babe," she said softly, her eyes darting around as if she was expecting a surprise attack.

I did as instructed. "How did you know I'd need these?" I asked in amazement.

She raised an eyebrow. "This is far from my first rodeo, girlfriend. Though, I know it's yours." Her brows furrowed and she resumed dragging me to the beat up hatchback we shared. Funds didn't allow for us to both have a car.

"Fucking bikers," she muttered under her breath.

Once we were safely in the car and had the compound in her rear view, worried eyes darted to me.

"Want to talk about it?"

I looked out the window. "Not really."

I saw her nod in my peripheral. "Just need to know, did the fucker hurt you?" Her voice was ice.

I didn't move my gaze. "No," I whispered, "that's the problem."

CHAPTER SIX

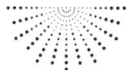

TWO DAYS LATER

"CANCER?" I repeated in a tortured voice.

My mom smiled a sad smile, squeezing my hand. "Yeah, baby. Not the best news I've had."

I gaped at her, tears welling in my eyes, refusing to believe this. "No, no. They've made some kind of mistake. Doctors do that all the time, take out the wrong organ, mix up babies. This is wrong," I declared firmly.

My mom was calm. "As much as I admire your distrust of the public system, they are right this time," she said, her voice light.

I shook my head, a thousand thoughts dancing around in it. I'd only just arrived home, Mom had called me and asked me to come home for dinner. I had sent her a text two days before, explaining I was going straight back to Tasman Springs, lying about an assignment I needed to get done.

I'd assumed she wanted to grill me about my night with Asher, as I had been dodging any contact for two days, wallowing in pity, unable to handle having to provide the details I knew Mom would demand. I was bracing, rehearsing it, reopening wounds that hadn't even begun to heal.

Instead, she told me this.

One little word tore through every inch of me.

I stared in her eyes, the vibrant ice blue ones with little to no wrinkles around them. The only lines that were there were a result of eleven years of happiness, of laughter. The horror that she endured for years before that was nowhere to be seen on her face, those scars lay down somewhere, I knew.

Her beautiful blonde hair was yet to be streaked with gray, and she had it bound in a braid to the side of her head. She was wearing her usual array of colors and textures. She didn't look sick. She looked as she always did.

"When d-did you f-find this out?" I stuttered, grasping at what this meant.

She squeezed my hand. "Yesterday," she told me quietly.

Yesterday.

Razorblades chewed at my stomach. I had been worrying about my own inconsequential self, my mom was facing this news alone. I'd been avoiding contact with her because I couldn't cope with voicing something that was dwarfed by the news she'd been dealing with.

I blinked away tears. "Why didn't you tell me?" I whispered. "I would have come, I would have—"

"Peanut, I didn't want you to have to be dragged along to some depressing hospital." She wrinkled her nose in distaste. "Those places are full of germs anyway. I wouldn't want you catching something for my sake," she continued, thinking of anyone but herself, like always.

"Mom, I would've come. I would've been there for you," I declared shakily. "It's fixable, right? They can fix you?"

My frantic mind clung to the fact that she didn't look sick, so she couldn't be *that* sick. They found it early. They'd fix her.

She squeezed my hand. "We give this positive thought, and I'm sure the universe will heal me. It wouldn't be so cruel to take me away without seeing my baby girl set the world on fire," she replied with a small smile.

She was wrong.

The universe was that cruel.

Cruel enough to plague my mother, the woman who ate only organic, vegetarian, didn't smoke, didn't drink, with a disease that took everything from her.

That also took everything from me.

I OPENED the door to the persistent pounding that had penetrated the sound of the loud music playing in the house. Mom was in the studio out back, switched off to the world. She was feeling inspired again, I didn't want to interrupt her if painting got her through right now, I'd give it to her.

I'd been lying on my old bed staring at the ceiling, feeling too numb to cry, or to do anything. I'd been Googling Pancreatic cancer for a while, but the low survival rates and the description had me first running to the bathroom to throw up, then bursting into a fit of tears.

My mind had been whirling, swimming in the complexities that came with that evil word.

Cancer.

We were going back to the doctors tomorrow. I was meant to go back home today, back to school tomorrow, but there was no way mom could convince me to. I wouldn't let her go through one step more of this alone. I'd drop out of college and move back here if that's what it took.

I'd had multiple calls on my cell from a blocked number throughout the past few days, and had ignored them initially because of shame. Shame at the realization that I'd never be able to be whoever Asher needed. That I couldn't function in his world. He may have taken my breath away, but situations like the one I'd been in the other morning stole it from me, left me gasping.

He had texted me first. I had no idea how he'd even gotten my number.

ASHER: *Babe. Thought I made myself clear, I didn't want you going anywhere. Where the fuck are you?*

THERE WAS no greeting nor sign off. Obviously, Asher decided he needed no introduction. I had immediately deleted the text. I'd desperately wanted to respond, to answer the calls, but I didn't even know what I'd say. What explanation could I give?

My phone had dinged earlier today, before the news.

ASHER: *You don't want this? Then let me know. But I know you do. We both do. Don't run from this.*

I HAD ENTERTAINED the idea of responding, of trying to be brave and follow my heart, try to ignore my traitorous head. He'd still been in the back of my mind throughout all this. That was the problem. How selfish could I be? My mom was just diagnosed with cancer, I was worrying about my love life? No. I had to take care of her. *That had to be over.*

It never would have worked anyway. I could barely function in the world my mom had brought me up in, the one with happiness and free love and no judgment. Their world—the scary, enticing and dangerous world would chew me up and spit me out.

So when I'd opened the door, I hadn't been ready. I had been raw.

"What the fuck, Lily?" I was immediately greeted with a hot and enormous biker taking up the doorway. His eyes were blazing with anger.

I jerked in surprise then whipped my head behind me to make sure Mom wasn't in the immediate vicinity. She did not need this. I quickly stepped out of the door, closing it behind me. This motion caused me to get right in Asher's grill, my body brushing his. I tried to scramble out of his manly stratosphere, but hands on my hips stopped me.

I ignored this. Or tried to. "What are you doing here?" I hissed. "Are you stalking me?" I added, registering the fact that he not only knew where my mom lived, but also the fact that I was here and not in Tasman Springs.

His brows furrowed and the hands tightened. "I've been asking myself the same thing since the moment I got off my bike," he responded, his eyes on mine. "You left. Normally I'm not one to chase, to try to figure out what goes on in women's heads with this kind of shit…" he paused, his face gentling and brushing my hair out of my face, "but this particular head, I want to know what went through it to make you leave. To make you run. From us."

A lance of pain joined the agony I had surrendered to since my mom told me. This was different. I couldn't let it in.

I frowned at him. "How do you know where I live?" I asked, dodging the beautiful words he'd uttered. "How did you know I was even here?"

His eyes turned hard at my response. "Your roommate informed me, after treating me to an impressive array of curse words, I didn't even know existed. That's saying something, considering the men I call brothers," he explained with a twinkle in his eyes.

"Bex," I muttered.

I'd told her little about what happened with Asher, though I hinted at the fact that I didn't belong in *that* world. That I wasn't strong enough. She had argued vehemently with this and had urged me to answer Asher's calls. It seemed she was taking matters into her own hands by disclosing my location.

His face hardened once more. "You wanna let me in on the reason why I came back to an empty bed two days ago? Why I got no explanation? Why you've been ignoring me?" he asked in a brisk voice. "Shit move, Flower. After what we had."

Normally, the face of such fury, or the mere presence of a male, let alone one like this would turn me into a mute mess, I failed to flinch in the face of his anger. Not this time. I didn't know whether it was the shock of the news my mom had dumped on me, or the fact I felt different with Asher. It wasn't up for inspection right now. Or ever. He needed to leave.

"I thought I'd do us both a favor and do what you wanted me to do and leave," I told him flatly.

I'd been lying to myself the reasons why he'd been calling me, texting me, was because of the fact he didn't like someone disobeying his alpha orders, not because he felt for me what I felt for him.

His already dark face turned stormy. He leaned in. "What are you talking about? Did anything about my actions that night, and the morning after, communicate the fact I wanted you to leave?" he asked slowly.

Somewhere deep down, I realized the truth in his statement. He had wanted me to stay. Treated me like I was something more than I was. I was too easily swayed to think otherwise. My mind was too quick to think the worst.

"Yeah, Flower. I know you're innocent, not experienced, so I was trying to be patient. But I can't. Not with you. You already fuckin' consume me. One goddamned night and you're under my skin," he whispered, his anger melting away.

My stomach dropped and my heart flew at his words, and the tenderness of the voice. The look in his eyes. His wasn't mincing his words, wasn't playing games or pretending he didn't feel this. It was real, honest. I couldn't believe it. The fact this man, this beautiful, rugged man, wanted me. In a way, a man wants a woman. Me. Ordinary, boring me.

But then reality came back in. I couldn't do this. Couldn't be consumed with him like I already was when my mom needed me. All of me. I could not put something as frivolous as my heart before her.

Asher's hand stroked my cheek. "This is more, babe. Special. You know it. I wouldn't have taken your virginity if I hadn't intended on treasuring that gift, treasuring the woman who gave it to me."

I stared at him. I tried to blink away the tears, tried to imprint this moment into my memory. The moment of someone actually seeing me. Wanting me.

"No. It's not," I whispered, brokenly at first. Then I found my strength, stepped out of his arms and put what I hoped was a blank expression on my face. "This was nothing more than one night. Not for me," I told him, my heart breaking.

Asher regarded me with cool eyes. I succeeded in hiding my flinch at the juxtaposition of that, and the tender look that had warmed my heart moments before.

"You're screwin' with me, right?" he clipped, hands crossing across his chest.

Don't look at the way his biceps flex at that gesture. I told myself. *It'll ruin everything.*

"I'm not," I informed him, impressed at the lack of emotion in my voice. "I don't want this." I waved my hand between us. "It was one night. That's it. Nothing more. So you need to leave," I instructed in a cool voice while white hot pain sliced through my insides.

Asher stared at me. "Whatever it is screwing with your head, saying that shit, you better straighten it now, 'cause I ain't coming back. You kicking me to the curb like this, playing some sort of game? I don't play games, Flower. I'm disappointed it seems you do, it means you're not who I thought you were."

I flinched. "You don't know me," I whispered. "You spent one night with me, you don't know anything about me."

He stepped forward. "That's where you're wrong," he declared hotly. "I spent that night inside you, exploring every inch of you, not just your body, but your fuckin' *soul*, Flower. You opened up to me, not just your legs, you gave me everything. Now in the harsh light of day you're running scared? Don't do that shit, you'll regret it," he growled, his hands moving to my neck.

I blinked a couple of times, trying to clear my vision of the tears obscuring them.

"You need to leave," I told him, ignoring the beautiful sentiment, and truth behind his words. As insane as it was. He was right. It had been more. The most it could be. And the only thing it could be. The best night of my life. Who knew the best night of my life would be followed up with the worst day of my existence in the space of a couple of days?

His face wiped of all emotion. "You better be sure of this shit, flower," he ground out. "I'm not fuckin' around. I ain't waiting for you."

"Please leave," I repeated, unable to say anything else.

Asher's cold expression searched my face and he stepped back, shaking his head. "Fuck this," he muttered.

He turned his back, giving me one last view of his cut, of him, before he mounted his bike and roared off.

I stood woodenly on the doorstep, watching him go, my heart bleeding, and my expression blank.

He didn't look back, once.

~

PRESENT DAY

ASHER

He lied.

He did fuckin' wait.

Three years Asher waited for Lily to get her shit together, for her to grow up, realize what was real between them, to come back.

Three years of agony, of dreaming of her, trying to forget her, fuck her out of his system.

He didn't grovel. He wasn't gonna follow her around like a puppy dog, trying to convince her to take a chance on them, on him. Nope. He wasn't exactly sure whether she was playing fucked up games, or was genuinely scared of the depth between them from just one night.

He knew one thing, though, she was a fuckin' liar. She felt something. He knew that. That night, being the first man into her sweet pussy, the first to explore her sweet little body, best of his miserable life. Superseded the night he got patched into the Sons.

That scared him shitless. That one night and one bitch could get under his skin, and play games with his mind. Worse that she stayed there for three fuckin' years. He watched his brothers find it. Grab a hold of that shit, claiming their Old Ladies, happily being pussy whipped.

Even fuckin' *Bull* found that shit.

But not him. No. For a year he watched her, in agony and anger at her coldness, at the way her gaze flickered over him as if they were strangers. He didn't miss the fleeting times when her mask slipped, the times that gave him some kind of fucked up hope. Then he saw nothing of her. She stopped working at

Gwen's store. That was worse. He wanted to watch her, follow her, make sure she was okay.

He didn't do that. Not only would that make him a lovesick pussy, but a stalker also. So he waited. Though he tried to lie to himself and say he didn't. Tried to act like she wasn't all he thought about when he drilled into club whores—it wasn't her milky white skin, her long blonde hair, her fucking piercing eyes that he pictured.

"Asher?" Lucky brought him out of his pining.

Good thing too. He needed to stop this shit. Now. Needed to move the fuck on and stop acting like a fucking chick. Enough was enough. He had been holding onto this shit for too long. He'd been holding onto the feeling she had given him that night. The feeling of home.

He'd never had one, not a real one, not since Benjamin. With her soft body in his arms was when he felt it. He knew it had been fucked up, insane even, the way he felt about her. The certainty he had for what was between them. He'd held onto insanity for too long.

"Yeah?" he jerked his head from where he was working on a car in one of the bays.

Lucky leaned casually on the car. "Just wanted to know if you were going to the funeral," he asked with a blank expression.

Asher straightened from the hood of the car, giving his brother his full attention. "Whose funeral? Yours? Your bitches finally found out about each other?" he joked.

Lucky didn't smile, unusual, fucker was always smiling, even at jokes made at his own expense.

"Nah, bro. Lily's mom's funeral. Gwen, Amy, and the girls are going. The club's going, to show support. I thought you'd want to go." Something worked behind the fucker's usually teasing eyes.

Asher hadn't forgotten the anger he'd unleashed on him three years ago.

He'd gotten back from the business, which was taking care of some tweaker fucking up one of their shipments, anxious to wipe the blood from his hands and then erase the deeds in Lily's body. Lucky had slammed him up against the wall, in the hall next to his door.

"WHAT THE FUCK?" he clipped.

He was not prepared for the anger coming from his usually care-free friend. Nor did he have the time or patience to inspect the reason for it.

"Tell me you didn't fuck her over," Lucky growled, getting in his face.

Asher shoved him back, with effort. He was a big fucker. But didn't mean Asher didn't pump iron five times a week for nothing.

"What are you talking about?" he shot, straightening his cut.

Lucky glared at him with empty eyes. "Lily."

Asher's entire frame jerked at the mention of her name. Anger he didn't know he was capable of feeling toward his brother simmered at the mere mention of her name.

"Not a bitch to fuck around with. Not her," Lucky continued, not flinching in the face of his fury. "She's not some club slut, so you treating her that way is not fuckin' acceptable. She's a fucking kid. Innocent as they come. You corrupted that shit? Bruised that innocence," his voice was flat but anger, no, fury simmered beneath the surface.

Asher's voice was not flat when he replied, nor did his anger simmer. It was right there. He stepped forward dangerously. "I fuckin' know that, brother," he spat. "What the hell does she have to do with you?" he asked quietly, curiosity underneath his anger.

The fact he was going to bat for a woman was not unusual. As much as he fucked them around, he respected them. Asher didn't know why he was going to bat for his woman. Why he seemed so furious. The fact he was having such a reaction to Lily, when Asher was reasonably sure he hadn't even spoken to her, grated him.

"She has nothing to do with me. Or you, for that matter. Fuck, brother, anyone could see a girl like that does not belong in our world. If she somehow finds herself there, she should not be running outta here half dressed with tears in her fuckin' eyes," Lucky shot with a level stare.

Asher jolted in surprise as Lucky's words sunk in. "What the fuck?" he muttered.

He didn't wait for a response, merely pushed into his room, swearing as he was presented with an empty, and mussed bed.

"Fuck!" he yelled at the empty room, at the bed where he experienced the best night of his life.

The next two days were miserable.

He didn't do miserable, especially pining over a chick. But Lily was different. He knew it the moment he laid eyes on her. He knew she was innocent when he first spoke to her, shy. But he had no fuckin' clue she was a goddamned virgin. He reasoned that a woman who looked like that could never be a fuckin' virgin.

White blonde hair, tight tanned body. Eyes as blue as the ocean. He figured the whole innocent act was just that, an act. He'd been around women all his life, who played various roles to get into bed. He'd quickly realized there was nothing fake about Lily or about how he felt for her.

Which is the reason he turned into a borderline stalker. He knew it was fucked up, but he couldn't stop.

After finally getting her address after unanswered texts and calls, Asher decided to go around. He'd ridden to Tasman Springs with nerves, and he never got fuckin' nervous. Not when going into situations where he was dodging bullets. So he couldn't figure out the reason for them when he knocked on a door of a shitty apartment building in an even worse part of town. Somewhere where Lily did not belong. He didn't expect the woman on the other side of the door.

Her black rimmed eyes regarded him and rested on his cut. They hardened. "The biker," *she spat with distaste. "And what in the fuck could you be wanting? Didn't get enough jollies hurting her the first time around?"*

Asher had been taken aback by her hostile demeanor and then her words.

Hurt Lily?

He'd sooner saw off his own arm. He'd finally been able to extract the information out of the small, but mouthy roommate. His determination intensified on the ride back to Amber. He needed to know what the fuck happened, that had her running out when he'd left her sated with a lazy smile on her face.

He'd not been happy with what he found. Dead eyes, emotionless voice. Her beautiful voice spouting lies about what they were. What they weren't. It surprised him that those words were like a blow to the stomach. That there was nothing he could do to convince her differently when shit had turned her resolve rock solid. He knew it in her face.

No way he'd grovel. Plead. No. So he left. The only girl who punctured his iron clad soul. The one who crawled under his skin.

"So you goin'?" Lucky asked, jerking him back into the present.

He didn't reply, just wiped his hands on a rag then strode in the direction of the clubhouse. He needed to shower, then he needed to get to his girl.

When he got to the cemetery, he was surprised. Not as surprised as Cade, Brock, and their women were to see him there, though he ignored that.

He only had eyes for one woman.

The one standing beside a casket covered in all sorts of crazy shit. The one wearing a bright yellow dress, one that showed just how much this shit had drained her. Her eyes were dead. He clenched his fists at the sorrow etched in her gaze. He near exploded at the fucker with his arms around her. He actually stepped forward without even noticing.

"Easy brother…"

He felt a firm hand on his shoulder.

He whipped his gaze to Brock, who had stepped away from his woman to restrain him. He regarded him levelly.

"Funeral isn't the best place to start a brawl," he stated quietly. "Won't do any good, 'specially won't do any good for her." He nodded his head at the woman staring into space.

Asher nodded tightly.

Brock stared at him a second more, satisfied he clapped his shoulder and moved back.

Asher watched the whole thing woodenly. Some part of him found it fuckin' insane that no one here, apart from the Sons, were wearing black. All of them were decked out in crazy colorful shit. Hippy shit. They were obviously Lily's people.

Surprised the shit out of him. Lily did not seem like she came from a free love household. Girl was as timid as a mouse, with everyone but him anyway. She wore fancy shit. Understated, as if she was trying not to draw attention to herself, but when you're that beautiful, you'd have to don a fuckin' sack to go unnoticed.

His entire body turned to stone when Lily got up, in front of the entire fuckin' crowd and spoke in her soft and throaty voice, speaking beautiful words about a woman who was obviously her world. She spoke like someone who didn't battle with crippling shyness, who wasn't wrestling with the demon of death.

His heart swelled with pride, admiration, and need. He couldn't go without her anymore. Couldn't let her go through this shit alone. During her speech, he had realized the reason for those dead eyes, that dismissal years ago. The reason why she'd quit the store, near dropped off the face of the earth—her mom. And he knew Gwen and the women had been oblivious to the fact her mom was even sick. He knew Lily would have some fucked up reason for that shit. Not telling people, not looking for help or support.

His gaze narrowed at the man who yanked her into his embrace when she finished.

First, he needed to eliminate that fuck.

CHAPTER SEVEN

LILY

WE ARRIVED BACK at the cemetery that was illuminated by the rising sun.

The place where my mom was buried.

The thought chilled me. But the morning sun shining on the place where she rested filled me with some warmth, even with the crispness of the morning air. She was surrounded by beauty. I was the one who had to live with the ugliness death left behind.

Asher stood with me as I regarded the scene silently. He didn't seem to find it uncomfortable, he didn't press to speak. Just stood there silent and sentinel, watching me, giving me strength. I forgot about that. The comfortable silence I'd enjoyed with him. I had gone over the words, I hadn't realized how the silence was just as important. It was only someone special you could be silent with. Once in a lifetime special.

"I'm going home now," I croaked, motioning to my car.

He nodded. "I'll follow you, babe," he declared as if it was some kind of foregone conclusion. As if my protests before were inconsequential.

I turned to fully face him. "No, you won't," I told him firmly.

He frowned at me, pushing off his bike, which he was leaning on. Leaning well I might add. He stood in front of me, not touching me, thankfully.

"I thought we'd discussed this," he said quietly.

I glared up at him. "*We* hadn't discussed," I snapped. "You did the whole 'I'm hot and alpha and my word is law' thing and expected me to obey. I don't obey."

Some strength, some backbone had emerged from God knows where. Maybe I had changed with the darkness that entered my soul. There was no reason to be timid and shy when I'd already realized my worst fears and lived them.

Asher's face turned dark. "You obey when I tell that tight little pussy to clench around my dick," he replied roughly.

I jolted. Both with shock and arousal. "We're in a cemetery, you can't say things like that," I chastised, redness creeping up my cheeks.

He grinned. "Babe, there's no one living here to hear us," he teased.

I flinched at his words and he immediately saw his mistake.

His hands grasped my hips. "Fuck, sorry, Flower," he muttered softly.

I blinked away my tears, gazing at him through my lashes. "I need you to give me space. Time," I whispered.

Asher frowned, stroking my cheek. "That's what I've been doing for three years, babe. Gotta say, I'm not fond of givin' you more," he grumbled.

I opened my mouth to argue, but his finger on my lips silenced me.

"Said I wasn't fond of it, not that I wasn't gonna give it to you," he continued.

I let out a breath of relief. As much as every fiber of my being wanted him, I knew I couldn't handle the complications. I needed to sort myself out. Figure out how to pick myself back up, rearrange my life around the gaping hole that was left in it.

"One condition. The boyfriend is out on his ass."

I sighed. "You don't get to dictate that," I told him quietly. I didn't have the energy to snap anymore. As quickly as the fire started, it burned out, leaving only the ashes of me left.

He opened his mouth, his jaw hard.

This time I was the one to silence him. "I'm going to be breaking up with *Aiden*," I enunciated his name, "because it's not fair to him. Because I don't need nor want a boyfriend right now," I said firmly, hoping my point came across.

His eyes softened slightly. "Good thing I don't wanna be your boyfriend," he stated flatly. "What I *am* is your man."

He kissed me firmly, silencing whatever weak protest that would've come from my mouth. I sank into his body as his arms went around me and his lips worked their magic.

When he released me, my brain was free of the troubles that been plaguing it.

He brushed my hair out of my face. "I'm givin' you time 'cause you need it, babe. Don't need too much of it, though, okay? We've got three years to make up for," he said softly against my mouth.

I didn't respond. I was still recovering from the kiss.

He smiled slightly. "You need anything, I'll be there. In a second, just a phone call away. Don't hesitate."

He waited for my nod and when he got it, he kissed my head softly.

"Get in the car, babe," he ordered.

"Okay," I murmured and turned to walk toward my car. Halfway there, I turned back. Asher was still in the same spot. "Thanks, I needed ... you," I told him, my stomach dropping at the declaration, and the truth behind it.

I hadn't let myself think about it during my grief, but I had been craving him, yearning for him to be my port in the storm. It was that yearning that stopped me from even entertaining the idea of calling him. Needing someone that much, meant heart-breaking agony when they were taken away. That's what scared me about this. No, terrified me.

His frame tightened and his eyes blazed at my words. "I'll always be here when you need me, Lily," he uttered. "And I'll always need you, too," he said in a much quieter voice.

I gave him one last look, then climbed into my clunky car and drove off. I looked in my rear vision mirror. Asher stood watching my car until I turned out of sight.

The troubles he erased with his kiss came hurtling back, as soon as my eyes lost sight of him.

"LILY," a frantic voice exclaimed as the front door slammed behind me.

Aiden rushed to me and grabbed my shoulders, a too little tightly.

"Where have you been?" he demanded. "I woke up to you gone, your phone still here, no note. You scared the hell out of me, Lil."

"I told him, you were unlikely to be tied in a basement some-where considering your car was gone," Bex added from the kitchen, clutching a coffee and looking bleary eyed. "Most likely you just needed some *alone* time, since you haven't had that in a while," she emphasized the word "*alone*" staring at Aiden's back —no, glaring.

She directed a softer look at me. A look of understanding. She knew me. Knew I needed my own space to process, and to sort my head. I didn't do well with people living in my pocket. I liked my own company. Needed it. She'd been living with me for three and half years. She got it. Most people, like Aiden, didn't get it.

Aiden ignored Bex.

"Where were you?" he demanded, rather sharply.

I squirmed in his grip. "Aids, you're hurting me," I told him quietly.

He looked down at his hands as if he was surprised they were there. He immediately released me and I rubbed my shoulders absently.

"Sorry," he said quickly, frowning at his hands. "I was just worried. You disappearing, going through what you're going through. I didn't want you to be alone."

I inwardly cringed. I wasn't alone. I was with the man who'd haunted my dreams for the past three years. I'd let him fuck me on his bike. Correction, I had done the *"fucking."* Guilt washed through me, turning my stomach.

"Coffee," Bex declared from beside me, handing me a cup.

I took it gratefully. She gave me a knowing look. Like she knew exactly what I was doing.

"I'll be in my room, sleeping until a normal hour, now that we don't have to call in *Liam Neeson* to retrieve Lily from a hostage situation," she declared drily.

She moved in to kiss my cheek. "Here if you need me, Lils babe," she said quietly in my ear, her eyes darting to Aiden in disdain.

I gave her a smile. "Love you," I whispered, needing her to know how much her quiet support and even her snarky remarks helped.

"Ditto." She winked, scowled at Aiden then walked to her room.

"Want to tell me where you went?" he asked softly.

I paused. "Let's sit down," I stalled, pointing to our floral sofa. It had a giant hole in the arm, which was covered by a printed pashmina. Apart from that, it was actually awesome. Covered in sequined cushions and fluffy throws.

The perfect space to break up with someone.

Not.

Once we were situated, with Aiden holding my hand, I spoke.

"I went for a drive, just needed some time to think," I started in a small voice. I wasn't lying, only omitting the truth. "On my drive I realized that I need to have some space right now. Need to get my life back together." The thought of doing that without my mom made me taste bile, but I focused on the task at hand. "I can't do that to you. Can't give you what you want the way I am now," I whispered.

Aiden's face was soft, he stroked my cheek. "It's not about you giving me anything. I'm here to give you whatever *you* need, Lily. I'm here for the long run. I care about you, a lot."

"You're *such* a nice guy," I whispered. "But I wasn't in the right frame of mind when this started. I needed someone for comfort. It isn't fair to you. We're better as friends."

Aiden sat back, his face blank. "You're not budging on this," he stated his eyes hard.

I shook my head. "I'm sorry."

He nodded. "Yeah," he muttered.

Silence descended. Unlike with Asher, it wasn't comfortable. I fiddled with my fingers, my anxiety rearing its head. I didn't do well in situations like this. Nervousness crawled all over me like hives.

"I guess I knew it," Aiden said finally. "Knew you didn't feel the same as I did for you. You're so reserved. I never know what you're thinking. It just makes you that much more intriguing. I wanted to be the man that opened you up, got inside that shell," he sighed, "but I'm not that man, am I?" It wasn't really a question, he was resigned to the fact.

I shook my head slowly.

He nodded again and leaned forward kissing my head softly. "This is not what I want, I'm just clarifying that now," he told me quietly. "You change your mind, I'm here. But if not, I'm still your friend, okay?"

Such a nice guy.

I nodded and smiled. "You'll find her. The one that's right for you. It's just not me."

He gave me a sad smile. "We'll agree to disagree there."

He stood. I stood with him, awkwardly walking to the door.

"You'll call if there's anything you need?" he asked firmly.

"Yeah," I whispered, knowing I wouldn't, not for a while anyway.

What I needed was my mom back. He couldn't give me that. What I needed was solitude. That he could give me.

He gave me a sad look.

I sank against the back of the door when he was gone, letting out a breath of relief.

"Thank fuck for that, thought I'd have to flea bomb the place to get him out," Bex exclaimed.

I glanced over at her. She was leaning against her door jamb and eating straight from a tub of peanut butter.

My eyes widened at her. "You were eavesdropping?"

She rose her brows. "Um ... of course," she replied as if I was crazy for even asking her this.

I screwed my nose up at the container in her hands. "Please don't tell me that's your breakfast."

She shrugged. "Good protein," she mumbled.

I shook my head, making my way to the kitchen to make us breakfast. I wasn't hungry, I hadn't been for weeks, but it gave me something to do. Idle hands were the Devil's instruments. And with the Devil came the demons.

"You did the right thing," Bex declared, following me to plonk herself down on a barstool, peanut butter in tow.

I pulled eggs and milk out of the refrigerator, sitting them beside a loaf of bread.

She spied that and the pan I was getting out. "French toast? *Fucking sicko*," she exclaimed in an Aussie accent and put her peanut butter down.

I rolled my eyes. "I know I did the right thing. It didn't make hurting him any easier," I told her.

She rolled her makeup smudged eyes. "Ugh. Seriously, I love you more than life itself, Lilmeister, but stop caring about other people, especially douchebrain. Focus on yourself, for once in your life. Let this shit process. Yell, scream, cry, eat two tubs of ice cream while watching *The Biggest Loser*. I'm down for it all. Or to completely leave you in solitude," she offered, knowing me too well.

I leaned against the counter, putting my head in my hands for a moment. "I'm scared," I whispered then looked up at her. "For three years it's been constant motion. Taking care of Mom, studying, working, rinse and repeat. I haven't stopped. Haven't contemplated any of it. I'm terrified if I do let myself realize that she's gone, I'll get lost. I'll disappear in this chasm left in my life and never come out," I told her brokenly. "Mom's dead. Gone. It doesn't feel real." I stared at the door. "I'm expecting her to walk in here, paintbrushes in hand, declaring she's going to paint our living room to brighten it up," I said, choking on my tears.

Bex's face was a mask of grief, a mirror of mine. She pushed up off her stool and rounded the counter to take me in her arms.

"Fuck, Lils, we'll get through this, promise. I won't let you lose yourself," she whispered into my hair.

In that moment, I clung to my best friend like she was my lifeline. Maybe she was. I tried not to think about the other raft in the sea of grief I was floating in.

The one named Asher.

～

ASHER: *Thinking of you, Flower.*

. . .

A SMALL SMILE tickled the edge of my mouth as I re-read the text I'd gotten shortly after lunch. I hadn't even been without him for twenty-four hours, and I yearned for his touch. It was as if the three years of distance had been three minutes. As if I hadn't just broken up with my "*kind of*" *boyfriend* that morning.

ME: *It's been four hours. How can you be thinking of me already? I'm sure you've got much more important things to think about, like slinging back hooch and shooting guns.*

I BIT MY LIP, re-reading what I had typed. I erased it.

ME: *I'm thinking about you, too.*

I REPLIED SIMPLY. He hadn't written anything back; he was giving me space like I'd asked. I was grateful for it.

"Lil, you deserve a drink. Hell, I think it's medically necessary," Bex informed me, holding out a bottle. "I know you're not a drinker, and that you haven't touched a drop in three years. Haven't had *fun* in three years. Not that I'm suggesting any of this is going to be fun, but alcohol makes you think it is, for a while anyway," she told me sagely.

It was late afternoon. We had done exactly nothing. Ate french toast. Sat on our sofa and watched crappy reality television. Joked. Talked about Mom. Told funny stories.

It was weird. Sitting on the sofa in my PJs, with nothing to do, nowhere to be. I'd temporarily dropped out of college to work enough to support Mom, and have enough time to take care of her. My job at the bar had given me a few paid days off.

It might have been a dive, but my boss was pretty awesome, and she'd loved Mom.

So I had nothing. No hospital to visit. No research to do for last minute cures. No bills to pour over—apparently medical bills died with the patient—apart from the usual.

My mom always shined bright. Shined beautiful. When I was around her, I was bathed in that light too. I was intoxicated, like everyone, by her zest for life. It was contagious. She was brilliant. The ying to my yang. The only reason I felt okay about being me, about my shyness, was because I had her to balance me out. To tell me that who I was, was exactly who I was meant to be.

Without her, I was in danger of drifting away from who I'm meant to be. Or losing it altogether. Who was I without my ying? This was all too hard. The bottle Becky presented me with, offered the easy solution—oblivion.

I JERKED AWAKE, wiping drool from the side of my mouth.

So attractive.

I blearily regarded where I was.

Sofa.

Why was I on the sofa? My eyes touched an empty bottle of Jägermeister. Oh yeah, that's why. Might explain the headache too. The headache was worsened by the knocking at the door. It wasn't loud, but it seemed to echo off my skull.

"Whoever that is, you shoot them. Shoot them right in their hand, so they can't inflict this horror on anyone else," Bex mumbled from her spot on the floor.

I squinted at her, feeling more than a little fuzzy, I vaguely wondered why she was on the floor when her room and her bed were meters away.

After a second, I got up, deciding to save the person on the other side of the door from getting maimed by a sleep zombie Bex.

I flinched at the bright light that assaulted me when I opened the door, and it took a second for the people on the other side to come into focus. I blinked rapidly.

"I told you it was too early," Amy hissed knowingly at Gwen, who was gazing at me with a soft look on her pretty face.

She ignored Amy. "Lily, sweetheart. I'm sorry, we can come back." She motioned to turn around.

"Or," Amy cut in, "we can take you out for a nice greasy breakfast with a Bloody Mary on the side, it'll fix you right up."

"You had me at Bloody Mary," I heard Bex yell from somewhere behind me.

I flinched at the sound, too loud.

Amy grinned. "It's settled then." She pushed past my zombie form to make her way into my apartment.

My hungover brain realized I should have been embarrassed at these glamorous women seeing my far from glamorous home. Being in this neighborhood and looking at the crumbling paint covered by posters, the faded carpet disguised with colorful rugs, the ancient appliances.

I'd been to their place many times. It looked like the pages of a magazine, mirrored the images in my head of what I hoped my life might be like one day. Seeing Amy standing in the middle of my living room clutching a bag that cost the same as three months' rent had me cringing. And realizing my life might never get better than this.

She didn't seem ruffled. "Point me in the direction of your room, Lily. I'll get you an outfit together. Gwen will make you coffee." She directed a pointed glance at Gwen, who was still standing in the doorway.

I stood silent, still bathing in the shame that had begun to wash over me. And trying not to vomit as my hangover intensified.

"That way." Bex pushed herself off the floor and answered Amy with her hand. "I'll shower first. Knock down the door if I'm not out in twenty, it means I've passed out," she instructed seriously.

I nodded woodenly, watching Amy disappear into my room.

"Coffee," Gwen declared with a soft smile.

She did as Amy did, strutting through the door in her designer duds, not blinking at the rundown apartment and the damaged vintage furniture.

"Diggin' the boho vibe." She winked at me. "I'll totally have to get you to take me vintage shopping."

I didn't reply and her cheerful face changed, and she stepped forward, grasping my forearms lightly.

"I'm not going to ask how you are because that's a stupid question," she murmured. "I am going to tell you you're not going to feel like this forever. It seems like it, I know. But I promise it won't last that long. It gets better."

Her eyes twinkled with unshed tears, and I knew she was thinking of the brother she lost a couple of years ago. Her voice was so convincing, I almost believed her—almost. Gwen had strength—family. Bex was all I had. I didn't have family. And I knew what little strength I had was keeping me upright. It wasn't going to chase away the Big Bad, or the demons. Wasn't going to wrench the weight off my chest.

Gwen continued, "I know you don't like to talk about yourself. You think that you need to handle all of your problems alone. You don't," she squeezed my arms, "you've got people around you. Whatever you need. If you want to talk or just go to a crappy romance movie, I'm here for you, girl," she said quietly.

I blinked away the tears at the support she was offering, but managed a small nod.

"Thanks, Gwen," I choked out, unable to say much more.

She gave me a small smile, not making me feel awkward at my inarticulate response.

"It's what friends are for, Lily, remember that." She released my arms. "Now, let's get you caffeinated, and then we can set to repairing that hangover," she said with a knowing grin before she moved toward the kitchen.

She skirted past a wayward wine bottle to reach the coffee pot. She was dressed all in white, her chocolate hair piled atop her head. Her body didn't betray the fact she'd had two children, she seemed to be some kind of freak of nature. You'd expect someone like that to be frightfully awful and stuck up. Gwen was neither.

I tried to let her words penetrate. To give me a sense of hope that she might be right. Maybe one day I'd find a way to believe those words.

But right now, the darkness of grief had a firm clutch on me, so firm that I worried I'd never see the light again.

CHAPTER EIGHT

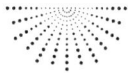

I GLANCED down at the name flashing on my ringing phone.
Asher.

My stomach did a somersault. I downed the remainder of
wine in my glass and stood. Bex gave me a small knowing grin,
but didn't say anything as I put the phone to my ear and walked
toward my room.

"Hey," I greeted quietly, closing the door.

It was early evening, Bex and I had recovered from our
hangovers, largely thanks to Amy and Gwen taking us out for
food. Since we were recovered, Bex declared the only logical
thing to do was to go out. I was happy to.

Alcohol promised numbness. Distraction. Anything that
quelled pain that had stitched itself to my soul was welcome.
We'd just started our *"pre-drinking"* and were getting ready to go
somewhere. I didn't care where. Anywhere that hid me from the
Big Bad that little bit longer.

"Flower," Asher's husky greeting sent tingles to my toes
much more effectively than my wine had done.

"Hey," I repeated.

I heard a throaty chuckle at the end of the phone. "Hey," he murmured.

There was a pause, a long one. It would have been awkward with anyone else, silence was kind of the opposite goal of a phone conversation, but it somehow wasn't.

I waited for the inevitable *"how are you going?"* that everyone asked the grieving relative. The question everyone knew the answer to, but the safe, expected social interaction.

"What's your favorite food?" Asher surprised me by asking.

I blinked. "What?"

"Your favorite food. See, I was sitting here thinking of you, and realizing I don't know much about you. Only how I feel about you. I want to know more. I want to know everything, Flower," he explained.

My stomach dropped again as I digested his words. He didn't say anything else as I was silent a moment. A long moment. He wanted to know me? Everything about me? I wanted to ask him why, why he seemed so interested in me when I was the most uninteresting person on the planet. I didn't.

"Steak," I said finally. Nothing else, no beautiful articulate reasoning that mirrored his own. I didn't do well with articulate in most situations.

There was a small pause. "Steak?" Asher repeated in disbelief. "The tiny waifish girl who looks like she eats salads for breakfast, lunch, and dinner, loves *steak?*"

I smiled, relaxing onto my bed. "Yeah. I love it. It was the only rebellious thing I've ever done in my mom's eyes. She was a vegetarian. My meat eating tendencies were her secret shame," I joked. Then I realized I was talking about her in past tense. My gaze flickered to the painting on my wall. The pain returned. It had never left, I guessed.

Asher didn't let me focus on it. "Well, I'll have to take you out for a giant steak for our first date."

"First date?" I repeated.

"Yeah," Asher confirmed. "See, we haven't had one of those, and I'm mighty keen to take you out. Show you off. When you're ready," he added.

I was silent for a long time. Again, he didn't press. "What if I don't know when I'll be ready?" I asked quietly.

Asher didn't pause. "Then I'll wait," he replied firmly, seeming unperturbed. "As long as you'll consent to me talking to you, calling you. Need to hear that beautiful voice at the very least. I wouldn't object to dirty pictures either," he teased.

I surprised myself by letting out a small giggle. "I'll consent," I said finally. "So, what's your favorite food?" I asked after another pause. I wanted to know him too, I realized.

Asher didn't miss a beat. "Tofu."

I surprised myself even more by bursting out with laughter.

And just like that, with a simple phone call, Asher seemed to salve some of the burn on my soul.

It felt good. Amazing in fact. I could get used to it.

That was the problem.

BEX WAS PAINTING her nails on the sofa while I made us lunch. I didn't think that putting frozen fries in the oven constituted *"making"* anything, but I was impressed I had the energy to do even that considering we hadn't arrived until the sun rose this morning.

"You know what? I'm not even hungover, or tired," I told Bex, straightening from the oven.

She didn't glance up from her task. "It's 'cause you're still a little bit drunk," she explained. "It'll hit you in a couple of hours, then you'll feel like you've been hit by a truck."

I screwed my nose up. "I'm not keen on that, alcohol is supposed to make you feel good isn't it?"

That was the whole reason I was doing this, being this person. This person who chugged beers at parties and did *Jell-O* shots. This person I didn't recognize. I didn't feel good. But I didn't feel anything. That was good.

Bex glanced up. "Yeah, it's not the alcohol that makes you feel bad the next day, it's the absence of it. Which is why we keep drinking," she told me cheerfully.

It was safe to say Bex was wholeheartedly on board with this new lifestyle I'd decided to adopt. The strip club where she worked had given her a few days off also.

Begrudgingly.

Her boss treated her like crap, but she was their main earner so he didn't have much choice but to give her the time off. She'd been a party girl since before I met her, but I knew even she didn't drink as much as we had been since ... since *it* happened. I guessed she was running too.

My heart did a skip when the sound of my phone jolted me out of my thoughts. I scrambled to snatch it off our counter, hoping it was him. I felt butterflies in the pit of my stomach at the name flashing on the screen.

"When the oven beeps you get up, take the fries out of the oven," I instructed Bex quickly. "If you don't, we both starve and die a fiery death when the oven catches fire," I warned.

Bex was not a cook.

She waved her free hand above her head. "Yeah, yeah, go and have your chat with your biker."

I didn't need to be told twice.

"Asher," I greeted softly as I closed the door to my room, sinking onto my bed.

"Flower," his raspy voice mumbling the name only he called me, and it was the best sound in the world. "You busy?"

"No," I answered quickly.

I may not know why he wanted to call me, to talk to me, but I knew I didn't want it to stop. I knew it was unhealthy.

Becoming this attached to someone who wouldn't be in my life for long, but I couldn't help myself. Calls with Asher went hand in hand with the fried food and alcoholic drinks, only they were unhealthy for my emotional wellbeing.

"Are you?" I asked.

There was a chuckle at the end of the phone. "Not right now, Lily. That's why I called you."

I felt my face flame. "Oh, right," I muttered. I was even awkward on the phone. Great.

"Even if I was busy, there's nothing that will stop me from speaking to my Flower," he told me as if I wasn't an awkward dork. As if I was special.

I swallowed. He was so candid. So free with his feelings. It was unnerving.

"Aren't guys like you meant to be mysterious and hide their feelings underneath a thick wall of muscle and testosterone?" I blurted, staring at my ceiling.

There was another throaty chuckle at the other end of the phone. "Guys like me?"

I fiddled with my comforter. "Hot guys. Bad ass biker types that leave feminine jaws dropping in their wake," I explained.

This time there wasn't a chuckle, there was a full out roar of laughter.

Usually, this would have me wanting to hang up the phone and hide underneath the comforter I was playing with. But he wasn't laughing at me. Not in that way.

"Flower, I'm not sure how I'm meant to act, or how mysterious I'm meant to be since I've never been in this situation," he replied.

"Situation?" I repeated.

"A situation where I've been unable to get a beautiful blonde out of my head for going on three years," he explained, his voice serious. "One where I've never wanted anything more than I want that particular blonde. I don't know what's going on in that beautiful head, I know she's going through shit, I know she's shy and oblivious to the effect she has on me…" he paused, and my stomach did somersaults, "so I'm trying to make it explicitly clear just how serious I am about her without scaring her off. Without her letting doubt corrupt that head. How am I doing?" he asked quietly.

I stared at the wall for a long moment. "You're doing pretty good," I whispered finally.

"Good," he said firmly.

He didn't let the conversation continue down this dangerous road. He moved on to topics mundane and decidedly less serious.

It didn't mean I didn't let those words rotate in my mind, and that I didn't think of it long after we'd said our goodbyes. I thought about it until I didn't think of much at all. Until I welcomed the blissful oblivion.

"WHAT MADE you want to patch into the Sons?" I asked shyly the next day, tired of him asking all the questions, desperate to know more about the man I'd loved for three years.

Asher paused. "I was a fucked up kid, shit at home wasn't good and I sought escape as soon it was offered. For a start, that escape took me down a bad road…" he paused again as if he was measuring his words, figuring out what to tell me, "I got out of that shit, joined the Navy, found discipline, order. Family. I got my shit together. I was good at it. The problem was I started to question the shit they asked me to do. Told me to do. I met Brock, he was serving the same time as me. He didn't like being told what to do either. So we got out. I followed him back to Amber, patched in as soon as I saw the club for what it was. A brotherhood. Family. The rest, as they say, is history," he explained.

I caught on to one thing he'd said. "You didn't have a family?" I asked quietly.

Asher paused. "I didn't. Till I did. I've got a huge, motley and loud family. They might not be blood, but the club, that's stronger than blood."

That hit me. Hit me hard. I yearned for that. A place that offered that. But no one could replace what I had. I moved my mind from those thoughts and focused on something else he said.

"How long have you been in the club?"

"Going on seven years," he replied.

I paused. *Seven years.* "I assume you had to probate, or whatever it is for a time before that?"

Asher choked out a laugh. "Prospect, babe," he corrected. "Yeah, for six months. Fuckin' misery, though I'm glad I didn't have to prospect when Gage was around, he puts those poor shits through Hell."

I pondered this. Seven and a half years with the Sons, time in the Navy. I assumed you had to be in the Navy for a while to become a SEAL.

"How old are you?" I asked finally. I had him pegged not much older than me, but he'd have to be way older if I factored all that in.

He seemed caught unaware. "Twenty-nine, why? You got an age limit on men you date?" he teased.

"Twenty-nine?" I repeated in disbelief. "But that's not enough time," I exclaimed.

"Not enough time for what?" he sounded amused.

"To become not only a bad ass Navy SEAL and then a bad ass biker," I blurted.

Asher choked out another laugh. "I joined the Navy at seventeen, flower. Trained for a year then served for four. Joined the Sons straight after."

"Seventeen," I repeated. "That's so young. You were just a

kid," I murmured. Too young to go down whatever dark road he went down. One I wanted to ask about but felt too shy to. I may have been coming out of my shell with him, but I'd never abandon it.

There was a pause. "Yeah, I was a troubled kid. Fucked up. I came out a man. Still fucked up in a way, differently 'cause of the shit I saw. The club showed me different kinds of fucked up, but it fixed what could be fixed," he replied.

I was taken aback. He shared so readily with me. Talked ... like really talked. Didn't grunt or speak in monosyllables. He was telling me about his life. Like he wanted me to know about it. Like he wanted me to be a part of it.

"What could be fixed?" I repeated. "What about what couldn't?"

"I'm starting to think only one person could fix that, I just have to be patient enough to wait for her," he murmured softly.

I let out a small gasp at the meaning behind his words at who *her* meant. I fiddled with the cushion on our sofa uneasily. He couldn't mean *me*. He had to know I couldn't fix him when I was beyond repair myself.

"You think that's me," I clarified.

"No," he said immediately. "I know it's you."

My heart sank and soared at the same time. "How do you know? You don't know everything about me, about what I'm not. Not that girl," I whispered, staring around our apartment. I was like this very apartment. Desperately covered with things to distract from what was underneath. Instead of crumbling paint, it was a crumbling soul that was poorly hidden.

"I know enough," he replied firmly.

I took a deep breath, feeling the effort it took to do so. If he was being so candid with me I had to tell him the truth.

"I'm not up for fixing anyone, I can't even fix myself," I declared finally.

"You can't expect to fix yourself, losing your mom, it's not something you get over quickly. It's not something you get over full stop. You learn to live with it," he told me softly. "You can't expect to fix yourself, 'cause you're not broken, flower, just bruised."

"It's not just that, Asher," I choked out. "I've been broken since before ... that, before she got sick," I admitted.

There was a loaded silence. "I don't follow, Flower."

I stood and wandered around our apartment, unable to be stationary a moment longer.

"Since before I can remember, I've been different. Weaker than everyone else. At first, I was just shy…" I paused, "then it turned into something else. A weight on my chest I couldn't escape. A constant awareness that situations could turn that weight into a vice that made me feel like I couldn't breathe."

I didn't tell him about the condition that actually stole the breath from me. I couldn't dump all of my weaknesses on him in one go. He'd realize I couldn't live in his life. He'd leave. I knew it had to happen, but I couldn't say goodbye to his voice at the other end of the phone just yet.

"Some people think I'm quiet. Shy. Others think I'm rude. The vast majority of people don't understand what it's like being unable to control your mind's reaction to situations. Crowds. Strangers. Anything unexpected really. It's like an illness you can't cure. One that you can only manage." I took a strangled breath, even talking about it made me anxious. "I used to wish that it was a physical illness. Because then at least there'd be a cure. An end. Being trapped in your own head is not something I'd wish on anyone," I whispered brokenly.

I blinked.

I couldn't believe I'd just said all that. I hadn't told anyone just how much my anxiety affected me. How weak it made me.

"Flower," Asher murmured with sympathy. The single word held so much. Even on the other side of the phone, miles away, I could hear it.

I had to nip that in the bud. "I don't pity myself," I said quickly. "There're worse things than being ... shy. I just needed you to know. The real me. Not who you think I am," I told him slowly, knowing this is when I'd get the goodbye I feared. I couldn't believe I'd even verbalized this part of myself. I never talked this much about how I felt, not to anyone. But the distance that the phone offered, let me and Asher become closer despite being in different towns.

There was a long pause. "Jesus," Asher muttered finally. "You don't know how much I wish I could get on my bike and see your beautiful face. Look into those ice blue eyes and tell you you're not who I think you are..." he paused, "you're better. I hate that for you, Lily. That you have to struggle with something I can never fix. It doesn't define you. How you handle it, who you become in spite of that shit defines you. Who you are, it's pretty fuckin' impressive," he said. "I'm strugglin' babe. I've gotta admit. I know I said I'd give you time. Wait until you were ready before this turned into what I want it to be. You saying shit like that, not being able to be there, to hold you, see your face. It's killing me," he admitted.

I swallowed. I couldn't stand that pain and frustration in his voice. I also couldn't handle what he wanted us to turn into right now. I couldn't handle what he'd just said. I stared out the window in shock. He didn't sound confused, disgusted or detached. He sounded proud. The only other person who repeated a familiar sentiment was the person who understood me better than anyone in the world. The person I buried days ago.

That realization hit me like a freight train. I couldn't do this. Talk about this with him. Not when I was still trying to escape the big sad.

"I've got to go," I said quickly, wiping away my tears.

"Lily," Asher's voice protested.

"I've got to go, I'm sorry," I whispered, then hung up the phone.

I stared out the window at the view of depleted homes and gray apartment buildings for a long time after that.

"Tequila?" Bex asked from behind me.

I turned to regard her strangely bright eyes focused on me and her hands holding up a bottle that offered numbness.

"Tequila," I nodded.

CHAPTER NINE

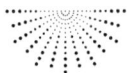

IT WAS MY NIGHT OFF, not from work, but from partying.

The past few days had been a blur. A blur of cocktails, wine, and clothes that I didn't feel comfortable in. After said cocktails and wine, I didn't care. I didn't care about anything.

Parties where I didn't know a soul except Bex. Clubs that were so crowded, I felt like I couldn't take a step without brushing someone's arm. A cocktail of things that usually would have had me a hyperventilating mess. Would have had me running away to the solitude of my own company.

The thing was, my own company didn't offer solace, only demons that wine and loud parties promised to chase away. There wasn't time to think. Time to remember. There was only the immediate, the now, the next drink, the next song. Then when I woke up, my thoughts would be on curing my headache. Whether it be with trash television and junk food, or burying my head back in the pillows. When the headache was cured it was the next drink. It was so far from what I would have done, I felt comfort in the uncomfortable environment.

"You sure you don't need a couple more days off?" Jude asked, eyeing me skeptically.

I knew I didn't look like me. My long hair was teased into a messy ponytail. My eyes were rimmed with dark liner I never wore. My clothes showed more than they concealed. I was wearing Bex's skin tight oil coated jeans and a teeny white crop top. Like I said, comfort came from the uncomfortable trapping of this adopted persona.

"I'm sure," I replied firmly, giving her my fake smile. I was getting mighty good at it. I almost convinced myself it was real.

She peered at me once more. "Okay," she said finally. "I don't do mushy shit, but I did lose my mom young." Her hard eyes softened a smidgeon. "Know what that pain is like, Lily. Feel for you girl." She gave my arm a quick squeeze.

Jude was pushing fifty and the years weren't kind to her. I wasn't talking about her looks, she looked five years younger than she was. Her inky black hair was free from any gray strands giving away her age. Her skin was perpetually tanned, and wrinkles touched the corner of her eyes and mouth.

If she looked five years younger, she dressed fifteen years younger. She was wearing a tight red tee with a plunging neckline, tucked into tight black jeans, her spike heeled boots coming up to mid-calf. She was wearing enough silver jewelry to sink the *Titanic*. None of that betrayed what she had endured in her life. It was her eyes. Demons danced beyond them.

"Thanks," I replied quietly.

She nodded briskly and turned to retreat back into her office.

I took a breath and braced for all the hugs and sympathetic words that the girls had for me as soon as Jude left. The women I worked with were all nice, lovely in fact. That was the problem. Lovely people offered sympathy. Sympathy reminded me of what I was trying desperately to forget.

"You're so strong, Lily. Coming back to work so soon?" Skye squeezed my hand once she released me from the hug, her eyes kind. "I'd never be able to do that."

"And you look great," Emma added from beside me, her made up eyes scanning my body. "Different, but great."

"Not that you didn't look great before," Skye added quickly, narrowing her eyes at Emma.

Emma's eyes widened in confusion. She had no filter and wasn't the brightest bulb in the box, but she had a good heart. Both girls were bubbly, beautiful and not afraid to come to work in what was little more than underwear. Which was why they always raked in more tips than me. Prior to tonight, I'd never shown this much skin, wore this much makeup, no matter how desperate I'd been for the money.

"Let's get ready for a big night." Emma winked, lining up shot glasses.

Skye handed me one. "To Lily's mom," she said quietly.

I swallowed the lump in my throat and clinked the tiny glass against theirs. I savored the fire of the alcohol as it burned my throat and numbed my fingertips. I immediately grabbed the bottle and filled up our glasses once more, lifting mine to them and downing it.

Both girls held their still full glasses and regarded me in amazement. I never drank at work. They did. Everyone did. It wasn't frowned upon by Jude, hell, she encouraged it. Especially when the customers paid for our drinks, which they routinely did. As long as we could still pour beer and string together sentences, it was fine. I was happy for that particular job benefit right about now.

The bar we worked on straddled the invisible line between the 'good' side of Tasman Springs and the 'dodgy' side. That and our reputation for having pretty young bartenders wearing little to no clothes flirting with the customers. That meant our clientele was always mixed with drunken frat boys and rougher, more dangerous men. We didn't have much trouble, probably because Jude was well known and respected, and she had a shotgun behind the bar.

"To a big night," I muttered, holding up my third glass.

I sat on a nearly empty bus at three in the morning, blearily regarding the empty streets passing me by. My mind was fuzzy at the edges, I wasn't blotto, considering I'd switched to water halfway through my shift. I may have been taking to my new lifestyle like a fish to water, but I was yet to find the ability to drink like a fish.

I was a lightweight. I also needed this job. My money was getting dangerously low, and my expenses were dangerously high. Oblivion was tempting, but homelessness was a deterrent. I was right on one thing, my tips drastically improved with my new wardrobe and drinking habits.

My eyes flickered down to the screen of my phone. I'd missed Asher's call tonight. I'd been working, but I didn't know if I could speak to him after the way we left things the previous day. Despite what he made me feel, the pain speaking to him ushered in, I missed the sound of his voice already. I took a breath.

Me: *Sorry I missed your call, I was working. Talk tomorrow?* I paused typing while chewing my lip, then added *xxx*

Kisses at the end of a text may have been a stupid thing to obsess over, I'd lost my virginity to the man for goodness sake, but I still felt a strange closeness about the gesture. I didn't put kisses at the end of any other text message, apart from with my mom and Bex. That and I rarely texted anyone but my mom and Bex.

I jumped when my phone rang in my hand, the sound seeming louder in the quiet bus.

"Hello?" I whispered, feeling self-conscious about being the obnoxious person talking on the bus.

The woman in the nurse's uniform a couple of seats down, and the homeless man across from me didn't seem worried.

"Lily," Asher greeted softly.

"What are you doing up so late?" I asked, frowning.

"Babe, it's Friday night," he said by explanation.

I screwed my nose up. "And?"

He laughed a little. "I forget sometimes, you don't know this stuff," he paused, "Friday night, it's unofficial party night here. Like clockwork. And since I reside at the club, it's kind of hard to sleep with that shit going on. If you can't beat 'em join 'em." There was humor in his voice, a lightness. He was slightly tipsy if I didn't know any better. As I was slightly tipsy, I did know better.

"Right, I knew that," I said, almost to myself.

My heart dropped as a thought struck me. Parties. Like the ones the girls at my school were desperate to go to. I guessed this party would have girls just like the ones at my school. Beautiful girls. Confident girls. Women like the one three years ago.

"Flower?" Asher's voice coaxed me out of this toxic thought. "What?" He seemed to sense something in my silence, different from my usual.

"Nothing," I replied quickly. I couldn't say anything. I didn't have any claim over him. We spoke on the phone. Had had sex twice. It may have meant everything to me. It didn't mean it meant everything to him. That we were anything.

"It's not nothing," he answered firmly. "If you've got something to say, you say it. You might swallow your words with other people, not with me."

I paused. "You were at this party," I started slowly.

"Yes," Asher replied patiently.

"And there were girls there," I stated, feeling like an idiot.

I heard Asher's sigh at the other end of the phone. "Yeah, there's always girls here, babe."

My heart dropped.

"I don't see them," he continued, his voice hoarse. "They all blur into one. They're all the same. Trying to be something different, to play a part. I see right through them. They're transparent. No substance. You..." he paused, "you're different. There's no one that can equal you. I can't see through you, babe. You take up every inch of my sight. It takes every inch of my concentration to see into you. You're not pretending to be anyone. You're just you. There's no comparison."

My breath left me in a whoosh. "So you're not...?" my voice trailed off, unable to voice that particular concern.

Asher's reply was instantaneous. "Since I laid my mouth on yours that morning on my bike I would never pollute it by touching anyone else. I'm yours, babe. I know that scares the shit out of you at the moment, but it's a fact."

I wasn't an idiot. I knew his behavior, the way he called me every night, the way he spoke to me meant he cared about me. I knew what was between us. I struggled to believe it. I'd spent my whole life convincing myself I was painfully ordinary, I couldn't understand why I had this extraordinary connection with someone like Asher.

My eyes moved to the dark, desolate world outside. "Drat," I hissed into the phone, launching from my seat. I pressed the button on the bus and it started to slow, the driver's eyes meeting mine.

"Not the answer I was expecting," Asher replied with humor in his tone.

I rushed down the aisle as the driver came to a stop. I gave him a grateful smile, stepping out into the chilly night.

"No, it wasn't because of you," I reassured him as I started walking. "I missed my stop and my feet hurt. I just tacked an extra ten minutes of pain onto my journey," I informed him, walking quickly along the lonely streets.

There was a long pause. "Your stop?" Asher repeated, the humor gone from his voice.

"Yeah, my stop," I agreed, rubbing at my shoulders, wishing I'd worn a thicker jacket.

"Please do not tell me you are on a bus," he said slowly.

"I'm not on a bus," I answered. "I'm *off* the bus and walking home."

Another loaded pause. "Walking home?" His voice was granite.

I screwed up my nose. "Yes, why do you keep repeating everything I'm saying? Is there a bad connection?" I asked in confusion.

"No, Lily. I can hear you loud and clear, I just can't quite believe what I'm hearing," he said tightly. "You're walking home at three in the morning, *alone,* in your neighborhood, am I correct?" His tone was flat.

"Yes," I responded slowly, registering his anger, even on the phone.

"Fuck," he shouted and I jumped. "Do you know how difficult it is knowing this shit and being half a fuckin' hour away?"

"It's fine—" I started.

"It's not fine," he cut me off angrily. "You live in a seriously shady part of town. It's the middle of the night, you're walking home alone. Have you got any goddamned sense of self-preservation?" he bellowed into the phone.

I straightened my spine, glancing around me. The neighborhood wasn't great, I'd admit. And it wasn't my usual habit to be out and about at this time, but I'd done it a handful of times and didn't encounter problems. There were even a couple of scantily clad girls across from me stumbling home. A lot of college kids lived in this area, thanks to cheap rent.

"I have plenty," I hissed. "What I don't have is a horse drawn carriage to ferry me wherever I need to go whenever my heart desires. I live in the real world. Where I've got to eat and pay rent. Which means I need to work. I don't appreciate someone yelling at me, because he doesn't agree with the only choice of transportation available to me," I informed him sharply.

"Why are you taking the bus in the first place? You have a car," Asher's voice was still hard, and he ignored my small monolog.

"Bex is borrowing my car, which I couldn't even drive if I had it, considering I don't want a DUI," I informed him smartly.

Bex was going to pick me up, but she was working later than I was, hence the bus. I wasn't going to tell Asher that. I didn't owe him an explanation.

"You're fuckin' *drunk?*" Asher exclaimed in disbelief.

Shit. Maybe that wasn't as smart as I thought. "No. I've just had a couple of shots," I backpedaled.

I heard a long sigh at the other end of the phone. I let out my own sigh as my apartment building came into view. My feet thanked the Lord.

"Please tell me you've got protection," he said finally.

"Protection?" I repeated.

"Yeah, babe, pepper spray, taser, gun?" he listed off these things like grocery items.

"A gun?" I repeated. "Could you honestly visualize me knowing how to work a gun?" I asked him honestly, crossing my parking lot.

"No, which means I'm gonna teach you how," he bit out.

I blanched at the thought of handling a gun. "No, thank you," I replied briskly.

"Jesus, Lily. Do you know how crazy it makes me thinking of you in danger? Of someone hurting you?" he asked in exasperation.

I paused riffling through my bag for my key. "No," I replied honestly. "Asher, I've never had anyone care about me. Not like you. Apart from my mom, and she was different. A lot different. She swore a lot less that was for sure," I joked. I turned my key in the lock. "I'm not used to how intense this is," I explained, sinking onto our lumpy sofa once I got inside our apartment.

Asher sighed again. "I know. Shit. I'm sorry, Lily. I try and remind myself of that. To take it slow with you. Be gentle." He paused, his anger seeming to deflate immediately. "Where are you now?" he asked with concern.

"Home safe. Unmugged and unmolested," I informed him, the walk not sobering me completely, hence my flippant demeanor.

Asher growled. "Don't joke about that," he warned. "You're not bussing home again. You need a ride, it's on the back of my bike. We clear?"

I nodded. The thought of actually seeing him, not just hearing a voice at the other end of the phone enticing. Of having someone to care if I got home safely.

"You alone at home?" he continued, taking my silence as confirmation.

"Yeah," I responded quietly, expecting him to talk about the dangers of a woman in an apartment alone.

"Where are you?" he asked, something changing in his voice.

"On the sofa," I replied, yanking my boots off and laying back.

"What are you wearing?" he questioned, his voice thick.

My stomach dropped. Desire tickled in my stomach. "Did you really just ask that?" I squeaked out.

"Yep," he replied simply. "It's what I dream about, Lily. What that beautiful little body is clad in every day," he said. "You turned on, Flower?"

I swallowed. I'd never done this before. I never talked aloud about sex, not to anyone.

"Yes," I found myself whispering, my hand running over my breast.

"Me too," he growled. "My cock's hard as a rock every time I hear that throaty voice on the other end of the phone," he rasped.

I let out a little moan as I ran my finger over my breast at his words.

"You touching yourself, Lily?" he asked hoarsely.

"Y-yes," I stuttered.

"Where?" he demanded.

I couldn't do it. Even with residual alcohol running through my system, I couldn't verbalize this.

"Is it your nipple? Your beautiful breasts? Pinch those nipples for me, Lily," he instructed.

I did as I was told, breathing heavily into the phone.

"Is that good, baby?" he asked in a rough voice.

Arousal superseded my embarrassment. "Yes," I breathed the word.

"If I were there I'd close my mouth over those delicious peaks," he declared. "I want you to touch your pussy, Lily. It'll be wet for me," he continued in a voice thick with desire.

I didn't hesitate, my hand moved into the waistband of my jeans, touching my soaking panties.

"You're wet, aren't you, Flower?" he rasped into the phone. "For me."

"For you," I repeated, my breath coming in pants.

"That pretty pussy's all for me. For me to use my mouth on. Taste you. That's what I'd do to you, Flower. What I'm gonna do. For now, I want you to rub your clit, make yourself come. Let me hear it," he demanded.

I rubbed like he told me to, the fire in my belly growing into an inferno.

"Are you...?" I choked out.

"Yeah, baby," he responded. "I'm rubbing my cock thinking of you touching yourself for me," he grunted.

That's what did it. The vision of him lying there, doing that to himself, thinking of me. I exploded into a million pieces, crying out Asher's name as I shuddered through my release. As I was coming down from my beautiful climax, I heard the unmistakable sounds of Asher's own release. It was one of the most erotic things I'd ever heard.

I lay there for a moment, breathless and silent. Asher the same.

"That was..."

"Amazing," Asher finished for me. "You're amazing, Lily," he murmured, his voice tight.

I stared at the ceiling taking in what had just happened.

Asher didn't seem to mind my silence. "It's late, Lily. Get some sleep," he told me.

I wasn't ready to lose him yet. I was exhausted, which meant my defenses were down. I didn't filter my thoughts or my words.

"Will you stay?" I asked quickly. "While I go to sleep?"

"Yeah, Flower," Asher replied in a soft voice. "Sleep," he commanded.

And with my hand cradling the phone, curled on the sofa, Asher silent at the other end, I did just that.

CHAPTER TEN

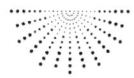

ONE WEEK LATER

"Do you know where we are?" I mumbled up at the stars.

My gaze moved to the outdoor patio area to my left which had a lot of people milling around, drinking, dancing, laughing. I didn't know a soul, apart from the person lying beside me.

Bex didn't move her gaze from the sky. "At a party," she replied dreamily.

I turned my head, regarding her profile. "But *whose* party?" I probed, the details lost in my muddled head.

I watched one of her brows furrow. "Jack's, or Jason's or Sylvia's. Fuck if I know," she replied casually.

Usual Lily, sober Lily, would have most likely freaked out about this, or gone into a mild panic attack, but this was not sober Lily. I had discovered the beauty of alcohol and what it did to my shyness, my emotions. Numbed them, kept the big sadness at bay. It was awesome.

A phone ringing jolted me out of my drunken, yet calm reverie. It stopped then started again. It was coming from somewhere nearby. I moved my head.

"That's your phone, Bex," I pointed out.

She acted like she hadn't heard me, then jumped abruptly. "Shit," she muttered. "Yo," she called into the phone.

There was a pause.

"Oh fuck, sorry, I completely blanked. I'll be there in," she glanced down at her watchless hand, "about twenty minutes?" She finished, the question in her voice most likely due to the fact that she had no idea where we were.

She sat up after she hung up and glanced over at me with a vacant gaze. "We've gotta bounce, babe," she instructed.

I squinted at her. "What? Why?"

I was quite happy in my current position, watching the sky, listening to the sounds of strangers having a good time, pretending that I was someone else.

She yanked on my arm and I reluctantly moved.

"Because," she said, standing. "I was meant to be at work, like an hour ago. And I need my job 'cause I need to eat and more importantly, buy booze."

I sighed and struggled to my feet, swaying slightly as I got accustomed to being vertical. Another ringing added to the sounds of the night. I looked at Bex. Her boss must really be pissed. She didn't move and stared at me.

"Lilmeister, that's yours," she informed me with a grin.

"Oh, right," I muttered, rifling through my bag.

Because I was flustered and drunk, I didn't even look at the number, which I would have screened at this moment, had I been a smidgeon more sober. Alas, I wasn't, and I didn't understand the logistical nightmare of chatting to my protective... whatever he was, while navigating a crowded party, severely wasted.

"'Lo," I slurred as Bex dragged me inside, through the party.

"Lily," a voice greeted softly.

"Asher," I half squealed in excitement. He hadn't called as was per usual tonight, and I had missed him. "I thought you'd forgotten about me," I declared, alcohol taking away my filter.

And sense of self-preservation apparently. Letting him know just how attached I was to our phone calls would not have been sober Lily's preference.

"I could never forget about you, Flower."

"Good," I yelled over the music that was getting louder as we walked into the dance area of the party.

I giggled slightly and was pushed against various bodies as Bex pushed us through the crowd.

"Where are you?" Asher's voice turned hard.

"Umm…" I hedged, looking around at the unfamiliar surroundings. "That's a mighty good question," I giggled again.

I felt a pinch on my behind.

I tugged on Bex's arm. "Oh my gosh, that guy just *squeezed my ass*," I whisper yelled at her, not realizing I was speaking into the phone.

Bex narrowed her eyes and glared into the crowd before yanking us again.

"What the fuck? What did you just say?" Asher yelled into the phone. "Lily, tell me where you are, right now," he commanded.

I took a deep breath as we emerged out the front door and I squinted at the unfamiliar street in what I deduced was a reasonably nice neighborhood.

"Who the heck do we know to get us ending up here?" I asked Bex in confusion. I said *"we,"* but I meant her. I hardly knew anyone well enough to get invited to any parties, let alone one in this area.

She shrugged her shoulders, with her eyes on her phone. "Fuck knows, Uber's on its way now, though," she muttered, rubbing her bare arms even though there was no chill in the air.

"Lily," a firm voice clipped in my ear.

"Oh right, on the phone," I muttered to myself.

"You're drunk," Asher stated.

"Affirmative on that Captain Jack," I replied breezily.

I hadn't educated Asher on my new lifestyle, he always called early afternoon, before the drinking could commence. There was a reason for that, me not telling him, I mused. I couldn't think of it at this moment, it didn't seem important.

"Please tell me that's not doucheface," Bex cut in, nodding at the phone.

"Don't call him doucheface," I snapped at her. "It's not him," I added, giving her reason to smile. Aiden had been absent from our lives for over a week, much to Bex's delight.

"Lily," Asher demanded softly but firmly.

I sighed. My head hurt from the difficulty of having two conversations.

"Tell me where you are. I'm coming to get you," he declared.

"I don't know where I am, Asher," I repeated impatiently. "That's the point, we've got an Uber—" My explanation was cut short when the phone was ripped out of my hands.

"If this is the Asher I've heard about, we're going to Mermaids in Tasman Springs, bring your biker buddies," Bex ordered into the phone before hanging up.

I gaped at her. "I can't *believe* you just did that."

She shrugged, grinning mischievously. "I want to meet this guy. Properly. One heated conversation on our doorstep three years ago is not sufficient. Plus, I've got a terrible memory, it may or may not have something to do with alcohol. I need to see *the Asher* you've been running off to have whispered phone calls with for the past week. Over a week, dude. It's about time you guys talked face to face, and did other things face to face." She waggled her eyebrows. "Plus, I need to figure out if he's good enough for my friend. We don't need another doucheface. It all depends on results of the test," she explained.

I frowned at her. "Test?" I repeated.

She nodded. "Only time will tell. A lot of it rides on how well his hotness has held up over the years. And how hot his friends are."

I sighed and decided to relent.

I couldn't lie and say I didn't want to see him. In my week long bender, I hadn't thought of much, I'd made a conscious effort to think of nothing. Apart from the times he'd called, I gave myself the luxury, to let his voice wrap around me, let our conversations take me away from it all. I tried not to think about him in the moments we weren't speaking, but Asher's face, his touch, the way he made me feel, that all crept into my dreams.

"COME ON, you know you want to," Bex whined.

I gazed up at her. She was slightly drunk, but she still looked kick ass. Her emergency hair and makeup procedures to get stage ready were rather impressive. Her inky hair was tumbled into messy ringlets around her face, false eyelashes were expertly applied, and her trademark heavy cat eye was sharp and fierce. Since her particular job description required her to take her clothes off for men, she was wearing a skimpy skirt, fishnets with a visible garter belt, and combat boots. Yeah, no stripper heels for this girl. The punters loved it apparently.

"Um. No," I told her and Adam, the bartender who was smirking at me.

"You'll be totally great, it's like a double act," she persuaded. "I know you're a good singer, I've heard you in the shower." She winked. "Plus, you're hot as balls."

I snorted. "Yeah, right."

She was my friend of course she'd say that. And she was drunk. And trying to get me up on stage.

Of a strip club.

Though I would admit that I didn't look like myself, hadn't for the past week. I'd embraced my inner wild child, or more accurately, let my wild child best friend have control over my outfits, hair, and makeup.

I was wearing the shortest shorts I'd ever been clothed in, with a sheer top tucked in, a lace bralette visible underneath. The sky-high heels I was wearing were the only part of the outfit that was mine. She'd teased my long blonde hair and stuffed it into a messy ponytail. My makeup was intense. I could barely recognize the intense smoky-eyed, contoured girl in the mirror.

That was good, though. Being someone else. It was the only way to escape the Big Sad. I'd decided to adopt this new persona. Though I was drawing the line at singing to my friend's stripping routine. I didn't judge her, not for a moment, but I knew there was no way I was going to be able to do that without vomiting.

"Adam," Bex's voice snapped my attention back to the present moment.

I took a sip of my vodka, such intense thought needed alcohol to discourage it.

"Do you or do you not think that Lily is the sexiest bitch you've ever laid your baby blue's on?" It was a question, but the way her eyes were narrowed I could tell she would only accept one answer.

I swatted her shoulder. "Bex," I scolded.

I turned to Adam, who was staring at me with a small grin on his face.

"You don't have to—"

"I work in a strip club. It means I see a lot of lookers," he began, leaning against the bar. "It's the God's honest truth you are the sexiest gal I've ever laid eyes on," he continued with a wink, his southern twang sharp.

I gaped at him. "Really?"

His smile got bigger. "Really darlin'," he said firmly. He gave me one more look before going to serve a customer.

Bex whirled my stool around to face her. The motion made me slightly dizzy.

"See?" she snapped. "No matter what crazy thoughts are floating around in that pretty little head, you're a ten. Adam doesn't bullshit," she told me firmly.

I raised my eyebrow at her. "Slathered in this much makeup, *Fiona* off *Shrek* would look like a supermodel," I stated. "Plus, my you-know-what is almost showing in these shorts."

Bex rolled her eyes. "You're twenty-three and not a virgin anymore. Call it what it is. Vagina. Pussy. The word doesn't bite," she teased.

I didn't answer, just sipped my vodka. "I'm not doing it," I declared when she wouldn't stop looking at me with that expectant stare.

Her shoulders sagged, but she wasn't mad. She kissed my cheek. "Yeah, babe, thought that'd be your final answer. This place," she waved her hands around, "isn't you."

There wasn't judgment or sarcasm in her voice, just something sad. It was quickly masked, and she propped up her boobs in a way every male in the immediate vicinity looked our way.

Bex was oblivious. "Gotta go make rent." She blew me a kiss and winked, then strutted toward backstage.

I frowned at her back, something niggling at the back of my mind at her strange demeanor. Her eyes had been darting around everywhere, and she seemed more hyped than she'd been in the car. The thought was quickly lost.

I leaned on my chair, saving myself at the last minute when I realized my chair had no back, because it was a bar stool. That would've been embarrassing. I leaned forward, plonking my elbows on the bar, putting my chin in my hands and chewing on my straw with my mouth. While I did that, I also chewed over Bex's words.

"This place, it isn't you."

"Who am I?" I half whispered to myself.

I asked that question, that pivotal question of my identity and was coming up blank. I didn't know who I was without my mom to be loud to counteract my quiet. Without me to tamp down her eccentricity. I took care of her. Even before the cancer, I was the responsible one. She was a great mom, but her unique spirit meant she didn't ride me about homework, curfews, or anything. It meant she didn't think like other moms.

I was responsible. I did homework. I made dinner for us when she'd locked herself away in her studio. We were a team. I was her partner. That's who I was.

Up until now. Now I was no one. So why couldn't I be the girl who danced with her girlfriend at a strip club? Why couldn't I let go of all of my inhibitions that had crippled me half my life? What's the worst that could happen? I'd already had the worse—hit rock bottom.

"What was that, babe?" Adam's voice made me jump and I met his dancing eyes.

"Nothing," I said quickly, not needing the hot bartender to know I was talking to myself.

Adam knew me a little. Well, as well as someone as hot as him could know a girl like me. I barely spoke to him on the rare occasion I came here to hang out with Bex. More like she dragged me here when I'd been cooped up in my room for too long studying, or staring at hospital walls.

Staring at strip club walls wasn't much better, but it did serve to take my mind off things. The girls were nice, Adam was the only bartender that spoke to me, all the other males in the joint leered. Including her boss, who made me feel more than a little uncomfortable. Luckily I'd flown under their radar, thanks to the fact I near shrunk into myself every time they tried to talk to me. They quickly lost interest, in a mousy mute.

So, because Adam knew me, his eyes softened slightly. "Want me to call you a cab?" he asked, having to yell over the music.

I did want him to call a cab. I wanted to go home to our four walls with crumbling paint and pretty posters and fairy lights. Though the pictures that decorated those same walls hindered me, that and the promise of solitude. I usually loved it. Now being alone with my thoughts was the last thing I needed. I was worried the silence my own thoughts offered would swallow me up.

Plus, Asher was coming. As much as I knew he would mess up my brain, how the attachment I felt to him was unhealthy, my drunken mind didn't need to focus too hard on that. Only the promise of his touch, his presence. I'd been talking to him on the phone every single day. He'd patiently waited for me to be ready for more. I wanted it. Craved it. But something stopped me. Something that didn't seem important right now.

"Nah, I'm good." I grinned at him drunkenly.

He gave me a long look then scanned the room quickly. "You stay here during Becky's routine, 'kay darlin'?" he ordered. "Big crowd tonight, a lot of rowdy men lettin' loose. You're a sweet girl who's had a drink too many, it's like blood in the water to these sharks."

I giggled slightly. Adam was protecting my honor. It was sweet. "Don't worry, men aren't going to trouble themselves with little old me when there's women taking off their clothes in front of them," I said decisively.

Adam gave me a look with furrowed brows. "Just stay here," he repeated.

I saluted him. "Yes, sir."

He shook his head and gave a small laugh. His eyes turned slightly sad, and he looked like he was going to say something before someone called him. He gave me a stern look to stay put before he left.

I swirled on my stool, sucking the last of my drink, regarding the scene. Adam was right, the place was packed. Tables full of men crowded the room. Females were peppered throughout these groups, but they were few and far between. It wasn't exactly the classiest strip club, not that I had much to compare it to.

It was dimly lit and the décor and tables dated. Most of the men who worked here were paid extra to convince the waitresses to turn to stripping, and most tried aggressively to get into bed with them. Luckily, Bex didn't let anyone pressure her into anything, but it didn't mean I liked the way it was. But it was her choice. She worked here at first to support herself through medical school. Now she just worked here to support herself. Medical school was a distant memory.

"Lily, it's so good to see you," a familiar voice drawled.

I inwardly cringed, swiveling on my bar stool.

Bex's sleazy boss stood in front of me, shamelessly leering. He was wearing black slacks, terrible snakeskin shoes, and a shirt with too many buttons undone. His huge belly protruded over his belt buckle. A tacky gold chain around his neck completed the *Sopranos* look.

"Tony, so good to see you," I greeted him with a straight face.

Carlos looked momentarily confused. He wasn't used to me being so articulate, let alone flippant. His face then turned into a sly grin.

"I'm sure you know by now that it's Carlos, though, by the looks of it, you've indulged in a lot of cocktails, name mix-ups are inevitable." He nodded to my now empty glass.

I didn't say anything, merely shrugged. I was hoping he'd get bored of me like he normally did.

"When are you going to decide to come and work here?" he asked, stepping into my personal bubble. "You could make a lot more money than you do at that bar. Men like the schoolgirl thing," he gave me another once over, "the sex kitten thing you've got going tonight could make you a lot of money also." His chubby finger trailed on my bare thigh. "Enough to put you through college and pay any pesky medical bills left over," he continued, his voice sending shivers down my spine. Not the good ones.

I screwed up my nose, trying not to gag. My insecurities came creeping back in. Vodka only gave me so much bravado, and the fact the creep was touching me when I had no one to back me up, had me retreating back into my shell.

"You wanna keep that hand, I suggest you take it off my woman," a tight voice cut in.

Both Carlos and my head whipped around. I sagged in relief to see Asher standing close to Carlos, glowering at him his arms crossed. His jaw was hard, and he looked unlike the man who had treated me with tenderness almost two weeks ago, three years ago. He looked dangerous.

A man I didn't recognize stood behind him, face tight. His cut told me he was in the Sons, as did the fact he was huge, muscled, and attractive. I was starting to think it was an entry requirement. Lucky stood beside him. He didn't look as mad as the rest of them, but his usually carefree face was dangerously blank.

Carlos scowled at them, then his eyes found their cuts and he moved his hands off me quickly, stepping back.

"My apologies, gentlemen. I didn't know this one was claimed by the Sons of Templar," Carlos's tone was pleasant, but his weasel eyes were narrowed on the attractive men like they were insects on his shoe. The way he said the club's name held something behind it like the words were unpleasant on his forked tongue.

I didn't think this was an appropriate moment to educate all of them that I wasn't claimed. I would never be like Gwen and Amy, who could throw sass at their scary bikers and turn them to puppy dogs. I didn't have enough confidence in myself to throw attitude, to voice my irritation in front of people I didn't know.

Silence was the lesser of two evils right now. Not that being *"claimed"* by Asher was evil, it was a dream. That was the problem. Dreams were fleeting. Nightmares were more likely to be the reality.

Asher advanced as soon as Carlos retreated, moving to step beside me and put his hand on the back of my neck.

"Now you do," he murmured dangerously, giving my neck a gentle squeeze.

I relaxed against his simple touch. I hadn't been near him for almost two weeks, the voice at the other end of the phone had me craving this every day. Now I had it, I didn't know how I'd live without it. I knew I'd have to, eventually. My drunken mind was all about instant gratification.

"I suggest you take better care of her, considering how dangerous it is to have a girl like that," he nodded to me, "in places where ... unsavory things could happen to her. You've got your own club in Amber, you want her to hang out in strip clubs, may I suggest your own?" he suggested pleasantly, though even I wasn't oblivious to the threat beneath his words.

The tall one stepped forward, danger seeping off him and Asher's body went tight beside me, he yanked me closer to his body protectively.

"Now I know you're a stupid son of a bitch, but I didn't realize you were suicidal, threatening my brother's Old Lady right in front of him," the tall one bit out, face dangerous.

Carlos didn't appear rattled. "No threat. Just a friendly observation from one business owner to another," he replied calmly. "You boys want to stay, have a drink, enjoy the show, you're most welcome." His eyes flickered to Adam, who'd been standing silently watching the exchange. "First round's on me. Though, if you're thinking about swinging any fists, I'd advise against it." He nodded his head to a corner where someone who looked like he abused steroids stepped out of, hand on his hip like there was something dangerous underneath it.

Something dangerous that shot people full of bullets.

Carlos's head moved to another corner where meathead's long lost brother did the same thing. My stomach dropped with concern. Not for the men beside me, they could take care of themselves, but for Bex. I may have had too much vodka to think with complete clarity, but I realized that a strip club that required this kind of security, a man who was prepared to give veiled threats to the club, it was dangerous. It was more than it seemed.

Carlos treated me to a look that made my skin crawl then gave the men a patronizing smile. "Enjoy the show, boys," he said, before turning on his tasteless heel and disappearing into the crowd.

"Wow," I exclaimed before any of the men could say a thing. "I knew he was an asshat, but Bex's boss is officially a massive *dick*," I declared with drunken certainty.

There was silence, the big guy turned slowly, Lucky stared at me, and Asher gave me a look, then they all burst out laughing. Well, Lucky and the big guy did, Asher's mouth turned up slightly hinting at amusement.

"Wanna educate me as to what the fuck you're doing at a strip club, alone?" Asher asked lightly, though his jaw was hard.

The big man and Lucky leaned on the bar on either side of me, people dispersing with a look from each of the men.

"Man, I wish I could do that, give someone a withering look and get them out of my bubble," I observed with amazement.

Lucky smirked again. The big man shook his head.

Three beers were set on the bar. Adam's was focused on me. "Everything okay here, Lily?" he asked me with concern, his focus on Asher's cut.

I gave him a grin. "Everything's fine," I declared. "Asher's not a shark." I winked.

Adam didn't look convinced. "You need me to call you that cab, just give me a holler, darlin'," he responded firmly.

"She doesn't need a cab, I've got her. My thanks for looking out for her," Asher answered for me.

Adam gave him a weary gaze. He nodded, looked at me a second more then moved down the bar.

Asher raised a brow. "Sharks?" he questioned.

"The men who frequent such establishments." I held my hands out to the room.

Lucky choked on the beer he was taking a tug of. "That's one thing to call them," he said dryly.

Asher gave him a hard look, then moved his gaze to me. "Such establishments are not somewhere you need to be spending your nights, Flower," he informed me. "Especially not alone.

"I'm not alone, I was with Bex," I explained.

Asher didn't seem happy about my answer. "Was. I don't see her anywhere, and this is not a place you should sucking down drinks. We're leavin'," he declared.

I smiled. "Wow, I think you may be the only man to say he wants to *leave* a strip club," I teased, not knowing where my cheerfulness was coming from. I had a niggling feeling it was coming from the man whose body was claiming mine.

Lucky let out another strangled chuckle, his eyes roving around the room.

Asher's face changed at my words, I didn't get time to think too hard on it as the music came on and the lights dimmed slightly.

"Plus, we can't leave, Bex is about to come on." I threw my hand out toward the stage where music had just started blaring.

Three sets of male eyes focused on the place where Bex emerged, strutting her stuff. Her eyes found mine as she rounded the poll, bugging out slightly at the men I was with, though her step didn't falter. She recovered quickly and winked at me.

"Jesus Christ," Asher muttered under his breath, his eyes

darting away from my scantily clad best friend the moment he realized it was her.

"Holy shit," Lucky exclaimed, his eyes glued to the stage. "I think I'm in love," he proclaimed dramatically.

The tall guy didn't say a thing, his eyes were glued on Bex and stayed there, his jaw hard.

Asher pulled me lightly out of my seat. "We're leaving," he said, or more aptly, ordered, his eyes on me.

I frowned at him. "We're not. Bex has only just started," I protested.

Asher gave me a hard look. "I'm not sitting here watching your friend strip, and more importantly, I'm not sitting in a strip club with you wearing those shorts," he bit out, his eyes moving over the length of me. He leaned into me, so his mouth tickled my ear. "Seeing you in those shorts means I'm going to have to fuck you in the next twenty minutes, and I'd rather not do it in a strip club bathroom," he added, making my stomach drop.

I gaped at him when he leaned back. "Okay. We're off then," I decided and the men grinned.

I didn't have time to give them proper goodbyes as Asher dragged me away, I only waved over my shoulder.

"Wanna give me some explanation as to why you've been spending your nights at strip clubs?" Asher asked softly, his finger trailing up and down my arm.

I took a long pause. "I told you, I needed time," I said finally.

Asher squeezed me. "I don't think you did, Flower. Now I've got you in my arms, thoroughly fucked, I know the last thing you needed was time. You were scared," he observed, correctly I might add. "And when I said I'd give you time, I didn't expect you'd spend it in strip clubs with sleazy fucks like Carlos Leith," he added in a hard voice.

Thoroughly fucked was one way to put it. Asher had damned near pounced on me the moment we made it through my door. Well, after he made me stand at the front door and do a *"walk through."*

"No boogeymen hiding under my bed?" I deadpanned when he'd stopped in front of me after his inspection.

He had frowned. "Don't like you in this place, and I'm fixin' that window. Tomorrow. Now, I fuck you."

And he had. Against the door. Then in my bed.

Now we were here. My body felt like jelly, and everything was delightfully fuzzy around the edges, thanks to residual alcohol and the ability for the world to fall away when Asher was with me.

I realized we were in that silence, one Asher hadn't tried to fill, hadn't urged me to talk. He merely resumed lightly tracing my arm, letting me process.

"You don't mind silence," I observed.

He tilted my chin so chocolate eyes met mine. "I've got you in my arms, I'm in your bed. After almost two weeks of only hearing that sweet voice on the other side of the phone. I know you don't like yabberin' at the best of times, unless you're with me, angry, or liquored up, somethin' I learned tonight." His eyes twinkled. "You need time to sort shit in your head, need time to process. I get it. I'm quite happy to give you that, as long as you're naked in my arms," he told me softly.

My belly did a little dip. He knew me. Saw right into me. After one night three years ago, and a few hours in my presence since then. It was unnerving.

"This is unnerving," I vocalized my last thought. "This, us ... it's too intense. Too quick. I'm not ready," I whispered.

Asher gave me a long look. "It is too intense," he agreed. "Don't know how to make it any other way. I know I wouldn't have it any other way. It's right, you know it. You're ready. You're just scared. Shit that went down with your mom, Flower, that's marked your beautiful soul. Damaged it," he stroked my cheek lightly. "Bruised those delicate petals. It'll heal. Might not mend quite the same, it'll always hurt, but I plan on being right here while you figure out how to heal it," he promised. "I'm done with the space. With the frustration of hearing the pain in that voice on the other end of a phone."

I blinked away the tears his words were causing. The pins and needles I felt as he prodded at my mind, the place where the big sad was hiding, lurking.

"I don't know if I can do that, be what you want me to be," I choked out, truth to my words but also self-preservation.

I'd just suffered a devastating loss, and I was setting myself up for it all over again. Cancer might not steal him, nor death, but probably boredom, reality. Realization that I wasn't that girl, whoever he thought she was. I wasn't special.

Asher's eyes were resolute. "I don't need you to be anything but who you are. My girl," he replied with certainty.

At that moment, I didn't want to argue, didn't want to push him away in order to save myself. I was willing to sacrifice the future Lily's emotional health for the current Lily's survival. Because right now, being Asher's girl, for however long, was something that I needed.

CHAPTER ELEVEN

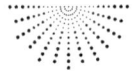

"Bex!" A high pitched voice screamed as soon as we tumbled out of our ride.

"Nat!" Bex's less high pitched scream was directed at a slim woman with a head full of ashy blonde hair.

Her outfit had me openly gaping at the sheer amount of skin the silvery bandage dress was showing, her sky-high heels looking like something even I would tumble down from. She was grinning warmly and drunkenly at us as we approached.

It was the night after Asher had told me I was *"his girl."* Something that would have normally had me floating on cloud nine, yet it barely had me paddling in the ocean of grief I was stranded in.

Belonging to the man I'd loved for three years may have been something good, something great, but it didn't automatically erase everything else bad in my life. Especially when he had to leave early this morning for work, with no time to talk about him turning up at the strip club, or about what the heck was going on between us.

I hadn't been mad.

A little part of me had been glad. Looking into to his eyes

was like forcing myself into looking into me. Into what I was running from. I didn't need that. I needed oblivion. Hence the fact I was in yet another of Bex's outfits, filled with Bex's home-made cocktails and at a club that was nowhere near my scene.

"Perfect timing," Nat exclaimed as we cut in the front of the line beside her.

There were a couple of whiny grumbles from a group of girls behind us. We ignored them. Well, I ignored them, trying to shy away from any potential conflict. Bex flipped them the bird before turning to hug Nat.

"This is my best bitch, Lily. Once a hermit, now party girl," she introduced with a slight slur, gesturing to me.

I did a lame little wave. "Hey," I muttered, focusing solely on staying upright. The transition from sitting in a car to standing on a sidewalk messing with my mind slightly.

She grinned at me, looking me up and down, but not in a bitchy way. Her gaze was warm. Friendly. "Bex has told me all about you, I'm glad to finally meet you in the flesh."

She surprised me by engulfing me in a hug. I wasn't a hugger. I avoided human contact with strangers if I could possibly avoid it. I wasn't one of those girls that hugged their friends every time they saw them. I didn't like it. But maybe it was the alcohol in my system, or the fact that this new Lily was a hugger or the weird sort of comfort in the perfume and alcohol laden hug had me relaxing.

"Sorry about your mom, babe," she whispered in my ear.

I jolted slightly at the reminder of my old life. The life I'd left behind when I put on clothes I didn't normally wear, drank things I didn't normally drink. Of that big sadness I was trying to escape. As if she knew what I was trying to do, the sympathetic look was quickly wiped from her face, and her drunken grin replaced it.

"Let's party, bitches," she said as the bouncer moved the rope aside to let us in.

Bex winked at me over her shoulder, and I followed, intent on forgetting everything.

∼

I was on a bar.

Like on top of it.

Dancing. Grinding.

Never in my twenty-three years had I thought I'd be on top of a bar in a crowded nightclub, dancing with my best friend and her posse. I was pretty sure most of them worked at Bex's club, on account of their mad dance moves. The old Lily, given the choice, would have rather wrestled with an anaconda than dance on a bar.

But I wasn't the old Lily. I was the new and improved and appropriately liquored Lily. This Lily thought dancing on a bar was awesome.

Bex grinned at me. "You all good, babe?" she yelled over the music, her hands going to my hips. Her eyes were bright, unusually bright, with the shots we'd just done I guessed.

I beamed at her, having a feeling it was slightly crooked. I was feeling slightly crooked.

"I'm great," I yelled back.

We were currently dancing to *"Timber"* by Pitbull and everyone was cheering us on. There were more cheers as Bex executed the perfect *"slut drop"* against my body, a term I had learned, and practiced this past week. I threw my hands in the air, twirling, closing my eyes. I soaked it all in. The cheers, the music, the exhilaration that masked the exhaustion. I tried to let it fill me up to replace the emptiness. It didn't work. It didn't make me forget about it, but made it seem somehow distant, or more removed.

When I opened my eyes, I was facing the crowd. It was

blurry, a mix of bodies moving. But somehow, between the bodies I spotted him.

Maybe because he was hard to miss.

He wasn't laughing, dancing, or grinding on anyone. He was standing near the edge of the gyrating sea, his arms crossed and his eyes firmly on me. They captured me from across the room. He had a couple of other men behind him I noticed, one was them was from the strip club, the other I couldn't see properly and not really worth focusing on. Not at that moment.

Instead of turning red, of scurrying off the bar and escaping this situation, the burning behind those distant eyes, I gave him what I hope was a sexy grin. I moved my hips, threw my hands up in the air again, and moved my body against the music.

My eyes didn't leave his the entire time. My whole body burned with need, and somehow, this new Lily had the boldness to execute this way of communicating it.

"Holy fuck," Bex shouted in my ear. "That's the biker? My memory does not do him justice," she declared in amazement, stopping her movement to gape at Asher.

We had talked about him, in great detail this afternoon, when she had stumbled out of bed, but she hadn't gotten a proper glance at him the night before. Well she had, but she said she'd been too *"shitfaced"* to remember him. And three years was a long time in Bex's world, especially when she didn't dream about him every night like I did. I guessed she was getting an eyeful now.

I didn't move my eyes from him. "Yep."

At that moment, Asher's burning eyes seemed to change, and he pushed from his spot to part the crowd like the Red Sea, his cut, his general menacing air making people scurry out of his way. I didn't miss the way women's eyes roved over him as he passed them. He didn't notice. He only had eyes for me.

Me.

A warm feeling settled in me at this. One right between my legs.

"You're so getting laid tonight," Bex informed me with a grin.

It wasn't lost on me the only time I'd felt whole since this all started when I was on the back of his bike. When he was inside me. When his hands were on me. When I spoke to him on the phone.

I barely realized I had stopped moving. Stopped breathing. That was until he reached the edge of the bar, his head tipped up at me, his jaw hard.

He didn't have to speak, his eyes said it all.

I turned to Bex, whose eyes were in danger of popping out of her head. "I'm gonna go," I shouted in her ear.

She nodded, not moving her eyes. "Yeah, you are!" She winked at me, kissed my cheek and gave me a little shove.

I stumbled a little, which was not her intention, I didn't think she realized the extent of my intoxication. Luckily I righted myself and moved to step down. That was until hands fastened around my hips and I was lifted down, my body running over a hard one as I came down to earth.

I was set lightly on the ground, firm hands biting into my hips.

"Hey," I whispered to his glittered eyes.

Asher's jaw was hard. He didn't say a word, his hands tightened even more and before I knew what was going on, he yanked me to his body, plastering my mouth on his.

Again, normally I would be highly embarrassed over someone as hot as Asher sucking face with me in the middle of a crowded bar. Nothing worried me at the moment. I thought of nothing but his mouth on mine. The flame his touch ignited. When he released me, I was breathing heavily and swayed slightly. Again, he didn't say a word, merely grasped my hand and tightly yanked me toward the exit.

I was so in for it. In a good way.

We hadn't spoken. He had texted me earlier in the night, asking where I was, after I'd told him I had gotten radio silence. I had guessed he would have been checking in, since I knew he was all protective. All of them were.

I saw how Cade was with Gwen, I guessed it was contagious. I didn't expect him to turn up at the bar, not that I had complained when he dragged me out without a word only that smoking kiss. He had silently fastened my helmet, got me situated on the bike, and we roared off into the night.

Then again, sex spoke in volume. Or was it sex sells? Whatever it was, words were not needed when attraction shouted.

The breeze against my skin served to sober me up slightly, even with the jacket Asher had draped over me. Too soon we were pulling into the parking lot of my building, the lights illuminating reality that was easy to escape on the back of the bike.

Again, Asher silently divested me of my helmet and snatched my hand to half drag me toward the stairs leading to my second-floor apartment. I scuttled slightly to keep up with his pace. I didn't complain. I wanted to be somewhere with a bed as soon as possible, even if it was my shitty apartment. I didn't even find myself embarrassed by it. Not at this moment.

"Give me your keys," Asher demanded when we reached my door.

I riffled through my purse quickly and handed them to him silently.

When we made it inside my apartment, I thought it might be pertinent to speak. To explain something, my shabby décor maybe. Or the array of empty wine bottles littering the table, which was usually pristine. I hadn't thought about it the night before, I'd been too focused on Asher.

"Asher," I began, closing the door behind us.

He whirled on me, his eyes seeming to glow. He pushed me

against the door. Not gently, but not so much that it was painful. It was the opposite.

"Do not speak," he commanded against my mouth, his hands running up my sides. "I'm gonna fuck you senseless." His breath tickled my ear. "I need to relieve the pressure in my cock that started the moment I saw you on top of that fuckin' bar," he hissed, his eyes meeting mine. "So do not speak," he ordered roughly. "Not until after I've fucked you. Then we've got a lot of fuckin' speaking to do."

I didn't speak, not at that moment. I didn't want to. I wanted to obey him. Do whatever it took to have him *"fuck me senseless."*

Luckily I didn't need to do anything, his mouth captured mine the way it had at the bar, but this time it was leading somewhere. His hands roved, squeezing my breasts roughly, causing me to moan into his mouth. I wrapped my leg around his hip, needing him closer, as close as humanly possible.

His hands moved, lower, snaking up my skirt. "You better be ready for me, Flower," he growled. His breath came out in a hiss as he felt just how ready I was.

I felt his movement as he freed himself, pushing my panties to the side.

He didn't mess around and plunged inside me, one hand on my leg, cocking it up, the other on my collarbone.

This wasn't gentle, slow, or tender. It was furious, animalistic. Everything I needed at that moment.

His strokes brought me closer and closer to my release, his eyes holding my gaze, making this moment more intense. The deep part of me, the one I tried not to listen to, told me this was more than fucking. This was claiming.

I closed my eyes, in an effort to silence that voice, to focus on the imminent explosion. The hand moved from my collarbone to the back of my head. My eyes snapped open.

"You keep looking at me," Asher ground out, his jaw taut as he continued pounding. "Your beautiful eyes will be looking into mine every second, so you know what this is. What you are. Mine," he grunted.

With those words came my climax, the unforgettable almost unbearable release that I'd been craving since the moment he left me this morning. He was like a drug, one I was hopelessly addicted to already. My nails bit into the back of Asher's cut as I rode the wave, as I let it wash over me.

I was breathing heavily when I came down. Asher's eyes hadn't moved from mine. He had stopped moving, but he was still hard inside me.

His hands went to my butt, and he lifted me.

I let out a little noise of surprise at the moment, at the way it made my tender skin tingle.

"We're far from fuckin' done," he growled, striding toward my bedroom.

In that moment, I didn't think of much. In the moments following, I didn't think of anything but Asher.

A BRUSHING on my jaw woke me up. Then a pounding headache swiftly followed.

"Flower," a rough voice tickled my ear.

I normally would have welcomed this, but not at the present moment.

"Too loud," I murmured, not opening my eyes.

I heard a chuckle. "Open your eyes, Lily," the voice commanded.

I sighed, then complied. I may have been reluctant to welcome the daylight into my brain, but that reluctance melted away with the sight in front of me.

Events from last night came rushing in.

Asher.

In the club. Against my door. In my bed.

First, it was the fucking, then it was the slow, glorious love-making. Now he was fully dressed, sitting on the edge of my bed, in the crook of my hip, my body facing him. His handsome face was soft and had a dark shadow of stubble maximizing his attractiveness. I gazed into his chocolate eyes, traveled down to his muscled body, his sinewy arms drool worthy underneath his leather cut.

"You're hot in the morning," I observed, speaking without thinking. Something I was not known for doing. Every word I spoke was usually carefully considered. Not with Asher it seemed. Everything was different with him. Even I was.

A small grin teased the side of his face. "Fuck," he muttered, shaking his head. "You make it damned near impossible to be angry with you."

I furrowed my brows. Why would he be angry? That was cause for too much brainpower, not something I was capable of first thing in the morning, especially with a hangover.

He stroked my jaw again. "I wanted to stay. Talk. Fuck you again," he murmured roughly, and my stomach did dips. "But, I've got club shit that needs taking care of," he continued his mouth turning a grim line. "I'll be back when it's done." He regarded me a moment, something seeming to work behind his eyes. "Doesn't sit well with me, the fact I've not had a proper moment with you, since the night at the strip club, since all that shit went down."

I did an inward flinch, and his words woke me up. By *"shit"* I assumed he was referring to my mother's death. Not something that needed to be in my mind right now. I was still running.

He didn't seem to miss it. "I'll be back," he repeated.

It wasn't a question, it was a foregone conclusion that phone calls were a memory and that he was going to be in my life. Like physically. Looking at his physique, I failed to remember why this was a bad thing.

"Okay," I repeated, nodding.

"Good. You gonna be at home tonight?" Again this seemed more like a command than a question.

I screwed up my nose, the warm feeling of waking up to him dissipating. I sat up slightly, ignoring the sharp pain in my head as I did so.

"What's the day?" My voice was husky and so not attractive.

Asher's jaw turned tight. "Thursday," he clipped, though he looked like he wanted to say something more.

I searched my mental banks. "Thursday," I repeated, knowing there was something important about this day. A light bulb dinged.

"Nope," I said finally. "I'm at work tonight."

"Work?" he repeated with a hard jaw.

"The thing people do to make a living." I surprised myself with the sarcastic answer.

Asher didn't seem amused. "Didn't know you worked so much, Flower. What happened to college?" His voice was hard. During all of our phone conversations, I'd managed to escape this particular topic.

My stomach flipped. "Well, I've been on a ... break from school for the past year and a half," I said slowly, wincing at the pain the heart-wrenching pain that was coming back. "The bar meant I had days free for Mom. It paid the bills, still does." I shrugged.

Asher's brows drew together as something worked on his face. He didn't say anything, but he looked pissed. Not pissed at me exactly, but something far away. His eyes went back to mine.

"Okay. Text me the address. I'll pick you up when you're done," he said firmly. "No more buses," he reminded me. And before I could argue, his mouth pressed onto mine and he straightened, giving me one more look before he left the room.

I stared at the closed door for a long while.

What had I gotten myself into?

Something I knew I couldn't handle. Something I wanted to

get out of if I was to keep swimming in the ocean of grief that had no end. Something I also wanted to drown in.

But then that was dangerous. Those feelings are not okay.

Luckily, I didn't have time to inspect this. To think too hard. My door opened and to my surprise, Bex poked her messy head through it. She was grinning as she rushed into the room, jumping on my bed.

I was jostled, belatedly realizing I was naked, so I quickly yanked the covers on top of me. She wasn't fazed at my nakedness, I shouldn't be surprised considering what she did for a living. I was surprised at the mere fact she was conscious.

"What are you doing up at," my gaze flickered to the clock on the wall, "eight am? That's equal to dawn in your world." My realization that she'd been sleeping less than I was lately didn't have time to come to fruition.

She moved onto her side, her head resting on her hand. "You were dragged off by a biker last night, Lil, I need to know the deets, like as soon as … I wasn't in the proper state to get the lowdown yesterday," she said as if it was obvious.

I struggled to sit up without puking. "How are you all … chirpy? I feel like someone hit me with a car," I exclaimed, rubbing my head.

Bex waggled her eyebrows. "I bet you do, you saucy minx. If that kiss last night was anything to go by, I'm guessing that biker *ruined* you," she said mischievously.

I screwed my nose up at her wording. "Yeah, well, he may have ruined me for all other men."

"I need to know everything," she ordered. "Positions, length, girth, width. Everything."

I gave her a look. She knew I didn't like talking about that kind of stuff, it just wasn't in my nature. I may have been transitioning into a party girl, but I wasn't going to change everything about me.

She rolled her eyes. "Okay, nana. Just tell me one thing, did he take care of you?"

I nodded slowly. "Oh, yes."

She grinned.

"How about you?" I asked, needing to change the subject. "Any lucky man reel you in last night?" I remembered the men with Asher, thinking Bex would have loved them.

"Dylan's asleep in bed still. I was the one who ruined him last night." She winked at me.

I held my tongue at this. It was hard. Bex may have disapproved of Aiden because her character did not gel well with someone like him, but Dylan was different. He was a bad guy. Period. He and Bex had a turbulent on again off again relationship.

I called it toxic. Bex called it passionate. I was worried about the fact he was in our house again. I knew that he was shady. He hung in circles I didn't have anything to do with, and I'm pretty sure he had connections to a street gang that caused trouble around here. I didn't know much about them, but I knew they were bad news.

Bex liked her men bad, the badder the better. I just hoped it wouldn't bite her in the ass.

"I'LL HAVE a shot of tequila, and one for yourself too, sweetheart." The guy in front of me winked.

I cringed on the inside. "Sure thing," I replied with a bright smile. One I perfected over the years to hide whatever anxiety I had from social situations.

You'd think someone battling with social anxiety would cringe away from jobs where you actually had to interact with people and be charismatic to earn tips. I would if I could. Not a lot of choice out there for me when I wanted to spend my days taking care of my mom.

Night work was synonymous with bar work or stripping. I chose the former. I would have loved to keep my job at Gwen's store, in Amber, where the patrons were less likely to squeeze my ass and have me on the edge of a panic attack every shift, but I didn't get to choose. I did what I always did. Sucked it up and got on with it.

I clinked my class with the guy in front of me.

"Cheers to pretty bartenders," he drawled.

I downed the shot, doing an inner eye roll. I savored the burn, the tingle that it gave me. Jude was watching me out of the corner of her eye. It wasn't disapproval in her gaze, most of the bartenders were half way to blotto by the end of every shift. It was part of this place's charm. The waitresses and bartenders were renowned for partying with the patrons, and mostly all of them were young pretty girls. Which was why it was always packed.

"You got a name, sweet thing?"

I smiled at him. I hoped it seemed genuine and not like I was suffering a stroke.

"Lily," I replied lightly. The tequila was doing its job to help make the exchange easier and maybe even guarantee me some tips.

He leaned forward on his elbows, his eyes roving over me. "What's your story, Lily?"

I paused. My story? I restrained a bitter laugh. If I told him *"my story"* I could kiss my tips goodbye. I would tell him how I was raised by a single mom after finally escaping the clutches of an abusive father. How I struggled with not being like anyone else, not being able to shine bright like my mom, and how I was crippled by self-awareness. How I fell in love with a biker after losing my virginity to him. How I watched my mother die slowly before my eyes. Quit college, so I could take care of her and watch while she faded away, while I faded away myself. Admit that now she was gone I was drifting like a ghost, barely feeling corporal, fighting the emptiness with spirits I normally wouldn't touch. Trying to stay afloat.

I gave him another smile. "Nothing interesting," I told him on another grin.

Luckily any further conversation was drowned out by more patrons needing their drink orders filled. During the course of the night, my mask stayed on, helped by the fact I downed every shot that was bought for me, so everything began to blur around the edges.

"Holy shit on a cracker," Skye muttered under her breath, her eyes glued on the entrance.

I was focusing on pouring a cocktail, so I didn't follow her eyes. I should not have had that last shot, I decided. It was trial and error figuring out how much I could take, how much I needed to stop the Big Sad, but still make me stand upright.

"How about your number, along with that drink?" the man asked me when I pushed the drink toward him.

I was a little shocked. The dude just ordered an Appletini. I'd been certain he was gay—my gaydar was malfunctioning.

My shock gave me pause, and so it gave time for someone else to answer for me.

"You can't order a decent drink, you definitely can't handle a decent woman," a voice declared from behind Appletini dude.

Appletini dude turned around, Skye and I both followed his gaze.

Asher stood there, something ticking in his jaw, his arms crossed, eyes firmly focused on me.

"Excuse me?" Appletini dude asked, seeming affronted.

Asher stepped forward, not saying a word. Then again, when your muscles bulged out of your tee, your jaw could cut a bitch and your cut communicated your connection to a well-known motorcycle club — maybe you didn't need words.

My guess was confirmed as soon Appletini paled, darted his eyes to me, then pushed through the crowd.

Skye, who had been watching the whole exchange, darted her eyes between Asher and me.

"You know this dude, Lily?" she whispered to me, despite Asher stepping up to the bar, well within earshot.

I let out a little giggle. One that sounded foreign to my own ears. I didn't giggle. Well, not until recently.

"You could say that," I replied, not taking my eyes off him.

Skye looked generally amazed. I guessed I couldn't blame her, she knew the before Lily. The before Lily didn't giggle, didn't take shots on shift, and she certainly didn't have hot bikers visit her and scare off men asking for numbers.

"Skye, Asher, Asher, Skye," I introduced, filling the silence.

Asher gave her a chin lift.

Her mouth was still agape so she managed a little wave.

Asher turned his focus back to me. His brows were knitted as he took in my outfit. Again, this was something new Lily chose. It was conductive with the outfits I'd been wearing for two weeks. Tonight, I'd gone for tight jeans, heels and a cropped top which showed off a lot of midriff. His gaze flickered with desire when he finished his top to toe inspection, though his jaw was tight.

"You're early," I pointed out, leaning against my side of the bar. It helped stop the swaying.

Asher frowned. "Yeah," was all he said.

"You want a drink?" I asked finally after he didn't give me more of an explanation.

"Yeah. Beer please, babe," he replied, his voice soft, even though he had to raise it to be heard over the music.

I handed him a beer, the brand I knew he liked, what I had seen him drink the limited times I'd been in his presence. Those torturous times in the beginning when Gwen or Amy had dragged me along to some gathering he'd be at. Where I'd have to put on my mask of indifference and pretend my heart didn't bleed every time his chocolate eyes touched mine. I shook myself out of the past and the demons it held. The present had enough for me to battle with.

"You didn't have to pick me up," I told him after he'd taken a pull of his beer.

He regarded me. "Yeah, I did, Flower," he replied tightly.

I chewed my lip, not knowing what else to say. We didn't exactly do small talk, which the only kind of talk we could have in a crowded bar.

He frowned, eyes on my lips. Without warning, his beer crashed down on the bar, and his hand tagged the back of my neck. His mouth fastened on mine before I knew what was going on. He kissed the ever living hell out of me for long enough that a few catcalls sounded in the distance. I say the distance because the background seemed to melt away with Asher's lips on mine.

He finally released me and rested his forehead on mine before he let me go and leaned back on his stool, taking another pull of his beer.

I gaped at him, touching my tingling lips absently. "What was that for?" I strangled out.

Asher's desire-filled gaze rooted me to the spot. "I wanted to kiss you," he said simply.

My gape stayed firmly in place until I jumped when my name was called.

"I've got to..." I gestured with my thumb.

Asher nodded tightly. "I'm not going anywhere, babe," he told me firmly.

I stared at him a second longer, then rushed to the other end of the bar, feeling his eyes on me. They didn't leave me for the whole night.

~

"Bye," I shouted to the girls and Jude who watched Asher, and I leave with something akin to amazement.

He wove us through the crowd effortlessly, though most people, drunk or sober seemed to move for him anyway. It might be close to closing, but the place was packed. Always was. Jude had let me go home early with a soft look on her usually hard face.

"You get some sleep, darlin'. You need it," she had rasped and squeezed my hand. That was the closest to kind and fuzzy my tough as nails manager got. She wasn't unkind, just brisk but fair.

Asher had seemed more than happy to drag me off. The only reason I managed to stay upright was because of the firm hand at my waist. I didn't think much about anything else, apart from the warmth that emanated from his hand, and the desire that intensified with his touch. We made it into the parking lot, which was well lit and mostly empty. A few people loitered around, smoking or waiting for taxis, I guessed.

"Asher, can we slow to a brisk walk? I've been on my feet all night, I'm not really prepared to break the land speed record to make it to your bike." I pulled back slightly, surprised at the fact I was slurring my words.

Asher stopped us completely and twisted so he faced me, both his hands went to my waist and he looked down at me. No, he glared at me.

"You're drunk again," he stated flatly, his jaw hard.

I squinted at him. "No, I would use the term appropriately liquored," I answered with a grin. Although, without the lack of noise and tasks to distract me, coupled with the fact I was seeing two of him, I realized Asher might have been closer to correct.

He looked up into the sky for a moment then back down to me. "What are you doing?" he asked quietly.

I tilted my head in confusion. "Well, I thought we were going home, but now we're standing in the middle of the parking lot, having this conversation."

His gaze didn't move from mine. "No, Flower. *What are you doing? That.*" he nodded his head at the doors, "the drinking, partying, dancing on fuckin' bars. That shit ain't you."

With his words, my drunkenness seemed to wash off like dirt. Clarity settled into my mind. As did cold fury.

I ripped out of his arms, able to do so because he wasn't expecting it. "You don't know me!" I yelled. "Who I am. How are you meant to know me when I have no fucking clue?" I continued to scream and scuttled backward when he tried to step closer to me. "You don't get to ride in here after three years, up on your high Harley and dictate who I am, tell me what actions are appropriate for the Lily you thought you knew. The one you thought you had figured out after one fucking night. She's gone," I choked out, breathing heavily. "Maybe she never existed, I don't know. But I know you're not saving me. You're not *'taking care of me.'* I do that for myself. I always have. Always will. And if you want this," I waved my hand between us, glad he kept his distance, "you have to realize I'm not going to cling to your leather cut and let you figure out life for me. Shield me from it. Tell me what to do. I'm not an Old Lady. I can't give you that," I whispered, surprised at the wetness on my cheek. I angrily swiped the tears away. I didn't need them at this moment.

There was silence after my shouting. Well, not really silence, since the dull thumping of music in the background was pretty loud. Asher just watched me for a second, his face still soft, not showing an ounce of anger that had been there before. He stepped forward slowly.

"Flower—"

"Is there a problem here?" a voice interrupted.

Asher didn't even turn. "Fuck off," he muttered, his eyes on me.

Because I wasn't a rude alpha male, and because I recognized the voice, I turned my voice to look at the figure who had stepped close to me.

"Aiden?" I asked, his attractive face was moved into a hard line.

"You okay, Lil?" He tore his gaze from Asher, who made a noise when he came to my side, touching my elbow lightly.

"Yeah, I'm-I'm fine," I stuttered.

Aiden frowned, then glared at Asher, which was pretty brave considering the murderous glint on Asher's gaze.

"I don't believe you. How about I take you home?" he suggested softly.

Asher stepped forward. "I'll be taking her home, and I'd appreciate it if you take your hand off her," he bit out.

Aiden stepped slightly in front of me. "I don't think I'll be letting her go home with the biker she was screaming at in a parking lot with tears streaming down her face," he told Asher, looking at him with disdain.

I put my hand on his shoulder hoping to defuse the situation. "Aiden, we're fine, really," I reassured him. "What are you doing here anyway? This place isn't really your... scene."

I put that lightly. He had routinely urged me to find other employment since he found out I worked here. His upbringing made him unable to fathom the idea that I could stomach working somewhere like this. He didn't understand that people like me didn't get a choice.

Aiden turned his head, frowning at me. "I haven't seen you in weeks. You weren't at home and I knew you'd be here. I wanted to make sure you were okay," he explained.

"By lurking in a fuckin' parking lot?" Asher clipped, standing like a stone.

Though I didn't like the cursing or the general aggravation in his tone, I had to agree with the sentiment.

"You're right," Aiden spoke to me. "This isn't my scene. I also knew you would be finishing about this time, taking the bus home. That's not safe. Not to mention your state of mind. I was waiting in my car to take you home."

"Right, man, that's firmly in stalker territory, so I'd greatly appreciate it if you stopped and stayed the fuck away from Lily," Asher ground out, fists at his sides.

I raised a brow at Asher. "Pot, meet kettle..." I gestured at Aiden, reminding him of the night he stayed outside my apartment.

He glared. "That was different and you know it, baby. This fucker needs to realize who you belong to," he sneered at Aiden as if I hadn't just informed him I belonged to no one, not moments ago.

"Asher, I've got this," I snapped.

Asher gave me a look but stayed silent.

Aiden looked between the two of us. "This is why you dumped me, Lily? You get a taste for biker?" he asked, a cruelness I didn't recognize creeping into his tone.

I said, "No," at the same time as Asher said, "Sure as fuck is."

I glared at Asher. "Shut up," I hissed.

Aiden's eyes flared. He took in my attire, the way I swayed slightly. His jaw turned hard and he turned to face Asher.

"So you think you can take advantage of a grieving girl, get her to drink too much, show too much skin, turn her into some kind of biker slut?" he accused, and I gasped at the last of his words.

I also gasped when Asher's fist plowed through Aiden's face, causing him to tumble to the ground.

"Holy shit," I yelled, bending to check on Aiden, who was bleeding from the nose.

I glared at Asher. "You really had to punch him? Really? Can you keep your testosterone under control long enough not to use your fists?" I snapped at him.

Asher ignored me and stepped over Aiden. "You ever refer to

Lily like that again, I'll make sure that pretty face is messed up so much even Mummy's best plastic surgeon won't be able to fix you," he promised coldly.

Aiden glared at him for a long moment, then his eyes moved to me. "Is this who you want to surround yourself with, Lily? You're better than this. This isn't you."

He struggled to his feet, shrugging me off when I tried to help him. "I'll be here when you remember who you are," he said, giving me a long look and Asher a glare before wandering into the parking lot.

I watched him for a moment. People kept telling me what wasn't me. I wished they'd enlighten me for a second, what was me.

CHAPTER TWELVE

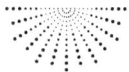

I SLAMMED the door as we got into my apartment. "What the heck was that?" I yelled at Asher.

The bike ride had made yelling impossible. And gave me a great opportunity to get even angrier.

Bex's eyes bulged from her position on the sofa, a spoonful of cereal halfway to her mouth.

Asher turned. "What was what?"

I scoffed. "Seriously? You're going to act like that senseless act of violence against my friend didn't happen?" I asked in disbelief.

"Dude, please tell me it was Aiden," Bex put in from the sofa.

I swear I saw Asher's mouth twitch slightly before he focused on me once more.

"I wouldn't call him referring to you as a *biker slut*, senseless. He should be glad he's not eating through a straw right now," he clipped tightly.

"Mother fucker said *what?*" Bex hissed.

"It was nothing, he was upset," I reassured her quickly.

Asher's eyes hardened. "Talking to a woman like that, that's never nothing. No matter how upset you are. Talking to you like that? That's something. Something not fucking acceptable. Something never fucking acceptable," Asher clipped. "You've gone through enough shit. Life's already handed you ugly. You're not having ugly words spat in your direction. Not when there's not one ounce of truth in them. Not when I'm around. And I intend to be around a lot," he promised.

I sucked in a breath. It was hard to argue with a guy when he said shit like that. And as much as I abhorred violence, a tiny piece of me agreed with Asher. Aiden was definitely out of line.

I sighed, plonking my bag down by the door. "Whatever," I relented trying to act like his words hadn't made my legs shaky. "I'm hungry." I stepped forward, pointing at Asher. "Use your words next time," I ordered.

He grinned, though there was something behind the grin. I didn't get time to analyze this, as he tagged my hips and yanked me to his body.

"I'm thinking I wanna do something that doesn't require any words," he murmured against my mouth.

I was caught by surprise, and my body responded accordingly, my heart thumping and breathing heavily.

"But, I'm hungry," I protested.

His eyes flared. "So am I ... starving," he said roughly.

I swallowed.

"Um ... guys, I'm still here," Bex called from the sofa. "Take it to the bedroom."

Asher smiled into my mouth. "What do you say, Flower?"

"Food can wait," I whispered.

"Good answer," he murmured.

"You're good at that," I whispered, breathless.

He had just finished making love to me. That was after he had *"eaten"* me like promised. It was more than amazing.

Asher's chest vibrated as he chuckled. "Glad you think so, Flower. Though how hard you came had me thinking you were enjoying yourself." His voice was husky.

I felt myself go slightly red at his statement. Asher seemed to sense my reaction because he pulled me from my position curled against his chest to lie half on top of him. He stroked my hair out of my face, eyes searching mine.

"You don't need to worry about that shit with me," he told me quietly.

"What shit?" I whispered.

His thumb ran over my cheek. "Whatever shit that runs through that beautiful mind to make you curl into yourself. Turns you quiet. Gives you that glow. Don't get me wrong, I love seeing that you get affected by shit like that," his voice was rough, "but I don't want you ever crawling to that place, being embarrassed of anything. Not when you're in this bed with me. Not when you're with me, full stop," he said firmly.

I stared into his eyes, his words filling a little of that empty space inside me. It frightened the shit out of me.

He continued. "I know that whatever turns you like that seems to turn off with me, most of the time. I want it to stay like that, Flower. I want to be the one to take that weight off your chest, to take down that shield you've constructed, I want you to just ... *be* when you're with me," he murmured into my mouth. "And when you feel comfortable enough, I want to get to the bottom of why you think you need to hide behind that shield. As if your life depended on it." He paused. "And now, we're going to talk about what that was in the parking lot."

I stared at him. I was silent, letting those words wash over me. I traced his jaw with my fingertip, amazed at the fact this man, this beautiful man was saying these beautiful words to me. Those beautiful words also catapulted me back in time, back fourteen years to memories that should be weathered and blurry with age, but instead they were clear as if they happened yesterday.

I WAS SCARED. Terrified. The headlights that illuminated our small living room meant he was home. That meant the red rage, the yelling, him hurting Mommy, saying bad words right in front of me. Sometimes saying those bad words to me.

"Okay, Peanut." Mom knelt in front of me, smiling that weird smile that didn't seem quite right. "I need you to do your special trick and don't say a word. Go to your place in your head. If you be really quiet, quiet as a mouse, it'll all be okay. I promise." She kept smiling that smile. "Just be my little quiet peanut for a little while longer, then Mommy will keep you safe. Can you do that, Lily?

I nodded, deciding to start being quiet as a mouse, right now because I could hear his key in the door.

Mommy did too because she kissed my head and stood, smoothing the pretty dress she was wearing underneath her apron.

I curled up as small as I could be on the sofa, my eyes glued to the pictures on the screen, trying not to make a sound, I even tried to make my breath silent. If I were quiet enough maybe I'd disappear, be invisible to him.

I ESCAPED the memory before its venom could taint this beautiful moment.

"Be me," I repeated.

"Yeah, Flower," he responded, not taking his eyes off me.

"What if I don't know who that is?" I asked in a strangled whisper.

Asher's hands clasped my neck firmly. "Then we'll find out, together."

His voice was so firm, so resolute, it made my stomach dip. Not in a good way.

"What if you find out you don't like, who I find out I am?"

His eyes hardened. "Not fuckin' possible."

I chewed my lip. Emotions like I was feeling, this, I didn't know how to figure it out. I didn't know how to figure out anything in my life. I could barely figure out my past, apart from the fact the last time someone looked out for me was when my abusive father had a heart attack in our kitchen, while my mother lay bloodied on the floor, after he caught her trying to leave. He would have killed her in that moment, even my nine-year-old eyes could have seen that. Something intervened to give her escape, freedom, a life. For fourteen more years at least. That same thing decided to rob of her of that. Rob me of that.

Asher put firm pressure on my neck to direct my eyes back to him. "The partying, the drinking, that shit helping?" he asked softly.

I regarded him, blinking away my demons and letting the feeling of warmth spread through me at his gentle words, his soft voice.

"No," I admitted. "But it helps delay it all. The feelings, the big sadness that I'm afraid I'll get lost in. Makes me forget. Be someone else. Someone different. Someone better," I told him truthfully.

There was a pause as Asher's face turned blank. Then he sat up, resting on the wall and positioning me so I was straddling him.

"You need to listen to me now, Flower," he began seriously. "There's no such thing as better. You are who you are. The fact you think that being someone else is better is not acceptable. I stand by what I said three years ago." His eyes burned into mine. "I don't know if there's such a thing as perfect, but I'm looking at as close as I can get right here." His hand squeezed my neck. "You aren't perfect because you're drop dead fuckin' gorgeous, your tight little body makes my cock harden in my jeans every time I see it. Not because you're kind, caring, soft when you need to be, but your claws come out when you decide to be a smart ass. Perfect isn't superficial shit it's who you are in here," he tapped my chest lightly, "and here." He brushed a hair off my head.

"I'm not," I argued. "I'm not beautiful. I know that. We both know that."

Asher's entire body jerked. Flinched. His eyes turned dark. "You seriously think that?" he asked in a hard voice.

I glanced down. "I know it," I replied in a small voice.

"Fuck," he muttered. "Wish more than anything else I had the gift to bring back the dead. First, I'd get your mom back, then I'd get your father. Kill that piece of shit all over again. I'd make it slow. Death is too easy of an escape for what he did to this beautiful soul," he said fiercely, his voice almost shaking with fury.

His finger moved underneath my chin, gently moving my eyes to meet his.

"Listen to me, Flower. You are the most beautiful, amazing woman I've ever laid eyes on. Everything about you. Your hair that shines like the sun. The eyes that look like someone's taken a piece of the ocean and put it in those beautiful things." He paused, stroking my face. "Beauty is on the surface, Flower. Temporary. Something that fades, withers. Being truly beautiful is when you've known suffering, fought demons at the depths of despair and managed to claw your way out. Managed to smile again. Managed to laugh, to live, to love. That's eternal. That's you."

His certainty. His resolve, almost had me believing him. His words caused tears to trail down my cheeks. But a lifetime of my own certainty stopped me. I knew arguing was pointless, so I just leaned down and placed my mouth gently on his.

Gently was where I started, hungry and claiming was where he finished it.

"You still want to try and look for answers at the bottom of a bottle, I won't approve, but I'll be there. You'll do it at the club," he said firmly against my mouth.

I nodded more on instinct than anything else. I was questioning the answers that lay at the bottom of any of the bottles I'd emptied. I knew that nothing of value was there, and it wasn't exactly a long-term plan.

"Can I ask you one question?" he murmured softly, searching my face.

I nodded.

"Do you want to be with me? Do you feel this, us, right down to your soul?" he asked in a raspy tone.

I swallowed. "That's two questions," I whispered, my heart beating one hundred miles a minute.

Asher gave me a look but didn't say a thing. He seemed to realize my need for silence. So he let the quiet expand while I searched my head.

"Yes," I said finally.

I opened my mouth to say the reasons why it wasn't that simple. How he'd realized that I wasn't right for him. How I was a broken shell that wouldn't fool him for long. His finger at my lips silenced me.

"It's that simple, Flower. You want this, you feel this. I want you. I've fuckin' craved you for three years, babe. I'm holding on as tight as I can without bruising you, and I'm not letting go anytime soon," he declared hoarsely. "That's all there needs to be right now. You want me. I want you. The other shit doesn't matter."

I wanted to believe that. With all of me, I did. I wanted to believe that fate had finished screwing with me, and somehow in the midst of all the turmoil in my life we could make it work. I knew doubt would creep in, later, in the future. But right now I did believe him, did feel the warmth settle in at his promise.

"Okay," I whispered.

He nodded, kissing my nose. He moved me off him to tuck me back into his chest.

"Sleep now," he commanded softly.

I snuggled closer to his warm body, squeezing my eyes shut. Hopefully, the presence of it would help make the nightmares go away.

I JOLTED awake with a pounding heart and a panicked mind. I was suffocating, choking, air trapped in my chest. My throat closed up, and I struggled to get any oxygen into my lungs, no matter how hard I sucked it in desperately.

The light switched on, Asher's worried face was illuminated, and he clutched my shoulders.

"Holy fuck, Lily, what is it?" he commanded urgently, his eyes darting over my entire body as if he was looking for a wound.

I struggled to catch my breath, to get words out. It wasn't lost on me, I hadn't told him about my asthma, so he wouldn't know about the terrifying attacks that had plagued me since I was a kid. Right after I turned nine, in fact. I hadn't had one in a long while, the terror was not unfamiliar, but unexpected.

"Lily?" he shouted as I wheezed, unable to speak.

Be calm. Try to be calm, I told myself.

I knew panic made it worse. Calm is hard when an invisible hand tightened around your throat, making you drown with no water in sight. I moved my shaking arm to the drawer beside my bed where my inhaler lived.

"I'm calling a fuckin' ambulance," he bellowed, his eyes saturated with panic he couldn't disguise. "Breathe, Flower, hold on," he pleaded.

The door opened and Asher's eyes cut to it, his body tightening even further. Bex didn't even say a word, as soon as she laid her eyes on me, she knew what was going on. She rushed to the bed, pushing Asher's hands off my shoulders. He moved, more with shock than anything else I think.

"Lilmeister, look at me," she commanded calmly. "Go to your place," she ordered softly.

"What the fuck's going on?" Asher yelled his phone at his ear.

Bex didn't glance at him. "Get off the phone and get me the inhaler and nebulizer from the drawer beside her bed," she snapped.

Asher's face jolted for a spilt-second in surprise, then he moved.

"Lils, at me," Bex commanded.

I locked my frantic eyes onto her calm ones.

"Think of the horizon," she whispered as she fiddled with the inhaler Asher thrust into her hands. "You're on a beach, remember? The air's clear, it's so warm it sinks into your bones, and you can hear the waves crashing in your ears. Take a deep breath, taste the saltwater air," she commanded softly, her voice serene, eyes on me.

"What the fuck is going on?" Asher shouted, juxtaposing Bex's gentle tone. His eyes locked on mine with something I'd never seen behind them.

Fear.

"She's having an asthma attack," Bex replied quickly.

She placed the nebulizer over my mouth and pressed the button on the inhaler.

"Breathe," she instructed calmly.

I focused, remembering my mom doing the same thing when I was little. She'd be calm, not panicked as I struggled to catch a breath. She'd told me to think of a sunset, go somewhere else and close my eyes and focus on that, not the strangling feeling in my chest. She'd sat holding my inhaler, describing in her melodic voice the place where I could go to find a way to breathe, to get through. She was never frantic. Though I'm sure she felt it, she never let it show, not until after at least. Then she'd rush me to the ER.

I closed my eyes fastening my shaking hands around the nebulizer. I tried to slow my heartbeat, picture the beautiful sunset, the horizon, my mom living beyond that, in that better place.

It took a while, to get past the panic that came with getting robbed of breath, of realizing I could suck it in once more, but I got there.

I opened my eyes to Bex and Asher's worried gazes. I slowly lowered my inhaler.

"I'm okay," I rasped after sucking in some more oxygen.

Asher stared at me, his face was blank, blinking a couple of times. Then his whole body sagged with relief. He moved closer to me, to cup my neck, his eyes intent on mine, searching my face.

"I'm still calling an ambulance," he declared, glancing down onto his phone.

I put my hand on his arm. "I'm okay. I don't need an ambulance," I protested in a husky voice.

His eyes cut back to me. "You stopped fuckin' *breathing*," he said slowly, his voice ragged.

"It's not the first time it's happened," I replied softly.

"It may be scary as shit, biker boy, but Lily's right," Bex put in from the other side of me, squeezing my hand. "She's gone through this before. Not much the hospital can do now anyway. Trust me, I dragged her ass there the first time it happened," she informed him with a shaky smile.

I knew she was trying to mask her own fright. It wasn't exactly cake when you watched someone suffocate on their own lungs. It wasn't cake experiencing it either.

I smiled a sad smile at this. She had. She'd also called my mom in hysterics and then put her on the phone to me after locating my inhaler and thrusting it at me. Mom's gentle voice had helped me focus on getting my breath back. That would never happen again. I'd never get that voice coaxing me out of the vortex of terror that came with my attacks. I blinked away the tears that came with this realization.

I unfastened the nebulizer and took a puff of the smaller part of the inhaler.

Asher's eyes narrowed. "I didn't even know she had asthma," he muttered quietly. His voice was defeated as if he was angry at himself.

Bex gave him a sad smile. "Well, our Lily's not about sharing much with the general public, in case you hadn't noticed." She winked at me. "She keeps this particular nugget close to her chest, excuse the expression." She squeezed my hand again, her eyes turning serious. "You okay now, Lils babe?"

I nodded, my throat feeling too dry to speak. Plus, I was too busy trying to catch my breath, it was hard to both breathe and speak after an attack. Bex knew this, and reached over to the glass of water beside my bed, handing it to me. I gulped the water greedily, trying to swallow in between breaths. I gave her a smile in thanks.

She watched me drink with her eagle eye, as did Asher, but his gaze was intent, alert, as if he was expecting me to drop dead at any moment.

"Okay, my work here is done," Bex exclaimed, pushing off the bed. "As much as I hate seeing you like that, at least I got a glimpse of your man shirtless. That'll turn anyone breathless." She winked at me then left the room.

I giggled slightly, the sound wheezy. Only Bex could make me laugh moments after an asthma attack.

Asher was not smiling. He was staring at me, his hand reached out to touch my throat lightly, then moved to my chest, laying it there for a moment. We were silent, his eyes didn't leave mine, his hand moving on my chest with my breaths.

"Been in a lot of scary situations, babe," he began quietly.

"Been shot at, had to shoot at other people. Thought death might be around the corner on many of those occasions," he continued, his eyes never leaving mine.

My heart started pounding under his hand, the image of Asher getting shot at causing more panic than the breath that had been stolen from me moments before.

"I've never been more afraid than just then, waking up to see you not being able to fuckin' breathe. Not knowing what was going on, or how to help you. Thinking you were going to fucking die, right in front of me. Not being able to do a fuckin' thing. I'd take bullets over that any day," he declared hotly. His hand moved to my jaw. "Me watching it was scary as shit. You experiencing it, fuck, Flower."

He actually grimaced, shaking his head. He was silent for a moment, looking down at my hand which was loosely grasping my inhaler. His own moved to cover it before he met my eyes once more. I almost flinched at the tortured look in his usually strong gaze.

"Why didn't you tell me?" he asked softly.

I shrugged. "Well, we haven't exactly had much time to get to know the details of each other's lives, if you haven't noticed," I pointed out, taking another puff of my inhaler.

Asher's jaw went hard. "We've had two weeks of getting to know details," he clipped, staring at my inhaler. "That's a pretty important detail, Lily. Especially when you're dancing on goddamned tables, and drinking yourself into the ground." He paused, grimacing. "Jesus, letting me fuck you like that…." he trailed off sounding disgusted in himself.

My stomach dropped. "That…" I whispered hoarsely, "that right there, is why I didn't tell you. It's not … sexy. This," I waved the inhaler, "I don't want you treating me like glass. I like that you treat me like I won't break, I never want you to look at me like you are now. Like I'm weak," I whispered.

I'd already had enough things that crippled me, my shyness,

my inability to be bad ass in scary situations like Gwen and Amy, my utter normalcy.

"I don't want you to see me like I'm some weak flower, some damsel needing to be rescued. Someone you need to take care of. I'm not that. I don't want to be your burden," I continued, voicing my worst fear.

Asher's whole body stilled, and his jaw turned tight. He didn't say a word. Not for a long while.

"You're angry," I observed after I couldn't stand the silence any longer.

"Not angry, just thinking," he replied tightly.

"Thinking about being angry," I clarified.

His face softened. "No, Lily. Just thinking. About how I can educate you on how amazing and how far from weak you are. How I can make you see you're special. How I can make you understand that there's nothing that can make me think otherwise," he murmured. "How you're not a delicate flower, but the most beautiful, most resilient woman I've had the pleasure of knowing. A flower that gets trampled on by life, but somehow manages to emerge, unbruised, and more beautiful than ever after it." He cupped my face. "You don't need anyone to take care of you. I want to. It's a privilege to be given a beautiful flower to nurture, to protect."

The breath left me, but this time in a good way.

"I'm coming to the conclusion there's not much I can say. Not right now anyway," he continued. "I don't think it's about me saying anything. I think it's about showing you. Every single day. Starting tomorrow."

He moved so his back was against the wall, and I was buried in his chest once more.

"That's tomorrow. Which you need rest for. Now you sleep," he ordered firmly.

Usually, I didn't sleep, not after an attack. I'd lie awake terrified for hours, trying to remind myself breath was coming easy, my mind taunting me with how easy that could change. I prepared for that. To my utter surprise, I let sleep claim me, encircled in Asher's arms.

Because I fell into oblivion so quickly, I didn't notice Asher watching me. Didn't realize he spent the rest of the night with his hand on my chest, only surrendering to sleep when the daylight kissed the corner of the room, chasing away the demons of the night.

CHAPTER THIRTEEN

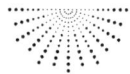

"I KNOW I said you needed your rest for today, but I didn't plan to let you do anything that would require energy...not until later at least," Asher murmured, his arms going around my stomach and mouth at my neck. "I'm also not fond of waking up without you, I've had enough mornings of that," he added on a grumble.

"You look so cute when you're sleeping, I didn't want to ruin it," I replied, my eyes on the pan I was cooking breakfast in. "Plus, you said you wanted to get to know each other right? Getting to know me means tasting my world famous French toast," I told him seriously.

Asher squeezed my waist. "I'm sure it tastes good, Flower, but not as good as the breakfast I planned on having this morning." His hand moved down to the waistband of my shorts.

I swallowed, doing my best to focus on the task at hand.

"And I'm not cute," he continued, his hand tickling the top of my panties. "I'm manly and rugged, handsome if you must, but never cute."

I couldn't help it, I burst out laughing. I'd never really seen the playful side of Asher, I liked it. The juxtaposition of his muscled and hard exterior with such silliness was refreshing. It was also the first genuine laugh I'd had in a long time, in recorded memory it seemed.

Asher moved the pan off the stove and twisted me in his arms, hands going to my neck.

"I'll forego my planned breakfast to hear that any day," he told me quietly, his eyes serious. He stroked the corner of my eye. "See those light up." His eyes moved to my mouth, which was still miraculously turned up. "You've got the sweetest smile I've ever seen," he whispered. "I'll move Heaven and earth to give you more reasons to show it to me."

I blinked. "You have to let me finish our breakfast," I muttered, not needing those feelings, the ones that came with those words.

Not first thing in the morning. Not when they chased away the demons I'd been waking up with. I had to learn how to chase them away myself. Relying on Asher to do so would result in disaster.

He gave me a long look then leaned in and kissed me firmly. I expected him to move back and let me do my thing. He stayed, searching my face.

"You okay today, Flower?" he asked with obvious concern, his large hand moving to my chest, letting it rise and fall with my breath.

I glanced down at how large and powerful it looked against my chest and gave him a shaky smile. "I'm fine."

He gave me a look, his jaw hard and eyes plagued with worry, the playfulness of before long gone.

"It takes me a few days to get over the shock of it all, but physically, I'm fine," I reassured him, placing my hand on top of his.

He searched my eyes, obviously looking for a lie. He nodded then kissed my head.

"I don't want you hiding shit like that from me anymore.

You're feeling anything out of the ordinary, you tell me right away," he commanded.

I nodded. It was the only way to get him off my case, I knew.

"Lily, I mean it. *Anything*, we're going to the hospital."

I wanted to roll my eyes. I also wanted to embrace the warm feeling that seemed to settle in my broken soul and start to jostle the broken pieces back together. The feeling of him taking care of me. Worrying about me. Caring about me.

I was lost in thought I didn't notice he was staring at me expectantly, obviously waiting for a verbal response.

"Yes, Asher, I promise," I said quietly.

"Good," he replied simply, stroking my neck. "I don't like that shit," he muttered. "A girl like you shouldn't struggle with something as simple as breathing, the world's already taken enough from you. Trying to steal your ability to exist? To breathe easy? That shit's not okay." He played with a tendril of my hair. "I don't want you breathless when you deserve to have every breath on this earth easy."

I stared at him. "If you don't want me breathless then you might need to remove yourself from my immediate vicinity," I half whispered. "Or make that my life. You steal my breath when you say things like that, but in a good way. In the best way," I told him, surprising myself with my honesty. My shield was lying in tatters at my feet, and I stared at him with nothing protecting me. I trusted him not to hurt me.

His entire frame jolted and his face went blank. I waited for a couple of seconds for him to answer, but he stayed silent, his eyes moving over every inch of my face like he was committing them to memory. The intensity in his gaze told me my words had just changed things, shifted them. A large part of me did a happy dance at this, but a smaller, more powerful part urged me to run, rebuild that shield as quickly as possible.

"Can I cook our breakfast now?" I asked with fake impatience, trying to chase away both parts for now. Just live in the moment.

"I'll allow it," he said dryly. "Only if you tell me what I can do to help," he added, completely surprising me.

My eyes bulged slightly. "You, Asher, manly biker type, want to help cook breakfast?" I clarified.

He pretended to look offended. "Don't look so surprised, Lily, I'm not a man to sit on my ass and let my woman run after me. Especially after shit last night." He sounded serious on the end. Though, he stepped forward to squeeze my ass. "And, being on this side of the counter means I'm within grabbing distance if I feel like it." He winked.

Winked!

I was enjoying playful Asher. "You're like this, and you haven't even had coffee," I pointed out in amazement.

Asher gave me a hungry look, yanking my body to his. "Who needs coffee when I've got you to get me out of bed?" he said seriously.

Before I could melt in a puddle at his feet, Bex came in to save the day.

"Seriously. If I put a hidden webcam in here I could make thousands off the two of you," she grumbled as she padded into the kitchen, aiming for the coffee pot.

"Good morning to you, too, sunshine," I called from Asher's arms, grinning.

Bex turned to me, sipping from her coffee mug. When her eyes caught mine, something in them turned sad, though she smiled. It was quickly masked.

"If I have to endure PDA from two beautiful people, you've got to tell me you're cooking me breakfast, too," she said as she sat herself on a barstool.

I gently pulled out of Asher's arms and put the pan back on the stove.

For the first time in weeks, no months, I was actually looking forward to the day ahead of me.

~

"HOLY HELL IN A HANDBASKET," Gwen yelled from across the room when Asher and I walked into the clubhouse.

I felt self-conscious about my attire as I hadn't been prepared for a club party when leaving the house today. I was wearing high-waisted, form-fitting, light denim jeans, a white boyfriend shirt and strappy maroon heels. My hair was piled atop my head and I wore little makeup.

"I wish you'd let me go home and change before we came here," I hissed in his ear on our approach.

Gwen was glam as usual. Even from across the room I could spy her strappy electric blue Manolos. The woman had a kid for chrissakes, two of them!

"You're beautiful," he replied firmly. "And if I'd let you go home you wouldn't have come," he added.

I was silent. He had me there. Gwen's eyes weren't focused on my outfit, they were glued to our intertwined hands as we approached the sofa where she was cradling her little boy, Knox. Cade was at her side, a sleeping Belle draped over his chest. He regarded us with his normal blank badass stare. His badassness was not hampered by the tender hand he had placed around his daughter's small body, nor the other one around his wife. That was not an easy feat.

I swallowed, trying to calm the fear that had choked me when we'd pulled up to the compound. That had turned me mute when Asher had walked us through the outside where people had been milling and shouting greetings to each other.

I had seen many of the men before, but not in such large numbers, and definitely not on their biker turf. It was safe to say

177

my shyness was back with a vengeance. It had all but disappeared after a day with Asher. He'd taken me on a ride, somehow knowing after the strangling claustrophobic feeling of last night I needed openness, fresh air, to feel alive. I was already feeling touched by death, my attack had me feeling caressed by it. Asher, his mere presence, his body against mine, it chased away the reaper. I'd fallen even deeper in love with him. That was until his ride finished at a familiar brick building. One that once held excitement and the promise of future. Now, it only held the ghost of the life before.

"What are we doing here?" I asked flatly after the roar of the Harley had silenced, and Asher had gotten off his bike.

He stared at me, I hadn't moved from my seat, only yanked my helmet off so I could speak and not look like a dork.

"You're going in, to sign up for your classes again," he stated, crossing his arms.

I stared at him. He didn't offer further explanation, so I stared some more my serenity quickly replaced by cold anger, one that masked the mild panic and despair that was simmering beneath my façade.

"Do we need to take you to the hospital?" I asked seriously.

Asher's brows furrowed together. "Not sure I get that statement, Flower."

I sat a little straighter, wanting to get up to even up our stances, but not wanting to look like I was conceding one bit.

"I'm assuming you're suffering from some disease that messes with your brain function, primarily thinking you have the right to take me here and try and dictate any part of my life," I hissed with a venom I didn't know I was capable of.

Asher didn't flinch nor change his expression in the face of my anger, if anything, his eyes softened slightly and he stepped forward, arm extended. I gave him a look that warned for the fate of said arm if he used it to touch me. Obviously, I wasn't good at the threat of dismemberment because his rough hand caressed my cheek.

"You need to do this, Lily," he told me quietly, eyes not leaving mine.

I jutted my chin out. "And you know what I need better than I do?"

He paused. "I'd like to think I know you better than you know yourself," he began. "But, that's not true. I look forward to knowing every inch of you. You know yourself, what you need, you're just scared of it. I'm in a better position to show it to you, to give you the opportunity to give yourself what you need." He nodded to the building. "You need to go back to college, babe, back to your future, your life. You need to start living it. Not running from it," he said sagely.

I refused to look away from him. "I'm not running from anything," I lied.

His face turned sad and the hand at my cheek tightened slightly. "Yeah, babe, you are. You're sprinting. You're breathless, running for your life. You need to realize it's gonna catch you, and it's not gonna be the end."

I blinked at him. He saw so much more than I thought anyone did. Than even I did. My anger fell away quickly, the energy of holding it up was something I couldn't keep up, when I was too busy trying to hold myself together.

"You don't know that," I whispered. "What it'll feel like when it catches me. I'm not strong enough to take it. It'll bowl me over, I won't be strong enough to get back up," I choked out.

Asher stepped forward and lifted me completely off the bike, encircling me in his arms, holding me in the air for a moment before settling me on the ground. He didn't let me go, nor did he release me from his intense gaze.

"It might," he agreed. "But I'll be here to pick you back up, make sure you can fly again. Not that you need me. You're strong enough."

I shook my head, both to disagree and to shake off the tears. "I'm not," I argued softly.

"Strength comes in lots of different forms, Lily. It doesn't make you weak if you let life knock you down. It makes you strong that you can stay standing for this long," he said. "I know what it's like to run, Flower. To believe if you change who you are it might mean that it won't recognize you, that you won't feel the extent of the loss the old you endured," he spoke quietly, with something underneath his raspy words.

Something I recognized. Sorrow.

"Trust me, I know it doesn't end well. You can't hide from yourself. Can't disguise yourself from grief..." he paused, a faraway look in his eyes. He focused on me. "I lost my little brother when I was fifteen. He was two years younger, but we were close. All we had was each other. Our dad was too drunk to notice us half the time, and our mom ran out when we were young." He sucked in a breath. "We were in a car wreck. I walked away. He didn't," he stated flatly.

I had my hand over my mouth, my eyes on Asher. I felt his pain. Beneath the words was the sorrow that I knew because my own grief recognized it.

"I didn't want to believe it," he continued hoarsely. "That it even happened. That I lost my best friend." He paused. "Then I realized it did happen, he was never coming back. Went down a dark road. Darker than the blackest midnight. Turned into someone who I didn't recognize, didn't respect. Thought that was the way to get out from under it. The way to survive." His clear eyes wouldn't let me go. "It was the way to die, Flower. I realized that. Dragged myself out from under that shit. Found new brothers. Found a new family. Met that shit I'd been running from. I faced what I thought would kill me. I lived." He stroked my face. "I'm not gonna let that happen to you. Let you know the blackest midnight. Let you venture any further into that shit. I'm not gonna let my flower wilt. I watched you amble down that road I'm so familiar with for long enough. I'm done watching." He nodded to the building once more. "So it starts with this, you going back to where you belong. We'll figure the other stuff out. First, you need to stop running. I'm gonna be here, every step of the way," he promised.

I stared at him, tears running unbidden down my cheeks. I didn't even notice the world around us. There wasn't a world around us right now.

"What was his name?" I whispered finally.

Pain, pure agony that my kindred soul recognized swam at the depths of his eyes.

"Benjamin," he replied softly with a sad smile.

"Does it ever stop hurting to say his name? To remember his face?"

Asher's hand tightened on my neck. "No," he said slowly. "But you get stronger, learn how to recognize that you can handle the hurt, that it won't kill you."

I chewed my lip. I wasn't strong. I couldn't even handle public speaking, crowds, meeting new people. How could I ever be strong enough to live with this pain?

Asher's hand went under my chin to make me meet his eyes once more. "You're strong," he declared, reading my mind. "I know you spend your life doubting that, but I'm standing right here in awe of the strength that my little flower has without even recognizing it," he promised. "Stop running, babe. You can handle it."

I stared at him for a long moment, then glanced at the building in front of us. I turned my head back to him.

"Okay," I whispered.

Asher smiled again, he bent to kiss my nose gently before releasing me, moving his hand firmly to clasp mine. And we walked in together, me trying to lift my feet with the weight of grief that had been like a dumbbell for weeks. It wasn't any lighter, but Asher was right, my ability to carry it around had seemed to increase. I was stronger. Only a little, but it was enough to make a difference.

~

"You and Asher? You're a thing?" Gwen squealed when we made it to them. "You're a sly little minx." She winked at me with a smile. "Of course, we all knew he had eyes for you."

I felt myself go red with embarrassment. Asher pulled me into his body as if he could sense me crawling back into my shell. He kissed my hair.

Gwen watched with a huge smile. "Oh, holy shit balls, if that isn't the cutest thing I've ever seen, I don't know what is," she exclaimed.

"Gwen, language," Cade clipped, his eyes twinkling but his tone scolding. His eyes pointedly resting on his daughter's head.

Gwen's eyes darted to her husband's. She rolled them. "Seriously? The man with the mouth of well ... a *biker* is chastising me for cursing in a decidedly curse-worthy situation? Belle didn't even hear," she told him firmly.

As if on cue, a little dark head popped up. "Shit balls," she parroted in her cute little toddler voice, her beautiful eyes glued on her father. Cade gave Gwen a pointed look then shook his head.

We were all silent for a moment then I burst out laughing. Like, proper, actual laughing. When I stopped, I saw Gwen was wiping a fake tear from the side of her eye, Cade even had a small smile. I glanced up at Asher to see his face devoid of any kind of humor. Instead, he was staring at me with blazing eyes. I didn't have time to inspect it because Gwen pushed off the sofa, the bundle in her hands being transferred to her husband who expertly jostled Belle so he could cradle Kingston in his huge arms. I would be lying if I said my ovaries didn't pulse just a little at that sight.

"This occasion, as with most occasions in life, calls for a cocktail," she declared, her twinkling eyes on me. "You can help me make them," she decided, snatching my hand and yanking me out of Asher's arms.

Before I had any chance to say anything, I was being dragged across the clubroom to the bar in the corner. I looked over my shoulder at Asher, who was grinning with his arms crossed and he shook his head. I surprised myself by grinning back.

"Okay, so I'm not technically allowed to drink cocktails since I'm breastfeeding." Gwen scrunched up her nose as she pushed a prospect out of the way and bustled behind the bar. "But I've pumped for the night so I should be able to have one," she informed me, and the prospect went pale. She glanced over at him. "Dude, if you're going to patch into the Sons you're going to have to deal with a lot more scarier things than my breast milk," she informed him with a straight face.

He blanched even further, his panicked eyes darting between us before making his escape. Gwen grinned as soon as his back was turned. I let out another little laugh. The happiness took me by surprise. Sorrow still tainted it, and I was aware of the slight pressure in my chest at being in an uncomfortable environment. But Asher was right, I was stronger.

Gwen started to mix drinks, unearthing two cocktail glasses. It was pretty comical seeing the bar at a biker clubhouse equipped with cocktail making implements, but I didn't think the Sons were worried about losing their bad ass reputation. It was firmly in place.

"So," she said, turning serious. "You and Asher. That's new?"

I sat down on the stool in front of the bar. "Um ... kind of?" My voice rose up at the end, betraying me.

Gwen's eyes narrowed, and she placed the bottle in her hand down on the bar to give me her full attention.

"Kind of?" she repeated with a raised brow.

My eyes darted back to where Asher was sitting with Cade and a couple of other men I didn't recognize. He was playing with Belle. Cue womb squeeze.

Fingers clicked in front of my face.

"Lily. Do not go into a fugue state perving at your man. I need details," she commanded.

I focused my eyes back on her. "Well, we may have had a ... thing three years ago," I explained slowly.

Gwen gave me a silent look to urge me to explain.

I chewed my lip. I didn't talk to anyone about this. I had only told Bex, I hadn't even told Mom. Now I wished I had. Asked for her advice. Somehow that thought had it all tumbling out right here in the clubhouse where anyone could overhear. And I didn't care.

When the last word had tumbled out of my mouth, Gwen was staring at me with her mouth open. She closed it abruptly.

"You've always got to watch the quiet ones," she muttered to herself.

She handed me a cocktail glass filled with amber liquid. I thought of Asher's words the previous night about how I was running. About how alcohol helped me do that. I took a sip. I may have been stronger, but I wasn't ready to feel it all yet. The full extent of it. To go back to the old Lily. I needed the new Lily right now. I wouldn't make it through the night without her, not with more men and women arriving at the clubhouse as Gwen and I spoke. The weight in my chest intensified as I entertained the prospect of having to face the blonde woman again.

"You two acted like you hadn't even shared a latte let alone a bed," she mused in amazement.

I didn't know what to say, so I stayed silent, sipping on my drink.

She rounded the bar with her own glass, sitting beside me. "I know you're shy, honey, that you're quiet. But why did you feel the need to keep this secret? There's too much of that around here," she added with a sad glint on her pretty face.

I considered her words a moment. "I had to forget," I told her quietly, my eyes downcast. "If I talked, shared it, I wouldn't be able to breathe, be able to do what I needed to do for Mom." My blurry eyes met hers. "I needed to breathe," I whispered.

Her eyes twinkled, and she nodded in understanding. "You're a pretty amazing person, Lily," she informed me.

I glanced at her in disbelief. This woman, who'd survived a kidnapping, a shooting and losing her brother without losing the ability to laugh was telling me *I* was amazing?

"No, I'm just normal," I replied.

Her hand found mine and squeezed it hard. "No, honey. You're the furthest from normal I've ever met." Her eyes found her husband's. "Not that I've got much experience with normal," she added lightly. Her eyes moved back to me. "You're special. I'm sure your mom told you that, that Asher will remind you of that. But I just want to know I think that, too."

I blinked through the tears at the words coming from the woman I admired and wanted to emulate in some way.

She seemed to sense I didn't know what to say because she stood, plastering a grin on her face.

"Right, we've got a sitter for the rugrats picking them up at any moment. It's time to show you how an Old Lady parties."

"You drunk, Lily?" Asher's voice tickled my ear, and his hands circled around my mid-section.

I turned my head to meet his chocolate eyes. They were blurry. "Yes," I admitted sheepishly. I knew he didn't approve of my coping mechanism and I expected him to be angry. To my surprise, he shook his head and smiled. Kissing my forehead.

Rosie, who I'd been chatting to, grinned wide. She elbowed Gwen. "You were right. Hottest couple I've ever laid eyes on. Sorry, sis, they might even knock you and Cade out of the park," she exclaimed, looking between Asher and I and Gwen and her husband, locked in a similar embrace.

I felt my face flame. I'd done my best to fly under the radar tonight. It was hard considering Asher and I seemed to be hot news. Luckily Gwen and Rosie hadn't left my side. It had helped, but the weight in my chest was still heavy as the night wore on and the clubhouse became more crowded. It wasn't late, and I was glad for Asher's arms and the solace they offered.

"Want to go to bed?" he murmured, his voice holding erotic promise that made me squirm. His hand ran up and down my hip.

"Yes," I said immediately, hungry for him.

He chuckled. "Say your goodbyes," he ordered softly.

Rosie, who had been watching avidly, waved her hand. "Oh, don't you worry about trivial things such as goodbyes. You crazy kids go and have some fun." She winked at me.

I giggled. I liked Rosie. I felt a connection with her. She was easy to talk to, and she didn't mind I didn't say much as she did enough talking for the both of us.

I did a little lame wave at Gwen and Cade as Asher began to drag me off. Cade grinned and lifted his chin. Gwen flat out smiled and blew me a kiss. A warm feeling settled in my chest, one that chased away the weight. These people were a family, and they were welcoming me into it like it was nothing. Like I belonged.

"I've had a beer too many, babe. I'm not gonna be able to drive us back to your place. I don't want to risk my precious cargo," Asher informed me as he led us through the common area into a quieter hallway. One I hadn't been in for three years. One that held memories, both good and bad.

He opened the door to his room, gently leading me inside.

"You okay, Flower?" he asked me with concern when he closed the door.

I knew he was referring to my asthma. My anxiety in situations like this. His eyes had been on me all night when he wasn't by my side. Worried, protective, alert to swoop in and save me if need be. I didn't want that right now. I didn't need to be looked at like I was an unexploded grenade. I wanted to just be looked at. So I crossed the distance between us and fastened my mouth to his.

My boldness paid off as his arms fastened around me, and he returned my fevered kiss with an intensity that told me fire had lurked under his concerned gaze all night.

I pulled my head back, hazy from the kiss. My eyes locked on chocolate irises, dark with desire.

"I want you," I declared throatily.

His arms tightened around me, one squeezing my ass firmly. "You've got me," he growled.

"I want *you*," I repeated. My hand moved to the hard length covered in denim, surprising myself with my boldness. His eyes flared. "I want to taste you."

His body stilled and his jaw turned hard. "Taste away, Flower," he said, voice thick with desire.

I grinned and pushed him against the door. He let himself be pushed, eyes never leaving mine. I kissed his throat, my hands massaging him above his jeans as I did so. He hissed out a breath. I moved my hands to the edge of his cut, pushing it off his shoulders and letting it fall to the floor. I looked at him through my lashes and trailed my hands down his tee, feeling the hardness of his muscles underneath. I didn't move my eyes from his as I grasped the bottom of his tee.

"Arms up," I commanded softly.

Asher's eyes darkened even more, as he did as I commanded, silently.

My entire body was pulsing with desire, I felt high off the control I already felt I had.

I trailed my hand across his bare abs, running my fingertips across the ridges. I bent and followed my fingers with my mouth, running soft kisses along his stomach. I moved down slowly, taking my time, savoring the moment. When I finally freed him from his jeans, I didn't hesitate, didn't worry about whether my inexperience would hinder me, or that Asher would be disappointed, I went in.

"Lily," he hissed when I fastened my lips around him. His hands went to my head, raking through my hair and freeing it from its bun.

I didn't stop, didn't slow at his movement.

"Fuck," he muttered as I continued, trailing my tongue along the underside of his length.

The power I felt intensified, my arousal pulsing through my entire body. I itched to touch myself, to give myself relief, but I focused on Asher.

He put gentle pressure on my head. "Babe, you got to stop. Unless you want me in your mouth," he declared roughly.

I stopped and gazed up at him, relishing the cords pulsing in his neck, the fact I was responsible for this.

"I want to taste you," I repeated my earlier sentiment.

His eyes blazed as I went back to my job.

"Fuck," he ground out, his hands raking through my hair.

I felt his entire body tense as his yelled my name and emptied himself into my mouth. I swallowed everything he gave me without hesitation. When he was finished, I slowly pulled back, wiping my mouth. Asher's hands circled my jaw gently and he gazed down at me in disbelief.

"Fuck, Lily, sometimes I wonder if I dreamed you up," he muttered.

I grinned.

He lifted me to my feet gently. "Your turn," he murmured against my mouth.

My stomach dipped as he pushed me against the bed and set to ravaging me for the rest of the night.

"Morning lovebirds," a familiar voice greeted Asher and I in the kitchen of the clubhouse.

This time I wasn't the one making breakfast, Asher had seated me firmly at the breakfast bar and was cooking. It was welcome, considering my head felt delicate, and my entire body was delightfully sore after what Asher did to it last night.

I smiled shyly as Lucky sat himself next to me. "Morning," I greeted.

I felt slightly self-conscious at the fact I was only clothed in one of Asher's tees, though it came down to my knees. It was strange that his home was a clubhouse full of other men. Scary men. Hot men like Lucky. Covered in tattoos and sporting beautiful tanned skin and muscles, he was impressive. The fact he was perpetually cheerful when he looked menacing on first glance was comforting. It didn't mean that ever present weight wasn't on my chest at being in his presence, being in somewhere like the clubhouse, but I was doing my best to ignore it. To be strong. So I could have more of this with Asher.

"Kitchen bitch, eh?" He nodded to Asher's back. "Good call, Lily, gotta train 'em early." He winked at me.

I giggled. Asher ignored him.

"So," Lucky continued, reaching to a fruit bowl to grab an apple and take a bite out of it. "Your friend Bex, the stripper. What's her story?" he asked casually.

"Do not go there, bro, she'll chew you up and spit you out," Asher warned, rounding the bar with two plates.

Lucky narrowed his eyes and rubbed his hands together. "Excellent. I enjoy a challenge," he declared.

I couldn't help but laugh. Asher was right. Bex would chew him up and spit him out. He was friendly, funny and hot. He had the required bad ass status, but wasn't a low life asshole, Bex's usual suspect.

"What's so funny squirt?" Lucky asked, snagging a piece of bacon off my overflowing plate, abandoning his apple.

He got a glare from Asher at this, which he ignored.

"Asher's right," I told him. "You've got no chance. Take that as a compliment, Bex excels at finding the shadiest and meanest men she can find," I said honestly. "You are neither."

I tucked into my breakfast and I noticed both men turn serious on either side of me.

"Shady?" Asher bit out, his eyes hard.

"Mean?" Lucky repeated, all playfulness gone from his face.

I looked between them. "Down boys. She can take care of herself," I reassured them.

Neither looked convinced, and I would come to ask whether bikers had some sort of sixth sense when their concern held considerable merit.

CHAPTER FOURTEEN

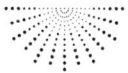

THREE WEEKS LATER

I WAS JUGGLING various grocery bags between my hands, somehow performing the feat of unlocking the door without dropping anything on the ground. I wasn't used to carrying this much, but with Asher practically living with me, we needed the extra food. Food he insisted on paying for after considerable debate.

"Put that away." Asher had growled last week while we were at the supermarket together. Growled. Like a dog. Right in front of the checkout clerk.

I scowled at him, and the fact he was pulling out his own wallet. "What are you doing?" I hissed. "Despite killing my buzz?"

Asher handed the clerk a card and gave me a sideways look. "Your buzz?"

I stepped forward, so it wasn't visible I was having an argument with my hot boyfriend in the middle of a grocery store.

"Yes, my buzz. The pleasant feeling I had, up until a moment ago, from wandering around the supermarket with my hot boyfriend," I informed him snippily. "One you just killed by doing the obvious alpha thing and insisting on paying, when I have the ability to do so."

The last part was a lie. I barely had the ability to do so. Bills seemed to be piling up, and since I had started back at college, I needed supplies and books that weren't covered in my scholarship. I should have been working more, but I'd been accepting the lesser hours I'd been offered by a worried Jude in order to spend more time with Asher. This was all beside the point, though.

Asher's face changed, he pulled me to his body. "I like this," he told me softly, brushing my hair out of my face, making it impossible to be angry with him. "That my girl gets a kick out of fuckin' grocery shopping. That your light is shining brightly again," he murmured against my mouth. "Though I'm not your boyfriend, I'm your Old Man," he corrected.

I tried to wriggle out of our intimate position. Asher's hands were a vice.

"Um ... Asher, we're in a grocery store," I said quietly.

He smiled. "You mentioned." He didn't let me go.

"Well, it's a public place, people can see us," I told him.

He grinned against my mouth again. "I don't give a fuck," he murmured.

Then, right in front of the cashier and shoppers, he kissed the ever loving shit out of me. A gesture that I thought would have had me purple with embarrassment. Instead, when he released me, I didn't give a fuck either.

It was only when we got back to my place that I realized he'd managed me out of my hissy fit about who paid.

I turned to face him from where he was sitting at the breakfast bar, frowning into his phone.

"You can't do that," I declared, my hands on my hips.

He glanced up from my phone, his eyes focusing on my stance. He obviously recognized said stance because he gave me his full attention.

"What? You said I couldn't help unpack that you had a 'system.'" He finger quoted with obvious amusement.

I glared at him. "Not that, the groceries, paying for them. You can't do that again," I told him firmly.

The amusement disappeared from his face. "I can and I will," he replied.

I glowered at him.

Before I had time to launch into a monolog about how I was a strong independent woman, Asher kept talking. "I spend all of my free time here, babe. You're busy. I'm busy. So the time we get to spend together, I relish. Which means my free time is spent under your roof, in your bed, and eating your food. You're my woman, I take care of you." He clocked my bulging eyes at this and held up his hand to let him continue, "You're also running yourself ragged. Studying, workin' at that bar." He didn't hide his distaste for my job. "You're running on empty, babe. Money is one thing you shouldn't have to worry about. I work full time. I've got it to spare. Plus, it makes me feel good to put it to something worthwhile like feeding my woman. Please just let me fuckin' do it."

I stared at him. I was quiet for a long time. He was used to this, the fact I didn't reply immediately. His sentiment, his words were beautiful. The fact I'd found someone who wanted to take care of me was beautiful. That this man, who seemed so hard on the outside, turned soft for me. I could get used to it. That was the problem. I'd stopped my partying, stopped running and embracing the uncomfortable. Asher was comfortable. Too comfortable. That was the problem. I couldn't explain this right now. I didn't want to. For now, I just wanted to be taken care of.

"Okay," I relented.

Asher had smiled and rounded the breakfast bar to give me a kiss. One that escalated to him fucking me on the counter.

It might have not been smart of me to throw myself into what Asher offered. To jump straight into a relationship that felt like we'd been together for years. It wasn't smart because it wasn't real. The bubble would pop at some point. But I had decided to think of that later.

I was proud of myself. Not just for my measly bicep strength, but of myself in general. It was an unfamiliar feeling.

I'd never really felt proud of myself. Comfortable in my own skin. My own life. It was like I hadn't found a way to fit yet, I was always tugging at the figurative sleeves of my existence, trying to stretch it into shape. After doing something as mundane as grocery shopping after almost a month back at college, I felt it. I had taken the sweater off, was just me. It felt good. The gaping hole in my life was still there, the pain was constant but manageable. I had hope. Asher was a huge part of this, I knew. It both comforted and worried me. Another person I'd build my life around. Another one that would tear it apart when he left.

All of this was running through my mind, plus being mindful of the glass jars in my bags that would break if I surrendered to my screaming arms. So when I walked through the door I was preoccupied. I didn't see it at first. When I did, the bags went hurtling to my feet and the smashing of the glass went unnoticed.

Bex was being held up against the wall, by what I recognized was Dylan's large form. Her lip was bleeding and her cheek red. I didn't think. The sight of my friend clawing at the hands cutting off her air supply had me acting on instinct. I rushed forward.

"Get off her," I screamed, yanking at the muscled shoulder attached to the equally muscled arm killing my friend.

His head moved a smidgeon, eyes barely resting on me before he jerked his entire arm, sending me flying toward the coffee table. I hit the corner of it at speed, pain radiating through my skull as the impact jarred my vision and something wet trickled down my head.

"Don't tell me what to do, bitch," he spat at me, his hands not loosening. "No woman tells me what to do. No woman breaks it off with me." His head whipped back to Bex, whose eyes were bulged in panic, her feet kicking out as they dangled off the floor.

I blinked furiously, and tried to push myself up, but my body wouldn't cooperate, blinding pain in my forehead crippled my movement.

"It's over when I say it's over," he spat.

One of Bex's flailing feet made impact with his crotch, not hard, but enough to make him release her and send her crumpling to the ground.

"It's so over," she rasped, glaring at him in hatred, rubbing her neck.

His entire face went red, like an angry bull. "Insolent bitch," he yelled, kicking her brutally in the stomach.

My body started to obey the moment my eyes bulged out in horror. White hot fury pulsed through my veins at the image of my strong best friend being brutalized before my eyes. Just like my mother had been years ago when I was powerless and small.

I would kill him.

My eyes rested on Bex's bag, overturned amongst the chaos. I scrambled over to it with blurry vision.

"You're just a filthy whore," he continued while I rifled through it desperately, wiping the blood obscuring my vision. "You're going to make me some money off that pussy," he yelled.

My hands found the cool steel just in time, and I unclicked the safety, getting to my unsteady feet.

"Get away from her and out of our house," I croaked, bringing the gun up to shoulder height.

He didn't even glance at me.

The shot I set off into the floor got his attention.

"Get away from her," I bit out as he turned to face the gun I had pointed at his head.

He grinned. It was a sick, chilling grin. He stepped forward and I scrambled back.

"You won't shoot me, you're afraid of your own fuckin' shadow," he sneered, taking another step forward.

The chilling truth to his words sank deep as he advanced on

me. My finger twitched on the trigger unable to do anything more.

"She might not, but I sure as fuck will," a cold voice declared from behind me.

ASHER

"You sure you know what you're doing, turning up here unannounced?" Asher asked his brother as they both swung off their bikes in Lily's lot.

He hated the decrepit apartment building in front of them, the shady neighborhood surrounding it. It was ugly. His girl did not deserve ugly. She deserved beautiful. He was determined to give it to her. But getting her out of this place would take time. She was stubborn and fiercely independent. He admired that. Loved that. It also pissed him off in moments such as this.

"I'm not unannounced," Lucky replied. "I've been invited to dinner with my brother and his girl. The hot roommate just happens to be a delightful coincidence," he continued, grinning.

Asher shook his head. "You're a crazy fuck," he declared.

Lucky didn't look offended. "Thank you."

Lucky had been determined to get Bex into bed. He'd even lost interest in his other bitches in his pursuit. He was having trouble getting through to her. She wasn't interested, as both Lily and Asher had predicted. He wasn't giving up. It was amusing. Though it didn't take much to amuse Asher these days. He had a reason to smile. He finally had his girl. Three years of waiting turned out to be well worth it. He'd wait for thirty if he knew that this was at the end of it. The shy, beautiful girl that crawled under his skin and took up residence there. The haunted sadness behind her ice blue eyes still irked him, but it was slowly depleting and her smiles seemed to reach those eyes every now and then. He wasn't stupid. He knew most of those beautiful smiles were conjured up to fool those around her. He wasn't fooled.

A gunshot jerked him out of his mind. A gunshot coming from Lily's apartment. His blood turned to ice. Neither he nor Lucky hesitated. They yanked their guns out of their cuts and sprinted toward the door that he only now noticed was ajar.

LILY

Both of us turned our gazes to Asher and Lucky, who were standing in the doorway with blank expressions, bodies taut. Their muscled arms were both extended, each aiming a gun at Dylan's head.

Asher's gaze flickered over me, stopping at my eyes and then his fury turned palpable.

"Come here, Flower," he ordered tightly. "Behind me."

I considered it. The safety he represented. My eyes flickered to my best friend curled in the corner. For a moment, my mind showed me the image of my mom in a similar position all those years ago. I made a split second decision. Not lowering my gun, I skirted around Dylan to rush to Bex's side, crouching down so I could gather her in my arms.

"Are you okay?" I whispered urgently.

She groaned and pushed herself up from the wall slightly. "Yeah, fucker hits like a girl," she replied shakily.

"This bitch a whore for the Sons now?" Dylan asked conversationally, jerking his head at Bex and I. "You've got no power here. This one's mine, you're both as likely to shoot me as the little mouse over here," he gloated, obviously not clocking the fact that he had three guns pointed at him and two very murderous stares directed his way.

A gunshot made me jump and cover Bex protectively with my body. I gaped at Lucky as Dylan sunk to his knees in pain, clutching a bloody shoulder. Asher stared at him too, expressionless.

Lucky shrugged at the attention on him. "My finger slipped," he explained nonchalantly, though fury danced in his eyes.

"You'll pay for that," Dylan bit out in fury. "You don't fuckin' shoot me without—"

He was cut off as Asher stepped forward and cold cocked him with his gun, his body crumpling to the ground. Asher stared at the unconscious body in disgust for a split second before his eyes cut to me. Lucky was already kneeling at my side, his face gentle and focused on Bex.

"You need the hospital, sweet thing?" he asked softly, though his jaw was hard.

I moved my eyes from Asher to Bex, wincing at the red mark already forming on her cheek, the marks at her neck. She flinched slightly as she pulled away from me slightly to try and get up.

"No, I'm fine. A couple of bruises," she rasped, her voice raw.

I tried to stop her from getting up, but Lucky beat me to it. His muscled and tattooed arms gathered her gently to lift her. He stepped over Dylan's body as if it were a downed log and set her on the sofa. I watched in amazement as he ran his hands over her body, talking softly, his eyes hard.

Involuntarily, my mind hurtled back to the times I'd sit beside my mom's bed, my little hands gently trying to bandage cuts with Mickey Mouse Band-Aids, trying to hold in my tears as Mom smiled and told me stories. I didn't even realize I was still pressed against the wall, clutching the gun until Asher gently removed it from my hands, his eyes glued to my head.

"Flower, I need you to look at me," he ordered flatly, in a voice devoid of emotion.

I struggled to push off the floor. "Bex," I protested loudly, needing to make sure she was okay.

Hands at my shoulders stopped me. "Lucky's got her," Asher

told me firmly. "Right now, I need to make sure I don't put another bullet hole in our friend over there." He nodded his head to the body currently staining our carpet with blood. "The only way that's going to happen is if I'm certain my little flower is going to be okay," he clipped, lightly pressing on my head with a bandana from his pocket.

I winced as the pressure radiated pain through my skull.

Asher's jaw turned granite. "Are you feeling any dizziness? Nausea?" he asked softly.

"No," I replied distractedly. "Lucky, you just shot someone," I said to the biker's back.

"Sure did, squirt," he replied breezily, frowning at Bex, who was now sitting up, glaring at the place where Asher was wiping.

"Give me your gun," she commanded him, holding out a shaky hand. "I'll kill that mother fucker myself for totally ruining my ability to wear a tank top for the next month and for hurting my best friend," she hissed with venom. Though she wasn't convincing considering her face was pale and slightly tight with obvious pain.

Lucky, for once, didn't smile at her. "Killing someone requires effort. You need to rest. Let us unbattered men do the killing."

I gaped at him. "Killing?" I repeated. "You're joking, right?"

Lucky glanced at me, and for once, his face held no hint of humor.

"Holy shit," I whispered. "Killing is against the law," I informed the room at large. I didn't think that was something people would need educating on, obviously, these people — my boyfriend, best friend and Lucky needed reminding.

"So is shooting someone," Lucky pointed out. "That ship's already sailed. Go big or go home I say."

"Yeah, but that was self-defense," I replied, although I didn't know how that was really going to hold up considering Lucky wasn't actually in need of defending.

"No, that was me teaching someone the beginning of a very long lesson," Lucky informed me, in a tone that was unfamiliar and brutal.

Asher's gentle touch contrasted the brutality, yet his eyes glittered with fury, something about the way he held himself had me thinking his thoughts lined up with Lucky's.

"Let's get you up, Flower," he said quietly, arms hooking under mine to place me on unsteady feet. His hand moved to frame my head as he squinted at the source of the stinging pain.

"I don't think you're gonna need stitches, but I'm getting our doc here. He needs to look at Bex anyway," he told me, glancing over at her.

I followed his eyes with concern. Bex met mine and she winked. *Winked.* Had I tumbled down the rabbit hole?

"You have a doc?" I asked in disbelief.

Asher nodded.

"One that has experience patching up bullet holes?" I continued.

Asher looked at me. "Yeah, Flower. Not that he's going to be patching up any bullet holes tonight."

I gaped at him once more. "Um ... hello?" I waved at him, then pointed at Dylan, who was steadily leaking more blood, it didn't look life threatening from here, but three years of nursing school weren't for nothing. He needed a doctor.

Asher's hard gaze followed me. "A man who did that to you, to Bex, isn't getting any medical help from me. He'll be lucky to leave with his life."

I stared at him for a long moment. The man who'd treated me with unbelievable tenderness was showing me what wearing that cut meant. I looked at Bex, brutalized like my mother. I looked back at the body that had caused it.

I pushed past Asher, only being successful because he wasn't expecting it.

I knelt beside Dylan, using all my effort to push his body face up to examine his wound. I may not have finished my nursing degree, but I knew how to stop someone from dying from a bullet wound. I hoped.

"What the fuck are you doing?" Asher asked urgently at my side, trying to pull me away from Dylan.

I moved my gaze away from the wound in his shoulder to glare at Asher for a split second.

"I'm making sure he doesn't die," I replied icily.

Asher stared at me. "It's a flesh wound, he'll be up and abusing more women in no time," he stated sarcastically.

"Unless you do the *right thing* and put a bullet in his skull?" I asked with fake sweetness.

"That's my vote," Lucky put in from the sofa.

"I'd be partial to the bullet in the skull option, too," Bex added in, blowing my proverbial socks off. I knew Bex came from a rough background, but I didn't think condoning murder would be something she'd be doing.

I ignored them, putting pressure on the wound with the pashmina from our sofa.

"Dude, that's my favorite pashmina, it'll be ruined now," Bex whined.

I ignored that too, putting my fingers to his wrist to take his pulse.

"Lily, I don't want you here, near him, touching him," Asher clipped.

"Well, sweetheart, we don't always get what we want, it's character building," I replied, mentally thinking about what else I could do at this moment.

Lucky's laugh pierced through the tension of the current moment.

"Shit, brother, you gotta watch the quiet ones," he joked.

Asher didn't smile.

"I'm not letting him die. And you're not killing him," I ordered.

Asher continued to stare at me.

I didn't think I'd have to have an argument with my boyfriend over someone's life.

"He hit you and Bex," he clipped.

"I'm aware," I said sharply. "But it's not up to us to decide if those actions require his life to be ended," I continued coldly. "He'll have what he did on his soul, you don't need it on yours."

Asher gave me a long searching look, and it seemed demons danced beyond his eyes before he sighed.

My entire body relaxed.

"You know where he lives?" he asked Bex.

She nodded. "South side of town, near Aimless," she replied, talking about an infamous bar which had regular shootings. One I steered well clear of. One Bex visited many times in the past, where she met Dylan incidentally.

Lucky and Asher both cursed simultaneously.

"What?" I asked, recognizing something change in their demeanor.

"Nothing," Asher replied quickly, too quickly. "We'll get him out of here, educate him on the fact he'll never be coming near either of you again. He does, I'll kill him myself," he promised with a hard glint in his eyes.

We stared at each other, me swallowing the bitter taste that he was serious. That he'd end his life. That he was prepared to. That violence was a way of life for Asher. That death was. It came with the cut. With the club.

"I'd like to order a pizza delivery," Lucky's voice shattered the moment as he spoke into his phone. "Yeah, I've got a big old hankering for pepperoni, one that's gonna need a van to deliver," he continued strangely. "Yeah, at Lily's place. See you in twenty." He hung up and glanced at me and shrugged his shoulders at the obvious confusion in my gaze. "Couldn't exactly say I'd clipped some gangbanger, and needed a body dump. Phones might be tapped," he said casually. "We do not want our friends at the ATF coming to this party."

Once more, I found myself hurtled into the reality of being involved with Asher. The reality of phone tappings, speaking in code, and ATF.

"Keep the pressure on this," I ordered Asher, nodding to the pashmina.

He gave me a long look before doing as I asked.

This got another laugh from Lucky, who I swear muttered, "whipped," under his breath.

I ignored this, my attention going to Bex, who was sitting rigidly on the sofa. My fingers gently touched the marks on her neck, my eyes examining the purplish tint on her cheekbone.

"Becky," I whispered brokenly.

"I'm okay, Lilmeister, promise," she reassured me in a strong voice.

"You're far from okay," I protested. I slowly lifted her shirt to reveal a bruise blossoming over half of her stomach. Lucky let out a hiss, his smile gone.

"I've changed my mind. Fucker is going to the ground," he growled, standing and yanking the gun from his pants.

I opened my mouth to argue, but Bex beat me to it.

"Stop. Lils was right. You can't murder him," she argued. I sagged with relief. "I don't want any more blood ruining the carpet," she deadpanned.

Lucky gave her a long stare but put his gun away.

"I never get to have any fun," he muttered.

I ignored this disturbing comment, focusing on making sure Bex didn't have any internal bleeding.

"I think you've got a couple of cracked ribs," I surmised.

Bex raised her eyebrow. "A couple? I'd say all of them," she bit out. "Which means I won't be able to work unless I want to do private stuff for fucked up men who enjoy battered women," she said with a scowl.

Lucky stepped forward with a stormy face. "That'll happen in no universe," he declared firmly.

She scowled at him. "It'll happen in the universe where I have to pay rent and feed myself, which happens to be this one," she shot back.

I whipped my gaze between the two of them in confusion. We didn't need that right now.

"We'll figure it out," I reassured her. I'd pick up extra shifts, cover both of our rents if I had to. She was the only family I had left. Though I didn't accept handouts from anyone, I would give Bex my last dollar if I had to. She was all I had left. "What happened?" I asked softly.

Bex sighed. "Turns out Dylan doesn't handle rejection well," she stated. "I don't handle being pimped out too well either, hence the rejection," she explained.

All of the air seemed to be sucked from the room with her words.

"Pimped out?" I repeated with a shaky voice.

Bex nodded. "You know Dylan's connected with Carlos somehow, and they've been trying to diversify their whores," she explained with a scowl. "Dylan thought I'd be perfect for his little scheme. I disagreed."

There was a loaded silence that followed her words. I could feel the male fury in the room. I wasn't exactly feeling calm either.

At that moment, Dylan decided to emit a moan and wake up.

With reflexes that stunned even me, I pushed off the sofa and shoved Asher's hand away from his shoulder. I pressed my finger into the hole, and Dylan screamed in pain.

"You lay a hand on her again, try to pimp her out again, I'll shoot you myself," I hissed into his pain-drenched eyes.

I was gently pulled back from his twitching body and evil glare.

"He won't breathe your air again," Asher whispered in my ear.

I sank back into Asher's body, squeezing my eyes shut. I decided to believe him. To trust him. To let him take care of this. Whatever that meant.

ASHER

"You come near either of those women again, we won't be dropping you home, you piece of shit. We'll be digging your grave," Asher hissed at the fucker they'd thrown on the side of the road.

He clutched his shoulder and chuckled. "The big, bad Sons of Templar," he sneered. "Do you have any idea who my family is?"

Lucky stepped forward. "I don't care if you're the President of the United States' long lost son, you come near them again, I'll rip your cock off and make you eat it," he promised. He then reared back and kicked the fucker savagely in the head, knocking him out cold.

He looked around. "Let's bounce, this isn't a place we want to be stopping for ice cream," he stated casually, climbing back into the van.

Asher gave the body one more look. His hand touched on the gun in his cut, thinking of the blood on Lily's face. Of her beautiful skin bruised. Of the haunted look in her eyes when she had been pressed against that wall clutching a gun.

"Bro, as much as I want to say otherwise, your Old Lady was right," Lucky called from the van. "Killing him would not be smart. It'd most likely start a war."

Asher realized the truth behind his friend's words and nodded, turning his back and climbing into the van.

There was silence as they pulled away. "Still might start a war," Bull muttered finally.

"Good," Gage cut in. "I've been itching to try out my new piece." He smiled, rubbing his gun thoughtfully, the sick fuck.

Bull's body tightened. "War with the Tuckers means bloody. They do not fight fair, and they'll target anyone connected to us. That's not fuckin' happening," he growled.

Asher raised a brow at his normally silent brother. He was usually on Gage's wavelength about a fight. He relished it. Shit he'd been through, sometimes Asher thought killing was the only thing that kept the fucker breathing. But he was different. Human, now that Mia had chased away the demons that used to define him. Fucker damned near cheerful ever since he married her.

"Bull's right," he agreed. "The Tuckers are crazy fucks, arguably crazier than you," he told Gage. "But that shit, shooting that stupid fuck, I'm doubtful it'll start anything. They may be crazy, but they're not stupid. Word's gotten around about Dylan Tucker. He's a pain in even that crazy family's ass. They won't start anything with us over a flesh wound..." he paused, his fists tightening, "especially when they find out it's a result of the bashing of two our women."

Bull leaned forward. "How will they find that out? That fuck's not likely to tell the truth."

Lucky grinned. "I'll set about educating the right people so word gets back to them."

Asher nodded. "Good. We'll be on alert, just in case. Let Cade know. But I'm doubtful it'll turn into anything more..." he paused, "and if it does, we'll burn their entire fucked up empire to the ground."

LILY

"You're quiet," Asher observed, stroking the hair from my face.

"I'm always quiet," I returned from my position against his chest.

"Not with me." He jostled me so my face tilted to meet his.

"We haven't been together long enough for you to make generalizations about how am I am not with you," I replied with a slight bite to my voice.

His eyebrows rose. "We've been together long enough for me to know when shit is swirling in that head."

We were in bed. We hadn't made love, we had barely spoken. The afternoon had been taken up with dealing with the bleeding man in our living room, with the battered Bex, and with some very angry bikers.

"Why do you guys have all the fun without us?" Gage whined when Asher had opened the door to him, a man I didn't recognize with a 'Prospect' patch and Bull.

The joking atmosphere had quickly dissipated when three sets of eyes focused on me. On the patched up cut on my forehead, which I'd done myself after convincing Asher we didn't need his doc. My nursing training had me able to patch up Bex and myself. Manly rage saturated the air when their eyes moved to Bex, on the sofa beside me, her bruises worsening with every hour.

"Please tell me we're dumping a body," Gage spit out, his eyes moving to the prone Dylan.

A groan emitting from his body answered the question.

He grinned. "So you did save some for me," he rubbed his hands together, "much obliged." His face had turned cold, and the glint in his eyes sent a shiver down my spine. He was not the man who'd been joking with me at the club days earlier, the man who'd been playing with Belle. This was a killer.

"This one's catch and release brother," Lucky informed him, putting a hand on his chest when he tried to advance further.

207

Gage scowled at him. "Come again?"

Lucky sighed. "It's not my first choice either, but the women in the building voted against us."

Gage's scowl deepened. "Since when do women get to dictate how we dole out justice?"

"Since women got the vote, I'm sure even alpha bikers have noticed a little thing called feminism," Bex interrupted from her perch on the sofa.

His hard gaze settled in on her face, I watched him visibly flinch at the state of it. His scowl deepened.

"Men who do that," he nodded to her face, "need to meet the reaper. Preferably slowly," he gritted out.

Bull stepped forward, surprising me by speaking, "Can't say I don't agree with you, brother, but be mindful of our audience." His eyes touched mine. "These women have been through enough shit. They don't want to become accessories to murder, I say we oblige them. Cade will also appreciate us not risking the club with this fucker," he continued in a rational voice.

Gage glowered at him. "What the fuck ever," he ground out finally, stepping back.

The men moved away from him, giving him the opening he needed to advance on Dylan's body. His motorcycle boots connected with Dylan's crotch savagely, and he cried out, curling into himself.

No one said anything, Lucky raised a brow.

Gage shrugged. "We can't kill him. No one said anything about making him a eunuch."

Lucky chuckled, and even Bull grinned.

You'd think at that moment I would have been focused on the fact I had multiple bikers and a man bleeding from a gunshot wound in my small living room. Instead, my attention was on Bull. On the way his attractive mouth was turned up. How his eyes seemed clearer, not haunted by those demons I recognized years ago. This amazed me and gave me hope.

"Flower, how about you take Bex, both of you pack a bag." Asher's voice tickled my ear and his hands tightened on my hips.

"Pack a bag?" I repeated, confused.

Asher turned me so I faced him. "Yeah, you're coming to the clubhouse until we can ensure it's safe to come back here." He frowned at my front door. "We'll get you a decent security system," he added.

I really wanted to argue with this. With him commanding me to leave my apartment, however shabby it was, it was where I felt comfortable. The mere prospect of leaving what little sanctuary my apartment offered me had my chest feeling heavy. But there was a man bleeding in my living room. A man that had attacked Bex. So my anxiety would take a backseat for safety, for her safety.

"Okay," I replied quietly.

Asher jerked in surprised, as did Bex, they were both obviously expecting an argument.

"Okay?" Bex repeated shrilly before anyone else could speak.

"Bex..." I tried to calm her before she got on a full rant. That failed.

She pushed off the sofa, grimacing slightly in pain. She pointed at Lucky, who advanced as if to steady her.

"Don't even think about doing the whole protective alpha shit. I'm fine," she ground out.

"Your face and ribs speak a different story, sweetheart," Lucky clipped.

She glared at him. "Does this biker clubhouse have mystical healing powers? Can it make all of my injuries disappear along with all of my problems?" She didn't wait for a response from anyone. "I know you all like to gather up the poor helpless females to help ascertain your position as bad ass bikers, but I'm not going for that shit," she declared.

I chewed my lip. Bex was serious and stubborn. Someone would have to drag her bodily from this place and by looking at Lucky's tight face that could be a possibility. If she wasn't going anywhere, neither was I. I felt relief at this fact. Bex threw the hissy fit I couldn't.

"Fuck," Asher muttered under his breath, obviously recognizing the look on Bex's face.

"You are going," Lucky gritted out.

Bex glared. "Care to make me?" she asked sweetly.

"Oh, I care to make you, sweetheart," he replied with menace in his tone. Menace that didn't belong there.

"Shit, if they want to stay, let them fuckin' stay," Gage cut in, playing peacemaker, as if he hadn't just argued murder moments ago. "No fucker is stupid enough to cause trouble with our bikes outside."

Lucky's murderous gaze settled on him. I didn't have the opportunity to watch the stare off.

Asher's hand moved to my neck, directing my gaze to his. "I guess I can't convince you to come to the club?" he asked sounding defeated.

I shook my head slowly. "If Bex is staying, I'm staying," I replied quietly.

Asher shut his eyes for a split second and then nodded. "How about you go and hang out in your room, we'll sort this." He nodded to Dylan's body.

I gave Bex a look, one that told her to listen to Asher. She rolled her eyes and walked toward my room. She paused and turned. Her face had lost its bravado, its fury. She looked small and vulnerable.

"Thanks..." she half whispered to the room, her eyes dancing over the men and settling on Lucky, "for arriving when you did. I don't doubt Lily's ability to pull the trigger if she had to." She paused. "But I'm glad she didn't have to." Without waiting for a response, she turned to disappear into my room. Lucky's eyes focused on the closed door, his brows furrowed.

Asher's hand touched my forehead lightly. "You sure you're okay, Lily?" he asked with concern.

I nodded quickly, not liking the fact all of the men were standing, looking at me.

He kissed me lightly on the mouth. "Go see to your friend. She may like to think she's tough as nails, but I doubt she's as okay as she's acting," he murmured, surprising me with his perception.

I stared at him for a long moment before I stepped out of his embrace.

"Can I get anyone a drink? Beer? Before you commence..." I trailed off, my gaze darting to where Dylan was situated.

There was a short course of clipped nos.

"I'll take that beer," Lucky replied, his eyes now focused on the situation at hand.

All the men gave him a look.

He held out his hands. "What? She offered."

Asher shook his head at him. "We're fine, babe," he reassured me.

"Okay, well, just let me know," I replied quietly. "Thank you," I said a bit louder, echoing Bex's sentiment. "I know this hasn't got anything to do with you, and I appreciate you doing it anyway," I blurted quickly.

Asher frowned at me.

"You're family, Lily. Someone hurts you, they hurt us. We don't stand for that. Appreciate the sentiment, sweetheart, but it's unnecessary," Gage said softly. "Plus, it was gearing up to being another boring Wednesday, I do love a good body disposal." He winked at me.

Despite the situation, I smiled shyly. "Thanks all the same," I repeated firmly.

I turned to go to my room, Asher still frowning at me.

I didn't focus on what the reason for that could be, nor ponder how he could still look hot as anything with furrowed brows. I had a friend to look after.

"I'M THINKING," I said finally.

"About today," Asher clarified.

"Yes. About your friend shooting someone, and both of you being prepared to kill that someone. No talk of calling the proper authorities was even entertained," I answered.

Asher sighed and sat up, taking me with him. "You may not have been an Old Lady for three years, but you've been connected to the club. You know the way we live our life, our distaste for law enforcement," he said slowly.

I looked into his clear eyes. "Yeah, I guess it's different being on the sidelines and having to argue with your boyfriend over not killing someone." I never thought I'd utter a sentence like that in my life. "It's a lot to deal with. I'm already trying to pick myself up, this is something that has me in danger of falling down," I whispered, the truth of my words slicing through my soul.

I was still trying to figure out who I was after my mom's death. Trying to understand whether being a nurse was what I wanted, if being who I used to be was what I wanted. If I did decide being a nurse was what I wanted, I had to study. Hard. I had to work harder to be able to survive. One of my scholarships had been dropped which meant I would need to pick up more shifts. My life would already be crazy. I didn't need shootings in my living room. I didn't need Asher consuming me.

His whole body tightened at my words. "I'm here to make sure you don't fall, babe. That shit, it wasn't exactly our fault," he ventured carefully, and rightly so.

I leaned back. "The man getting shot by your brother was not your fault?" I repeated.

"He put his hands on you. Almost killed your best friend. What the fuck did you expect me to do?" he bit out.

"Call the police instead of discussing the dumping of his body?" I suggested.

Asher's face was granite. "Shit that Tucker's connected to, means half the police are in his pocket," he said.

It was my turn to freeze. "What do you mean, shit that he's connected to?" I repeated. "And how do you know Dylan's last name?"

Asher seemed to contemplate something before speaking. "Everyone knows the Tucker family, babe. They're crazy sons of bitches with a lot of money and a heap of power. Crazy plus power, plus money means dangerous. Dangerous as fuck to be exact," he clipped. "His family is into everything. Prostitution, drugs, arms. You name the pie, their fingers are in it."

"Dylan's rich?" I asked in disbelief "He never even chipped in for groceries when he was here, regardless of the fact he ate everything in sight," I complained. "What a ... dick," I said finally.

Asher raised his brows in amusement. "I'd say dick is a kind word to call him, though you're focusing on the wrong details, babe. He's dangerous. His family is off the charts crazy." His face turned serious. "The fact he's been in your presence, in your house without you knowing who he is, what he is," he grimaced, "fuck babe." He ran his hand over his mouth.

"Well, I don't exactly run in those type of crowds, I just thought he was your regular run-of-the-mill douchebag," I explained, not liking that yet again I was a clueless naïve girl needing to be saved.

Asher's face softened, as he stroked my cheek. "Of course, you didn't know, babe, I didn't expect you to." He paused. "Bex would have. It's not a secret, and she does run with those type of crowds, Lily. As much as you wouldn't like to admit it," he added, seeing me open my mouth to argue, "she should've been smarter."

I leaned back. "So you're saying it's her own fault that she got beaten up?" I asked in a quiet voice.

"Shit no, Flower, of course not. The blame for that lies firmly on Tucker's shoulders. Any man that does that shit is no man." He paused again. "But she should've known the danger in getting involved with a man like him."

My anger was tamped down slightly. "Bex doesn't exactly live a cautious life. You don't know what she's had to go through," I defended my friend.

Asher gazed at me. "No, babe, I don't. Everyone has their own demons. I know that. I don't presume to know hers. But when her demons cause my woman to get involved..." he stroked my face ... "to get hurt, it gets to me, Flower. I don't want you to face any more demons, your own or anyone else's. I'd slay dragons for you, babe," he murmured quietly.

I stared at him, a cocktail of emotion swirling in my belly. How do you respond when someone says that to you?

"You scare me," I said finally.

Asher didn't betray any emotion at my strange response, nor did he say anything.

"Saying things that like, it terrifies me," I confessed. "Having you come in with your brothers, talking about bodies and killings like it's a plan to go bowling, that scares me, too," I whispered. "I feel afraid all the time. Afraid to be with you. Be without you. A girl that's always afraid, that's broken, isn't ever going to be strong enough for *that* life. For *your* life," I told him. "Bex was wrong before. I wasn't going to do it. Shoot him. Even if it meant he hurt us, killed me even, I wouldn't have had the strength to pull that trigger," I choked out, feeling ashamed.

Asher moved me so I was straddling him, his hands grasping my hips tightly.

"You're strong enough, Flower," he told me with certainty. "When someone breaks, they heal, twice as strong as before. You were strong before, babe, you're stronger now. You're strong because you're gentle when most people would be rough. You stand when most people would fall. Strength comes in different forms," his hand crept up my hip, "and you would've done it. As much as it pains me to say, you don't have enough sense of self-preservation. You might not have done it for yourself, but you would've done it for your friend. I know that, because you'd do anything for the people you love," he said with pride in his husky voice. "If I could have dreamt up my perfect Old Lady, she wouldn't have been as good as you," he murmured. "And that's what you are. It might scare you, I'm man enough to admit it scares the shit out of me. When the world hands you something you treasure more than anything else you've ever had, all you can think of is the agony of losing it." His hand moved to the waistband of my panties.

I sucked in a breath.

"But the feel of it, of you, in my hands is enough to make me forget that fear," he murmured, his finger moving to caress my bare skin.

My body moved against him, tingles of pleasure radiating to my fingertips.

His eyes blazed with desire as his finger plunged into me. "You want this?" he rasped.

I let out a little moan and started to move with him. "Yes," I whispered.

He sat up, grasping my neck with his free hand. "Then that's all that matters," he declared, flipping us so I was on my back.

I barely registered the change in positions, his finger continuing to move inside me.

"Top off," he commanded.

I quickly complied, wrenching my tee off. The moment I'd tossed the fabric to the floor, Asher's mouth fastened on my nipple. My hands drove into his hair and I arched my back slightly, moaning as his teeth grazed my sensitive peak. The cold air bit my bare skin as Asher's mouth left my breast to travel downward.

"You're going to come in my mouth, Lily," he instructed, pulling his finger out of me.

I writhed in frustration at the loss, but my fingers grasped the sheets in expectation from Asher's words.

"You're going to come in my mouth, then you're going to come on my dick," he growled.

"Yes," I hissed, my voice husky with desire.

I cried out as his mouth fastened on me, licking me, working his magic. My back arched even more, and my hands fisted the sheets ever tighter at the blinding pleasure that erupted from the base of my spine and shattered through the rest of me.

Asher moved from between my legs, his body moving atop mine and grabbing my legs so they were pressed up close to my ears.

I felt him poised at my entrance and he paused. "This is us, flower, all that matters," he declared before plunging into me.

I cried out once more, this angle intense on my sensitive flesh. Asher held my ankles, pounding into me mercilessly. The pleasure was all-consuming, almost too intense, almost to the point of pain. But it danced that glorious line. Asher released my legs so he could settle his body completely atop mine and slow his strokes. His hands cradled my head and his mouth claimed mine. I could taste myself on his lips.

"Open your eyes, Lily," he commanded.

I did as he commanded, not even realizing I had them squeezed shut.

"This is one of them," he whispered while he made slow love to me. "One of the million and one moments that makes the fear worth it," he continued as he built me up to my second orgasm. "Every second, every moment I'm with you, it's worth it," he said, the cords in his neck tight, his eyes tender.

I didn't say a word, my climax hit me without warning, and I rode it without tearing my eyes from his. I rode the wave of pleasure while my heart pounded with the power of his words, of his gaze. And when I was done, the aftershocks started all over again as he poured into me without moving his eyes from mine.

"It's worth it," I whispered in a small voice after minutes of loaded silence. "Every moment."

Asher pulsed inside me and his mouth covered mine. We didn't speak any more that night.

"THIS IS A CHANGE," Asher observed lazily from his spot in my bed.

I glanced at him over my shoulder as I buttoned my blouse. "W-what is?" I stuttered over my words at the view I was getting. Asher was propped up on pillows, shirtless, with the entirety of his muscled form on display. The background of my mom's mural intensified his beauty.

"Me lying leisurely in bed while you rush off." He frowned. "I don't like it," he added.

I stood, slipping my feet into my mules. "Well, I wouldn't be rushing if *someone* had let me get up when my alarm went off," I scolded lightly.

His eyes turned dark. "Your beautiful, naked body was pressed against me. You're lucky I only fucked you once. That I let you leave this bed at all," he growled.

My stomach dipped with desire, despite the fact I'd had a thoroughly satisfying orgasm not moments ago. I distracted myself by piling textbooks into my tan slouchy leather bag. My one beautiful, designer accessory—one I'd never be able to afford in a million years—a Christmas present from Gwen and Amy.

"Jesus, how does someone as tiny as you carry around all of those books?" His tone was drenched in disbelief as he watched me stretch the expensive bags seams to the limit.

I eyed the beautiful bag in distaste. "With great difficulty," I answered truthfully.

Asher put his hands behind his head, my eyes attached themselves to his biceps and appreciated the way they flexed with this movement.

"Maybe I should blow off the club and walk around carrying your books all day," he suggested.

I laughed. "Yeah, and then we'd have a trail of drooling girls following us wherever we went," I teased.

Asher rolled his eyes. "I'm more worried about the drooling

boys," he shot back lightly, though his eyes weren't as teasing as they were moments before. "One boy in particular."

I raised my brow. "You're not going to let that pretty face be distorted by a green-eyed monster are you now?" I asked sweetly.

He didn't answer, and his eyes traveled down the length of me when I straightened.

"I thought you said you had classes all day," his tone was questioning.

"I do," I replied, scanning my messy desk for anything else I might need. My gaze stuttered over a forgotten flyer. One promising miracle cancer results. A blade went through my heart.

"And you're wearing that?" Asher's question jolted me out of my pity party.

I glanced down at my outfit self-consciously. "Yeah, what's wrong with it?"

My white blouse was a reminder of the days I worked at Gwen's store and could get some pricey items at a serious discount. It was white silk, and I had it half tucked into tight white jeans. The shoes were also a gift from Gwen after she had to clean out her closet when moving in with Cade. They were tan mules with a chunky heel, and I loved them.

Asher pushed out of bed, stalking over to me. It didn't escape me that his ability to stalk naked was impressive and drool worthy. His finger traced over the bandage hiding under my hair, his other hand on my hip.

"Not one single thing is wrong with what you look like, apart from this," he told me, lightly touching my injured forehead. "You're beautiful," he stated, his eyes running the length of me again. "I just thought college girls wore ripped jeans and baggy hoodies," he continued, his tone teasing.

I regarded him. "When have you ever seen me in a baggy hoody?" I asked him seriously.

Asher pondered. "Every time I've had the pleasure of seeing this tight little body, it's always been encased in a delightful package," he replied, nuzzling my neck. He pulled back, his eyes serious. "You sure you're okay today?" He brushed the bandage once more.

I nodded. "I'm more worried about Bex, you'll check on her before you leave?"

Asher nodded tightly. "Yeah, Flower. Not that I think she'd admit to me that she wasn't okay. Seems like that girl could be bleeding from a bullet wound and cover it with a Band-Aid and declare there was nothing wrong," he said seriously.

"Well, at least I know what a bullet wound looks like should that ever happen," I replied, looking at my feet. The events of yesterday invaded my mind. Worry that seemed to pile on top of everything else weighing me down.

Asher seemed to sense my growing panic. His hand tightened. "I'm gonna take care of this, Flower. I'm gonna take care of you," he promised.

I didn't want to, but I sank into his hold, into the warm cocoon his words provided. I should have argued. I should have told him that I would take care of myself, that I had to. Otherwise, I'd get lost in him. But I didn't.

He kissed my lips gently. "See you tonight?" he asked when I reluctantly pulled back.

"I'm working tonight," I groaned. "And the next, and the next, maybe until the end of time. Or until Bex heals and I don't have to cover both of our rents." I frowned at the prospect of surviving all of this even more tired than I usually was. At how I was going to keep my GPA high enough to keep my scholarship. Pressure hit my chest, and I felt a vice around my lungs.

Asher's jaw tightened. "I said I'd take care of you, Lily. That means you don't have to work at that place anymore," he told me flatly.

My panic was momentarily forgotten. It would never be

truly forgotten, the pressure on my chest told me that. But anger seemed to be a good distraction.

"I'm late," I snapped. "That means I cannot articulate everything wrong with that sentence. I'll condense my rant. You won't pay my rent. You won't turn me into a helpless woman reliant on you for everything from orgasms to electricity bills," I informed him in a tight voice.

His face turned hard at my words, and I didn't give him a chance to respond.

"I've got to go," I said tightly, hoisting my bag onto my shoulder, and turning my back on him.

Asher's hand fastened around my wrist, and he yanked me back into his body, plastering my lips with his before I could protest. It was embarrassing that even though I was annoyed, I didn't fight one bit.

"You don't get it, Flower. I'm the one who's reliant on you," he murmured against my mouth. "Just trying to find a way to even the scales."

My anger dissipated in an instant. My fragile emotional state had my state of mind in a precarious position.

"You're late," he reminded me gently.

"I'm late," I agreed.

He rested his forehead on mine for a moment longer before I sighed and used all my willpower to walk out the door.

CHAPTER FIFTEEN

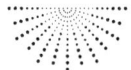

"LILY?"

It took me a moment to register my name being called. I jerked my head up from its position bent over a medical textbook.

"Aids?" I blinked at the sheepish figure standing beside the table I'd claimed in the corner of the library. All of my books were scattered atop of it. I think most of my wits were hiding amongst the pages.

"Mind if I sit?" He gestured to the seat across from me.

I shook my head, moving books around.

He sat, regarding me anxiously. "I'm surprised you're talking to me. That you didn't just tell me to screw off," he said slowly.

I tilted my head. "Of course I'm talking to you, why would I tell you to screw off?" I asked, perplexed.

He frowned, then the sheepish look returned. "That night, outside your work? I met your boyfriend's fist? Said some pretty ugly things to you. Some things I want to apologize profusely for," he said.

I nodded. "Oh that, sorry, my head's not exactly doing its

best with the whole thinking thing," I joked lightly. "I'm the one that's sorry. Asher was out of line."

I inspected his nose, thankfully it was still straight and perfect. I hadn't seen him since that night, hadn't heard from him. I was a bad person, I didn't even try and contact him. I should have. He'd been a good friend to me. But with everything else going on, I'd just never found the time. I was surprised I was only just running into him now, after being back for almost a month. Then again, I was almost always hurrying to my next class or camped out in the library.

Aiden shook his head. "No, he did the right thing. I was out of line..." he paused. "I was just surprised. You looked so different, you were acting so different and him," he looked at me in the eye for the first time, "he's not someone I ever expected you'd be with," he said carefully. His eyes ran over me. "You look more like yourself."

"You mean I'm sober and not wearing midriff-baring outfits?" I asked with sarcasm.

Aiden's face changed slightly at my response. He wasn't used to replies like that from me.

"Um ... yeah. That's one way to put it," he said slowly. "I'm so happy that you're back at school. It's where you belong. You're better now? Doing okay?" he asked with genuine concern.

It was the genuine concern that stopped me from laughing coldly like I felt like doing. Was I doing okay? After burying the only family I had left? After witnessing a shooting, after being assaulted the night before?

"Yeah, I'm getting there," I replied softly, not completely lying.

I may still have that vice threatening to strangle me, the pressure on my chest, the pain in my soul, but I also had Asher. I really had him, and he really wanted me. The thought warmed the ice of my grief.

Aiden smiled warmly at me. "Good," he proclaimed and paused. "You're not still with that biker are you? That was just a phase, a response to the turmoil in your life?"

I sat back, pursing my lips at his condescending tone. I knew he meant well, but I couldn't help being pissed right off at the way he decided to show concern. It wasn't the first time I'd felt patronized by him, I had come to accept it as part of who he was, before. But now, I felt unable to timidly accept it.

I pushed my hair back in frustration. "Asher is not a phase," I began tightly, about to launch into an uncharacteristic monolog about what exactly Asher was to me.

I stopped because Aiden's eyes focused on my forehead and bulged out in horror.

"He did that?" he exclaimed in fury. "Jesus, Lily."

"Of course he didn't," I snapped, letting my hair fall back down. "What, because of something you think you know about what he is, makes you think he's capable of violence against women?"

Aiden's face turned icy. "I know he's capable of violence. I know what his gang gets up to. They're scum, Lily. The dregs of society. You should not be with the dregs. Your friend no doubt introduced you, those are the kind of people she ... *entertains*," he spat.

I stared at him, not recognizing whoever just uttered those words. "You should go," I told him firmly. "I've got a lot of studying to do." I looked down to my books. I had to. Otherwise, I might just reach across the table and strangle him.

Aiden's eyebrows shot up. "You're dismissing me?"

I glanced at him. "I'm informing you of the fact I'm quite eager to pass this paper, and to do so I need to study, and also not get kicked out of the library for breaking your nose with this textbook," I said flatly. "Which is exactly what I'll do if you say another word about my boyfriend or my best friend."

Aiden gazed at me in amazement. "I'm trying to look out for you, Lily," he explained.

I raised my brow at him. "Uh-huh. I'm quite capable of doing that. And capable of deciding who should be and should not be in my life," I said pointedly.

He stared at me in silence for a moment and stood up. "I really wish that were true," he uttered with disappointment.

I stared at his retreating back, the exchange leaving a sour taste in my mouth. I thought Aiden was my friend. Things had gotten mixed up when we tried to make it more, but I thought he was a decent guy, and I'd missed him. I found myself questioning whether he had ever been a decent guy. Maybe now, I had taken off whatever glasses I'd been looking at the world through before. Maybe now, I was stripped down bare, I saw people for what they were. Or maybe Aiden was just an asshole. I couldn't ponder it. I had books to bury myself in for the remaining hour I had left before I had to rush home to change and go to work.

I GOT HOME EXPECTING to be greeted with a giant bloodstain staring at me. I was surprised when my gaze hit the clean carpet, with a faint ring of pink where Dylan had been shot. Other than that, nothing.

I glared at Bex, who was lounging on the sofa.

"What?" she asked defensively. "It wasn't me. I listened to your strict instructions and haven't moved my ass off the sofa," she informed me.

She nodded to the silent man sitting in the armchair across from her. The one who had shocked me for a moment until I spotted his prospect patch and remembered Asher calling earlier today informing me they'd have *"someone on us"* until they could be sure Dylan wasn't going to do anything further.

"Stan over here did it, quite impressive really, he could have a career in stain removal if the biker thing doesn't work out," she mused with a straight face.

I rolled my eyes. "Thanks, Stan," I addressed the skinny redhead staring blankly at the television. He surprised me, not looking like a biker at all. But I wasn't one to judge books by their covers.

His eyes cut to me. "You're welcome, Ma'am. But my name's not Stan," he informed me. "It's Skid."

"Oh, okay, sorry, Skid," I said quickly, feeling my face flame slightly. I glared at Bex. "Why are you calling him Stan?" I hissed under my breath.

She glanced at him. "Because I refused to believe his actual name is 'Skid' and he won't tell me his real name. Ain't that right, Andrew?"

He didn't move his gaze from the television, just shook his head slightly.

Bex grinned. "It's a game we're playing," she informed me.

I rolled my eyes before narrowing them on the nasty purple bruise on her face and the ring of red around her neck. I flinched slightly.

"How are you?" I asked in a softer voice, stepping forward to bend down in front of her.

Bex's grin dimmed slightly. "I'm fine," she reassured me. She shook a little bottle in front of me. "Silas brought me the good stuff." Her gaze went to the corner, where she must have gotten another imperceptible head shake.

I frowned at the bottle, snatching it off her to inspect the label. I was just reading about prescription medicines. "Don't take too much of that, these are strong and easy to get addicted to," I said seriously.

Something had flickered in her eyes before she snatched the bottle back from me.

"Okay, okay, Nurse Ratchet," she teased. Her face turned

serious once more, and she pushed my hair back and flinched when she saw my head. "I'm sorry, Lilmeister," she whispered.

I squeezed her hand. "I thought we agreed this was not your fault," I told her firmly. "I've got to change for work, you two okay here?" I asked, my gaze darting between them.

Bex's smile returned. "Me and Jordan are fine."

I shook my head. "Have you spoken to Carlos about not being able to work?" I asked with concern.

She scrunched up her nose. "Yeah, I did talk to that weasel. He said he was disappointed in me for letting him down, as if turning into a dickwad's punching bag was my decision," she scoffed.

"He's a dick," I informed her.

She nodded. "That he is," she agreed. "But he's a dick that signs my paychecks. Or he will when I can get back to work. Until then, he's got me on unpaid leave."

My back straightened in anger. "Unpaid?" I repeated. "You're entitled to paid sick leave."

She shook her head. "I'm not entitled to shit, I'm lucky I've got a job to go back to. Not that Carlos has much choice, I'm one of his top earners." She paused, worry tainting her face slightly. "This better get better, quick smart," she gestured to her body, "my rainy day fund is seriously lacking, and by lacking I mean nonexistent." The bravado in her voice was long gone and now only worry remained.

I grabbed her hand and squeezed once more. "Don't worry, I've got us covered," I reassured her with a smile.

She frowned at me. "I'm not putting my shit on you. I don't want you working yourself into the ground. You've got enough crap to deal with. You've got college to ace, a sex hunk boyfriend to ravage. I'm not your responsibility," she said quietly.

I smiled at her. "Newsflash. You're my best friend. You're the only family I've got left. I'm taking care of us," I told her firmly. "And to do that, I've got to go get ready for work," I continued. And before she could argue, I rushed into my room to change so I could make it to work.

IT WAS hours later when I had tried to distract myself from being dead on my feet and field lame pickup lines from sleazy guys that I thought of the answer to our problems.

Mom's house. A lawyer had called days ago about her *"estate."* Not that there was anything left. Bank accounts were all but drained from medical bills, and what little that was left I spent on her funeral. The only thing she had left was her house. I didn't think of that before. I couldn't. I couldn't go back to the place I'd grown up in after we escaped my father. The place that held so much happiness within its walls.

Now it was a tomb, a tomb of memories that would haunt me if I went in there. But I had to. If I wanted to continue college without failing, I had to cut down hours at the bar. I couldn't do that if I had to keep paying rent for the place we were in now. Unlike Bex, I had a rainy day fund. One that would be dry when I had to cover the both of us. But if we moved to the house my mom owned, my house, we wouldn't have to worry about rent. I just had to find a way to walk through the front doors without being ripped apart by the memories within its walls.

ONE WEEK LATER

I stood staring at the door. I must have stood there for minutes, but it felt like hours. I squeezed the key so tightly I felt the jagged edges imprint in every one of my fingers. I stared at the swirling colors on the wood. Mom had painted it when we moved in. My gaze moved to the flowerbeds, once blooming with the same color that Mom filled her life with, dead and wilted. It would all be like that. Inside, all the color would be damp, lifeless.

I didn't want to go in. The heaviness on my chest was almost too hard to bear. I almost reached into my bag for my inhaler, but I stopped, having to remind myself this wasn't a physical problem. The air trapped in my chest was not a failure of my lungs, but a failure of my mind. Trapped in my own head, I was the only one who could repair it.

I wished Asher was here. That Bex was here. That I could have them beside me, borrow their strength. But Bex was back at the club, practicing her routine for the next night. Her bruises had finally faded, and Carlos had grudgingly taken her back as if she'd inconvenienced him by being brutalized.

Asher was away on a "run." I didn't get much more of an explanation, only that he would be gone for a few days. We had just lost our constant shadow *"Skid,"* as Asher had been reassured we'd seen the last of Dylan. He left three days ago, and although he called me every day so far, I missed him. That too had left a sour taste in my mouth. Three days. Three days I felt lost without him. How would I handle the rest of my life when something happened to tear us apart?

So I had to find the strength to walk through that door and to withstand the memories. So then I could try to build my life around the ghosts that haunted me. The pain that plagued me. I ignored the pressure in my chest as I took a tentative step forward and put my key in the lock.

I PUSHED THROUGH THE SWEATY, inebriated sea of people toward the line for the bathroom. I too, may have been slightly inebriated. I situated myself at the end of the line, trying not to focus on the fact that I was alone in the crowded bar — drunk as I may be, being in a place full of people I didn't know, dressed like I was. It had ants tickling the bottom of my belly.

I had to find Bex.

She had melted away with the crowd when we were dancing, I hadn't been able to find her in what felt like hours. In reality, it was probably only a handful of minutes. Time moved differently when you were full of alcohol, and when people kept bumping into you, stumbling around. Apart from this small detail, I was happy with the way alcohol was making me feel. Or more accurately, not feel. The afternoon sorting through Mom's stuff was nothing short of torture. The pain, I thought could never have gotten worse, showed me a newer depth and a further emptiness. Asher's absence contributed to it. So it had been a small victory that Bex's demeanor seemed to mirror mine when I got home and she declared we get, "shitfaced."

If I'd been of a more stable frame of mind, I might have asked her what haunted her eyes. But I was too wrapped up in myself. A fatal mistake.

I took another deep breath as my eyes darted around me in a line that felt like it never moved.

"Do you think he's good looking?" a girl in front of me asked her friend.

Her friend squinted over my shoulder, looking toward the bar. "Yeah, I think so...." she paused, swaying slightly. "Definitely."

The other girl followed her gaze, her eyes glazed over with the slightly vacant look I had seen on myself in the mirror at home. The one where alcohol made everything fuzz at the edges.

"Yeah, I'm so taking him home tonight," she exclaimed before they both burst out laughing.

My mind started to wonder about my current situation with

a man who I didn't have to ask anyone about his looks. I knew he was swoon worthy. Sexy as sin. I had known for years. Now he was back in my life. Somehow wanted to be part of the mess that was my life.

The dull ringing of my phone was almost lost underneath the pounding of some song I didn't recognize, the only way I noticed was the buzzing coming from the tiny bag I had clutched to my side.

"Hello," I shouted as I fumbled to answer it just in time.

"Where are you?" a voice growled on the other end of the phone. His husky voice seemed to cut through the music, the conversations around me.

I stepped forward as the line moved, taking me into the bathroom and away from the music.

"Where am I?" I repeated. "What kind of way is that to begin a phone call? Most people go with 'hello,'" I snapped, surprised at my irritation. Why was I irritated? The sound of his voice, even laced with anger calmed the churning feeling I was battling with being in this place alone. Maybe that was why. He had the ability to control something even I couldn't grapple with.

"Hello, Flower," he said slowly.

I smiled, despite myself. I took a look in the mirror, the smile was slightly wonky, and my eyes did indeed have that vacant look the girl in front of me was wearing.

"Hello, Asher," I replied.

There was a pause. "Where are you?" he asked again.

"Why do you want to know where I am?" I hedged, frowning at the fact the dirty bathroom only had two stalls, and only one seemed to have women coming in and out of it, hence the reason for the long wait.

"You're in a club," he surmised.

"What makes you think that? I'm not," I lied, for what reason, I had no idea. Maybe it was the undertone of disapproval in his voice that penetrated my haze. Since we'd officially become a *couple*, I'd tamped down on my short-lived partying lifestyle. Snuffed it out completely. I didn't need it with Asher. But without him, even for three days, after today, I needed something. To feel nothing.

"I can hear the music in the background, Flower. I know what a club sounds like," he clipped.

"I could just be playing loud music at my apartment," I protested.

He was away God knows where with God knows who, why I was lying was anyone's guess, but I didn't want to have an argument over me being out. I didn't want to hear the disappointment in his voice at my choice of coping mechanism. I wished I were stronger to not need this, that I could wade through the thorns of grief that surrounded me without anesthetic. But I wasn't.

"You're slurring your words," he pointed out, sounding exasperated.

"I've had a couple of wines," I replied. It was the truth. A couple of wines and a couple more cocktails.

"Okay, well, I'm standing outside your apartment, which is silent as a crypt," he growled.

Shit. He had me there.

I didn't exactly expect to outsmart him, but I hadn't exactly expected to be talking to him, but I didn't have the presence of mind to screen his call. Despite being caught out, a small feeling of elation bubbled in my stomach. He was back. At my apartment. I'd see him. I glanced down at my attire. Me seeing him meant he'd see me. I was wearing a tight, body con dress that clung to every bit of my curveless body. My makeup and hair was used to disguise the toll grief had taken on me. To hide me from myself. Not recognizing myself when I looked in the mirror was a good thing. But I felt ashamed. Looking into Asher's eyes was like looking into the truest mirror that showed me without the trappings I used to run from myself. I couldn't see myself right now. Not after this afternoon.

"What is going on in there? People need to pee, like badly," the girl in front of me pounded on the stall which hadn't opened for the entire time we'd been in there.

I frowned at the door, something starting at the pit of my stomach. Something that wasn't connected to social anxiety and crowds. Something I had trouble inspecting under the cloud of drunkenness I was struggling to escape.

"Lily, where are you?" Asher demanded, his voice sharp.

My back straightened with irritation. "Why do you want to know?"

There was a loaded pause, even on the other end of a phone call after more than a couple of wines, I could feel it. His intensity.

"Seriously, Lily? Could you stop with this shit? I want to know because you're mine. Because I want to see you. Because I haven't seen you four days and I want to touch you, taste you. At this moment, though, I want to make sure you're not about to be fuckin' groped at some fuckin' club," he bit out.

The girl in front of me went into the only stall that seemed to be working. Again, I frowned at the door that hadn't opened since I had gotten in here. I bent down, not too keen on getting any closer to the grime and who knows what on the sticky floor, but needing too at the same time.

"Lily?" Asher snapped in my ear, sounding concerned.

"Shhh," I commanded, bending enough so I could see underneath the stall. So I could see the shoes I'd helped Bex pick out tonight underneath. They were laying at a weird angle. Something sank in my stomach, I shot straight up.

"Bex!" I pounded on the door urgently.

"Flower, tell me what's going on," Asher asked, his tone hard.

I ignored this, my stomach curdling at the silence beyond the door.

"Bex! Open the door, now," I yelled, not caring that the other women in the stall were staring at me.

Again, nothing.

"Lily," Asher repeated urgently.

"How do you pick a bathroom lock?" I asked him, staring at the door in desperation.

"Why do you want to know that? Are you okay?" his voice was alert.

"That's not an answer," I snapped with impatience, looking behind me for some help. I didn't think the women behind me would be much help, considering they looked worse than I did. Ditto with anyone working in this bar, and even if they would help, I'd have to wade through the crowded dance floor.

"I'll have to kick it in," I whispered to myself.

"Jesus, kick what in? Where the fuck *are* you, Lily? Tell me so I can help," Asher's voice turned soft at the end, I could tell he was trying to mask the glimmer of panic in his voice.

I ignored him again, pushing at the door with my shoulder. It looked flimsy and moved slightly even with the small amount of pressure I was exerting. Maybe my laughable strength would be enough to get me in.

"Bex, I'm coming in," I yelled again, hoping I wouldn't give her a head injury if I did by some miracle get the door open.

The silence at the other side of the door gave me the strength I didn't think I had. I slammed against the door with all my might, stumbling slightly as it gave way, swinging on its hinges. It took me a moment to focus on what I saw.

"Oh my God," I whispered in horror. "No, no, no," I chanted, kneeling beside Bex's slumped body.

"Lily!" Asher shouted, but my phone tumbled out of my hand as my shaking fingers went to the needle at Bex's arm.

"No. Bex, wake up," I commanded, shaking her pale body with panic.

A thin film of sweat was covering her face, her lips tinged with blue.

"Someone call an ambulance," I screamed at the crowd gathering behind me, my phone smashed on the floor, forgotten.

I clutched my best friend. "Please wake up, please be okay," I chanted at her limp body.

CHAPTER SIXTEEN

I CLUTCHED THE COFFEE CUP, taking sips of the awful brew out of necessity more than anything else. I had been shocked sober at what I'd seen in that bathroom stall, at having to see paramedics struggle to revive what looked like the corpse of my friend.

"We've got a weak pulse," had been the only thing that stopped me from collapsing into hysterics.

They let me ride in the ambulance with her, pushed to one side, watching in horror as they connected all sorts of things to Bex, mumbling words like *"overdose"* and *"heroin."*

I stopped my pacing, staring down at the remains of my coffee, eyes blurring at the sides.

Heroin. Overdose.

They hadn't told me anything, not since we had arrived, hours ago. Terror pulsed through me like a living thing. At the lack of news. At the smell of these sterile walls, ones I had promised myself I'd never see again. Ones that held ghosts and haunted my dreams. If these walls took another person from me, I didn't know if I could stand it.

Heroin. Overdose.

I swallowed my tears. I didn't even know. My best friend had been taking heroin, enough to be doing it in club toilets and I hadn't noticed. So wrapped up in my own despair I hadn't noticed Bex drowning in her own. Hindsight is twenty-twenty, so they say. Now I think back to those days where Bex had looked twitchy, dark circles under her already dark eyes, her frame skinnier than usual. The fact she always seemed to be on her last dollar, even though she barely bought anything apart from wine and clothes from goodwill.

I sank into a chair in the waiting room, putting my head in my hands.

"Please don't die, please don't die," I chanted to the floor beneath me.

"Rebecca Bennett?" a voice penetrated my sorrow.

I shot off the chair and rushed to an older man in a white coat, glancing over a chart in his hands.

"Is she okay?" I demanded, wanting to clutch his lapels but restraining myself.

He regarded me. I was a mess, I knew. The outfit I was wearing was intended for a club floor, not fluorescent lights and a hospital waiting room. Mascara smudged under my eyes, brought loose from tears. I didn't care. I didn't care what he thought of me. He just needed to tell me one thing.

"You're Ms. Bennett's family?" he asked skeptically.

I resisted the urge to shake the answer out of him. "Yes, I'm her family. Her sister," I said firmly.

He paused a second then glanced at the chart in his hands. "Your sister is lucky to be alive," he stated, eyes moving back to me. "A heroin overdose causes the body to forget to breathe, it doesn't take long for brain damage to set in when the brain is deprived of oxygen," he told me with clinical detachment.

I didn't hear much beyond, *"alive"* which made my whole body sag. I felt it tighten back up at his words.

"She's going to be okay, though, isn't she?" I asked in desperation.

The doctor nodded. "Luckily, the paramedics could administer the right drugs and we could treat her. As I said, she's lucky. This could have easily gone another way."

"Can I see her?" I asked. I didn't want to sit at another hospital bedside. Not again. But I had to see her with my own two eyes.

The doctor nodded again. "For a short while. Then I suggest you go home, get some sleep. She'll need to be in here overnight at the very least."

I followed him down hallways that seemed like a second home, welcoming me with their sick satisfaction. I swallowed the lump in my throat at the memories that came with them.

When the doctor stopped outside the room, he turned to me. "Your sister needs help," he told me flatly. "We don't refer these cases to the police, but I urge you to get her into a rehab facility before they become involved, or before we are too late next time."

I nodded. "There won't be a next time," I replied firmly. I had been blinded by my own demons for long enough. I'd help Bex conquer hers. It didn't matter that mine hadn't been defeated yet.

The doctor's face softened slightly, and he seemed to regard me with a sort of pity.

"I hope that's true." He gave me a nod before he left.

I walked woodenly to the bed where someone vaguely looking like my best friend was lying hooked up to machines. The beeping of her heart monitor gave me hope.

I clutched the hand with chipped black nail polish. "You're going to be okay," I whispered to her sleeping body. "We're going to get you through this."

~

BY THE TIME I got out of the hospital, daylight was kissing the horizon. A new day. One I couldn't muster any enthusiasm for. I should have taken the bus. Should have realized that a taxi was an extravagance I couldn't afford. But I felt dead on my feet. To my bones tired. So I took the taxi, deciding I would worry about my dwindling funds later. After I caught enough sleep to make me mobile enough to get Bex home and to figure out how to take care of her.

When I fumbled my key in my lock, my thoughts were of bed, of researching rehabs that we had no way to pay for, of figuring out how to get more time off work to watch Bex. How to eat if I wasn't going to work. They weren't on being aware of another person in my apartment. I nearly crawled up the wall when Asher stood from the sofa, staring at me. It wasn't just a stare, his blazing eyes tore through me, running over every inch of me. His tight form relaxed slightly when he made it back up to my eyes as if he had been expecting me to be damaged in some way.

We gazed at each other for a long while.

"What are you doing here?" I asked after my heart had returned to its normal rhythm. "Did you break in? I added on an afterthought. Despite everything, my body yearned to touch him, to run into his arms. I stayed rooted to the spot, his stiff form and angry gaze communicating that he might not be feeling warm and fuzzy toward me right now.

"What am I doing here?" he repeated.

His eyes ran over me once more, and he must have seen it, whatever was painted on my face to give me away because his face softened and he advanced on me. My body immediately relaxed when it became enveloped in his musky scent, when his large hand rested on my hip, the other spanning my chin.

"Fuck, Lily. What happened? Are you okay?" His gaze flickered over my scantily-clad body in concern, looking for an outward sign of injury. Only it wasn't the outside of me that was bleeding, or that was damaged. Luckily even his eagle gaze couldn't spot that.

His eyes met mine.

I ached to tell him. To let his strong shoulders carry the weight that settled on top of me. I knew he'd do it. Take everything off he could, carry it for miles if he had to. I knew he was strong enough to help. That he would in a heartbeat once I uttered the truth. But I couldn't. This wasn't his problem. It wasn't what I wanted us to be. Him constantly having to pick up the pieces of the life that always seemed to be in tatters. He couldn't fix this anyway.

"Lily," he said softly, firmly. His tone was saturated with concern, though the hard edge hinted at anger.

"There was a small incident. At the club. Bex is in the hospital," I said slowly, knowing parts of the truth would be the best way to go.

Asher's body stilled. "Is she okay?"

I nodded. "She's fine," I lied. "I've been with her, just making sure."

"Who do I have to kill?" he growled.

It unnerved me that he sounded serious. The gun poking out the side of his cut reinforced the seriousness. The irony of the fact there was nothing the big bad biker and his equally bad gun could do to repair this situation was not lost on me.

"No one. It was an accident like I said. No heads for you to crack," I told him quietly, the only honest part of this conversation. I hoped this was an accident. The bile that I tasted over the fact it could've been done intentionally didn't go away with any rational thought. I focused on Asher. On getting him out of here.

"Jesus," he muttered again. "Why didn't you call me? I've been out of my mind with worry, Flower." The hand at my hip tightened.

My foggy mind thought back to the fate of my phone. "I

smashed my phone, dropped it," I explained, mentally groaning. There was no way I could afford another phone.

"Payphones exist for a reason," he shot back, an edge to his previously soft voice. "I've been tearing up this town lookin' for you, babe, worried out of my mind."

I cast my eyes downward. "I'm sorry, I didn't think. My mind was preoccupied," I told him honestly.

He looked at me, stared into my eyes in a way I was worried he'd see through all of my lies, he'd see the truth playing beyond my haunted gaze. I knew he had power, power over me, but I didn't think that translated to supernatural mind reading abilities. Lucky. Or else I'd be screwed. The man who was quickly consuming my entire shattered soul may have been hard on the outside, but the soft center was filled with a man who wanted to protect, to take care of me. The weak girl who couldn't even breathe without help.

He paused. "You're dead on your feet, let's get you to bed," he declared finally.

It wasn't lost on me that anger seemed to simmer below the surface. He had swallowed it for me, out of concern, despite his inner alpha that screamed at him to demand I tell him where I was at all times. I wanted to hate both parts of him. Instead, I loved them. Therein lay the problem.

All I wanted was to surrender to the pressure at my hips, to crawl into bed with him and forget the world. I couldn't. I had responsibility.

"I think you should go," I said slowly.

Asher's expression changed. "What?" he clipped.

"You should go home. You're right. I need to sleep…alone," I told him firmly, stepping out of his embrace, I felt the warmth leave me, the comfort of his presence. I held my back up despite the exhaustion knowing at the edges of my mind.

He stood woodenly, staring at my retreating form. "I thought we were done with this shit," he uttered quietly. "That you were done running from me, from us."

"I'm not running," I whispered.

He gave me a cold glare that chilled my already frozen bones. "You fucking are," he clipped.

"Having one night to myself, to catch my breath, to fricking sleep, is not running," I snapped in irritation. My emotions were raw, needing an outlet. Asher was the closest thing. "I can't have you claim every inch of me, every inch of my time when I need it. I need some time to myself. To rebuild the remains of my pathetic life. To figure out who I am," I yelled.

Asher stepped forward, his face soft. "I know who you are, Flower," he began softly.

I stepped back my emotions exposed, like a raw nerve. Everything came tumbling out. "What? Yours? Some ideal version of me you've constructed in your head from our time together. You can't know who I am when I don't even know. People keep telling me who I'm not, who I should be. I'm so tired of it," my voice was hoarse.

"I'm not people," he growled. "I'm your fucking person," he continued fiercely. "Yours."

I let him approach me, breathing heavily, my soul open, speaking more words than I ever had before.

"The emptiness, I don't feel it when I'm with you," I whispered brokenly.

Asher stroked my face. "That's good, Lily, 'cause you fill me up, to the brim. Never thought I was unfinished, till you came to complete me."

I ignored those beautiful words. I had to. "No, it's not good," I muttered, looking down a moment. I took a breath then looked into his eyes. "If I only feel whole when I'm with you, I open myself up to the emptiness whenever you're gone, whenever you leave."

Asher opened his mouth to protest. I put my finger over his lips.

"Don't tell me you'll never leave or any of that romance novel stuff," I requested softly. "This is real life. Shit happens. Stuff you have no control over. You can't make promises about that kind of stuff…" I paused, thinking of my best friend lying in a hospital bed, of her injecting herself with poison to escape the world I hadn't even known was wearing her down. "Even if it is some kind of fairytale ending and we ride off into the sunset together, what's beyond that? What happens after that? I can't attach everything I am to you because I have to know who I am in order to be with you. I have to be whole myself."

It was the truth. The inevitable truth that I had to acknowledge. The fact my responsibility to Bex made it pertinent for this truth to come out now was of little consequence. It needed to happen. I needed to be real.

Asher's beautiful rugged face searched mine, his jaw turning hard. "You're not going to change your mind," he declared flatly.

I shook my head slowly, battling the tears that came with it.

Asher sighed, his entire frame tightening. "You're so fuckin' convinced shit's gonna turn this sour you can't see what's right in front of you." His hand tightened on my neck. "That I'd do everything in my power to make sure what's beyond that horizon is just as beautiful as you deserve, and that I'll be there as long as my body is taking breaths," he murmured. "You're so convinced that you're some stranger to yourself, you don't know how you'd see yourself if you just opened your eyes. Looked at yourself through my eyes. Through the eyes of your friend who'd die for you. Maybe then you'd see that you can't search for anyone better than who you are, 'cause that person doesn't exist." He didn't wait for the sounds of my heart breaking at his words, he pressed his mouth firmly to mine. Then he was gone.

It was that best friend that would die for me that stopped me from chasing him. From stopping him. Instead, I sank down against the floor and surrendered to the Big Sad that engulfed me as soon as Asher's presence stopped chasing it away.

I SAT a steaming mug in front of Bex. She stared at it vacantly and silently. She'd been silent the entire ride back from the hospital, the silence saying everything and nothing at once. She didn't look like herself. Her face was pale, the sprinkling of freckles on her small nose usually covered by makeup were even more prominent on her naked face, making her look like a child. Vulnerable. The vibrancy, the presence she usually brought wherever she went, seemed extinguished.

I sat across from her, cradling my own cup. "When did it start?" I asked, my words seeming to echo in the quiet room.

She contemplated the cup for a second before her empty eyes moved to mine."

"Six months ago," she replied quietly, shame in her usually boisterous voice. "First, it was pills, to help keep me energized. Keep me up. Then..." she trailed off.

I sank back. Six months. I'd been blind for six months.

"Why?" I choked out.

A spark seemed to flicker in those lifeless eyes. "Why?" she repeated.

"Why did you do that to yourself?" I asked.

The spark that seemed to only flicker before fully ignited. "Why do I do it to myself, Lily? Why I didn't do it a fuck of a lot sooner is the better question," she snapped. "My life is a steaming pile of shit. Since I was born, I've been covered with filth. Parents that abandoned me like trash. Foster parents that in the best case, ignored me for a paycheck and worst case, came into my room late at night until I was old enough to fight them off." Her voice was broken. "Living a life where no one cares, no one gives a shit about you apart from what they can take from you. Your childhood for a paycheck, your innocence for some fucked up perversion. I would lie in bed and promise myself that there'd be a better tomorrow. That I'd be better than the filth that clung to me, that was me."

Her tearstained eyes met mine. "And somehow I did it. Tricked the world into thinking that filth was gone, even though it still seeped into my bones. I got myself out with a scholarship. Somehow a fucked up childhood may have invariably damaged my soul, but it didn't hinder my ability to do well in tests."

She laughed without humor and it was an ugly sound.

"Then it came back, the filth. The truth of who I was. I realized it would never leave, that I'd never live the life I dreamed of." She shrugged. "Why delay the inevitable. I traded textbooks for the pole, sold my body. The inside was so damaged I'd never get anything out of it, but my outside was worth something."

"You are worth something, you're worth *everything*," I said fiercely, tears running down my cheeks at the heart-wrenching story. I knew her background, but she'd told me breezily, as if it didn't bother her. I didn't know the extent of it. I should have known what lay underneath those joking words. Those scars beneath the surface. I was her best friend. I should have known.

Bex smiled sadly. "Yeah, that's what you told me. What Faith told me. The two of you, coming into my life, you're probably the reason why I didn't seek solace in the needle sooner," she stated quietly. "Then it got you. Faith. Life took it away from two people who didn't deserve it. I couldn't handle it. I'm not strong like you, Lil. I got Dylan treating my body like it was his, Carlos profiting off it, men claiming it. I needed to escape it all. Have something that took it all away. Made me forget for a while."

I sat back, blinking. "Why didn't you tell me?" I asked brokenly.

Bex smiled again. "Tell my sweet little Lils that I was shooting up whenever she was at the hospital caring for her dying mom? Letting my best friend see the filth, when she was the only one who treated me like it wasn't there? Put my problems on the girl already carrying the weight of the world on her shoulders?" She shook her head. "No. That's not what best friends are for. They're for taking some of that load, not adding to it," she whispered softly.

I stood quickly, moving to sit next to her, clutching her hands in mind. "That goes both ways you big idiot," I told her croakily. "You're all I've got. You can't check out, too. You can't decide you're not good enough. You can't put poison in your body anymore. Promise me," I pleaded. "You're worth so much more than that. You can be so much more. My mom knew that. She saw the real you. She wouldn't want you to give up." Playing the dead mom card was a low blow, but I was willing to do anything to make sure Bex didn't meet my mom, wherever she was, anytime soon.

Bex stared at me. "I don't want to," she said finally. "I don't want to live that life. I think I realized that when I was in that stall, shooting up. It was like I was back in bed years ago. I want something more," she whispered.

"You're going to get it," I reassured her.

Her eyes, the ones that had life in them, stared into mine. "I'm not going to some rehab where they do daily circle jerks and talk about feelings. I'm not being trapped in some state-run prison," she stated firmly.

"Okay," I replied quietly. I knew the reality of what Bex could afford, which was nothing, which meant places that rivaled the foster homes she grew up with. Only the rich had the luxury of rehabs with tennis courts and spas.

"You don't need this," she continued, shame back on her face. "You don't deserve to have to handle your drug addict friend going cold turkey on heroin."

I pulled her chin with my thumb and forefinger. "That's the last time you say something like that. In sickness and in health," I told her firmly.

She grinned. "That's marriage."

I shrugged. "Best friendship is like marriage. And you're my family," I told her simply.

"I'm DYING," Bex declared, her entire body shaking while a thin film of sweat trickled off her forehead.

I dabbed it with a damp cloth. "You're not," I promised.

"I am," she argued, any further protest silenced by her emptying the contents of her stomach into the toilet bowl.

I held back her hair and rubbed her back, my heart bleeding for my friend, my heart bleeding with the powerful flashback that hit me of doing the exact same thing with Mom. Only with Bex, her body was having trouble with the poison leaving her body, with Mom they were fighting her body with poison. Unlike Mom, Bex was going to win this battle. I had to believe that.

She wiped her mouth with toilet paper, her defeated gaze turning to me.

"I can't do this, Lil," she croaked.

"You can," I told her firmly, helping her off the floor.

We walked slowly to the living room, Bex relying heavily on me, her body weak. Days of withdrawals had turned her into a shadow of herself, I would have barely recognized her if it wasn't for the purple tips peeking out of her shaggy bun.

Once I'd settled her back on the sofa and watched her curl into the blanket with a grimace, I walked into the kitchen, where I could still see her.

I was at a loss. I had to work tonight. Had to. My funds were running seriously dry, funds that both Bex and I needed now she wasn't working. I knew there would be no way I could have afforded a new phone to replace my smashed one.

Then one had been sitting inside the door of the apartment when I got up. Someone had broken in. Someone who knew the code of the new security system we had.

Use it. Were the words that were scrawled on the box.

I had to ignore the pang that came with thinking of him. Of the fact, he was going to do everything he could to take care of me, even with the way I treated him the other night. I couldn't focus on that. I had someone else to take care of.

There was no way I could leave Bex alone. After snatching a couple of hours of restless sleep after Asher had left two days ago, I consulted a nursing friend who now specialized in treating people with addictions. Her help was invaluable, as were her pointers in finding Bex's stash. I had flushed various bags of powder, hidden in spots in Bex's room, including lipstick tubes.

I'd felt like I was violating her trust, but her survival was more important to me than her trust at that moment. Though my friend had been more than willing to help in any way she could, I knew having a stranger, no matter how nice, sit with her and witness this, would send Bex into a tailspin.

I was at a loss. Bex's friends from the club were uncertain, considering she had told me that was where she'd first been offered the bag presenting her with an escape.

Quite simply, I was fucked.

LATER THAT AFTERNOON, after finally realizing I'd have to forfeit another paycheck and figure the repercussions out later, my problems were solved by a small and slightly crazy woman.

"Rosie," I exclaimed in surprise when I opened the door.

She was clad in her normal glam. Every time I saw her, she

was wearing something completely different than the last time I saw her. She was all in black. Black sleeveless turtleneck tucked into a short black leather mini and black heeled ankle boots. Her shoulder length curls were tumbling out of a messy bun. I was wearing one of Asher's tees and leggings with holes in them.

"Please tell me the beautiful couple I had placed all my money on isn't already dust?" she greeted, hands on her hips.

I let out a breath, glancing back to Bex asleep on the sofa. I stepped forward obscuring Rosie's view of our interior.

"We're not over," I said slowly. "We're just on a break," I explained.

Her eyes narrowed. "Ross and Rachel were on a break, look what happened to them," she snapped, the only person that could use a *Friends* reference in serious conversation. "Asher's gone from smiling like a fat kid with cake, to grimacing like a fat kid deprived of said cake," she continued. Her eyes softened as she glanced at me. "You don't look so good yourself, Lil. What's going on? Why haven't you called? I'm your friend. I want to help."

Her words, her kind eyes maybe just the fact I was functioning on little to no sleep and suffering from Asher withdrawals was the reason I stepped out of the door and into her arms, sobbing. The entire story of Bex's overdose, everything came tumbling out.

After I had finished, she'd pulled me out her arms to regard me with sad eyes.

"Fuck," she whispered. "Life hasn't stopped delivering you punches has it?"

I laughed bitterly, rubbing my eyes. "I guess not," I said slowly.

"Well, I would ask why Asher isn't here, helping you with this, but I'm thinking it's the same reason why Gwen, Amy, and I aren't privy to this. You think you have to handle all this alone." She gave my shoulders a squeeze. "I'm not gonna tell you to call him, fill him in. That's your choice. I'm not going to offer to pitch in financially because I know you won't take a dime." She rose her brow slightly at how my frame flinched at this. "I am going to offer what I can. What you're going to accept. I'm going to stay here. Hang with Bex while you go to work," she decided.

I shook my head. "I can't ask you to do that."

She pursed her lips. "It's a good thing you're not asking then," she said.

I didn't have the energy to argue anymore. So I let myself take the help that she offered. The help she offered without judgment, without expecting anything in return.

CHAPTER SEVENTEEN

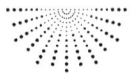

I DRAGGED myself into my car. I was tired. No, I don't think there was a word to explain what I was. My days were spent watching Bex like a hawk. Caring for her. Her entire body was crying out for a fix, and no matter what her mind wanted, the body was hard to say no to. So I watched. Didn't sleep. And when she was sleeping I opened my textbooks with bleary eyes, thankful that by some small miracle my teachers had let me study from home under the guise I was suffering from mono.

Somehow I managed to plaster a smile on my face for my entire shift, though my tips told me it wasn't as convincing as my recent tequila-filled grins. I was swearing off anything mood altering for the time being. My mind was taken up with the various things I had to get done, on top of making sure my best friend successfully survived heroin withdrawals and mentally calculating the days I had till my next assignment was due, one that my college career hinged on.

No pressure.

All of this had the underlying taste of longing. For Asher. Somehow, with my life being one kidnapping away from a soap opera or bad reality show, I missed him. I felt like I was going through withdrawals too. That my body was itching for him, yearning for my next fix.

I pulled up to my apartment with those things battling for the forefront of my mind, Asher winning hands down. It was then, a delightful sort of irony took over when my headlights illuminated a familiar Harley. Two of them in fact.

My tired body soared, renewed energy coming from the fact my next hit was so close. Reason went out the door. All the reasons why not. So it was in my eagerness to get to the elation his presence promised that I forgot to check. Do what I always did when I pulled into the parking lot of my dodgy apartment building in the bad part of town. I didn't need to. Asher's bike was there. Asher was there. It meant safety.

Safety that obviously wasn't guaranteed when I was slammed against the door I'd just shut.

"You think you can hide behind your dogs," a rough voice hissed, a huge body pressing me against the car.

I could only see a dim outline of the figure in the darkness of the parking lot. His hand pressed painfully against my throat. Terror pulsed through me.

"There'll be a time when they get sick of that snatch when they throw you aside." The hand not at my neck trailed down my side.

My heart beat furiously, and my eyes were glued to the door of my apartment, willing it to open. I struggled to contain my panic, my airway cut off both from the pressure of his hand and the terror creeping up my throat.

"Or maybe they won't," the voice continued slowly. "Maybe that pussy will keep them entertained. It doesn't mean that one day when they're not expecting it, we'll take what we are owed." The hand moved to my breast, and I cried out, the sound silenced by the pressure at my neck. "Maybe we'll just take it now," the voice mused.

"Dude, we gotta go." Another figure emerged from the darkness.

The hand at my throat loosened and the head moved. "We'll go when I say we go," he snapped.

His distraction gave me the opportunity to bring my knee up to connect with his crotch. I felt satisfied with the grunt of pain he emitted, and the fact he doubled over enough for me to dart out of his hold.

I didn't hesitate. "Asher!" I screamed with my husky voice, running past the stationary second form. I heard muttered curses from behind me as my apartment door opened.

"Asher," I screamed again as my run across the parking lot seemed to take forever.

"Lily!" I heard his bellow.

The screeching of tires had me looking over my shoulder to watch a black car zoom out of the lot. Because I was looking one way and running another, I smacked into something, hard. Luckily that something was warm and smelled musky and safe. Hands reached out to steady me.

"Flower," Asher said urgently.

"A-sh-ash," I wheezed, clutching his shoulders. A fist tightened around my lungs, the terror and the exertion of my short fight and run already catching up on me. This time, it wasn't anxiety or fear strangling me. This was real, my body's response to the incident moments before.

"Lily, your inhaler, where is it?" he demanded sharply, immediately registering the reason for my strangled breathing.

I was frozen for a split second, then out of instinct, I reached for my bag on my shoulder. My panic intensified when the realization hit that I must have dropped it in the struggle. I pointed at my car while the wheezing got worse.

Calm, I told myself. *You're safe. Asher means safe.*

"What's going on ... shit Lily, are you okay?" a familiar and concerned voice asked with urgency mirroring Asher's.

"Get her purse from the car, now," Asher demanded, lifting me into his arms. The dim light illuminated his attractive face, tight with concern. "You've got more inside, right?" he asked while striding with apparent ease up the stairs to my apartment.

I nodded. "Totally soap opera," I wheezed between strangled breaths. I would've laughed if I had the ability. And wasn't scared out of my wits.

"What?" Asher frowned down at me.

I didn't have time to reply.

"Lily! Oh my God is she okay?" A pale looking Bex leaned against the door, regarding us in horror.

"Get her inhaler, now," Asher barked at her, and she scrambled to comply.

"I'm fi-fine, it's n-not bad," I tried in vain to reassure him.

He frowned down at me once more and settled on the sofa, positioning me so I was on his lap.

Bex thrust my inhaler at me, and I self-consciously puffed on it, aware of the many sets of eyes focused on me at that moment. As my breathing calmed, I felt Asher's hand on my chest relax, though his body stayed tight and his hand didn't move.

"Okay, I had a fuckin' internal struggle the entire way back in here," Lucky said, bursting into the room, his attractive face worried. "I know handbags are like a chick's sacred space, and no man should venture in without express permission, but it seemed like life or death. Someone tell me what the fuck I'm looking for in here before my hand gets bitten off by some handbag urchin hiding in the depths of this colossal thing," he pleaded with his head bent, riffling through my purse.

His head snapped up, and he focused on me, on what was in my hand and realization dawned.

I couldn't help the giggle that burst out of me at his face, and the fact he was holding my baby pink tote, one tattooed hand still elbow deep. When he saw where my eyes were focused, the muscled arm immediately retreated. A tampon came attached to that muscled arm, he looked down in horror and quickly dropped it. He gingerly held the bag by its handles, holding it slightly away from his body like it was an undetonated bomb. This made me laugh even more.

"Is she okay? Are there drugs in that? If so, I'll take a toke when you're done," Lucky deadpanned, nodding to the bag.

Out of the corner of my eye, I saw Asher shake his head and Bex rolled her eyes from her spot in front of me. When my laughter finally faded out, the seriousness of what had just happened crept back in.

Asher lightly touched my chin so I was focused on him. Despite everything, I drank in every aspect of his features, as if we'd been separated for months. I was aching for my fix. For his lips on mine. His body on mine. My need almost outweighed everything else around us. Almost.

"What was that? Why are you guys here?" I asked before he could go all alpha and demand to know if I was unharmed and untraumatized. I was sitting on his knee close enough for him to see no immediate bloody bullet wounds.

His face searched mine, resting on my mouth for a moment. "Want to tell me if you're okay first, Flower? Then we'll get into explanations. On both sides," he added ominously.

See? Alpha male protectiveness. There must be classes on it.

My back straightened, and I felt my face flame upon the realization that both Lucky and Rosie, who was unusually quiet in the corner, had seen me sucking on my inhaler after having a small tussle with random men and running a couple of meters. These guys dodged bullets without a breaking a sweat — maybe not Rosie, but I knew she could take care of herself. Me? I wheezed and whimpered after a minor altercation.

"I'm fine," I said quietly, my eyes moving downward self-consciously.

Again, Asher's hand moved to make our eyes meet once more. I noticed his hand was still resting lightly on my chest.

"You were just attacked in your own parking lot, no one expects you to be fine, Lily," he told me quietly.

I met his eyes. "I am," I replied firmly. "I won't be if someone doesn't tell me what's going on." I moved my eyes around the room.

Lucky had gingerly put my handbag on the ground and was watching me with knitted brows, his gaze kept flickering to Bex, with something that looked like annoyance and concern. It was something I'd never seen on him. Granted, I didn't spend huge amounts of time with him, so I wasn't exactly flush with knowledge of his facial expressions, but it seemed unusual. Rosie was sitting across from us, her eyes were glued to Asher and me, her brows knitted with worry. Bex looked at her hands.

The silence hung heavy in the room for a moment before Bex looked up with watery eyes.

"It was because of me," she whispered in a voice I didn't recognize. Broken. Defeated.

"It is not because of you," Lucky interrupted with a face like a hurricane. "That's the last time you're laying the blame of this shit at your pretty little feet, got it?" he commanded roughly, his eyes locked in some sort of stare off with Bex.

I watched in amazement as she held it for a moment then nodded, looking away. Lucky's jaw was hard and he kept watching her. Bex never lost stare-offs, never. Even though Lucky may have been a scary, albeit well-tempered biker, she normally wouldn't have flinched at his stormy gaze. But today she did. Her mask had been ripped off, now she was battling with her demon, and the vulnerable girl underneath peeked out. It broke my heart. Reason number a million and one why I wished my mom was still here. To heal her. To help me fix her.

"They were here because they're the scum of the earth who

consider women property and don't like it when they get told otherwise," Asher cut in.

I restrained a snort. Despite the sorrow edging into the forefront of my mind, I couldn't help but see the irony.

Asher saw something in my face. "We never see women as property, Flower. Not our club. Women aren't possessions to be owned and traded. Any fucker that thinks that is someone that needs to taste lead," he declared hotly.

"And who are these specific ... fuckers?" I asked softly.

Lucky, who had been seriously regarding Bex, let out a choked sound. We all looked at him. He waved his hand.

"Sorry, shit. I'm well aware of the need to teach these fuckers a serious lesson. But I wasn't even sure you could utter the word *'fuck,'* Lily," he told me seriously.

Despite myself, I grinned. I was the only one.

"You know Bex's boss?" Asher asked, getting us back on track.

I nodded. "I've had the displeasure."

His face tightened. "The strip club serves as a recruiting tool for his main business, peddling flesh," he stated flatly.

I nodded again.

Asher looked at me in surprise.

"You knew?" he asked.

"No, but I'm not surprised. That guy gave me the serious heebie-jeebies," I declared, my concerned eyes on Bex. I didn't know where this story was leading, but it wasn't anywhere good for my troubled best friend.

"Bex?" I said slowly, needing the rest to come from her.

"I said no," she told me quickly, as if I would doubt her, judge her. I would never do either. We all did what we had to do to survive, to make it through. There were choices that people had to make that weren't pretty or ideal, but they were necessary.

"Or I may have used more colorful words than a one syllable response, just to get my message across." She grinned, a glimpse of the old Bex shining through. "I thought that was the end of it. Obviously not," she finished.

I felt like I'd missed something. "That's why those thugs were here? To bully you into prostitution?" I guessed.

The way the air turned wired had me thinking my guess was correct. I glanced over to a hard-jawed Lucky.

"Thing One and Thing Two came knocking at the door, trying to intimidate the little female into letting them in or they'd huff and puff and blow my house down. Didn't count on the fact I'd seen way worse than them. And I had bigger, badder, wolves on speed dial," Rosie spoke for the first time, grinning, as was her way. Growing up with bikers had her slightly insane. In a good way.

"I don't get it," I said, furrowing my brows. "Carlos may be an asshole, but he can't expect you to go back working there after that? What did he have to gain from it?" I asked Bex.

She shrugged. "The fact I've got nothing else. That I need to eat."

My eyes popped out. "You're not going back there?" I asked in disbelief.

She obviously hadn't been to work in the past few days, for obvious reasons. Reasons that hadn't been shared with the group. Reasons I tried to remind her of with her mind. The slippery slope of addiction was one thing that should have scared her off, this was another. Like she said, she had to eat. Sometimes we didn't have the luxury of choice.

"Since I've been *sick*," she enunciated the word as if to remind me. "I've obviously been missed. My ass is the only reason that place makes anything. That and my boobs." She winked.

"So you're going back?" I repeated with distaste.

"She's not fuckin' setting a toe in that shit hole's direction," Lucky growled, his eyes glued to Bex.

She straightened. "I am," she argued.

Another stare off. This time Bex won.

Lucky sighed and shook his head. "You wanna take your clothes off, show the world that sweet ass, you'll be doing it at *our* club. Where I can keep a fuckin' eye on that ass," he declared. "And where no one puts a hand on you trying to sell that ass," he added roughly.

Bex opened her mouth as if to argue. I knew she was doing it just to argue, the Son's club had a good reputation, and they treated and paid their girls well. No drugs were tolerated on the premises either. She'd talked about moving there before, but couldn't justify the commute. I had yet to tell her about my mom's house and the lack of commute. When I did, she would realize that Lucky was solving all her problems. Therein lay the rub.

Bex may be different than me in every other way, but in this, we were the same. We didn't want these men riding in on their Harleys fixing our problems as if we weren't capable of living life until they came along. On giving them power. Taking that agency away from us. No matter how decent, how good looking, how much we might care about said men, our lives were not set out to be sorted out for us. We needed this. To be in control of our lives. Or at least grab on to the illusion of control. Without it we had nothing.

"It's a good idea," I murmured before she could argue.

I knew how she felt, but I wasn't going to let her pride take her back there.

She glared at Lucky then glared at me and was silent.

Lucky took this as a yes. "You won't be swinging your ass around any pole until you're better. What's wrong with you? Have you been to the doctor?" he frowned at her, his eyes trailing over her sunken form, her pale skin. He was smart. He wouldn't stay ignorant for long. Especially, if he was interested in the way I thought he was.

"I'm fine," she ground out.

His brows furrowed further. "Bitches around here need to stop saying they're fine when they're obviously not. Every man worth his salt knows that if uttered by a woman, the word *'fine'* could signify a fuckin' apocalypse," he muttered.

He got three female glares at his words.

He held his hands up in surrender.

"We haven't seen the last of them," Asher ushered the conversation back to the more pressing matter than the semantics of women's vocabulary. "Carlos knows you're my Old Lady. For him to authorize this, for them to do that with my bike in the parking lot?" He paused, hands around me tightening. "They're not fuckin' around."

"If what they said to me was anything to go by, they most certainly are not," I said quietly, almost to myself. My stomach dipped. Or more accurately it felt like I'd swallowed razor blades. When it rained, it poured. Then it stopped raining and lightning set everything on fire.

Asher went rigid. "What exactly did they say?" he clipped dangerously.

"That we haven't seen the last of them," I paraphrased.

He glared at me. "Don't get cute, Flower, now is not the time. What specifically did they say?"

I scrunched up my nose. "Not something I'd care to repeat," I hedged. I didn't need any more alpha released tonight, if someone struck a match this place might explode the air was already so thick with it. Plus, Bex's state of mind was already delicate, to say the least, I was not letting these lowlifes be the catalyst for something taking away my best friend.

Asher's silence told me I wouldn't be able to get away with my own.

"They said when you got tired of our ... *snatch*, they'd take it for themselves," I said finally, my nose screwed up.

As expected, alpha anger rose to epic proportions the moment the words left my mouth.

Though I wasn't focused on that, neither was Rosie. Both of us were focused on Bex and her reaction. She seemed outwardly calm. That didn't mean much. She'd seemed outwardly normal when she'd been injecting herself with poison for six months. As much as I needed Asher here, I needed him gone. I needed to talk to my friend. Figure out how to get her through this.

Asher had other ideas.

"You're going to the club," he declared tightly. "Both of you," he added.

"No, we're not," I replied quickly and firmly.

No matter how much Carlos and his *"boys"* scared me, I was even more terrified at the prospect of losing Bex. Taking her to a biker clubhouse where no one knew what she was going through, where it was unfamiliar, and who knows what was on offer, had a distinct promise of shattering the precarious road she was on to recovery.

Two determined sets of male eyes told me my protests were in vain.

Bex surprised the living hell out of me by not releasing her inner banshee. "We'll go, Lil," she said quietly.

Both Lucky and I gaped at her in disbelief. He had been expecting the banshee also.

"That's the second time you got hurt as a result of my shit," she explained in a guilty voice. "It'll be the last," she promised, glancing at Asher.

I felt his form tighten around me. "Damned straight it'll be the last," he repeated the same promise in his voice, slightly more masculine and firm.

"I've got school here. And work. I can't exactly commute back to Amber at two in the morning. And I need that job," I protested.

Asher's face turned hard, and I knew he would have something to say about this. He wanted me out of the bar, and this was his perfect excuse. He'd get to exert all of his protectiveness over me, and I'd lose what little self-sufficiency I had left.

"Well, I can solve that particular problem," Rosie chimed in from the corner. "Gwen and Amy have been itching to get you back, but they were waiting for the right time to ask. For things to ... settle down with you." She paused, gazing around the room. "Things aren't looking to settle down anytime soon, so I'm declaring this the perfect time," she exclaimed with a smile.

Asher's form relaxed and a satisfied, edging on smug look replaced the tight one that had been there before.

There it was. Someone else solving all my problems for me. My chest felt heavy once more. I couldn't argue. This was a matter of my safety, of Bex's. I wasn't an idiot. I wasn't going to risk my life for pride. I certainly wouldn't risk Bex's. I glanced at her again. She was giving me a weak smile. Dark purple rings decorated her eyes. She wouldn't recover in a biker clubhouse, one with women like the one I met three years ago. Men who drank and smoked as was their right.

"Okay," I relented finally. "But we're not going to the club," I added quickly.

Both Asher and Lucky glared at me, and I felt like shrinking into myself at the power of both of their stares.

"I can't study, can't live ... there," I said quietly. "But there's a place in Amber, somewhere no one knows about, somewhere they, whoever they are, won't find us," I continued quickly.

Bex's face got even paler as she realized where I was talking about. "Lils," she began softly.

"Where would that be?" Asher asked in a hard voice, interrupting Bex.

I met his chocolate eyes. "My mom's."

There was a long silence as everything sunk in around the room.

"Okay, I know this is yet another drama that the club has to wade through, but can I just say, I'm glad you too are off your break. Totally knew this wasn't a *Ross and Rachel* situation," Rosie piped in with a grin.

I couldn't help it, despite the sorrow that crept up my throat at the prospect of the events ahead of us, I smiled. And it was genuine.

CHAPTER EIGHTEEN

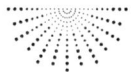

"LILY," a husky voice tickled the back of my neck.

I snuggled into the hard, warm body at my back, my mind blissfully blank and half asleep.

I felt desire rush into my fuzzy mind as Asher let out a throaty growl, and his hand pushed into the waistband of my shorts.

"I've missed this pussy, Flower," he murmured in my ear as his rough hand rubbed my magic spot.

I let out a little mew of pleasure, aching for him, aching for more.

"Dreamed about this pussy," he continued as he pushed into me.

I turned my head, not caring about morning breath or the possibility I looked like a swamp creature, I needed him. The split second before his mouth claimed mine had my stomach dip in a different way, his eyes, the utter devotion behind them had me losing my breath. His mouth ravaged my mouth while his fingers worked me up to my beautiful crescendo. I moved my body against his, kissed him with the ferocity and desperation I didn't know I was feeling.

Before I could succumb to my mind-shattering orgasm, Asher's hands left me and before I had time to protest he had me on my back. His body hovered over mine, eyes capturing me with that devotion, that reverence that I felt physically.

"This is where you're meant to be," he declared roughly, his expert hands divesting me of my shorts. "In my bed, with me. The shit on the outside is secondary, it's doable, as long as I've got you. As long as you've got me." He lowered down and positioned himself at my entrance, framing my face with his. "And you've got me, Lily. For as long as this body has breath, you've got me," he whispered, the weight of his words settling in conjunction with the beautiful explosion that came with him plunging into me.

His strokes didn't mirror his gentle words, the tender gaze he paralyzed me with. They were urgent, desperate, hard. I wrapped my legs around his waist, scratched his back with my nails, loving every brutal stroke.

He was right. At that moment, every problem, every torturous feeling that seemed insurmountable, didn't matter here. Not in this moment, not in any moment I had him. I got it.

"I love you," I whispered, my voice strangled by my imminent climax.

The frenzied thrusts stopped abruptly, Asher's entire frame stilled atop me. His gaze that had moments ago warmed my soul, stole every bit of breath in my lungs.

"I was searching for who I was without you, now I realize who that is. Nothing. I'm nothing without you," I continued in a shaky voice.

"You're wrong," he clipped, the cords in his neck tight. "You're everything without me. You just belong with me."

He pushed into me slowly, his eyes never leaving mine. "Three words seem fuckin' insignificant to describe what I feel for you," he grunted. "But that's all I've got. I love you, Flower."

Once the words had left his mouth he moved again, hard and

magnificent. The elation of those words rode the high of a climax that radiated to every part of me. I felt Asher tighten around me, and I clutched him as he found his own release.

We stayed like that, me holding him tightly, never wanting to let him go, to let this moment become a memory.

Asher gazed at me. "Those words, babe, they mean everything," he began roughly. "You've always been everything to me. It. My Old Lady. Whatever shit we went through to get here was worth it tenfold to hear you utter those three words." He brushed a wayward hair out of my face. "They mean nothing is keeping us apart now. It's you and me, Flower, shit out there," his eyes moved to the door, "that's shit we'll face together. You're not facing that alone, never again," he promised.

I blinked at his words, at the fact somehow this man who was rough and brutal on the outside softened for me. Normal, boring Lily.

"Okay," was all I managed to choke out.

Asher didn't seem bothered by my lack of response, his eyes crinkled at the side and he pressed a light kiss on the edge of my nose. After pulling out of me and cleaning me with a tenderness that matched his previous words, he gathered me in his arms.

"That said," he continued, "the shit out there is serious. I need you to take it seriously. I know you're concerned about your friend, I also need you to be concerned about you," he instructed. "'Cause this," he squeezed my body, "is precious to me. Every time this knows pain, mental or physical, I feel it too. I want you to remember that. Take care of yourself, Lily. You're taking care of me at the same time," he told me softly.

I glanced up at him, the beauty of his words wrapping around me and lifting the weight off my chest.

"I will, Asher," I promised.

He kissed my nose. "Good," he said simply. "As much as I want to stay, talk to you about why we were separated yet again, I've got to go and knock some heads together," he declared.

My stomach dropped. "Carlos?" I questioned.

He nodded.

"Be careful," I whispered. "What you said to me, it holds true with me, too. If you hurt, I hurt. I couldn't survive another person being taken away from me," I admitted quietly.

Asher's body tightened. "Nothing's gonna take me away from you, Flower. Not while I've got breath in my body," he promised.

I sank back into his chest. I knew he was telling the truth. What worried me was the things that had the ability to take breath from his body.

ASHER

"We can't just roll into Carlos's and try to reason with him. The man's a worm. His brain mirrors the size of that," Cade addressed the table, leaning back in his chair.

"Who said anything about reason?" Asher asked him, twisting his knife into the wood of the table.

His Prez regarded him. "I get what you want, brother, I do. But this could get messy. Bloody. We've had enough of bloody." He glanced over at Bull.

He was right. It seemed the club never caught a moment of respite the past few years. Bull's woman was kidnapped most recently, though that wasn't anything connected to club shit, when someone hurt a member of their family, they all bled. They struck back. The shooting before that had rippled through the club, they'd lost a brother. They'd bled. Though, again, they struck back. Hard.

"We could blow up the fucker's club," Gage suggested. "I'll light that place up like a Christmas tree. Say the word."

The entire table stared at the crazy fuck. He was serious.

Cade's face was blank. "We're not blowing up a building," he told him firmly like a father would tell a child they couldn't play with fireworks.

Gage's face mirrored that of a sulky child.

Cade focused on Asher once more. "They hurt your woman, they'll bleed for that. But Carlos is connected to the Tuckers—"

"Loosely," Lucky interrupted. "Only the stupid fuck we winged a couple of weeks back. Family hardly flinched at that. Shit, I wouldn't be surprised if they sent us a thank you card. Fucker's a spoilt little shit. Not popular within the family."

"But he's still family," Brock cut in, leaning forward. "Meaning if we push hard enough, they'll push back. They can't afford to look weak."

"Let them push, we're a lot stronger than those fucks," Lucky replied with a glint in his eyes.

Brock raised a brow. "Yeah, we are. But we've also got women, children to think about. We're not risking them," he replied firmly.

Asher clenched his fists. "I'll go in alone, no colors, no bike. No blowback for the club," he declared.

Lucky's eyes met his. "No way you're doing this alone. I'm in too," he told him.

Gage leaned forward. "If I don't get to blow anything up I'm at least coming on the field trip," he growled.

"I'm in too," Bull muttered, his eyes hard.

Cade leaned back. "Club's in on this," he told Asher. "Carlos has always been a pain in my ass, and he's a sick fuck. He also has big aspirations, ones that would mean shit for us down the line. Best to address it now," he decided.

Asher nodded, pulling his knife out of the table. Lucky's eyes stayed hard. Gage grinned wide. *Crazy fuck.*

"Don't kill him," Cade instructed. "Teach him a lesson. Let him know his place."

Asher nodded.

They didn't kill him, as much as they wanted to. They taught him a lesson. A long one. One that had Asher satisfied Lily wouldn't breathe his air again.

He'd wish much later that he'd put a bullet in the fucker's brain. They all would.

LILY

"Want to tell me whatever's really going on with Bex? The real reason you pushed me away that night?" Asher asked slowly with an edge to his voice.

I sighed. I knew he wouldn't stay ignorant for long. I doubted Lucky would either. I didn't miss whatever was between Bex and him. He was currently sleeping on the sofa in my mom's living room. I guessed it was my living room now. Mom would never dance through it with a smile, she'd never change it around when inspiration struck her.

The room I was in wasn't hers, not anymore, that was mine too. Asher had helped me pack up all of her things. He hadn't said a word the entire time, like he sensed I needed silence. He merely took the boxes I offered him to Mom's studio out back. I couldn't go out there. Not yet. I had moved into Mom's room, and Bex was in my old room. She was still *"sick."* Still pale, unable to hold much down, still a shadow of herself.

Asher had told us Carlos was taken care of, so I didn't know why Lucky was on our sofa. Then again, maybe I did.

I traced a circle on his naked chest, not wanting to lie, not wanting to betray my best friend's trust either.

Asher jostled me so I met his eyes. They weren't swimming with anger like I expected, but concern.

"Lily?" he probed.

I looked into his eyes for a long moment. He had already taken on so much of my problems. I didn't want to give him one more, but I also didn't know how long I could shoulder this burden alone. How much longer I could lie to him.

"It wasn't an accident that put Bex in the hospital," I whispered slowly.

Asher nodded as if he was expecting it, but his eyes swam with concern.

I took a deep breath. "It was an overdose," I continued.

Once the word left my mouth Asher's entire form tightened and his face turned blank.

I continued. "Heroin," I choked out. "The overdose was an accident, that what she says, what I have to believe," I told him in a small voice. "But the drugs? The needle in her arm? No accident. She'd been using for months. And I didn't notice. I was blind," I said, fighting the tears at the corner of my eyes.

Asher's hand tilted my chin so my wayward eyes would meet his. "Do not lay any blame on yourself for this, Lily," he commanded. "Addicts excel at hiding their addiction." He paused. "You were running yourself ragged taking care of your mom, you could never have expected this," he said firmly. There was another pause, this time, a loaded one. "You didn't tell me."

I shook my head. I didn't think he was finished speaking, and I really didn't want to get into why I didn't tell him. We never got what we wanted in these situations it seemed. He stayed still a moment, and I waited for him to say something more, for him to say he was here for me how I should share things with him, how he was going to take care of everything. He didn't. The silence lasted longer than I was comfortable with, it wasn't comfortable. It was the first time the absence of words with Asher had me feeling anxious.

He very gently gathered me up and lifted me off his chest, and placed me on the pillow beside him. I went up on my elbow, my stomach churning. I wanted to give him an explanation, but I felt tired of constantly justifying my reasons to him. To myself.

He pushed up off the bed, still silent, then padded over to the wall beside my armchair, staring at it a moment, then plowing his fist through it.

I jumped and sat up abruptly, pulling the sheets over my naked body. I regarded his tattooed back in horror. He placed both his hands on the wall, bowing his head and taking a deep breath before turning to face me. His face was blank.

I looked from the hole in the plasterboard to his fist, which was dripping blood.

This was the first time I'd seen Asher lose control, really lose control.

"You're bleeding," I observed in a small voice.

"You were in another hospital, facing the real possibility you could be losing another person in your life," he started quietly, ignoring me. "Facing more shit that doesn't seem to give you any respite. Facing that alone," he stated flatly.

"I didn't lose her," I replied softly.

Asher's gaze darted up. "You didn't know that at the time. I was too busy tearing the fuckin' town apart trying to find you, angry as shit at you, thinking you were fuckin' 'round at some club and you were alone," he clipped in a cold voice.

I stared at him, unsure of what to say, what to do. He had never acted like this, he seemed angry, that was obvious. And something else. Defeated.

"Asher," I began.

"When are you going to get this? *You're not fucking alone!*" he roared at the end, and I flinched.

Not at the anger, but the pain in his voice.

He stepped forward. "You're not alone, Flower," he said softly. "I don't know how else to tell you, to show you. I can't control that," he gestured to the door, "as much as I would like to stand in front of you and bear the brunt of everything that keeps coming at you, I can't. I can't stop it. I can't control it. But I can make sure you don't face it alone. You'll never be alone with this shit again, I want you, Lily. Not for now, not for a while, forever," he declared fiercely, kneeling beside the bed. He grasped my hands. "You're strong in ways I'm not. And

I'm strong in ways you aren't. That's why we work. I know shit is hard for you. That being around crowds, around people you don't know scares the shit out of you. I know you're suffering from a loss that gutted you. That you struggle every day with a condition that can make it feel impossible to breathe. That you get stuck inside your head and don't know how to get out." He paused and brushed a tear from my cheek. "All that should bring a person to their knees. Instead, my flower stands tall. Beauty blossoms where on most people it would wither. You're willing to give your all for the one person you've got left." His hand tightened on mine. "While I admire the shit outta that, babe. I'm not gonna let you do that. I need this," he trailed his hand down to my chest, to my heart, "I need you if I'm going keep breathing easy. So let me help you. Let's face this together," he stated, though there was a question in there too.

Tears were pouring down my cheeks unbidden at this point. I couldn't hold them in anymore. I knew he was perceptive, that our connection was out of the ordinary, that he saw more than other people. I didn't realize he saw everything. He didn't just see everything, he understood it. Even Mom, who knew what I struggled with, couldn't truly understand was I was—the was I was. She accepted it, unconditionally. I never thought I'd meet someone that understood it.

"Lily?" Asher said softly.

"I love you," I blurted through my tears. "I want forever, too. Beyond forever," I continued in a whisper.

Asher's face changed completely, softened completely. His chocolate eyes blazed into mine. "Marry me," he said in a voice husky with emotion.

I didn't hesitate. Not like I did with everything else. Overthink it, trying to find the sense. I didn't need to look for the sense.

"Okay," I whispered.

Asher's hand fastened at the back of my neck, and he pulled me in for the most beautiful kiss I had ever experienced.

"Marry me tomorrow," he murmured against my mouth.

Again, I didn't hesitate, didn't state the reasons why not, the stuff swirling out there. Instead, I smiled into his mouth, letting the feeling of elation lift me up.

"You can't get married in one day, there's forms, hoops to jump through," I protested weakly.

Asher grasped my head. "I got it, babe," he promised.

And for once, I didn't question him.

"Let's do it," I whispered.

Asher grinned against my mouth, it was safe to say he beamed. Then he made love to me, slowly, beautifully. In a way that the outside world failed to exist, and it was just him and me.

"You're beautiful, Lils," Bex whispered, wiping a tear from her made up face.

I regarded myself in the mirror. My white blonde hair tumbled down my back in soft curls, two small plaits were pulled back on either side of my face. My makeup was natural, understated.

Me.

It was the dress, the dress that caused my fingers to tingle and my eyes to prickle. What had Bex's heavy eye makeup running down her face. My mom bought it for me.

Two months before she died, she gave it to me.

"I've got a present for you, Lily," Mom exclaimed softly, leaning on the doorframe to the living room.

I pushed off the sofa, closing the lid to my laptop abruptly. Mom didn't need to see the sites I was surfing. Scouring actually. Searching for some last minute cure.

"Mom, you shouldn't be out of bed," I scolded gently, my stomach turning at the way she held that frame for support, the way her colored pants hung off her emaciated frame. "And you most definitely shouldn't be giving me presents," I added.

Her bright eyes lit up, and she gave me a mischievous grin. "I'm the mother here, I say when I should and shouldn't be out of bed," she teased. "And, as the mother, it is my prerogative to give my daughter gifts. Now come on." She waved her hand at me.

Despite the sorrow swimming in the depths of my soul, I smiled and walked toward her. I was getting good at making it look genuine. She linked her arm in mine, and I didn't miss how heavily she leaned into me.

"Sit," she commanded when we made it to her brightly decorated bedroom.

I did as she commanded and planted myself on the quilt that she and I had made when we first moved here. My eyes flickered around the room at the photos, at the scarves draped over lamps, antique perfume bottles arrayed on her dresser and clothes messily strewn across the floor. It looked normal. Like nothing had changed. My eyes touched the multiple pill bottles scattering her nightstand. Harbingers of change. Of doom.

"Here," she exclaimed.

I moved my weary gaze to where she was standing by her overflowing closet, blinking away my tears. That didn't really work when my eyes caught what she had in her hands.

"Mom," I choked.

She gave me a chastising look. "No tears. Put it on," she commanded, thrusting it at me.

I took it woodenly and as if on autopilot, I divested myself of my clothes and put on the garment she handed to me.

She zipped me up and stood behind me as we both looked in the mirror.

"*Prettiest girl I've ever seen, my Lily,*" *she whispered in my ear.* "*I knew the moment I saw it, it was you. It would be what you wore on your wedding day, to help you shine. The day you walked down to meet the man who appreciates everything my beautiful Lily is. Sees in you. Exactly who you are,*" *she continued in a bright voice.*

Tears streamed silently down my cheeks as I looked at the dress she'd bought for me. The wedding dress. The sheer long sleeves were flowing and tapered in with a button at my wrists. The entire bodice was delicate flowered lace. From underneath my breasts, it cascaded down to my knees in layers of sheer fabric. It was the palest yellow you could imagine, and it fit me like it was made for me.

"*I won't be there when you meet him,*" *Mom whispered, pulling my hair back.* "*I won't be here to watch that love blossom for my beautiful girl. I won't be able to walk you down that aisle. I won't be there in body, sweetheart. But I think the universe let me find this so I could be there in spirit,*" *she told me softly, pulling half my hair from my face.*

I stared in the mirror a moment longer, then whirled, curling into my mother's arms.

"*You will be, Mom,*" *I sobbed into her chest.* "*You will be there, it's not the end. You're not leaving me,*" *I choked out.*

She stroked my head and pulled back to hold me at arm's length. She gazed at me with twinkling eyes.

"*It's not the end, Lily. It's just a new beginning, I finally get to see what's beyond the horizon,*" *she whispered.*

I FINGERED the fabric on the dress, remembering that moment. The beauty of it. I didn't believe in that stuff like Mom did, the universe, fate, the other side. How could I when the universe, fate, took my mom away from me? Took everything away from me. I couldn't help but reconsider my cynicism. Because I felt her, right at that moment, looking at myself in the mirror. I didn't just see myself, I saw her. I felt her warm presence at my side.

I blinked away my tears and took the bouquet of daisies Bex handed me. "Are you okay?" I asked with concern. Her black dress hung off her, and even makeup couldn't cover the gray tinge to her skin.

She had refused to be anywhere but here, despite the fact she was still struggling with withdrawals. She hadn't been angry that Asher knew, the two of them had had a hushed conversation that I hadn't been privy to, but they seemed okay. Lucky seemed to be her shadow, much to her distaste. There was something between them. I think it scared her. He hadn't figured out the truth yet, and I knew that terrified her.

She gave me a faux frown. "This is your wedding day, Lil, you're not allowed to think about anyone but yourself," she instructed firmly and paused. "I'm okay. I will be okay. Seeing you find this … happiness. It makes me happier than anything, Lils babe. Your mom would be so proud of you," she whispered. "She would've approved, of him. Of the two of you."

I nodded. "I know," I replied with certainty.

She smiled. "Let's go get you hitched."

I let her lead me out of the little room attached to the city hall building in Amber. I didn't care about the location. I was glad of it, to be honest. Glad that Lucky and Bex were the only people who knew, who were serving as witnesses. I didn't want anyone else. I didn't need to be the center of attention. I didn't want the spectacle. I just wanted Asher.

We walked down the small hallway that led to the room Asher waited in. The nerves, the heaviness on my chest I expected didn't come. For once, I wasn't plagued with doubt, with the ever present fist threatening to squeeze the breath from me. It all fell away. And when Bex opened the doors to the room, my breath did leave me. But in a good way.

The room was empty, the rows of seats devoid of people. Three figures stood up on a small platform, but I only had eyes for one. Asher was wearing a simple black shirt, open at the collar. His cut was over the top. He wore black slacks and black motorcycle boots on his feet. His chocolate eyes were locked on me the moment I entered the room. His entire body jolted on my approach. Lucky elbowed him and whispered something in his ear, grinning widely.

Asher didn't respond, didn't act like anyone had spoken. He only had eyes for me. Me. Boring, normal, Lily. Except, I didn't feel boring or normal. I felt beautiful, special. Extraordinary.

I smiled shyly at him when I had climbed the small stairs, standing in front of him. His entire body was frozen, and he continued staring at me. I gazed in amazement at the water in his chocolate eyes.

"You take my breath away, Flower," he rasped finally.

I grasped his hands tightly, smiling. "Ditto," I whispered back.

The man between us smiled warmly, clearing his throat. "Should we begin?" he asked the two of us.

Asher didn't take his eyes off me. He didn't look like he was going to say anything; it didn't look like he could.

So for once, I spoke up. "Yes, I think we should begin," I responded firmly.

Asher's hands squeezed mine.

And in a few short minutes, there began the happiest moment of my life. The moment Asher's lips claimed mine and we were man and wife.

Lucky let out a whoop from beside us, the man who married us jumping in fright.

"Okay, we're hitched," he exclaimed, slinging his arms around our shoulders. He glimpsed at me. "You look beautiful darlin'," he told me, laying a gentle kiss on my cheek. He pulled back. "Now it's time to party!"

I looked over at Bex, who was wiping her eyes and beaming at me.

"I love you" I mouthed, not being able to move from Lucky's firm embrace.

"I love you too," she mouthed back.

"No party," Asher growled.

Lucky stepped back, hand on his heart as if Asher had just thrust a dagger through it.

"No party?" he repeated like a kid getting told he wasn't allowed dessert. "You get married all cloak and daggers, swear me to secrecy under the penalty of death and now you say *no party?*"

Asher's hard gaze didn't waver. "No party," he repeated firmly.

I knew why he was saying that. Because of me. Because he knew how I would do being the center of attention at a rowdy party at the clubhouse. I didn't think it was possible, but I loved him even more in that moment. I knew that club celebrations were part of the lifestyle. They did everything together, as a family. They may have lived a hard life, a misunderstood life, but when it came to celebrating that life, they didn't screw around. I opened my mouth to speak, but Lucky beat me to it.

"That might be hard considering I didn't blanch at the death threat uttered to me because I'm as brave as a lion," he gave me a cheeky grin, "and I love a good party. So there may or may not be a club full of very expectant people waiting back at the club-house to toast to Mr. and Mrs. Breslin." His bravado trailed off toward the end as Mr. Breslin's glare got more withering.

"For fuck's—" he grit out.

I put my hand on his arm. "I think what my husband is trying to say, Lucky, is thank you," I interrupted Asher, feeling a flutter at calling him, my husband.

Lucky grinned. "Awesome." He gave me a once over. "I'll take this one in the cage," he jerked his head to Bex, who stiffened slightly, "and you take your bike."

I smiled slightly at the fact the dress my mom picked out was suitable for the back of a Harley.

"See you there, kids, don't take too long." Lucky winked at us and clutched Bex's hand, dragging her off while she hissed in his ear.

Asher yanked me flush with his body, stroking my hair. "We don't have to go, Flower," he began softly.

I put my finger over his lips. "Yeah, we do," I replied. "That's your family. My family now, too. I want to," I told him firmly

He frowned for a moment before his face cleared and he regarded me. "If it gets too much, promise you'll tell me?" he said firmly.

I kissed him lightly on the mouth. "I promise. But it's already too much," I murmured against his mouth. "But that's a good thing," I continued.

Asher made a sound in his throat and kissed me, not lightly.

CHAPTER NINETEEN

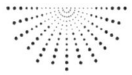

ASHER TOYED WITH THE SIMPLE, yet beautiful square cut vintage diamond on my finger.

"You happy, Mrs. Breslin?" he asked quietly.

I turned my head up to meet his eyes. "Yes," I replied simply. "I never thought it would be possible to be this happy ever again," I whispered.

Asher stroked my head. "I didn't think this kind of happiness even existed, babe. Being able to call you my wife, nothing's ever tasted sweeter on my tongue, apart from your pussy," he said in a low voice.

I squirmed, even though we had just thoroughly consummated our marriage, many times. We started in Asher's small room in the clubhouse. That was after we had a huge and boisterous welcome from a massive, intimidating crowd when we arrived.

I'd swallowed the lump in my throat and smiled brightly at them all, taking all the congratulations and gruff well wishes in stride. Asher hadn't let me go the entire time. Not until Gwen and Amy had both descended on me with tears in their eyes.

"I can't believe you got married," Gwen squealed when she let me go.

"And that you didn't tell us," Amy added with a grin. "Good call. Biker weddings are the hardest things to plan, trust me," she said seriously, looking over to her husband with a small grin.

"I can't believe you got married," Gwen repeated.

Amy gave her a look. "Are your batteries malfunctioning?" she asked. "We got that memo. Plus, the dress is divine." She touched the fabric. "You are divine. Asher's right to lock this down. You're stunning, honey, though we knew that already."

I smiled shyly. "Thanks," I replied.

Gwen beamed. "And you're moving back to Amber, which means you can come back to the store," she managed to get to complete sentences. "After the honeymoon," she added hastily.

I laughed. "We don't get much of a honeymoon. I've got class on Monday."

Amy waggled her eyebrows. "You'll be surprised what your hubby can fit into two days."

I reddened slightly, my stomach tightening in expectation. It was like I was a virgin all over again. As if Asher had telepathic powers, I felt his hands on my waist, and he pulled me back into a firm chest.

"Excuse me, ladies," he murmured. "I'm going to have to steal my wife away."

Amy winked at him. "Yeah, you do."

Gwen blew me a kiss as Asher dragged me through the bodies and directed me to a familiar room.

He closed the door, the party a dull rumble in the background.

"I know it's not hearts and flowers or glamorous," he explained, grasping my hips, "but this is where you gave me the greatest gift I've ever received. Where I fell in love with my shy and beautiful little flower. I wanted our first time as husband as wife to be here," he murmured against my mouth, his hand snaking up the skirt of my dress.

I sucked in a breath when his finger danced at the edge of my panties. "It's perfect," I replied throatily.

He smiled against my mouth. "You're perfect," he countered. His mouth covered mine at the same moment his finger entered me, and I gasped into his mouth.

The kiss that had started reverent and gentle turned frantic. I was suddenly desperate for him, to get him inside me. Asher seemed to feel the same as his finger left me and my panties came off in a rip. His mouth plundered my mouth while he lifted me, pressing me against the door. I wrapped my legs around his hips and clawed at his back.

"This isn't going to be gentle, Flower," Asher growled against my mouth.

"Good," I replied, breathless. "I don't need gentle. I need real. I need you. I need us," I pleaded.

Seconds after the words left my mouth Asher plunged inside me, rough, hard and amazing. His forehead rested against mine, and he pumped into me mercilessly. I took every inch he gave me, ecstasy overwhelming every inch of me.

"It's just us. You and me, babe," Asher grunted out. "Forever."

I cried out as he brought me to the edge of the precipice. "Forever," I repeated.

After he had rocked my world and cleaned himself from me tenderly, Asher straightened, a strange look on his face.

"I meant to show you this before, but I didn't realize how much of a sex demon my little wife was," he teased lightly, though his eyes were hesitant.

I grinned at him lazily. "Show me what?"

He stared at me a moment longer before unbuttoning the collar of his shirt. I gasped when he unveiled his chest.

My fingers trailed around the edge of the red skin of his pec. Tears blurred my vision as I stared at the skin covering his heart. At the fresh tattoo. It was beautiful. A watercolor lily that dripped with every color of the rainbow, my name scrawled underneath it. I remembered the words he had uttered in this very room, almost four years ago.

"Tattoos are for life, apart from the club, I've never loved anything that much to commit to a lifelong reminder of it on my body."

I looked closer and the breath got caught in my lungs. I tore my gaze up from his chest.

"Is this?" I choked out.

Asher's eyes softened. "Yeah, babe, saw it when I was in her studio," he told me gently

A single tear trailed down my cheek, and I moved my attention back to his chest. To the flower that my mom had painted. The one that was mounted on a wall in her studio.

"You're my muse, baby girl. My beautiful Lily. The thing that lights up my life," Mom had told me when I was twelve, right after we moved to Amber. It was the first thing she painted.

"Do you like it?" he asked, a strange kind of uncertainty in his voice.

"Like it?" I repeated. My eyes met his once more. "There aren't words to describe how much this means to me. How perfect this is," I whispered. "This is the greatest thing anyone's ever done for me."

Asher smiled and wiped away my tear with his thumb. "Get used to this feeling, Lily. This is what you deserve. What I'm gonna give you," he promised.

After today, I found myself believing him. Believing the worst might be behind me. And that we might ride away into the horizon to something better.

Hours later, we lay in bed in a beautiful room in *"The Cottage."* It had been a surprise wedding gift from Mia and Bull. Mia, Bull's wife managed it. I had the pleasure of meeting both her and her daughter Lexie a few months ago, and though they had been through drama that dwarfed mine, they were happy. Bull's demons were gone and I was hopeful mine were going too.

We could hear the waves crashing through the French doors that opened onto a sea view balcony, the salt air clinging to our bodies. I didn't even appreciate the beautiful surroundings. I was too busy being ravaged by my husband.

We had lain in beautiful silence, letting the sound of the waves wash over us. Asher's hand trailed my back lazily.

"You got classes on Monday?" he asked quietly.

I didn't move my head from his chest. "Yeah," I sighed, not wanting to think about the work awaiting me.

"I don't want to rush you, but have you thought about where you want to live?" he probed softly. "If you don't want to be at your mom's, we got options. Apart from shit for my bike, I don't live an extravagant lifestyle, I've got a nest egg. A significant one. Enough to get us a house." He paused. "I haven't used it 'cause I've never had a home, not since Benjamin. The place I grew up in was four walls that held pain, memories that were tainted with my father's whiskey stained imprint." He pushed the hair from my head. "The club was my home. I didn't want four walls of my own until I was sure I wanted to share those walls with someone. Make memories with," he stated.

I kissed his chest, his words making my heart soar and bleed at the same time. My neck craned so I could look at my husband.

"I'm sorry," I whispered. "That you don't have a place to remember him … Benjamin."

He smiled a sad smile. "I do, babe," he replied softly. He

moved my hand and placed it lightly over the tattoo on his chest. "Right here, I got the memories I need." He let that sink in a moment, the beauty of his sentiment, of his pain etching into my soul. "I don't want to rush you, but you're not going back to your apartment, and I'm not too crash hot on sharing our matrimonial bliss with my brothers," he joked lightly.

He had already *"talked"* my landlord out of letting us out of our lease, and we were in the process of moving all of our things to Mom's.

I regarded his tattoo, trailing my fingers around the red edges of healing skin. Asher was silent, giving me the time he knew I needed to think. I chewed over his words, what he said about Benjamin, about memories, about a home. When I thought of home, I thought of Mom's little cottage by the sea. Of the heavily decorated rooms. The vibrancy that hit you the moment you walked through the door. The vibrancy that hit me when I walked in there for the first time since losing her. That's what made it hard. Impossible. My house was missing the thing that made it a home. My mom.

But when I thought about home I also thought of Asher. He was my home.

"What do you want?" I asked finally. Asher hadn't ever had a home, he deserved a choice.

His hands tightened around me. "I've got what I want, Lily, right here in my hands. I've got my wife. I've got my bike, my club, everything else is a bonus," he declared.

I moved up on an elbow. "In that order?" I teased.

A grin tickled the corner of his attractive mouth. "You're always first, Lily. It's always you and me before anything out there."

We stared at each other a moment. "Every memory I have of that house is full of happiness. Until three years ago. Then it all turned dark," I spoke quietly, fighting the prickling of grief in my throat. "I don't want it to end dark. I want our lives to color it again."

Asher took me into his arms so I lay completely on top of him. He kissed my nose lightly.

"Then that's what we'll do, Flower. Color your world so you don't even want to remember what the darkness even looks like," he promised.

And his promise held true. For a time.

TWO MONTHS LATER

"You'll do great," Asher told me kissing me firmly.

I kissed him back distractedly trying to remember the correct terms and procedures for someone suffering a heart attack. My mind drew a blank. I was so screwed.

"I'm going to fail," I whined dramatically. The pressure on my chest seemed to intensify with the building in front of me waiting, staring, holding my future within its walls.

Asher grasped my neck, forcing my gaze to move to something else. My attractive husband.

"You're not going to fail," he replied firmly.

His eyes, the certainty in them had me believing him.

Despite the fact I'd been on clinical placement for the past two months, that my life was constant motion once more, I was happy. I found joy in nursing that I thought would be lost with my mom. I wasn't shy or anxious with my patients. I was confident, the only time I felt confident. I wasn't running on empty, dragging myself out of bed every morning. I seemed to float out of bed, only after my husband woke me up in the most delightful way possible. I loved it. Loved him. Being married to Asher was like living a dream. Though news of a marriage wasn't so well received everywhere.

I was hidden in my corner of the library once more, chewing on my pen with frustration. It was my day off from placement, but I realized how rusty I was, how much I needed to brush up on.

"Lily?" a familiar voice called my name,

I glanced up, and my body stiffened. "Aiden," I greeted him coldly, mindful of our last conversation.

He pretended not to notice my chilly greeting and sat down. "I haven't seen you around, I've tried calling you," he said, putting his books down on the table.

"My phone ... broke," I explained. "I haven't been around. I've been on placement."

Aiden glanced at my books. "You're obviously working hard. I'm happy for you," he told me quietly.

"Thanks," I replied softening. I was about to ask him how law school was going, but his eyes focused on my finger. My left hand.

"Please tell me that isn't what I think it is," he said quietly.

I followed his gaze, lifting my hand slightly. "Well, if you think it's an engagement ring, it is what you think it is," I responded.

His face paled. "You're engaged, to him?" he spat out.

"I'm married," I corrected.

Aiden's eyes bulged, and he sat back in his chair. "Married?" he repeated.

I nodded.

"Jesus," he muttered to himself. "You barely know him," he added.

I frowned. "I know him," I said firmly.

Aiden shook his head. "You've changed, Lily, you're not who I thought you were," he stated with disappointment.

I sat up a little straighter. "I haven't changed. I've just found someone who lets me be me. Who sees me," I informed him, gathering up my books. I stood, looking at the person I had thought was my friend. He wasn't, he just saw that I was someone he thought he could mold into someone he wanted.

"Goodbye, Aiden," I said quietly, turning my back on him.

Aiden wasn't the only person gone from my life. As soon as Lucky

found out the truth about Bex, the night of my wedding, in fact, he'd
spirited her away to some cabin in the middle of nowhere. I knew this
because she'd called me to let me know she was okay. Pissed off with a
certain alpha male, but okay.

She arrived back a couple of weeks later, looking much better than
when she had left. Though she and Lucky seemed to have some kind
of arrangement, she was refusing to be labeled "his" or turn it into
anything more. She also moved out of my mom's, much to my
dismay.

"You're married now, Lil, you don't need a roommate. Especially
not an ex-junkie stripper," she joked.

My eyes had narrowed. "You are never to refer to yourself in such
a way ever again," I commanded seriously. I clutched her shoulders.
"You don't have to leave. I don't want you to leave."

She smiled. "I know, but I'm not going far. Rosie's got a spare room
and has offered it to me. I'll be five minutes' drive," she reassured me.

I felt my eyes water. "Five minutes is too long. I've spent three
years having you two doors away," I choked out. She'd been with me
since freshmen year.

Her eyes turned sad. "It's time, as much as I would love to live with
you until you're old and gray, you're a married woman now, that's
your husband's job. That's the bad news, nothing lasts forever, not
even our kick ass living situation." Her kohl-rimmed eyes turned seri-
ous. "It's the good news too, Lil. Nothing lasts forever," she squeezed my
hand.

I PULLED up to the empty parking lot of the strip club owned by
the Sons. I'd been in a couple of times since Bex started working
there. It was a vast improvement on the last place. It had class.
An oxymoron for some, a strip club with class owned by bikers.
But they did it well. The bouncers were respectful, not that they
said much, and most of the women who Bex worked with were

friendly. It wasn't seedy, she was treated well and she seemed happy.

I frowned down at my phone.

BEX: *Pick me up from work. Then we'll party! xxx*

IT DIDN'T LOOK like there were any signs of life in the club, that being because it was a Monday afternoon and they weren't opening for another few hours. I had questioned why Bex was even here, it wasn't completely unusual as she came here to practice routines. I'd been with her a few times and gave her pointers. Not that I had much experience.

ME: *I'm outside.*

I TEXTED, not wanting to go in. It might be broad daylight but it was in an industrial part of town, not much else was out here and I couldn't see any signs of life. A glint of silver caught my eye and I recognized Lucky's bike out front. How I had missed it before I didn't know. I was relieved slightly, but I was also dubious to go in. I didn't need to see ... that. Bex swore that whatever was between them was purely physical, but I knew different.

BEX: *Come in. I'm not ready, need your help with something.*

I ROLLED MY EYES. Bex was never ready when she said she would be. I got out of my car just as my phone started ringing.

"Hello, hubby," I greeted with a grin.

"Hey, baby," his husky voice tickled my stomach. "How'd it go?"

I locked my door and strode across the empty lot, my heels echoing. "Good." I paused. "I think. Or I could have bombed completely. It's done. Out of my hands," I declared.

"You would have aced it, Flower. You've been studying like crazy over the past month, no one can produce that many flash-cards without some of that knowledge sinking in," he teased.

I grinned. He had dutifully tested me on everything from blood types to how to administer an IV without a compliant. He'd even insisted I practice my *"procedures"* on him. That always turned dirty within minutes.

"You on your way here?" he asked.

There was a small party at the club, celebrating me finishing mid-terms. One that didn't cause me to break out in hives. Over the past two months, whenever I wasn't on placement or working at the store, I spent my time with Asher at the club. My shyness had quickly fallen away, and I felt comfortable around all of the rough men. They were family. They took my silence in their stride and grew used to the fact I wasn't loud or sassy like Gwen and Amy.

"I'm picking Bex up from work and I'll be there," I told him, frowning at the front door, which was ajar.

"What's Bex doing there now?" he pondered.

I walked through the dark foyer. "I don't know, but Lucky's here. I hope my eyes aren't scarred for life when I go inside," I joked.

Asher's deep chuckle sounded at the end of the phone. "I hope so too, Flower. Or else I'll have to kick his ass for corrupting my sweet innocent wife."

I rolled my eyes. "You've already well and truly corrupted me, Mr. Breslin," I shot back, looking around the empty room gingerly, hoping not to encounter anything above G-rated.

"Well, hurry over here so I can corrupt you some more, Mrs. Breslin," he commanded roughly.

My stomach dipped. "I'll do that. Love you," I replied throatily.

"Love you, Flower," he returned.

I rang off.

"Bex," I called.

I was met with silence and something crawled up my spine, a sixth sense of uneasiness.

"What's a girl like you doing in a place like this?" a deep voice asked from the shadows.

I jumped and turned, my heart pounding in my chest. "Lucky! You scared the jeebus out of me," I scolded him, putting my hand on my chest.

He stepped forward, grinning. "I'd hate to rob you of your jeebus," he teased.

"What are you doing here?" I asked after scowling at him. Apart from Asher and Bex, Lucky was someone I felt like I could be my complete self with. He didn't treat my shyness like the cripple it was. His gentle teasing and easy manner coaxed me out of my shell quickly. He was like a brother.

He crossed his arms. "Had to pick up some paperwork shit," he explained with a grimace as if collecting paperwork was akin to shoveling horse manure.

"My heart bleeds for you," I shot sarcastically.

He grinned. "Kitten's got claws. What are you doing here? Practicing for your big debut? I think the only way your husband will let you on that stage is if he neuters every male within a hundred-mile radius," he said, crossing his arms.

I shook my head at him. "I'm looking for Bex, she texted me and told me she needed to be picked up. Have you seen her?"

Lucky's grin quickly disappeared. "No, she's not here. When did she text you?" he asked, instantly alert.

That feeling of foreboding returned. "Just now," I told him, looking down at my phone.

"I'm afraid Rebecca won't be coming to the phone right now," a voice declared from the shadows.

Lucky immediately stepped in front of me drawing his gun at the emerging figure. Carlos stepped into the light, not seeming to be bothered he was looking down the barrel of a gun. His fake tanned face looked overly smug in fact. He was limping, leaning heavily on a cane he hadn't had the last time I saw him.

"What have you done with her, you piece of shit?" Lucky spat, his voice vibrating with fury.

Carlos smiled and straightened his suit jacket casually. "Oh, I've taken her to where she belongs. A place where a girl such as her can serve her intended purpose," he replied breezily.

My heart sank, and I felt a vice tightening around my lungs.

No.

Not Bex.

Lucky's form turned to granite in front of me.

"Get out of here right now, call Asher the moment you're in your car," he instructed me tightly, not moving his gun.

"I'm afraid the new Mrs. Breslin will have to stay with us," Carlos exclaimed. "She's needed as a part of a message I'll be sending to your club," he finished the same moment I felt cold steel at my temple.

Lucky whirled around and pointed his gun at the man who yanked me into his body.

"Let her go motherfucker or I'll spray your worthless brains all over this floor," he clipped, voice shaking with fury.

The man behind me laughed. "Try it. Her head will be opened before you can even get your shot off," he said, and I tasted bile.

Lucky glared as two more men appeared at either side of him. His jaw hardened.

I battled against the growing pressure on my chest, my breath coming in slow pants.

Lucky's eyes softened as he focused on me. "Don't worry, sugar, you're gonna be fine," he promised.

Carlos laughed lightly. "It's not her you should be assuring of safety, you should be more worried about yourself," he stated. He made a small nod of his head and a gunshot echoed inside the cavernous room.

I didn't even realize I was screaming until the ringing in my ears stopped. My eyes widened in horror at Lucky's still form on the floor. Blood started pooling underneath him and he didn't move, didn't portray any sign of life.

This can't be happening.

"You bastard," I cried, tears streaming down my cheeks.

Carlos stepped over Lucky's prone body to stand in front of me. He tilted his head and trailed his hand along my cheek. I flinched back from his vile touch. He grinned and sucked on the finger that had trailed through my tears.

"It's a shame," he mused. "That we can't use you. You'd be much more valuable than your junkie friend. But, we need to send a message to your husband's little club." He paused. "We are not to be fucked with. And they need to learn what happens when people try." He nodded his head to the man holding me.

I struggled as he dragged me toward the stage. My efforts were laughable, my small body not even emitting enough strength to make a difference, regardless on the adrenaline pouring through my veins.

After he'd gotten me on stage, he pushed me roughly so my back met the cool steel of the pole. I stared down the barrel of a gun as he pointed it at my forehead.

"Move and die, your choice," he uttered with a grin.

I stood silently, paralyzed with fear, unable to think of some clever way out of this. Unable to think of anything beyond the roaring in my ears, the heavy pressure on my chest. I felt like a frightened shaking rabbit in the headlights.

I stayed still while he tied me to the pole, Carlos watching on with his arms crossed. His gaze flickered around the room.

"It's nothing personal, Lily," he stated conversationally. "You're just a bird really. One of two that I get to kill with one stone." He glanced down at Lucky's body. "Well, three technically."

Anger blossomed in the pit of my stomach. "They'll kill you," I hissed. "Every one of you. They'll end you for this," I promised not recognizing my own voice.

Carlos seemed unperturbed at his perilous future. "I expect they'll try, but I've got powerful partners. Partners that have a vested interest in my survival," he informed me.

I flinched as the rope tightened painfully around my wrists. Something registered in my mind.

"The Tuckers," I said, half to myself. Asher said they were powerful, Dylan had been ranting about making Bex his *"whore."* I thought it was the rantings of an insane pig. So had Asher and Lucky, they'd made sure there was a message sent to not only him, but his family that Bex was off limits. They said they made an agreement. The same with Carlos. My eyes narrowed on the cane he was leaning on. The agreement, I guessed.

He regarded me. "Correct, Mrs. Breslin. I see it's not true what they say about blondes, there's some brains in that pretty head. It's a shame they won't be of use to you much longer." He buttoned his jacket, gesturing to the men he was with. "Well, I wish I could stay and chat, but things to do, junkies to punish," he informed me with an apology.

My throat closed up in fear for my best friend. "They'll find you. Find her," I croaked.

He grinned. "I sure hope so, I'm looking forward to the day that the Sons of Templar realize not everyone scuttles away into their corners when they throw their weight around. That old friends that they thought they'd extinguished are emerging from the ashes," he replied with a glint in his eye. "Though I don't expect that day will be today, they'll be too busy scouring the ashes of their business for remains of their family," he added, turning on his heel.

The vice around my chest tightened as his words sunk in, and with the smell of gasoline that wafted into my nostrils. I watched in horror while they poured it along the bar as they strutted out of the building. I struggled savagely with my bonds, not feeling the skin being ripped from my wrists at this motion. I had to get out. Survive.

The door closed and the flames surrounded me.

ASHER

Asher glanced at his phone in irritation. Something chewed in the bottom of his gut. Something he hadn't felt since the moment he slid the diamond on his wife's finger.

Dread.

"Why the long face, brother?" Brock asked, slapping him on the back and sitting beside him at the bar. "Married life not all it's cracked up to be?" he teased.

"We both know that married life is all it's cracked up to be, and more," Asher replied, grinning slightly.

He may be a sappy fuck, but he didn't even care. Finally, he had his Lily, his flower. Forever. He knew why Brock, Cade, and even Bull let their women drag them around by their dicks. Why they looked at them like the sun rose with them. Because it did. Because their world was filled with all sorts of shit, of all sorts of darkness. Women that came in and brought the light were one in a million. For Asher, Lily was one in a lifetime.

Brock grinned back and clinked his bottle with his. "Amen to that brother," he replied, glancing over at his own wife, who was laughing with Gwen and holding Kingston in her arms. "Just wish my woman would decide it's time for me to put a baby in her. I'm ready for one of my own, maybe it'll calm her down, make me stop worrying about what crazy shit she's up to," he mused, taking a pull of his beer.

Asher laughed. "I don't think anything's going to tamp down your woman's crazy shit, if Gwen's anything to go by." He grinned into his bottle. "What's the problem? You got lazy swimmers?" he asked seriously.

Brock moved his soft gaze from his wife to him, the expression on his face turning into a scowl.

"My swimmers are far from lazy, motherfucker. My swimmers are excellent," he growled.

His continued protests were silenced by Wire's approach, both men silenced at the look on his face. Asher felt that dread intensify tenfold.

"We've got a problem," Wire stated flatly when he got to them.

Wire's face was pale. Asher's stomach clenched. Fucker was never rattled. He sucked down energy drinks like they were water, and therefore was constantly twitching, eyes darting around whenever he wasn't surrounded by his computers. He wasn't twitching. His form was still. Shit was bad.

"We need to get to the Diamond Lounge, now," he demanded urgently.

Asher stood immediately, as did Brock, their beers rattling on the bar as they thrust them down.

"Shit's gone down. Fuck. They shot Lucky. Set the place on fire," he told them quickly. "The cameras have been down and I didn't think much of it. I've only just got them back on."

Asher stepped forward, shaking him by the shoulders. "Lily's in there," he barked. "Is she okay?"

Wire's expression turned his body to ice and fear clog his throat.

LILY

I coughed at the smoke invading my nostrils, my lungs, every part of me. My chest wheezed in response to the fumes strangling me. I ignored this. My bonds were loosening, I could feel the warm trickle of blood trailing down my fingers as my skin ripped away with the force I was rubbing it against the rough rope. I didn't feel the pain that should have come with this.

"You can do this," I gritted out, choking on the gathering smoke.

I could feel the heat of the approaching flames that were engulfing the building. I'd never felt anything so intense in my life. It felt like my body would burst into flames at any moment. My eyes zeroed in on Lucky's body, on the fire dancing around it. They moved to the small opening at the entrance to the building. Smoke distorted my vision, but I hoped that opening stayed like that. It had to. Otherwise, I'd have no chance.

I wasn't surrendering to the growing feeling I was going to die. I couldn't. I wouldn't. Asher's face filled my vision for a moment. His sharp jaw, his deep chocolate eyes.

I coughed again and my eyes focused back on the flames. A sharp twang of pain radiated up my arm as I got my wrist free. I yanked the other free and fell forward, painfully landing on my knees and wrists. I ignored the pain and scrambled around to unfasten the rope at my ankles. The heat was more intense now, the smoke made it nearly impossible to see, to breathe.

I knew I would pass out from smoke inhalation before the flames charred my body, especially with my already weakened lungs. My shaking and bleeding hands ripped off my cardigan and fastened it on top of my mouth. It wouldn't do much, delay my death from suffocation for a few moments, minutes if I was lucky. I scrambled up as my legs were released and stumbled off the stage to where Lucky's body lay.

I wouldn't let him be turned to ashes. I wouldn't leave him.

My hands hooked under his armpits, and I wrenched with all of my strength to drag him toward the opening. It looked miles away, especially with the flames moving closer at terrifying speed. I felt like the skin was melting off my body. My arms screamed, and my lungs felt useless as I coughed into the fabric at my mouth. I wasn't going to do this. I wasn't going to make it. I wasn't strong enough.

"You can do this, peanut," my mom's voice whispered in my ear. *"You're so much stronger than you know. I'm not ready to see you again, not yet. You can do this, baby."*

With every inch of my body telling me I wasn't going to do this, my mind reassured me I could. It urged me forward, renewed my strength to drag Lucky. Gave me the ability to suck what little air remained, just enough for me to chase away the black spots dancing at my vision.

My body sagged against the door and I let Lucky's body go, supporting him with one hand while the other fastened on the doorknob. I gritted my teeth at the blinding pain that erupted in my palm as the piping hot steel singed my skin. I ignored this and turned the handle, praying for it to open. I fell onto the ground as the door moved and cool air rushed at me. I sucked in the air greedily, choking on the cleanness of it as my polluted lungs struggled to expel the poison clogging them.

I hooked my hands under Lucky's body once more, using the last of my strength, of my breath to drag us onto the concrete, a safe distance from the flames. I collapsed against the asphalt as my body struggled to get a proper breath. My chest wheezed, and the invisible hand fastened around my throat.

I heard a roar. I didn't take much notice of it, thinking it was in my own ears, my body's response to dwindling oxygen. I didn't think it might be Harley pipes.

"Lily!" a voice bellowed.

I blinked and moved my eyes up. A blurry figure sprinted toward me.

"Fuck, fuck!" Asher's beautiful voice cursed as arms gathered around me pulling me further from the flames.

"Someone check his pulse," he barked, and I felt Lucky's body slide away from me. I tried to crane my head to watch, to hope beyond hope that they'd find one. That my eyes had deceived me when I'd seen them kill him.

Asher's hand stopped my head's motion. "Lily, look at me," he demanded urgently.

My lazy eyes moved to his, and my chest rose and fell frantically, a terrible sound erupting from it. The sound of my lungs giving out.

"Go to my saddlebags and get the inhaler out from there, *now*," he barked over his shoulder. His desperate gaze moves back to me. "Baby," he whispered.

I watched a tear stream down his cheek.

I wanted to speak. To tell him how happy I was to have two months as his wife. How I wanted my lifetime, but two months was beautiful. How he helped me to breathe easy.

"I love you," I choked out, spluttering.

"Don't," he rasped. "Don't fuckin' say goodbye. You're not going anywhere, babe. You're not leaving me," he demanded.

A figure returned, and Asher reached up to snatch what an outstretched hand gave him. He expertly attached my nebulizer and held it to my mouth.

"Breathe," he ordered. He pleaded.

I didn't move my eyes from his as I tried in vain to catch my breath. I continued to watch those tortured eyes as the spots on my vision got bigger. I let them warm me up as those spots took over entirely. Then there was nothing.

ASHER

He couldn't move. It felt like his body was frozen. He feared if he did move he'd overturn every table in this fucking waiting room, smash the glass encasing him in it, separating him from his wife. So he didn't move. He stayed with his elbows resting on his knees, his head in his hands. He couldn't get it out of his head. The image of Lily dragging his brother out of a burning building.

Of her small form sucking at the air desperately, at that horrible sound coming from her chest. Of the burnt mess on her palm, the bloodstained wrists. She had fought. His flower had fought against the flames.

It wasn't that that haunted him. No. It was the look on her soot-stained face as she rested in his arms. It wasn't panicked like the faces of many men he'd seen facing death. It was calm. Peaceful. She accepted her fate. Her beautiful eyes said goodbye to him, and she faced death with a bravery he didn't even know he'd have when the reaper came for him. Then there was nothing. Then he lost her. Her body turned limp in his arms, and he had placed his palm over her chest. Like he had many times when he watched her struggle. When she was asleep and he lay there, silent and sentinel, waiting for her body to betray her. Unlike those times, his hand didn't move with the rise and fall of her chest. His hand didn't move at all. His hands tightened on his head.

He felt someone enter the room. They stood in front of him. "Any news?" the voice asked.

Asher didn't look up. Didn't move. "No," he clipped, struggling to keep his voice from shaking.

He felt the air move as the figure sat beside him. A hand rested on his shoulder.

"She's going to make it through, brother. She's strong," Cade told him firmly.

"Yeah, she's strong," Asher agreed. Strength didn't guarantee survival. Today was a grim reminder of that. "Lucky?" he asked with resignation. His brother had taken two to the chest, inhaled major amounts of smoke. The paramedics were performing CPR the moment they had arrived on the scene. Like they did with Lily.

"Still in surgery," Cade replied tersely.

At this, Asher looked to his president's tight face. "He's alive?" he asked with disbelief.

Cade nodded. "For now."

Some part of Asher that had been coiled tight relaxed a smidgeon. Enough that the vice around his chest made him feel like he could breathe, barely.

"Got the women at the club on lockdown, till we figure out who the fuck this is," he continued, his voice hard.

Asher nodded, unable to usher up the required fury for those responsible. It would come. He'd rip the fingernails off every single person connected to this. For now, his energy was focused on his wife. On hope. That his beautiful woman would make it out of this.

"Whoever it is, they've got big balls," Cade bit out. "I'm going to fuckin' relish cutting them off."

"You got word on Bex?" Asher asked. Things weren't looking good for her, considering no one could get a lock on her, and it was her phone that lured Lily to the strip club in the first place.

"We've got Wire on it," Cade answered after a moment.

Both of their heads snapped up as a tired looking doctor entered the room.

"Which one of you is Mrs. Breslin's husband?" he asked, glancing at a chart.

Asher pushed out of his chair with such force it rattled to the ground.

He advanced on the doctor. "I am," he clipped. He couldn't say anything else.

"Your wife is breathing on her own now, Mr. Breslin," the doctor told him.

Asher's entire body sagged. "I need to see her," he demanded immediately, cutting off whatever else the doctor had to say.

That could wait. He needed to see with his own eyes. Needed to touch her. Or else those thoughts of her still chest would rip him apart.

"She's sedated and suffering from significant burns to her hand," the doctor tried to explain again.

Fury had its space to grow with the knowledge that Lily was okay, fury that he'd tamped down for the time being.

"I need to see her, now," he repeated. He wasn't taking no for an answer.

The man must have seen this on his face because he didn't say anything else, merely nodded.

"Follow me."

Asher sank into a chair beside the bed holding Lily's small form. His hand immediately darted out to cover her small chest and breathed easy for the first time in hours at the movement of his hand.

He grasped her small hand, it disappeared in his large one. He brought it up to his mouth and kissed it lightly.

"I'm here, baby," he whispered. "I'm here. You're not alone."

EPILOGUE

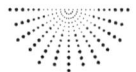

THREE WEEKS LATER

One week.

That's how long I was in the hospital for.

My lungs had sustained significant damage from smoke inhalation, and my hand was severely burned, the pain was like nothing I'd ever experienced. The skin was light pink now it was healing. It would scar, not that Asher would let me live with the physical reminder. We'd be seeing a plastic surgeon as soon as it was properly healed. I didn't care about the pain on the outside. It was the stuff on the inside that couldn't be repaired by a plastic surgeon. Not even my husband's gentle touch or his strong arms that encircled me every moment he wasn't out hunting for them. The people that did this. That shot Lucky. That almost killed me. That still had Bex.

I braced myself on the kitchen counter. Pressure built on my chest once more. I had an overwhelming urge to sink to the ground, to hug my knees to my chest and surrender to the weight that was pushing me down.

The moment I thought my strength would waver, that I

would collapse, strong arms encircled me and the weight lightened a fraction.

"Flower?" Asher murmured in my ear.

I sank back into his body, closing my eyes a second. Asher's hand moved over to my chest, as it did often in the past three weeks. He left it there and we stood in silence for a moment.

"Lucky's out today?" I said finally, turning into Asher's arms.

His worried gaze roved my face. He nodded. "Yeah, he's discharging himself. Against doctor's orders," he responded with a frown.

I touched the stubble on his chin. Moved to the heavy bags under his chocolate eyes. He wasn't sleeping well, I knew. The entire club was on alert after the events three weeks ago. Everyone was thirsty for vengeance, Asher more so than most. It killed men like Asher when they were unable to exert that vengeance. When they felt vulnerable. When Asher couldn't be around me, I had an escort wherever I went. Not that I was going many places these days, apart from college and home. It was a struggle even to drag myself out of bed every day Bex wasn't found. But I did.

"He's looking for her," I said finally.

Lucky had had to be sedated when they told him about Bex. He'd started to rip out all of the cords in his arms and get out of bed. Despite the fact he was recovering from two gunshot wounds that technically killed him. Stopped his heart and had him in a coma for days.

"Yeah," was all Asher said. His hand brushed the hair from my face. "You okay, Flower?" His voice was tight with worry. As it always was when he looked at me. He was waiting, I knew. Waiting for me to fall apart.

"No," I replied honestly, and his frame tightened. "But I will be. Somehow. We'll find her," I said firmly. "For now, we'll keep going. For now, I've got you."

His hands fastened at my neck. "Forever you've got me, flower," he promised.

"Forever," I agreed.

His eyes stayed locked on mine for a moment, then his mouth went to mine. He kissed me slowly, building a steady crescendo of need in my belly.

My hands fastened around his neck as the kiss deepened and he lifted me to set me on the counter. I moaned into his mouth when I felt his hard length pressing into my panties. His hand moved to caress my nipple.

"Asher," I breathed against his mouth.

"My Lily," he murmured, moving his hands downward.

I slipped my own hand underneath his tee, running it over the skin that had my name inked on his body.

He hissed as I raked my nails slowly across it and over to his muscled back.

My panties were pushed aside, and he positioned himself at my entrance. His hand framed my face and he paused, gazing at me in amazement.

"Perfect," he proclaimed quietly.

Then he pushed into me, causing the air to escape from my lungs.

Everything else melted away in that moment. The pain, the pressure, the sorrow. It all disappeared, and it was only me and Asher.

AFTER, Asher cleaned me up he carried me out to the conservatory, which looked out onto the waves. Mom and I had spent hours out here when I was growing up. She said the entire reason she bought the house was this spot right here. Where you could feel like you were witnessing nature's beauty and ferocity from a safe cocoon. It was hard to be out here at first, but now I felt the memories of Mom wrapping me in that same safe cocoon.

Asher sat us on the old ottoman facing the ocean, gathering me tightly in his arms. We didn't speak. We didn't need to. Words would chase in the reality of what lay out there. For now, we needed silence. Just each other. Just the moment where everything made sense.

The ringing of Asher's phone chased away that fleeting moment.

We both tightened as he jostled me slightly to retrieve it from his jeans.

"Yeah," he clipped tightly.

As with every phone call, I braced. For inevitable news. For the gut wrenching pain that would be at the end of it. For the less likely relief that it might hold.

Asher's frame tightened as he stayed silent. His hard gaze met mine.

My heart beat in my throat at his expression.

"We'll be right there," he replied tersely.

He paused a moment after he put the phone down. "We've got her," he declared huskily.

Every taut muscle I'd been holding for three weeks slackened and I collapsed against him. I jerked my head up.

"She's alive? Okay?" I managed to choke out.

Asher stroked my head. "Yeah, Flower. She's alive."

I closed my eyes a moment, sending out a thanks to the universe. She was alive. I let that piece of news wash over me. I felt the weight at my chest lift. She was alive. Everything else would be okay. Everything else Asher and I would face, together.

DAUNTLESS

Want to find out what happened to Bex?

This isn't a fairy tale. I'll save you the trouble by telling you that now.

This is the tale of a girl who spent her life bouncing around foster homes, who had her innocence stolen in the darkness before she knew it was something that could be lost. Her demons followed her everywhere, after that night. They chased her to the medical school she dropped out of, to the strip club she sold herself in, and finally caught her in a river of sin where they tried to drown her.

My name is Bex and this is my story.

I'm paddling, barely keeping my head above water. And even though I'm submerged, I'll never be clean. The layer of dirt that has clung to me since birth is a tattoo I'll wear for life.

He can't see it, though.

Even when I'm torn and tattered, and left in pieces, he wades into the filth to try to put those pieces back together.

He doesn't seem to understand there's nothing left to repair. To love. Just sullied fragments of a damned soul.

He's willing to damn himself in order to exact revenge on those who sent me to the pit.

Problem is, my name is at the top of that list, since I not only damned my own soul, but his too.

Buy here

ACKNOWLEDGMENTS

I want to extend a huge thanks to every single one of my amazing readers. I have the best job in the world and the best readers in the world. *Beyond the Horizon* was deeply personal and emotional for me to write, I know a lot of people struggle with issues touched on in this book. I'm sending my love and thoughts to every one of you. I know that you can find your own HEA just like Lily and Asher.

My mum. You're always going to be at the top of the list. I would never be here if it wasn't for you. You shared your love of reading with me and told me I could be anything I wanted to be.

Dad. You're not here to read this but I know you're watching over me. I wouldn't be the woman I am without you. I miss you everyday.

Emma and Polly. My crazy girlfriends. One of my mother's friends read this book and commented that it was like listening to the three of us. I took that as a huge compliment. I am lucky beyond belief to have such special friends. I don't know what's tighter, our jeans or our friendship.

I couldn't do this without my phenomenal betas. **Amy,**

Sarah, **Andrea**, **Jennifer and Ginny,** I seriously love you, ladies. This book would not be what it is without them.

I want to give a special mention to **Judy**. I can't thank you enough for beta reading this for me even though it touched on some sensitive issues. You're amazing, my thoughts are with you.

Thank you **Kay**, for editing this book. You are amazing.

If you liked this book, I would love it if you could take the time to leave a review. As an indie author, I rely on reviews to get the word out about my books and share the Sons of Templar with the world.

Until next time...
Anne
xxxx

ABOUT THE AUTHOR

Anne Malcom has been an avid reader since before she can remember, her mother responsible for her book addiction. It started with magical journeys into the world of Hogwarts and Middle Earth; then as she grew up her reading tastes grew with her. Her obsession with books and romance novels in particular gave Anne the opportunity to find another passion, writing. Finding writing about alpha males and happily ever afters more fun than reading about them, Anne is not about to stop any time soon.

Raised in small town New Zealand, Anne had a truly special childhood, growing up in one of the most beautiful countries in the world. She has backpacked across Europe, ridden camels in the Sahara, eaten her way through Italy, and had all sorts of crazy adventures. For now, she's back at home in New Zealand and quite happy. But who knows when the travel bug will bite her again?

ALSO BY ANNE MALCOM

THE VEIN CHRONICLES

Fatal Harmony

Deathless

Faults in Fate

Eternity's Awakening

Buried Destiny

STANDALONES

Birds of Paradise

doyenne

THE KLUTCH DUET

Lies That Sinners Tell

Truths That Saints Believe

RETIRED SINNERS

Splinters of You

Printed in Great Britain
by Amazon